Praise for Robert Galbraith's

Career of Evil

"Galbraith is one of our finest contemporary crime writers.... *Career of Evil* is the third—and best—novel in the engaging Cormoran Strike private detective series.... This perfectly paced mystery is packed with surprises, all of which play out with flawless crime-fiction logic."

—Jocelyn McClurg, *USA Today*

"Galbraith has created a pair of characters who live on in your head after the book is closed, and who make you wish desperately for a new installment.... It's an irresistible relationship.... We all know that Robin's the Nora to Strike's Nick; why don't they?... *Career of Evil* can be sparklingly witty and, as when we learn something crucial here about Robin's past, unexpectedly moving."

—Moira Macdonald, *Seattle Times*

"Hugely entertaining.... *Career of Evil* succeeds powerfully on its own terms."

—Lloyd Sachs, *Chicago Tribune*

"Strike and Robin are just as magnetic as ever.... Robin is the real star of this novel—as spirited, resourceful, and vulnerable as one of the heroines in a Shakespeare comedy—and readers cannot help but root for her and Strike to finally fall for each other. Their developing relationship propels this novel toward its conclusion."

—Michiko Kakutani, *New York Times*

"An entertaining novel.... The denouement is violent, unexpected, and satisfying."

—Marcel Berlins, *The Times* (UK)

"Galbraith's writing is velvety and fluid, making the book pure pleasure.... In *Career of Evil,* Galbraith's moral acumen is reserved not for the killer sucking his fingers clean of blood after the kill, but for characters like Matthew, Robin's fiancé, who subtly undermines her, who hates Robin's job for giving her independence and confidence. That's what makes these novels so good: they are clever, tightly plotted mysteries with all of the most pleasurable elements of the genre (good guy, bad guy, clues, twists, murder!), but with stunning emotional and moral shading."

—Annalisa Quinn, National Public Radio

"Bloody good.... The author's trademark plotting has lost none of its propulsive readability, and Strike and Robin reveal more of their backgrounds as well as their charms."

—Daneet Steffens, *Boston Globe*

"*Career of Evil* is delivered with such sheer gusto—and, crucially, such a confident hold on a deliriously clever plot—that most sensible readers will simply cave in and enjoy it."

—Christobel Kent, *The Guardian* (UK)

"Another triumph.... Its darkness is mitigated by its sparkling protagonists."

—Kim Hubbard, *People*

"Galbraith is nothing if not an accomplished plotter, and he handles all these different characters and strands with real aplomb.... The big reveal, when it comes, is thoroughly satisfying."

—Michael Prodger, *Financial Times*

"Galbraith's captivating third novel... deepens his lead characters, Cormoran Strike and Robin Ellacott.... Maintaining a high level of suspense throughout, Galbraith transforms Robin into a professional equal of Strike's and sets the stage for further complexities in their relationship in the next book."

—*Publishers Weekly*

"As with previous Strike novels, the relationship between Cormoran and Robin remains fascinating."

—Colleen Kelly, *Minneapolis Star Tribune*

"A gripping novel...fast and satisfying."

—Charles Finch, *New York Times Book Review*

"As Robin and Strike draw together strands of the past and present, Galbraith demonstrates a breezy command of the intricacies of both the central mystery and of the form itself. It's a genuine—and all-too-rare—pleasure to see a mystery cracked through dogged investigative work....Strike and Robin are a pleasure to watch, as powerful a fictional pairing as any in recent memory. Their relationship, which Galbraith has allowed to unfold naturally and shift over the course of three novels, is the true heart of these books."

—Robert Wiersema, *Toronto Star*

"Gripping....This is a thriller where the crime solvers are just as enigmatic as the criminal."

—Diana Duong, *Maclean's*

"A refreshing change to the genre....Every bit as impressive as *The Cuckoo's Calling*....Let's hope the sardonic Cormoran Strike is here to stay."

—Barry Forshaw, *The Independent* (UK)

Also by Robert Galbraith

The Cuckoo's Calling
The Silkworm

Career of Evil

Robert Galbraith

MULHOLLAND BOOKS
Little, Brown and Company
New York Boston London

The characters and events in this book are fictitious. Any similarity to real persons, living or dead, is coincidental and not intended by the author.

Mulholland Books / Little, Brown and Company
Hachette Book Group
1290 Avenue of the Americas, New York, NY 10104
mulhollandbooks.com

Originally published in hardcover in North America by Mulholland Books, October 2015
Published simultaneously in Great Britain by Sphere, October 2015
First Mulholland Books trade paperback edition, April 2016
First Mulholland Books media tie-in paperback edition, May 2018

Mulholland Books is an imprint of Little, Brown and Company, a division of Hachette Book Group, Inc. The Mulholland Books name and logo are trademarks of Hachette Book Group, Inc.

ISBN 978-0-316-34993-2 (hc) / 978-0-316-35245-1 (large print) / 978-0-316-39137-5 (int'l pb) / 978-0-316-35372-4 (signed edition) / 978-0-316-34989-5 (trade pb) / 978-0-316-48640-8 (media tie-in pb)
Library of Congress Control Number 2015948930

10 9 8 7 6 5 4 3 2 1

LSC-C

Printed in the United States of America

See page 493 for full credits.

To Séan and Matthew Harris,

Do whatever you want with this dedication,
but don't—
don't—
use it on your eyebrows.

I choose to steal what you choose to show
And you know I will not apologize—
You're mine for the taking.

I'm making a career of evil...

Blue Öyster Cult, "Career of Evil"
Lyrics by Patti Smith

Career of Evil

1

2011

This Ain't the Summer of Love

He had not managed to scrub off all her blood. A dark line like a parenthesis lay under the middle fingernail of his left hand. He set to digging it out, although he quite liked seeing it there: a memento of the previous day's pleasures. After a minute's fruitless scraping, he put the bloody nail in his mouth and sucked. The ferrous tang recalled the smell of the torrent that had splashed wildly onto the tiled floor, spattering the walls, drenching his jeans and turning the peach-colored bath towels—fluffy, dry and neatly folded—into blood-soaked rags.

Colors seemed brighter this morning, the world a lovelier place. He felt serene and uplifted, as though he had absorbed her, as though her life had been transfused into him. They belonged to you once you had killed them: it was a possession way beyond sex. Even to know how they looked at the moment of death was an intimacy way past anything two living bodies could experience.

With a thrill of excitement he reflected that nobody knew what he had done, nor what he was planning to do next. He sucked his middle finger, happy and at peace, leaning up against the warm wall in the weak April sunshine, his eyes on the house opposite.

It was not a smart house. Ordinary. A nicer place to live, admittedly, than the tiny flat where yesterday's blood-stiffened clothing lay in black bin bags, awaiting incineration, and where his knives lay gleaming, washed clean with bleach, rammed up behind the U-bend under the kitchen sink.

This house had a small front garden, black railings and a lawn in need of mowing. Two white front doors had been crammed together side by side, showing that the three-story building had been converted into upper and lower flats. A girl called Robin Ellacott lived on the ground floor. Though he had made it his business to find out her real name, inside his own head he called her The Secretary. He had just seen her pass in front of the bow window, easily recognizable because of her bright hair.

Watching The Secretary was an extra, a pleasurable add-on. He had a few hours spare so he had decided to come and look at her. Today was a day of rest, between the glories of yesterday and tomorrow, between the satisfaction of what had been done and the excitement of what would happen next.

The right-hand door opened unexpectedly and The Secretary came out, accompanied by a man.

Still leaning into the warm wall, he stared along the street with his profile turned towards them, so that he might appear to be waiting for a friend. Neither of them paid him any attention. They walked off up the street, side by side. After he had given them a minute's head start, he decided to follow.

She was wearing jeans, a light jacket and flat-heeled boots. Her long wavy hair was slightly ginger now that he saw her in the sunshine. He thought he detected a slight reserve between the couple, who weren't talking to each other.

He was good at reading people. He had read and charmed the girl who had died yesterday among the blood-soaked peach towels.

Down the long residential street he tracked them, his hands in his pockets, ambling along as though heading for the shops, his sunglasses unremarkable on this brilliant morning. Trees waved gently in the slight spring breeze. At the end of the street the pair ahead turned left into a wide, busy thoroughfare lined with offices. Sheet glass windows blazed high above him in the sunlight as they passed the Ealing council building.

Now The Secretary's flatmate, or boyfriend, or whatever he was—clean-cut and square-jawed in profile—was talking to her. She returned a short answer and did not smile.

Women were so petty, mean, dirty and small. Sulky bitches, the lot of them, expecting men to keep them happy. Only when they lay dead and empty in front of you did they become purified, mysterious and even wonderful. They were entirely yours then, unable to argue or struggle or leave, yours to do with whatever you liked. The other one's corpse had been heavy and floppy yesterday after he had drained it of blood: his life-sized plaything, his toy.

Through the bustling Arcadia shopping center he followed The Secretary and her boyfriend, gliding behind them like a ghost or a god. Could the Saturday shoppers even see him, or was he somehow transformed, doubly alive, gifted with invisibility?

They had arrived at a bus stop. He hovered nearby, pretending to look through the door of a curry house, at fruit piled high in front of a grocer's, at cardboard masks of Prince William and Kate Middleton hanging in a newsagent's window, watching their reflections in the glass.

They were going to get on the number 83. He did not have a lot of money in his pockets, but he was so enjoying watching her that he did not want it to end yet. As he climbed aboard behind them he heard the man mention Wembley Central. He bought a ticket and followed them upstairs.

The couple found seats together, right at the front of the bus. He took a place nearby, next to a grumpy woman whom he forced to move her bags of shopping. Their voices carried sometimes over the hum of the other passengers. When not talking, The Secretary looked out of the window, unsmiling. She did not want to go wherever they were going, he was sure of it. When she pushed a strand of hair out of her eyes he noticed that she was wearing an engagement ring. So she was going to be getting married...or so she thought. He hid his faint smile in the upturned collar of his jacket.

The warm midday sun was pouring through the dirt-stippled bus windows. A group of men got on and filled the surrounding seats. A couple of them were wearing red and black rugby shirts.

He felt, suddenly, as though the day's radiance had dimmed. Those shirts, with the crescent moon and star, had associations he did not like. They reminded him of a time when he had not felt like a god. He did not want his happy day spotted and stained by old memories, bad memories, but his elation was suddenly draining away. Angry now—a teenage boy in the group caught his eye, but looked hurriedly away, alarmed—he got up and headed back to the stairs.

A father and his small son were holding tight to the pole beside the bus doors. An explosion of anger in the pit of his stomach: *he* should have had a son. Or rather, he should *still* have had a son. He pictured the boy standing beside him, looking up at him, hero-worshipping him—but his son was long gone, which was entirely due to a man called Cormoran Strike.

He was going to have revenge on Cormoran Strike. He was going to wreak havoc upon him.

When he reached the pavement he looked up at the bus's front windows and caught one last glimpse of The Secretary's golden head. He would be seeing her again in less than twenty-four hours. That reflection helped calm the sudden rage caused by the sight of those Saracens shirts. The bus rumbled off and he strode away in the opposite direction, soothing himself as he walked.

He had a wonderful plan. Nobody knew. Nobody suspected. And he had something very special waiting for him in the fridge at home.

2

A rock through a window never comes with a kiss.

Blue Öyster Cult, "Madness to the Method"

Robin Ellacott was twenty-six years old and had been engaged for over a year. Her wedding ought to have taken place three months previously, but the unexpected death of her future mother-in-law had led to the ceremony's postponement. Much had happened during the three months since the wedding should have happened. Would she and Matthew have been getting on better if vows had been exchanged, she wondered. Would they be arguing less if a golden band was sitting beneath the sapphire engagement ring that had become a little loose on her finger?

Fighting her way through the rubble on Tottenham Court Road on Monday morning, Robin mentally relived the argument of the previous day. The seeds had been sown before they had even left the house for the rugby. Every time they met up with Sarah Shadlock and her boyfriend Tom, Robin and Matthew seemed to row, something that Robin had pointed out as the argument, which had been brewing since the match, dragged on into the small hours of the morning.

"Sarah was shit-stirring, for God's sake—can't you see it? *She* was the one asking all about him, going on and on, I didn't start it..."

The everlasting roadworks around Tottenham Court Road station had obstructed Robin's walk to work ever since she had started at the private detective agency in Denmark Street. Her mood was not improved by tripping on a large chunk of rubble; she staggered a few steps before recovering her balance. A barrage of wolf-whistles and lewd remarks issued from a deep chasm in the road full of men in hard hats and fluorescent jackets. Shaking long strawberry-blonde hair out of her eyes, red in the face, she ignored them, her thoughts returning irresistibly to Sarah Shadlock and her sly, persistent questions about Robin's boss.

"He is *strangely* attractive, isn't he? Bit beaten-up-looking, but I've never minded that. Is he sexy in the flesh? He's a big guy, isn't he?"

Robin had seen Matthew's jaw tightening as she tried to return cool, indifferent answers.

"Is it just the two of you in the office? Is it really? Nobody else at all?"

Bitch, thought Robin, whose habitual good nature had never stretched to Sarah Shadlock. *She knew exactly what she was doing.*

"Is it true he was decorated in Afghanistan? Is it? Wow, so we're talking a war hero too?"

Robin had tried her hardest to shut down Sarah's one-woman chorus of appreciation for Cormoran Strike, but to no avail: a coolness had crept into Matthew's manner towards his fiancée by the end of the match. His displeasure had not prevented him bantering and laughing with Sarah on the journey back from Vicarage Road, though, and Tom, whom Robin found boring and obtuse, had chortled away, oblivious to any undercurrents.

Jostled by passersby also navigating the open trenches in the road, Robin finally reached the opposite pavement, passing beneath the shadow of the concrete grid-like monolith that was Centre Point and becoming angry all over again as she remembered what Matthew had told her at midnight, when the argument had burst back into flame.

"You can't stop bloody talking about him, can you? I heard you, to Sarah—"

"I *did not* start talking about him again, it was *her,* you weren't listening—"

But Matthew had imitated her, using the generic voice that stood for all women, high-pitched and imbecilic: "*Oh, his hair's so lovely*—"

"For God's sake, you're completely bloody paranoid!" Robin had shouted. "*Sarah* was banging on about Jacques Burger's bloody hair, not Cormoran's, and all I said—"

"'*Not Cormoran's,*'" he had repeated in that moronic squeal. As Robin rounded the corner into Denmark Street she felt as furious as she had eight hours ago, when she had stormed out of the bedroom to sleep on the sofa.

Sarah Shadlock, bloody Sarah Shadlock, who had been at university with Matthew and had tried as hard as she could to win him away from Robin, the girl left behind in Yorkshire... If Robin could have been sure she would never see Sarah again she would have rejoiced, but Sarah would be at their wedding in July, Sarah would doubtless continue to plague their married life, and perhaps one day she would try to worm her way into Robin's office to meet Strike, if her interest was genuine and not merely a means of sowing discord between Robin and Matthew.

I will never *introduce her to Cormoran,* thought Robin savagely as she approached the courier standing outside the door to the office. He had a clipboard in one gloved hand and a long rectangular package in the other.

"Is that for Ellacott?" Robin asked as she came within speaking distance. She was expecting an order of ivory cardboard-covered disposable cameras, which were to be favors at the wedding reception. Her working hours had become so irregular of late that she found it easier to send online orders to the office rather than the flat.

The courier nodded and held out the clipboard without taking off his motorcycle helmet. Robin signed and took the long package, which was much heavier than she had expected; it felt as though some single large object slid inside it as she put it under her arm.

"Thank you," she said, but the courier had already turned away and swung a leg over his motorbike. She heard him ride away as she let herself inside the building.

Up the echoing metal staircase that wound around the broken birdcage lift she walked, her heels clanging on the metal. The glass door flashed as she unlocked and opened it and the engraved legend—C. B. STRIKE, PRIVATE INVESTIGATOR—stood out darkly.

She had arrived deliberately early. They were currently inundated with cases and she wanted to catch up with some paperwork before resuming her daily surveillance of a young Russian lap-dancer. From the sound of heavy footfalls overhead, she deduced that Strike was still upstairs in his flat.

Robin laid her oblong package on the desk, took off her coat and hung it, with her bag, on a peg behind the door, turned on the light, filled and switched on the kettle, then reached for the sharp letter-opener on her desk. Remembering Matthew's flat refusal to believe that it had been flanker Jacques Burger's curly mane she had been admiring, rather than Strike's short and frankly pube-like hair, she made an angry stab to the end of the package, slit it open and pulled the box apart.

A woman's severed leg had been crammed sideways in the box, the toes of the foot bent back to fit.

3

Half-a-hero in a hard-hearted game.

Blue Öyster Cult, "The Marshall Plan"

Robin's scream reverberated off the windows. She backed away from the desk, staring at the obscene object lying there. The leg was smooth, slender and pale, and she had grazed it with her finger as she pulled its packaging open, felt the cold rubbery texture of the skin.

She had just managed to quell her scream by clamping her hands over her mouth when the glass door burst open beside her. Six foot three and scowling, Strike's shirt hung open, revealing a monkeyish mass of dark chest hair.

"What the—?"

He followed her stricken gaze and saw the leg. She felt his hand close roughly over her upper arm and he steered her out onto the landing.

"How did it arrive?"

"Courier," she said, allowing him to walk her up the stairs. "On a motorbike."

"Wait here. I'll call the police."

When he had closed the door of his flat behind her she stood quite still, heart juddering, listening to his footsteps returning downstairs. Acid rose in her throat. A leg. She had just been given a leg. She had just carried a leg calmly upstairs, a woman's leg in a box. Whose leg was it? Where was the rest of her?

She crossed to the nearest chair, a cheap affair of padded plastic and metal legs, and sat down, her fingers still pressed against her numb lips. The package, she remembered, had been addressed to her by name.

Strike, meanwhile, was at the office window that looked down into the road, scanning Denmark Street for any sign of the courier, his mobile pressed to his ear. By the time he returned to the outer office to scrutinize the open package on the desk, he had made contact with the police.

"A leg?" repeated Detective Inspective Eric Wardle on the end of the line. "A fucking *leg?*"

"And it's not even my size," said Strike, a joke he would not have made had Robin been present. His trouser leg was hitched up to reveal the metal rod that served as his right ankle. He had been in the process of dressing when he had heard Robin's scream.

Even as he said it, he realized that this was a right leg, like his own lost limb, and that it had been cut below the knee, which was exactly where he had been amputated. His mobile still clamped to his ear, Strike peered more closely at the limb, his nostrils filling with an unpleasant smell like recently defrosted chicken. Caucasian skin: smooth, pale and unblemished but for an old greenish bruise on the calf, imperfectly shaven. The stubbly hairs were fair and the unpainted toenails a little grubby. The severed tibia shone icy white against the surrounding flesh. A clean cut: Strike thought it likely to have been made by an axe or a cleaver.

"A woman's, did you say?"

"Looks like—"

Strike had noticed something else. There was scarring on the calf where the leg had been severed: old scarring, unrelated to the wound that had taken it from the body.

How many times during his Cornish childhood had he been caught unawares as he stood with his back to the treacherous sea? Those who did not know the ocean well forgot its solidity, its brutality. When it slammed into them with the force of cold metal they were appalled. Strike had faced, worked with and managed fear all his professional life, but the sight of that old scarring rendered him temporarily winded by a terror all the worse for its unexpectedness.

"Are you still there?" said Wardle on the end of the line.

"What?"

Strike's twice-broken nose was within an inch of the place where the woman's leg had been cut off. He was remembering the scarred leg of a child he had never forgotten... how long was it since he had seen her? How old would she be now?

"You called me first...?" Wardle prompted.

"Yeah," said Strike, forcing himself to concentrate. "I'd rather you did it than anyone else, but if you can't—"

"I'm on my way," said Wardle. "Won't be long. Sit tight."

Strike turned off his phone and set it down, still staring at the leg. Now he saw that there was a note lying underneath it, a typed note. Trained by the British Army in investigative procedure, Strike resisted the powerful temptation to tug it out and read it: he must not taint forensic evidence. Instead he crouched down unsteadily so that he could read the address hanging upside down on the open lid.

The box had been addressed to Robin, which he did not like at all. Her name was correctly spelled, typed on a white sticker that bore the address of their office. This sticker overlay another. Squinting, determined not to reposition the box even to read the address more clearly, he saw that the sender had first addressed the box to "Cameron Strike," then overlain it with the second sticker reading "Robin Ellacott." Why had they changed their mind?

"Fuck," said Strike quietly.

He stood up with some difficulty, took Robin's handbag from the peg behind the door, locked the glass door and headed upstairs.

"Police are on their way," he told her as he set her bag down in front of her. "Want a cup of tea?"

She nodded.

"Want brandy in it?"

"You haven't got any brandy," she said. Her voice was slightly croaky.

"Have you been looking?"

"Of course not!" she said, and he smiled at how indignant she sounded at the suggestion she might have been through his cupboards. "You're just—you're not the sort of person who'd have medicinal brandy."

"Want a beer?"

She shook her head, unable to smile.

Once the tea had been made, Strike sat down opposite her with his own mug. He looked exactly what he was: a large ex-boxer who smoked too much and ate too much fast food. He had heavy eyebrows, a flattened and asymmetrical nose and, when not smiling, a permanent expression of sullen crossness. His dense, dark curly hair, still damp from the shower, reminded her of Jacques Burger and Sarah Shadlock. The row seemed a lifetime ago. She had only briefly thought of Matthew since coming upstairs. She dreaded telling him what had happened. He would be angry. He did not like her working for Strike.

"Have you looked at—at it?" she muttered, after picking up and setting down the boiling tea without drinking it.

"Yeah," said Strike.

She did not know what else to ask. It was a severed leg. The situation was so horrible, so grotesque, that every question that occurred to her sounded ridiculous, crass. *Do you recognize it? Why do you think they sent it?* And, most pressing of all, *why to me?*

"The police'll want to hear about the courier," he said.

"I know," said Robin. "I've been trying to remember everything about him."

The downstairs door buzzer sounded.

"That'll be Wardle."

"Wardle?" she repeated, startled.

"He's the friendliest copper we know," Strike reminded her. "Stay put, I'll bring him to you here."

Strike had managed to make himself unpopular among the Metropolitan Police over the previous year, which was not entirely his fault. The fulsome press coverage of his two most notable detective triumphs had understandably galled those officers whose efforts he had trumped. However, Wardle, who had helped him out on the first of those cases, had shared in some of the subsequent glory and relations between them remained reasonably amicable. Robin had only ever seen Wardle in the newspaper reports of the case. Their paths had not crossed in court.

He turned out to be a handsome man with a thick head of chestnut hair and chocolate-brown eyes, who was wearing a leather jacket and jeans. Strike did not know whether he was more amused or irritated by the reflexive look Wardle gave Robin on entering the room—a swift zigzag sweep of her hair, her figure and her left hand, where his eyes lingered for a second on the sapphire and diamond engagement ring.

"Eric Wardle," he said in a low voice, with what Strike felt was an unnecessarily charming smile. "And this is Detective Sergeant Ekwensi."

A thin black female officer whose hair was smoothed back in a bun had arrived with him. She gave Robin a brief smile and Robin found herself taking disproportionate comfort from the presence of another woman. Detective Sergeant Ekwensi then let her eyes stray around Strike's glorified bedsit.

"Where's this package?" she asked.

"Downstairs," said Strike, drawing the keys to the office out of his pocket. "I'll show you. Wife OK, Wardle?" he added as he prepared to leave the room with Detective Sergeant Ekwensi.

"What do you care?" retorted the officer, but to Robin's relief he dropped what she thought of as his counselor's manner as he took the seat opposite her at the table and flipped open his notebook.

"He was standing outside the door when I came up the street," Robin explained, when Wardle asked how the leg had arrived. "I thought he was a courier. He was dressed in black leather—all black except for blue stripes on the shoulders of his jacket. His helmet was plain black and the visor was down and mirrored. He must have been at least six feet tall. Four or five inches taller than me, even allowing for the helmet."

"Build?" asked Wardle, who was scribbling in his notebook.

"Pretty big, I'd say, but he was probably padded out a bit by the jacket."

Robin's eyes wandered inadvertently to Strike as he reentered the room. "I mean, not—"

"Not a fat bastard like the boss?" Strike, who had overheard, suggested and Wardle, never slow to make or enjoy a dig at Strike, laughed under his breath.

"And he wore gloves," said Robin, who had not smiled. "Black leather motorcycle gloves."

"Of course he'd wear gloves," said Wardle, adding a note. "I don't suppose you noticed anything about the motorbike?"

"It was a Honda, red and black," said Robin. "I noticed the logo, that winged symbol. I'd say 750cc. It was big."

Wardle looked both startled and impressed.

"Robin's a petrolhead," said Strike. "Drives like Fernando Alonso."

Robin wished that Strike would stop being cheery and flippant. A woman's leg lay downstairs. Where was the rest of her? She must not cry. She wished she had had more sleep. That damn sofa...she had spent too many nights on the thing lately...

"And he made you sign for it?" asked Wardle.

"I wouldn't say 'made' me," said Robin. "He held out a clipboard and I did it automatically."

"What was on the clipboard?"

"It looked like an invoice or..."

She closed her eyes in the effort to remember. Now she came to think of it, the form had looked amateurish, as though it had been put together on someone's laptop, and she said as much.

"Were you expecting a package?" Wardle asked.

Robin explained about the disposable wedding cameras.

"What did he do once you'd taken it?"

"Got back on the bike and left. He drove off into Charing Cross Road."

There was a knock on the door of the flat and Detective Sergeant Ekwensi reappeared holding the note that Strike had noticed lying beneath the leg, which was now enclosed in an evidence bag.

"Forensics are here," she told Wardle. "This note was in the package. It would be good to know whether it means anything to Miss Ellacott."

Wardle took the polythene-covered note and scanned it, frowning.

"It's gibberish," he said, then read aloud: "'*A harvest of limbs, of arms and of legs, of necks—*'"

"'*—that turn like swans,*'" interrupted Strike, who was leaning against the cooker and too far away to read the note, "'*as if inclined to gasp or pray.*'"

The other three stared at him.

"They're lyrics," said Strike. Robin did not like the expression on his face. She could tell that the words meant something to him, something bad. With what looked like an effort, he elucidated: "From the last verse of 'Mistress of the Salmon Salt.' By Blue Öyster Cult."

Detective Sergeant Ekwensi raised finely penciled eyebrows.

"Who?"

"Big seventies rock band."

"You know their stuff well, I take it?" asked Wardle.

"I know that song," said Strike.

"Do you think you know who sent this?"

Strike hesitated. As the other three watched him, a confused series of images and memories passed rapidly through the detective's mind. A low voice said, *She wanted to die. She was the quicklime girl.* The thin leg of a twelve-year-old girl, scarred with silvery crisscrossing lines. A pair of small dark eyes like a ferret's, narrowed in loathing. The tattoo of a yellow rose.

And then—lagging behind the other memories, puffing into view, although it might have been another man's first thought—he remembered a charge sheet that made mention of a penis cut from a corpse and mailed to a police informer.

"Do you know who sent it?" repeated Wardle.

"Maybe," said Strike. He glanced at Robin and Detective Sergeant Ekwensi. "I'd rather talk about it alone. Have you got everything you want from Robin?"

"We'll need your name and address and so on," said Wardle. "Vanessa, can you take those?"

Detective Sergeant Ekwensi moved forwards with her notebook. The two men's clanging footsteps faded from earshot. In spite of the fact that she had no desire to see the severed leg again, Robin felt aggrieved at being left behind. It had been *her* name on the box.

The grisly package was still lying on the desk downstairs. Two more of Wardle's colleagues had been admitted by Detective Sergeant Ekwensi: one was taking photographs, the other talking on his mobile when their senior officer and the private detective walked past. Both looked curiously at Strike, who had achieved a measure of fame during the period in which he had managed to alienate many of Wardle's colleagues.

Strike closed the door of his inner office and he and Wardle took the seats facing each other across Strike's desk. Wardle turned to a fresh page of his notebook.

"All right, who d'you know who likes chopping up corpses and sending them through the post?"

"Terence Malley," said Strike, after a momentary hesitation. "For a start."

Wardle did not write anything, but stared at him over the top of his pen.

"Terence 'Digger' Malley?"

Strike nodded.

"Harringay Crime Syndicate?"

"How many Terence 'Digger' Malleys do you know?" asked Strike impatiently. "And how many have got a habit of sending people body parts?"

"How the hell did you get mixed up with Digger?"

"Joint ops with Vice Squad, 2008. Drug ring."

"The bust he went down for?"

"Exactly."

"Holy shit," said Wardle. "Well, that's bloody it, isn't it? The guy's an effing lunatic, he's just out and he's got easy access to half of London's prostitutes. We'd better start dragging the Thames for the rest of her."

"Yeah, but I gave evidence anonymously. He shouldn't ever have known it was me."

"They've got ways and means," said Wardle. "Harringay Crime Syndicate—they're like the fucking mafia. Did you hear how he sent Hatford Ali's dick to Ian Bevin?"

"Yeah, I heard," said Strike.

"So what's the story with the song? The harvest of whatever the fuck it was?"

"Well, that's what I'm worried about," said Strike slowly. "It seems pretty subtle for the likes of Digger—which makes me think it might be one of the other three."

4

Four winds at the Four Winds Bar,
Two doors locked and windows barred,
One door left to take you in,
The other one just mirrors it…

Blue Öyster Cult, "Astronomy"

"You know *four men* who'd send you a severed leg? *Four?*"

Strike could see Robin's appalled expression reflected in the round mirror standing beside the sink, where he was shaving. The police had taken away the leg at last, Strike had declared work suspended for the day and Robin remained at the little Formica table in his kitchen-cum-sitting room, cradling a second mug of tea.

"To tell you the truth," he said, strafing stubble from his chin, "I think it's only three. Think I might've made a mistake telling Wardle about Malley."

"Why?"

Strike told Robin the story of his brief contact with the career criminal, who owed his last prison stretch, in part, to Strike's evidence.

"…so now Wardle's convinced the Harringay Crime Syndicate found out who I was, but I left for Iraq shortly after testifying and I've never yet known an SIB officer's cover blown because he gave evidence in court. Plus, the song lyrics don't smell like Digger. He's not one for fancy touches."

"But he's cut bits off people he's killed before?" Robin asked.

"Once that I know of—but don't forget, whoever did this hasn't necessarily killed anyone," temporized Strike. "The leg could have come off an existing corpse. Could be hospital waste. Wardle's going to check all that out. We won't know much until forensics have had a look."

The ghastly possibility that the leg had been taken from a still-living person, he chose not to mention.

In the ensuing pause, Strike rinsed his razor under the kitchen tap and Robin stared out of the window, lost in thought.

"Well, you *had* to tell Wardle about Malley," said Robin, turning back to Strike, who met her gaze in his shaving mirror. "I mean, if he's already sent someone a—what exactly *did* he send?" she asked, a little nervously.

"A penis," said Strike. He washed his face clean and dried it on a towel before continuing. "Yeah, maybe you're right. More I think about it, though, the surer I am it's not him. Back in a minute—I want to change this shirt. I ripped two buttons off it when you screamed."

"Sorry," said Robin vaguely, as Strike disappeared into the bedroom.

Sipping her tea, she took a look around the room in which she was sitting. She had never been inside Strike's attic flat before. The most she had done previously was knock on the door to deliver messages or, in some of their busiest and most sleep-deprived stretches, to wake him up. The kitchen-cum-sitting room was cramped but clean and orderly. There were virtually no signs of personality: mismatched mugs, a cheap tea towel folded beside the gas ring; no photographs and nothing decorative, save for a child's drawing of a soldier, which had been tacked up on one of the wall units.

"Who drew that?" she asked, when Strike reappeared in a clean shirt.

"My nephew Jack. He likes me, for some reason."

"Don't fish."

"I'm not fishing. I never know what to say to kids."

"So you think you've met *three men* who would've—?" Robin began again.

"I want a drink," said Strike. "Let's go to the Tottenham."

There was no possibility of talking on the way, not with the racket of pneumatic drills still issuing from the trenches in the road, but the fluorescent-jacketed workmen neither wolf-whistled nor cat-called with Strike walking at Robin's side. At last they reached Strike's favorite local pub, with its ornate gilded mirrors, its panels of dark wood, its shining brass pumps, the colored glass cupola and the paintings of gamboling beauties by Felix de Jong.

Strike ordered a pint of Doom Bar. Robin, who could not face alcohol, asked for a coffee.

"So?" said Robin, once the detective had returned to the high table beneath the cupola. "Who are the three men?"

"I could be barking up a forest of wrong trees, don't forget," said Strike, sipping his pint.

"All right," said Robin. "Who are they?"

"Twisted individuals who've all got good reason to hate my guts."

Inside Strike's head, a frightened, skinny twelve-year-old girl with scarring around her leg surveyed him through lopsided glasses. Had it been her right leg? He couldn't remember. *Jesus, don't let it be her...*

"*Who?*" Robin said again, losing patience.

"There are two army guys," said Strike, rubbing his stubbly chin. "They're both crazy enough and violent enough to—to—"

A gigantic, involuntary yawn interrupted him. Robin waited for cogent speech to resume, wondering whether he had been out with his new girlfriend the previous evening. Elin was an ex-professional violinist, now a presenter on Radio Three, a stunning Nordic-looking blonde who reminded Robin of a more beautiful Sarah Shadlock. She supposed that this was one reason why she had taken an almost immediate dislike to Elin. The other was that she had, in Robin's hearing, referred to her as Strike's secretary.

"Sorry," Strike said. "I was up late writing up notes for the Khan job. Knackered."

He checked his watch.

"Shall we go downstairs and eat? I'm starving."

"In a minute. It's not even twelve. I want to know about these men."

Strike sighed.

"All right," he said, dropping his voice as a man passed their table on the way to the bathroom. "Donald Laing, King's Own Royal Borderers." He remembered again eyes like a ferret's, concentrated hatred, the rose tattoo. "I got him life."

"But then—"

"Out in ten," said Strike. "He's been on the loose since 2007. Laing wasn't your run-of-the-mill nutter, he was an animal, a clever, devious animal; a sociopath—the real deal, if you ask me. I got him life for something I shouldn't have been investigating. He was about to get off on the original charge. Laing's got bloody good reason to hate my guts."

But he did not say what Laing had done or why he, Strike, had been investigating it. Sometimes, and frequently when talking about his career in the Special Investigation Branch, Robin could tell by Strike's tone when he had come to the point beyond which he did not wish to speak. She had never yet pushed him past it. Reluctantly, she abandoned the subject of Donald Laing.

"Who was the other army guy?"

"Noel Brockbank. Desert Rat."

"Desert—what?"

"Seventh Armoured Brigade."

Strike was becoming steadily more taciturn, his expression brooding. Robin wondered whether this was because he was hungry—he was a man who needed regular sustenance to maintain an equable mood—or for some darker reason.

"Shall we eat, then?" Robin asked.

"Yeah," said Strike, draining his pint and getting to his feet.

The cozy basement restaurant comprised a red-carpeted room with a second bar, wooden tables and walls covered in framed prints. They were the first to sit down and order.

"You were saying, about Noel Brockbank," Robin prompted Strike when he had chosen fish and chips and she had asked for a salad.

"Yeah, he's another one with good reason to hold a grudge," said Strike shortly. He had not wanted to talk about Donald Laing and he was showing even more reluctance to discuss Brockbank. After a long pause in which Strike glared over Robin's shoulder at nothing, he said, "Brockbank's not right in the head. Or so he claimed."

"Did you put him in prison?"

"No," said Strike.

His expression had become forbidding. Robin waited, but she could tell nothing more was coming on Brockbank, so she asked:

"And the other one?"

This time Strike did not answer at all. She thought he had not heard her.

"Who's—?"

"I don't want to talk about it," grunted Strike.

He glowered into his fresh pint, but Robin refused to be intimidated.

"Whoever sent that leg," she said, "sent it to *me*."

"All right," said Strike grudgingly, after a brief hesitation. "His name's Jeff Whittaker."

Robin felt a thrill of shock. She did not need to ask how Strike knew Jeff Whittaker. She already knew, although they had never discussed him.

Cormoran Strike's early life was documented on the internet and it had been endlessly rehashed by the extensive press coverage of his detective triumphs. He was the illegitimate and unplanned offspring of a rock star and a woman always described as a supergroupie, a woman who had died of an overdose when Strike was twenty. Jeff Whittaker had been her much younger second husband, who had been accused and acquitted of her murder.

They sat in silence until their food arrived.

"Why are you only having a salad? Aren't you hungry?" asked Strike, clearing his plate of chips. As Robin had suspected, his mood had improved with the ingestion of carbohydrates.

"Wedding," said Robin shortly.

Strike said nothing. Comments on her figure fell strictly outside the self-imposed boundaries he had established for their relationship, which he had determined from the outset must never become too intimate. Nevertheless, he thought she was becoming too thin. In his opinion (and even the thought fell outside those same boundaries), she looked better curvier.

"Aren't you even going to tell me," Robin asked, after several more minutes' silence, "what your connection with that song is?"

He chewed for a while, drank more beer, ordered another pint of Doom Bar then said, "My mother had the title tattooed on her."

He did not fancy telling Robin exactly where the tattoo had been. He preferred not to think about that. However, he was mellowing with food and drink: Robin had never showed prurient interest in his past and he supposed she was justified in a request for information today.

"It was her favorite song. Blue Öyster Cult were her favorite band. Well, 'favorite' is an understatement. Obsession, really."

"Her favorite wasn't the Deadbeats?" asked Robin, without thinking. Strike's father was the lead singer of the Deadbeats. They had never discussed him, either.

"No," said Strike, managing a half-smile. "Old Jonny came a poor second with Leda. She wanted Eric Bloom, lead singer of Blue Öyster Cult, but she never got him. One of the very few who got away."

Robin was not sure what to say. She had wondered before what it felt like to have your mother's epic sexual history online for anybody to see. Strike's fresh pint arrived and he took a swig before continuing.

"I was nearly christened Eric Bloom Strike," he said and Robin choked on her water. He laughed as she coughed into a napkin. "Let's face it, Cormoran's not much bloody better. Cormoran Blue—"

"*Blue?*"

"Blue Öyster Cult, aren't you listening?"

"God," said Robin. "You keep that quiet."

"Wouldn't you?"

"What does it mean, 'Mistress of the Salmon Salt'?"

"Search me. Their lyrics are insane. Science fiction. Crazy stuff."

A voice in his head: *She wanted to die. She was the quicklime girl.*

He drank more beer.

"I don't think I've ever heard any Blue Öyster Cult," said Robin.

"Yeah, you have," Strike contradicted her. "'Don't Fear the Reaper.'"

"Don't—what?"

"It was a monster hit for them. 'Don't Fear the Reaper.'"

"Oh, I—I see."

For one startled moment, Robin had thought that he was giving her advice.

They ate in silence for a while until Robin, unable to keep the question down any longer, though hoping she did not sound scared, asked:

"Why do you think the leg was addressed to me?"

Strike had already had time to ponder this question.

"I've been wondering that," he said, "and I think we've got to consider it a tacit threat, so, until we've found out—"

"I'm not stopping work," said Robin fiercely. "I'm not staying at home. That's what Matthew wants."

"You've spoken to him, have you?"

She had made the call while Strike was downstairs with Wardle.

"Yes. He's angry with me for signing for it."

"I expect he's worried about you," said Strike insincerely. He had met Matthew on a handful of occasions and disliked him more each time.

"He's not worried," snapped Robin. "He just thinks that this is it, that I'll have to leave now, that I'll be scared out. I won't."

Matthew had been appalled at her news, but even so, she had heard a faint trace of satisfaction in his voice, felt his unexpressed conviction that now, at last, she must see what a ridiculous choice it had been to throw in her lot with a rackety private detective who could not afford to give her a decent salary. Strike had her working unsociable hours that meant she had to have packages sent to work instead of the flat. ("I didn't get sent a leg because Amazon couldn't deliver to the house!" Robin had said hotly.) And, of course, on top of everything else, Strike was now mildly famous and a source of fascination to their friends. Matthew's work as an accountant did not carry quite the same cachet. His resentment and jealousy ran deep and, increasingly, burst their bounds.

Strike was not fool enough to encourage Robin in any disloyalty to Matthew that she might regret when she was less shaken.

"Addressing the leg to you instead of me was an afterthought," he said. "They put my name on there first. I reckon they were either trying to worry me by showing they knew your name, or trying to frighten you off working for me."

"Well, I'm not going to be frightened off," said Robin.

"Robin, this is no time for heroics. Whoever he is, he's telling us he knows a lot about me, that he knows your name and, as of this morning, exactly what you look like. He saw you up close. I don't like that."

"You obviously don't think my countersurveillance abilities are up to much."

"Seeing as you're talking to the man who sent you on the best bloody course I could find," said Strike, "and who read that fulsome letter of commendation you shoved under my nose—"

"Then you don't think my self-defense is any good."

"I've never seen any of it and I've got only your word that you ever learned any."

"Have you ever known me lie about what I can and can't do?" demanded Robin, affronted, and Strike was forced to acknowledge that he had not. "Well then! I won't take stupid risks. You've trained me to notice anyone dodgy. Anyway, you can't afford to send me home. We're struggling to cover our cases as it is."

Strike sighed and rubbed his face with two large hairy-backed hands.

"Nothing after dark," he said. "And you need to carry an alarm, a decent one."

"Fine," she said.

"Anyway, you're doing Radford from next Monday," he said, taking comfort from the thought.

Radford was a wealthy entrepreneur who wanted to put an investigator, posing as a part-time worker, into his office to expose what he suspected were criminal dealings by a senior manager. Robin was the obvious choice, because Strike had become more recognizable since their second high-profile murder case. As Strike drained his third pint, he wondered whether he might be able to convince Radford to increase Robin's hours. He would be glad to know she was safe in a palatial office block, nine to five every day, until the maniac who had sent the leg was caught.

Robin, meanwhile, was fighting waves of exhaustion and a vague nausea. A row, a broken night, the dreadful shock of the severed leg—and now she would have to head home and justify all over again her wish to continue doing a dangerous job for a bad salary. Matthew, who had once been one of her primary sources of comfort and support, had become merely another obstacle to be navigated.

Unbidden, unwanted, the image of the cold, severed leg in its cardboard box came back to her. She wondered when she would stop thinking about it. The fingertips that had grazed it tingled unpleasantly. Unconsciously, she tightened her hand into a fist in her lap.

5

Hell's built on regret.

Blue Öyster Cult, "The Revenge of Vera Gemini"
Lyrics by Patti Smith

Much later, after he had seen Robin safely onto the Tube, Strike returned to the office and sat alone in silence at her desk, lost in thought.

He had seen plenty of dismembered corpses, seen them rotting in mass graves and lying, freshly blown apart, by roadsides: severed limbs, flesh pulped, bones crushed. Unnatural death was the business of the Special Investigation Branch, the plainclothes wing of the Royal Military Police, and his and his colleagues' reflexive reaction had often been humor. That was how you coped when you saw the dead torn and mutilated. Not for the SIB the luxury of corpses washed and prettified in satin-lined boxes.

Boxes. It had looked quite ordinary, the cardboard box in which the leg had come. No markings to indicate its origin, no trace of a previous addressee, nothing. The whole thing had been so organized, so careful, so neat—and this was what unnerved him, not the leg itself, nasty object though it was. What appalled him was the careful, meticulous, almost clinical *modus operandi*.

Strike checked his watch. He was supposed to be going out with Elin this evening. His girlfriend of two months was in the throes of a divorce that was proceeding with the chilly brinkmanship of a grandmaster chess tournament. Her estranged husband was very wealthy, something that Strike had not realized until the first night he had been permitted to come back to the marital home and found himself in a spacious, wood-floored apartment overlooking Regent's Park. The shared custody arrangements meant that she was only prepared to meet Strike on nights when her five-year-old daughter was not at home, and when they went out, they chose the capital's quieter and more obscure restaurants as Elin did not wish her estranged husband to know that she was seeing anyone else. The situation suited Strike perfectly. It had been a perennial problem in his relationships that the normal nights for recreation were often nights that he had to be out tailing other people's unfaithful partners, and he had no particular desire to kindle a close relationship with Elin's daughter. He had not lied to Robin: he did not know how to talk to children.

He reached for his mobile. There were a few things he could do before he left for dinner.

The first call went to voicemail. He left a message asking Graham Hardacre, his ex-colleague in the Special Investigation Branch, to call him. He was not sure where Hardacre was currently stationed. The last time they had spoken, he had been due a move from Germany.

To Strike's disappointment, his second call, which was to an old friend whose life path had run more or less in the opposite direction to that of Hardacre, was not picked up either. Strike left a second, almost identical message, and hung up.

Pulling Robin's chair closer to the computer, he turned it on and stared at the homepage without seeing it. The image that was filling his mind, entirely against his will, was of his mother, naked. Who had known the tattoo was there? Her husband, obviously, and the many boyfriends who had woven in and out of her life, and anyone else who might have seen her undressed in the squats and the filthy communes in which they had intermittently lived. Then there was the possibility that had occurred to him in the Tottenham, but which he had not felt equal to sharing with Robin: that Leda had, at some point, been photographed in the nude. It would have been entirely in character.

His fingers hovered over the keyboard. He got as far as *Leda Strike nak* before deleting, letter by letter, with an angry, jabbing forefinger. There were places no normal man wanted to go, phrases you did not want to leave on your internet search history, but also, unfortunately, tasks you did not want to delegate.

He contemplated the search box he had emptied, the cursor blinking dispassionately at him, then typed fast in his usual two-fingered style: *Donald Laing.*

There were plenty of them, especially in Scotland, but he could rule out anyone who had been paying rent or voting in elections while Laing had been in jail. After careful elimination and bearing in mind Laing's approximate age, Strike narrowed his focus to a man who appeared to have been living with a woman called Lorraine MacNaughton in Corby in 2008. Lorraine MacNaughton was now registered as living there alone.

He deleted Laing's name and substituted *Noel Brockbank.* There were fewer of them in the UK than there had been Donald Laings, but Strike reached a similar dead end. There had been an N. C. Brockbank living alone in Manchester in 2006, but if that was Strike's man, it suggested that he had split up with his wife. Strike was not sure whether that would be a good or a bad thing...

Slumping back in Robin's chair, Strike moved on to considering the likely consequences of being sent an anonymous severed leg. The police would have to ask the public for information soon, but Wardle had promised to warn Strike before they gave a press conference. A story this bizarre and grotesque would always be news, but interest would be increased—and it gave him no pleasure to reflect on it—because the leg had been sent to his office. Cormoran Strike was newsworthy these days. He had solved two murders under the noses of the Met, both of which would have fascinated the public, even had a private detective not solved them: the first, because the victim had been a beautiful young woman, the second, because it had been a strange, ritualistic killing.

How, Strike wondered, would the sending of the leg affect the business he had been working so hard to build up? He could not help feeling that the consequences were likely to be serious. Internet searches were a cruel barometer of status. Sometime soon, Googling

Cormoran Strike would not return to the top of the page glowing encomiums on his two most famous and successful cases, but the brutal fact that he was a man in receipt of a body part, a man who had at least one very nasty enemy. Strike was sure he understood the public well enough, or at least the insecure, frightened and angry section of it that was the private investigator's bread and butter, to know they were unlikely to be drawn to a business that received severed legs in the post. At best, new clients would assume that he and Robin had troubles enough of their own; at worst, that they had, through recklessness or ineptitude, got into something way over their heads.

He was about to turn off the computer when he changed his mind and, with even more reluctance than he had brought to the job of searching for his mother in the nude, typed in *Brittany Brockbank.*

There were a few of them on Facebook, on Instagram, working for companies of which he had never heard, beaming out of selfies. He scrutinized the images. They were nearly all in their twenties, the age she would be now. He could discount those who were black, but there was no telling which of the others, brunette, blonde or redhead, pretty or plain, photographed beaming or moody or caught unawares, was the one he sought. None were wearing glasses. Was she too vain to wear them in a picture? Had she had her eyes lasered? Perhaps she eschewed social media. She had wanted to change her name, he remembered that. Or perhaps the reason for her absence was more fundamental—she was dead.

He looked at his watch again: time to go and change.

It can't be her, he thought, and then, *let it not be her.*

Because if it was her, it was his fault.

6

Is it any wonder that my mind's on fire?

Blue Öyster Cult, "Flaming Telepaths"

Robin was unusually vigilant on the journey home that evening, surreptitiously comparing every man in the carriage with her memory of the tall figure in black leathers who had handed her the gruesome package. A thin young Asian man in a cheap suit smiled hopefully as she caught his eye for the third time; after that, she kept her eyes on her phone, exploring—when reception permitted—the BBC website and wondering, like Strike, when the leg would become news.

Forty minutes after leaving work she entered the large Waitrose near her home station. The fridge at home had almost nothing in it. Matthew did not enjoy food shopping and (although he had denied it during their last row but one) she was sure that he thought she, who contributed less than a third of the household income, ought to bolster her contribution by performing those mundane tasks he did not like.

Single men in suits were filling their baskets and trolleys with ready meals. Professional women hurried past, grabbing pasta that would be quick to cook for the family. An exhausted-looking young mother with a tiny baby screaming in its buggy wove around the aisles like a groggy moth, unable to focus, a single bag of carrots in her basket. Robin moved slowly up and down the aisles, feeling oddly jumpy. There was nobody there who resembled the man in black motorcycle leathers, nobody who might be lurking, fantasizing about cutting off Robin's legs . . . *cutting off my legs* . . .

"Excuse me!" said a cross middle-aged woman trying to reach the sausages. Robin apologized and moved aside, surprised to find that she was holding a pack of chicken thighs. Throwing it into her trolley, she hurried off to the other end of the supermarket where, among the wines and spirits, she found relative quiet. Here she pulled out her mobile and called Strike. He answered on the second ring.

"Are you all right?"

"Yes, of course—"

"Where are you?"

"Waitrose."

A short, balding man was perusing the shelf of sherry just behind Robin, his eyes level with her breasts. When she moved aside, he moved with her. Robin glared; he blushed and moved away.

"Well, you should be OK in Waitrose."

"Mm," said Robin, her eyes on the bald man's retreating back. "Listen, this might be nothing, but I've just remembered: we've had a couple of weird letters in the last few months."

"Nutter letters?"

"Don't start."

Robin always protested at this blanket term. They had attracted a significant increase in oddball correspondence since Strike had solved his second high-profile murder case. The most coherent of the writers simply asked for money, on the assumption that Strike was now immensely rich. Then came those who had strange personal grudges that they wished Strike to avenge, those whose waking hours seemed devoted to proving outlandish theories, those whose needs and wishes were so inchoate and rambling that the only message they conveyed was mental illness, and finally ("Now *these* seem nutty," Robin had said) a sprinkling of people, both male and female, who seemed to find Strike attractive.

"Addressed to you?" Strike asked, suddenly serious.

"No, you."

She could hear him moving around his flat as they talked. Perhaps he was going out with Elin tonight. He never talked about the relationship. If Elin had not dropped by the office one day, Robin doubted that she would have known that she existed—perhaps not until he turned up for work one day wearing a wedding ring.

"What did they say?" asked Strike.

"Well, one of them was from a girl who wanted to cut off her own leg. She was asking for advice."

"Say that again?"

"She wanted to cut off her own leg," Robin enunciated clearly, and a woman choosing a bottle of rosé nearby threw her a startled look.

"Jesus Christ," muttered Strike. "And I'm not allowed to call them nutters. You think she managed it and thought I'd like to know?"

"I thought a letter like that might be relevant," said Robin repressively. "Some people *do* want to cut bits of themselves off, it's a recognized phenomenon, it's called…*not* 'being a nutter,'" she added, correctly anticipating him, and he laughed. "And there was another one, from a person who signed with their initials: a long letter, they went on and on about your leg and how they wanted to make it up to you."

"If they were trying to make it up to me you'd think they would've sent a man's leg. I'd look pretty bloody stupid—"

"Don't," she said. "Don't joke. I don't know how you can."

"I don't know how you can't," he said, but kindly.

She heard a very familiar scraping noise followed by a sonorous clang.

"You're looking in the nutter drawer!"

"I don't think you should call it the 'nutter drawer,' Robin. Bit disrespectful to our mentally ill—"

"I'll see you tomorrow," she said, smiling against her will, and hung up on his laughter.

The fatigue she had been fighting all day washed over her anew as she ambled around the supermarket. It was deciding what to eat that was effortful; she would have found it quite soothing merely to shop from a list that somebody else had prepared. Like the working mothers seeking anything quick to cook, Robin gave up and chose a lot of pasta. Queuing at the checkout, she found herself right behind the young woman whose baby had at last exhausted itself and now slept as though dead, fists flung out, eyes tight shut.

"Cute," said Robin, who felt the girl needed encouragement.

"When he's asleep," the mother replied with a weak smile.

By the time Robin had let herself in at home she was truly exhausted. To her surprise, Matthew was standing waiting for her in the narrow hall.

"*I* shopped!" he said when he saw the four bulging shopping bags in her hands and she heard his disappointment that the grand gesture had been undermined. "I sent you a text that I was going to Waitrose!"

"Must've missed it," said Robin. "Sorry."

She had probably been on the phone to Strike. They might even have been there at the same time, but of course she had spent half her visit skulking among the wine and spirits.

Matthew walked forward, arms outstretched, and pulled her into a hug with what she could not help but feel was infuriating magnanimity. Even so, she had to admit that he looked, as always, wonderfully handsome in his dark suit, his thick tawny hair swept back off his forehead.

"It must've been scary," he murmured, his breath warm in her hair.

"It was," she said, wrapping her arms around his waist.

They ate pasta in peace, without a single mention of Sarah Shadlock, Strike or Jacques Burger. The furious ambition of that morning, to make Matthew acknowledge that it had been Sarah, not she, who had voiced admiration of curly hair, had burned out. Robin felt that she was being rewarded for her mature forbearance when Matthew said apologetically:

"I'm going to have to do a bit of work after dinner."

"No problem," said Robin. "I wanted an early night anyway."

She took a low-calorie hot chocolate and a copy of *Grazia* to bed with her, but she could not concentrate. After ten minutes, she got up and fetched her laptop, took it back to bed with her and Googled Jeff Whittaker.

She had read the Wikipedia entry before, during one of her guilty trawls through Strike's past, but now she read with greater attention. It started with a familiar disclaimer:

This article has multiple issues.

This article needs additional citations for verification.

This article possibly contains original research.

Jeff Whittaker

Jeff Whittaker (b.1969) is a musician best known for his marriage to 1970s supergroupie Leda Strike, whom he was charged with killing in 1994.[1] Whittaker is a grandson of diplomat Sir Randolph Whittaker KCMB DSO.

Early Life

Whittaker was raised by his grandparents. His teenage mother, Patricia Whittaker, was schizophrenic.[citation needed] Whittaker never knew who his father was.[citation needed] He was expelled from Gordonstoun School after drawing a knife on a member of staff.[citation needed] He claims that his grandfather locked him in a shed for three days following his expulsion, a charge his grandfather denies.[2] Whittaker ran away from home and lived rough for a period during his teens. He also claims to have worked as a gravedigger.[citation needed]

Musical Career

Whittaker played guitar and wrote lyrics for a succession of thrash metal bands in the late 80s and early 90s, including Restorative Art, Devilheart and Necromantic.[3][4]

Personal Life

In 1991 Whittaker met Leda Strike, ex-girlfriend of Jonny Rokeby and Rick Fantoni, who was working for the record company considering signing Necromantic.[citation needed] Whittaker and Strike were married in 1992. In December of that year she gave birth to a son, Switch LaVey Bloom Whittaker.[5] In 1993 Whittaker was sacked from Necromantic due to his drug abuse.[citation needed]

When Leda Whittaker died of a heroin overdose in 1994, Whittaker was charged with her murder. He was found not guilty.[6][7][8][9]

In 1995 Whittaker was re-arrested for assault and attempted kidnap of his son, who was in the custody of Whittaker's grandparents. He received a suspended jail sentence for the assault on his grandfather.[*citation needed*]

In 1998 Whittaker threatened a coworker with a knife and received a three-month jail sentence.[10][11]

In 2002 Whittaker was jailed for preventing the lawful burial of a body. Karen Abraham, with whom he had been living, was found to have died of heart failure, but Whittaker had kept her body in their shared flat for a month.[12][13][14]

In 2005 Whittaker was jailed for dealing crack cocaine.[15]

Robin read the page twice. Her concentration was poor tonight. Information seemed to slide off the surface of her mind, failing to be absorbed. Parts of Whittaker's history stood out, glaringly strange. Why would anyone conceal a corpse for a month? Had Whittaker feared that he would be charged with murder again, or was there some other reason? Bodies, limbs, pieces of dead flesh... She sipped the hot chocolate and grimaced. It tasted of flavored dust; in the pressure she felt to be slim in her wedding dress, she had forsworn chocolate in its true form for a month now.

She replaced the mug on her bedside cabinet, returned her fingers to the keyboard and searched for images of *Jeff Whittaker trial.*

A matrix of photographs filled the screen, showing two different Whittakers, photographed eight years apart and entering and exiting two different courts.

The young Whittaker accused of murdering his wife wore dreadlocks tied back in a ponytail. He had a certain seedy glamour in his black suit and tie, tall enough to see over the heads of most of the photographers crowding around him. His cheekbones were high, his skin sallow and his large eyes set unusually far apart: the kind of eyes that might have belonged to an opium-crazed poet, or a heretic priest.

The Whittaker who had been accused of preventing another woman's burial had lost his vagrant handsomeness. He was heavier, with a brutal crew cut and a beard. Only the wide-set eyes were unchanged, and the aura of unapologetic arrogance.

Robin scrolled slowly down through the photographs. Soon the pictures of what she thought of as "Strike's Whittaker" became interspersed with pictures of other Whittakers who had been in trials. A cherubic-looking African-American called Jeff Whittaker had taken his neighbor to court for allowing his dog to repeatedly foul his lawn.

Why did Strike think his ex-stepfather (she found it odd to think of him in those terms, as he was only five years older than Strike) would have sent him the leg? She wondered when Strike had last seen the man he thought had murdered his mother. There was so much she did not know about her boss. He did not like to talk about his past.

Robin's fingers slid back to the keys and typed *Eric Bloom*.

The first thing that occurred to her, staring at the pictures of the leather-clad seventies rocker, was that he had Strike's exact hair: dense, dark and curly. This reminded her of Jacques Burger and Sarah Shadlock, which did nothing to improve her mood. She turned her attention to the other two men whom Strike had mentioned as possible suspects, but she could not remember what their names had been. Donald something? And a funny name beginning with B...Her memory was usually excellent. Strike often complimented her on it. Why couldn't she remember?

On the other hand, would it matter if she could? There was little you could do on a laptop to find two men who might be anywhere. Robin had not worked for a detective agency for this long without being perfectly aware that those who used pseudonyms, lived rough, favored squats, rented their accommodation or did not add their names to electoral rolls could easily fall through the wide mesh of Directory Enquiries.

After sitting in thought for several more minutes, and with a sense that she was somehow betraying her boss, Robin typed *Leda Strike* into the search box and then, feeling guiltier than ever, *naked*.

The picture was black and white. The young Leda posed with her arms over her head, a long cloud of dark hair falling down over her breasts. Even in the thumbnail version, Robin could make out an arch of curly script set above the dark triangle of pubic hair. Squinting slightly, as though rendering the image a little fuzzy somehow mitigated her actions, Robin brought up the full-sized picture. She did not want to have to zoom in and nor did she need to. The words *Mistress of* were clearly legible.

The bathroom fan whirred into life next door. With a guilty start, Robin shut down the page she had been viewing. Matthew had lately developed a habit of borrowing her laptop and a few weeks previously she had caught him reading her emails to Strike. With this in mind, she reopened the web page, cleared her browsing history, brought up her settings and, after a moment's consideration, changed her password to DontFearTheReaper. That would scupper him.

As she slid out of bed to go and throw the hot chocolate down the kitchen sink it occurred to Robin that she had not bothered to look up any details about Terence "Digger" Malley. Of course, the police would be far better placed than she or Strike to find a London gangster.

Doesn't matter, though, she thought sleepily, heading back to the bedroom. *It isn't Malley.*

7

Good to Feel Hungry

Of course, if he'd had the sense he was born with—that had been a favorite phrase of his mother's, vicious bitch that she'd been (*You haven't got the sense you were born with, have you, you stupid little bastard?*)—if he'd had the sense he was born with, he wouldn't have followed The Secretary the very day after handing her the leg. Only it had been difficult to resist the temptation when he did not know when he would next have a chance. The urge to tail her again had grown upon him in the night, to see what she looked like now that she had opened his present.

From tomorrow, his freedom would be severely curtailed, because It would be home and It required his attention when It was around. Keeping It happy was very important, not least because It earned the money. Stupid and ugly and grateful for affection, It had barely noticed that It was keeping him.

Once he'd seen It off to work that morning he had hurried out of the house to wait for The Secretary at her home station, which had been a smart decision, because she hadn't gone to the office at all. He had thought the arrival of the leg might disrupt her routine and he had been right. He was nearly always right.

He knew how to follow people. At some points today he had been wearing a beanie hat, at others he had been bareheaded. He had stripped to his T-shirt, then worn his jacket and then his jacket turned inside out, sunglasses on, sunglasses off.

The Secretary's value to him—over and above the value any female had to him, if he could get her alone—was in what he was going to do, through her, to Strike. His ambition to be avenged on Strike—permanently, brutally avenged—had grown in him until it became the central ambition of his life. He had always been this way. If someone crossed him they were marked and at some point, whenever opportunity presented itself, even if it took years, they would get theirs. Cormoran Strike had done him more harm than any other human being ever, and he was going to pay a just price.

He had lost track of Strike for several years and then an explosion of publicity had revealed the bastard: celebrated, heroic. This was the status *he* had always wanted, had craved. It had been like drinking acid, choking down the fawning articles about the cunt, but he had devoured everything he could, because you needed to know your target if you wanted to cause maximum damage. He intended to inflict as much pain on Cormoran Strike as was—not humanly possible, because he knew himself to be something more than human—as was superhumanly possible. It would go way beyond a knife in the ribs in the dark. No, Strike's punishment was going to be slower and stranger, frightening, tortuous and finally devastating.

Nobody would ever know he'd done it; why should they? He'd escaped without detection three times now: three women dead and nobody had a clue who'd done it. This knowledge enabled him to read today's *Metro* without the slightest trace of fear; to feel only pride and satisfaction at the hysterical accounts of the severed leg, to savor the whiff of fear and confusion that rose from each story, the bleating incomprehension of the sheep-like masses who scent a wolf.

All he needed now was for The Secretary to take one short walk down a deserted stretch of road...but London throbbed and teemed with people all day long and here he was, frustrated and wary, watching her as he hung around the London School of Economics.

She was tracking someone too, and it was easy to see who that was. Her target had bright platinum hair extensions and led The

Secretary, midafternoon, all the way back to Tottenham Court Road.

The Secretary disappeared inside a pub opposite the lap-dancing club into which her mark had gone. He debated following her inside, but she seemed dangerously watchful today, so he entered a cheap Japanese restaurant with plate-glass windows opposite the pub, took a table near the window and waited for her to emerge.

It would happen, he told himself, staring through his shades into the busy road. He would get her. He had to hold on to that thought, because this evening he was going to have to return to It and the half-life, the lie-life, that allowed the real Him to walk and breathe in secret.

The smeared and dusty London window reflected his naked expression, stripped of the civilized coating he wore to beguile the women who had fallen prey to his charm and his knives. To the surface had risen the creature that lived within, the creature that wanted nothing except to establish its dominance.

8

> I seem to see a rose,
> I reach out, then it goes.
>
> Blue Öyster Cult, "Lonely Teardrops"

As Strike had been expecting ever since the news of the severed leg hit the media, his old acquaintance Dominic Culpepper of the *News of the World* had contacted him early on Tuesday morning in a state of advanced ire. The journalist refused to accept that Strike might have had legitimate reasons for choosing not to contact Culpepper the very second he had realized that he was in receipt of a severed limb, and Strike further compounded this offense by declining the invitation to keep Culpepper informed of every fresh development in the case, in return for a hefty retainer. Culpepper had previously put paid work Strike's way and the detective suspected, by the time the call terminated, that this source of income would henceforth be closed to him. Culpepper was not a happy man.

Strike and Robin did not speak until midafternoon. Strike, who was carrying a backpack, called from a crowded Heathrow Express train.

"Where are you?" he asked.

"Pub opposite Spearmint Rhino," she said. "It's called the Court. Where are you?"

"Coming back from the airport. Mad Dad got on the plane, thank Christ."

Mad Dad was a wealthy international banker whom Strike was

tailing on behalf of his wife. The couple were having an extremely contentious custody battle. The husband's departure for Chicago would mean that Strike would have a few nights' respite from observing him as he sat in his car outside his wife's house at four in the morning, night-vision goggles trained on his young sons' window.

"I'll come and meet you," said Strike. "Sit tight—unless Platinum cops off with someone, obviously."

Platinum was the Russian economics student and lap-dancer. Their client was her boyfriend, a man whom Strike and Robin had nicknamed "Two-Times," partly because this was the second time they had investigated a blonde girlfriend for him, and also because he seemed addicted to finding out where and how his lovers were betraying him. Robin found Two-Times both sinister and pitiable. He had met Platinum at the club Robin was now watching, and Robin and Strike had been given the job of finding out whether any other men were being granted the additional favors she was now giving Two-Times.

The odd thing was that, little though he might believe or like it, Two-Times seemed to have picked an atypically monogamous girlfriend this time. After watching her movements for several weeks, Robin had learned that she was a largely solitary creature, lunching alone with books and rarely interacting with her colleagues.

"She's obviously working at the club to help pay for her course," Robin had told Strike indignantly, after a week's tailing. "If Two-Times doesn't want other men ogling her, why doesn't he help her out financially?"

"The main attraction is that she gives other men lap dances," Strike had replied patiently. "I'm surprised it's taken him this long to go for someone like her. Ticks all his boxes."

Strike had been inside the club shortly after they took the job and he had secured the services of a sad-eyed brunette by the unlikely name of Raven to keep an eye on his client's girlfriend. Raven was to check in once a day, to tell them what Platinum was up to and inform them immediately if the Russian girl appeared to be giving out her phone number or being overattentive to any client. The rules of the club forbade touching or soliciting but Two-Times remained convinced ("Poor, sad bastard," said Strike) that he was only one among many men taking her out to dinner and sharing her bed.

"I still don't understand why we have to watch the place," Robin sighed into the phone, not for the first time. "We could take Raven's calls anywhere."

"You know why," said Strike, who was preparing to disembark. "He likes the photographs."

"But they're only of her walking to and from work."

"Doesn't matter. Turns him on. Plus, he's convinced that one of these days she's going to leave the club with some Russian oligarch."

"Doesn't this stuff ever make you feel grubby?"

"Occupational hazard," said Strike, unconcerned. "See you shortly."

Robin waited amidst the floral and gilt wallpaper. Brocade chairs and mismatched lampshades contrasted strongly with enormous plasma TVs showing football and Coke ads. The paintwork was the fashionable shade of greige in which Matthew's sister had recently painted her sitting room. Robin found it depressing. Her view of the club's entrance was slightly impeded by the wooden banisters of a staircase leading to an upper floor. Outside, a constant stream of traffic flooded left and right, plenty of red double-deckers temporarily obscuring her view of the front of the club.

Strike arrived looking irritable.

"We've lost Radford," he said, dumping his backpack beside the high window table at which she was sitting. "He's just phoned me."

"No!"

"Yep. He thinks you're too newsworthy to plant in his office now."

The press had had the story of the severed leg since six that morning. Wardle had kept his word to Strike and warned him ahead of time. The detective had been able to leave his attic flat in the small hours with enough clothes in his holdall for a few days' absence. He knew the press would soon be staking out the office, and not for the first time.

"And," said Strike, returning to Robin with a pint in his hand and easing himself up onto a bar stool, "Khan's bottled it too. He's going to go for an agency that doesn't attract body parts."

"*Bugger,*" said Robin, and then: "What are you smirking about?"

"Nothing." He did not want to tell her that he always liked it when she said "bugger." It brought out the latent Yorkshire in her accent.

"They were good jobs!" said Robin.

Strike agreed, his eyes on the front of Spearmint Rhino.

"How's Platinum? Raven checked in?"

As Raven had just called, Robin was able to inform Strike that there was, as ever, no news. Platinum was popular with punters and had so far that day given three lap dances that had proceeded, judged by the rules of the establishment, in total propriety.

"Read the stories?" he asked, pointing at an abandoned *Mirror* on a nearby table.

"Only online," said Robin.

"Hopefully it'll bring in some information," said Strike. "Someone must've noticed they're missing a leg."

"Ha ha," said Robin.

"Too soon?"

"Yes," said Robin coldly.

"I did some digging online last night," said Strike. "Brockbank might've been in Manchester in 2006."

"How d'you know it was the right man?"

"I don't, but the guy was around the right age, right middle initial—"

"You remember his middle initial?"

"Yeah," said Strike. "It doesn't look like he's there anymore, though. Same story with Laing. I'm pretty sure he was at an address in Corby in 2008, but he's moved on. How long," Strike added, staring across the street, "has that bloke in the camouflage jacket and shades been in that restaurant?"

"About half an hour."

As far as Strike could tell, the man in sunglasses was watching him back, staring out across the street through two windows. Broad-shouldered and long-legged, he looked too large for the silver chair. With the sliding reflections of traffic and passersby refracting off the window Strike found it difficult to be sure, but he appeared to be sporting heavy stubble.

"What's it like in there?" Robin asked, pointing towards the double doors of Spearmint Rhino under their heavy metallic awning.

"In the strip club?" asked Strike, taken aback.

"No, in the Japanese restaurant," said Robin sarcastically. "Of course in the strip club."

"It's all right," he said, not entirely sure what he was being asked.

"What does it look like?"

"Gold. Mirrors. Dim lighting." When she looked at him expectantly, he said, "There's a pole in the middle, where they dance."

"Not lap dances?"

"There are private booths for them."

"What do the girls wear?"

"I dunno—not much—"

His mobile rang: Elin.

Robin turned her face away, toying with what looked like a pair of reading glasses on the table in front of her, but which actually contained the small camera with which she photographed Platinum's movements. She had found this gadget exciting when Strike first handed it to her, but the thrill had long since worn off. She drank her tomato juice and stared out of the window, trying not to listen to what Strike and Elin were saying to each other. He always sounded matter-of-fact when on the phone to his girlfriend, but then, it was difficult to imagine Strike murmuring endearments to anyone. Matthew called her both "Robsy" and "Rosy-Posy" when he was in the right mood, which was not often these days.

"...at Nick and Ilsa's," Strike was saying. "Yeah. No, I agree... yeah... all right... you too."

He cut the call.

"Is that where you're going to stay?" Robin asked. "With Nick and Ilsa?"

They were two of Strike's oldest friends. She had met and liked both of them on a couple of visits to the office.

"Yeah, they say I can stay as long as I want."

"Why not with Elin?" asked Robin, risking rebuff, because she was perfectly aware of the line Strike preferred to maintain between his personal and professional lives.

"Wouldn't work," he said. He didn't seem annoyed that she had asked, but showed no inclination to elaborate. "I forgot," he added, glancing back across the street to the Japanese Canteen. The table where the man in camouflage jacket and shades had sat was now unoccupied. "I got you this."

It was a rape alarm.

"I've already got one," said Robin, pulling it out of her coat pocket and showing him.

"Yeah, but this one's better," said Strike, showing her its features. "You want an alarm of at least 120 decibels and it sprays them with indelible red stuff."

"Mine does 140 decibels."

"I still think this one's better."

"Is this the usual bloke thing of thinking any gadget you've chosen must be superior to anything I've got?"

He laughed and drained his pint.

"I'll see you later."

"Where are you going?"

"I'm meeting Shanker."

The name was unfamiliar to her.

"The bloke who sometimes gives me tip-offs I can barter with the Met," Strike explained. "The bloke who told me who'd stabbed that police informer, remember? Who recommended me as a heavy to that gangster?"

"Oh," said Robin. "Him. You've never told me what he was called."

"Shanker's my best chance for finding out where Whittaker is," said Strike. "He might have some information on Digger Malley as well. He runs with some of the same crowd."

He squinted across the road.

"Keep an eye out for that camouflage jacket."

"You're jumpy."

"Bloody right I'm jumpy, Robin," he said, drawing out a pack of cigarettes ready for the short walk to the Tube. "Someone sent us an effing leg."

9

One Step Ahead of the Devil

Seeing Strike in the mutilated flesh, walking along the opposite pavement towards the Court, had been an unexpected bonus.

What a fat fucker he'd become since they had last seen each other, ambling up the road carrying his backpack like the dumb squaddie he had once been, without realizing that the man who had sent him a leg was sitting barely fifty yards away. So much for the great detective! Into the pub he'd gone to join little Secretary. He was almost certainly fucking her. He hoped so, anyway. That would make what he was going to do to her even more satisfying.

Then, as he had stared through his sunglasses at the figure of Strike sitting just inside the pub window, he thought that Strike turned and looked back. Of course, he couldn't make out features from across the road, through two panes of glass and his own tinted lenses, but something in the distant figure's attitude, the full disc of its face turned in his direction, had brought him to a high pitch of tension. They had looked at each other across the road and the traffic growled past in either direction, intermittently blocking them from view.

He had waited until three double-deckers had come crawling end to end into the space between them, then slid out of his chair, through the glass doors of the restaurant and up the side street. Adrenaline coursed through him as he stripped off his camouflage jacket and turned it inside out. There could be no question of binning it: his knives were concealed inside the lining. Around another corner, he broke into a flat-out run.

10

With no love, from the past.

Blue Öyster Cult, "Shadow of California"

The unbroken stream of traffic obliged Strike to stand and wait before crossing Tottenham Court Road, his eyes sweeping the opposite pavement. When he reached the other side of the street he peered through the window of the Japanese restaurant, but there was no camouflage jacket to be seen, nor did any of the men in shirts or T-shirts resemble the sunglasses-wearer in size or shape.

Strike felt his mobile vibrate and pulled it out of his jacket pocket. Robin had texted him:

Get a grip.

Grinning, Strike raised a hand of farewell towards the windows of the Court and headed off towards the Tube.

Perhaps he was just jumpy, as Robin had said. What were the odds that the nutter who had sent the leg would be sitting watching Robin in broad daylight? Yet he had not liked the fixed stare of the big man in the camouflage jacket, nor the fact that he had been wearing sunglasses: the day was not that bright. Had his disappearance while Strike's view was occluded been coincidental or deliberate?

The trouble was that Strike could place little reliance on his memories of what the three men who were currently preoccupying him looked like, because he had not seen Brockbank for eight years,

Laing for nine and Whittaker for sixteen. Any of them might have grown fat or wasted in that time, lost their hair, become bearded or mustached, be incapacitated or newly muscled. Strike himself had lost a leg since he had last set eyes on any of them. The one thing that nobody could disguise was height. All three of the men Strike was concerned about had been six feet tall or over and Camouflage Jacket had looked at least that in his metal chair.

The phone in his pocket buzzed as he walked towards Tottenham Court Road station, and on pulling it out of his pocket he saw, to his pleasure, that it was Graham Hardacre. Drawing aside so as not to impede passersby, he answered.

"Oggy?" said his ex-colleague's voice. "What gives, mate? Why are people sending you legs?"

"I take it you're not in Germany?" said Strike.

"Edinburgh, been here six weeks. Just been reading about you in the *Scotsman*."

The Special Investigation Branch of the Royal Military Police had an office in Edinburgh Castle: 35 Section. It was a prestigious posting.

"Hardy, I need a favor," said Strike. "Intel on a couple of guys. D'you remember Noel Brockbank?"

"Hard to forget. Seventh Armoured, if memory serves?"

"That's him. The other one's Donald Laing. He was before I knew you. King's Own Royal Borderers. Knew him in Cyprus."

"I'll see what I can do when I get back to the office, mate. I'm in the middle of a plowed field right now."

A chat about mutual acquaintances was curtailed by the increasing noise of rush-hour traffic. Hardacre promised to ring back once he had had a look at the army records and Strike continued towards the Tube.

He got out at Whitechapel station thirty minutes later to find a text message from the man he was supposed to be meeting.

Sorry Bunsen cant do today ill give you a bell

This was both disappointing and inconvenient, but not a surprise. Considering that Strike was not carrying a consignment of drugs or a large pile of used notes, and that he did not require intimidation or beating, it was a mark of great esteem that Shanker had even condescended to fix a time and place for meeting.

Strike's knee was complaining after a day on his feet, but there were no seats outside the station. He leaned up against the yellow brick wall beside the entrance and called Shanker's number.

"Yeah, all right, Bunsen?"

Just as he no longer remembered why Shanker was called Shanker, he had no more idea why Shanker called him Bunsen. They had met when they were seventeen and the connection between them, though profound in its way, bore none of the usual stigmata of teenage friendship. In fact, it had not been a friendship in any usual sense, but more like an enforced brotherhood. Strike was sure that Shanker would mourn his passing were he to die, but he was equally certain that Shanker would rob his body of all valuables if left alone with it. What others might not understand was that Shanker would do so in the belief that Strike would be glad, in whatever afterworld he was dwelling, to think that it was Shanker who had his wallet, rather than some anonymous opportunist.

"You're busy, Shanker?" asked Strike, lighting a fresh cigarette.

"Yeah, Bunsen, no chance today. Woss 'appening?"

"I'm looking for Whittaker."

"Gonna finish it, are you?"

The change in Shanker's tone would have alarmed anyone who had forgotten who Shanker was, what he was. To Shanker and his associates, there was no proper end to a grudge other than killing and, in consequence, he had spent half his adult life behind bars. Strike was surprised Shanker had survived into his midthirties.

"I just want to know where he is," said Strike repressively.

He doubted that Shanker would have heard about the leg. Shanker lived in a world where news was of strictly personal interest and was conveyed by word of mouth.

"I can 'ave an ask around."

"Usual rates," said Strike, who had a standing arrangement with Shanker for useful bits of information. "And—Shanker?"

His old friend had a habit of hanging up without warning when his attention was diverted.

"'S'there more?" said Shanker, his voice moving from distant to close as he spoke; Strike had been right to think he had removed the mobile from his ear, assuming they were done.

"Yeah," said Strike. "Digger Malley."

A silence on the end of the line eloquently expressed the fact that, just as Strike never forgot what Shanker was, nor did Shanker ever forget what Strike was.

"Shanker, this is between you and me, no one else. You've never discussed me with Malley, have you?"

After a pause, and in his most dangerous voice, Shanker said:

"The fuck would I do that for?"

"Had to ask. I'll explain when I see you."

The dangerous silence continued.

"Shanker, when have I ever grassed you up?" asked Strike.

Another, shorter silence, and then Shanker said in what, to Strike, was his normal voice:

"Yeah, all right. Whittaker, huh? See what I can do, Bunsen."

The line went dead. Shanker did not do good-byes.

Strike sighed and lit up another cigarette. The journey had been pointless. He would get straight back on a train once he had finished his Benson & Hedges.

The station entrance gave onto a kind of concrete forecourt surrounded by the backs of buildings. The Gherkin, that giant black bullet of a building, glinted on the distant horizon. It had not been there twenty years previously, during Strike's family's brief sojourn in Whitechapel.

Looking around, Strike felt no sense of homecoming or nostalgia. He could not remember this patch of concrete, these nondescript rears of buildings. Even the station seemed only dimly familiar. The endless series of moves and upheavals that had characterized life with his mother had blurred memories of individual places; he sometimes forgot which corner shop had belonged to which rundown flat, which local pub had adjoined which squat.

He had meant to get back on the Tube and yet before he knew it, he was walking, heading for the one place in London he had avoided for seventeen years: the building where his mother had died. It had been the last of Leda's squats, two floors of a decrepit building on Fulbourne Street, which was barely a minute from the station. As he walked, Strike began to remember. Of course: he had walked over this metal bridge over the railway line during his A-level year. He remembered the name, Castlemain Street, too...surely one of his fellow A-level students, a girl with a pronounced lisp, had lived there...

He slowed to an amble as he reached the end of Fulbourne Street, experiencing a strange double impression. His vague memory of the place, weakened no doubt by his deliberate attempts to forget, lay like a faded transparency over the scene in front of his eyes. The buildings were as shabby as he remembered them, white plaster peeling away from the frontages, but the businesses and shops were totally unfamiliar. He felt as though he had returned to a dreamscape where the scene had shifted and mutated. Of course, everything was impermanent in the poor areas of London, where fragile, fair-weather businesses grew up and faded away and were replaced: cheap signage tacked up and removed; people passing through, passing away.

It took him a minute or two to identify the door of what had once been the squat, because he had forgotten the number. At last he found it, beside a shop selling cheap clothing of both Asian and Western varieties, which he thought had been a West Indian supermarket in his day. The brass letter box brought back a strange stab of memory. It had rattled loudly whenever anyone went in or out of the door.

Fuck, fuck, fuck...

Lighting a second cigarette from the tip of the first, he walked briskly out onto Whitechapel Road, where market stalls stood: more cheap clothing, a multitude of gaudy plastic goods. Strike sped up, walking he was not sure where, and some of what he passed triggered more memories: that snooker hall had been there seventeen years ago...so had the Bell Foundry...and now the memories were rising to bite him as though he had trodden on a nest of sleeping snakes...

As she neared forty, his mother had begun to go for younger men, but Whittaker had been the youngest of the lot: twenty-one when she had started sleeping with him. Her son had been sixteen when she first brought Whittaker home. The musician had looked ravaged even then, with sallow hollows under his wide-apart eyes, which were a striking golden hazel. His dark hair fell in dreadlocks to his shoulders; he lived in the same T-shirt and jeans and consequently stank.

A well-worn phrase kept echoing in Strike's head, keeping pace with his footsteps as he trudged down Whitechapel Road.

Hiding in plain sight. Hiding in plain sight.

Of course people would think he was obsessed, biased, unable to let go. They would say his thoughts had jumped to Whittaker when he saw the leg in the box because he had never got over the fact that Whittaker had walked free on the charge of killing Strike's mother. Even if Strike explained his reasons for suspecting Whittaker, they would probably laugh at the notion that such an ostentatious lover of the perverse and the sadistic could have cut off a woman's leg. Strike knew how deeply ingrained was the belief that the evil conceal their dangerous predilections for violence and domination. When they wear them like bangles for all to see, the gullible populace laughs, calls it a pose, or finds it strangely attractive.

Leda had met Whittaker at the record company where she worked as a receptionist, a minor, living piece of rock history employed as a kind of totem on the front desk. Whittaker, who played the guitar and wrote lyrics for a succession of thrash metal bands that, one by one, threw him out because of his histrionics, substance abuse and aggression, claimed to have met Leda while pursuing a record deal. However, Leda had confided to Strike that their first encounter had happened while she was trying to persuade security not to be so rough with the young man they were throwing out. She had brought him home, and Whittaker had never left.

The sixteen-year-old Strike had not been sure whether or not Whittaker's gloating, open pleasure in everything that was sadistic and demonic was genuine or a pose. All he had known was that he hated Whittaker with a visceral loathing that had transcended anything he had felt for any of the other lovers whom Leda had taken up, then left behind. He had been forced to breathe in the man's stench as he did his homework of an evening in the squat; he had almost been able to taste him. Whittaker tried patronizing the teenager—sudden explosions and waspish put-downs revealed an articulacy he was careful to hide when he wished to ingratiate himself with Leda's less educated friends—but Strike had been ready with put-downs and comebacks of his own and he had the advantage of being less stoned than Whittaker, or, at least, only as stoned as a person could be living in a constant fug of cannabis smoke. Out of Leda's hearing, Whittaker had jeered at Strike's determination to continue his oft-disrupted education. Whittaker was tall and wiry, surprisingly well muscled for one who lived an almost entirely sedentary life; Strike was already over six feet and boxing at a local club. The tension between the two stiffened the smoky air whenever both were present, the threat of violence constant.

Whittaker had driven Strike's half-sister Lucy away for good with his bullying, his sexual taunts and sneers. He had strutted around the squat naked, scratching his tattooed torso, laughing at the fourteen-year-old girl's mortification. One night she had run to the telephone box at the corner of the street and begged their aunt and uncle in Cornwall to come and fetch her. They had arrived at the squat at dawn next day, having driven overnight from St. Mawes. Lucy was ready with her meager possessions in a small suitcase. She had never lived with her mother again.

Ted and Joan had stood on the doorstep and pleaded with Strike to come too. He had refused, his resolve hardening with every plea Joan made, determined to sit Whittaker out, not to leave him alone with his mother. By now, he had heard Whittaker talking lucidly about what it would feel like to take a life, as though it were an epicurean treat. He had not believed, then, that Whittaker meant it, but he had known him capable of violence, and had seen him threaten their fellow squatters. Once—Leda refused to believe it had happened—Strike had witnessed Whittaker attempt to bludgeon a cat that had inadvertently woken him from a doze. Strike had wrested the heavy boot from Whittaker's hand as he chased the terrified cat around the room, swinging at it, screaming and swearing, determined to make the animal pay.

The knee onto which the prosthesis was fitted was beginning to complain as Strike strode faster and faster along the street. The Nag's Head pub rose up on the right as though he had conjured it, squat, square and brick. Only at the door did he catch sight of the dark-clad bouncer and remember that the Nag's Head was another lap-dancing club these days.

"Bollocks," he muttered.

He had no objection to semiclad women gyrating around him while he enjoyed a pint, but he could not justify the exorbitant price of drinks in such an establishment, not when he had lost two clients in a single day.

He therefore entered the next Starbucks he encountered, found a seat and heaved his sore leg onto an empty chair while he moodily stirred a large black coffee. The squashy earth-colored sofas, the tall cups of American froth, the wholesome young people working with quiet efficiency behind a clean glass counter: these, surely, were the perfect antidote to Whittaker's stinking specter, and yet he would not be driven out. Strike found himself unable to stop reliving it all, remembering...

While he had lived with Leda and her son, Whittaker's teenage history of delinquency and violence had been known only to social services in the north of England. The tales he told about his past were legion, highly colored and often contradictory. Only after he had been arrested for murder had the truth leaked out from people from his past who surfaced, some hoping for money from the press, some determined to revenge themselves on him, others trying in their own muddled fashion to defend him.

He had been born into a moneyed upper-middle-class family headed by a knighted diplomat whom Whittaker had believed, until the age of twelve, was his father. At that point he had discovered that his older sister, whom he had been led to believe was in London working as a Montessori teacher, was actually his mother, that she had serious alcohol and drug problems and that she was living in poverty and squalor, ostracized by her family. From this time onward, Whittaker, already a problem child prone to outbursts of extreme temper during which he lashed out indiscriminately, had become determinedly wild. Expelled from his boarding school, he had joined a local gang and soon became ringleader, a phase that culminated in a spell in a correctional facility because he had held a blade to a young girl's throat while his friends sexually assaulted her. Aged fifteen, he had run away to London, leaving a trail of petty crime in his wake and finally succeeding in tracking down his biological mother. A brief, enthusiastic reunion had deteriorated almost at once into mutual violence and animosity.

"Is anyone using this?"

A tall youth had bent over Strike, his hands already gripping the back of the chair on which Strike's leg was resting. He reminded Strike of Robin's fiancé Matthew, with his wavy brown hair and clean-cut good looks. With a grunt, Strike removed his leg, shook his head and watched the guy walk away carrying the chair, rejoining a group of six or more. The girls there were eager for his return, Strike could see: they straightened up and beamed as he placed the chair down and joined them. Whether because of the resemblance to Matthew, or because he had taken Strike's chair, or because Strike genuinely sensed a tosser when he saw one, Strike found the youth obscurely objectionable.

His coffee unfinished but resentful that he had been disturbed, Strike heaved himself back to his feet and left. Spots of rain hit him as he walked back along Whitechapel Road, smoking again and no longer bothering to resist the tidal wave of memory now carrying him along...

Whittaker had had an almost pathological need for attention. He resented Leda's focus being diverted from him at any time and for any reason—her job, her children, her friends—and he would turn his flashes of mesmeric charm on other women whenever he deemed her inattentive. Even Strike, who hated him like a disease, had to acknowledge that Whittaker possessed a powerful sex appeal which worked on nearly every woman who passed through the squat.

Thrown out of his most recent band, Whittaker continued to dream of stardom. He knew three guitar chords and covered every bit of paper not hidden from him with lyrics that drew heavily on the Satanic Bible, which Strike remembered lying, its black cover emblazoned with a pentagram and goat-head combined, on the mattress where Leda and Whittaker slept. Whittaker had an extensive knowledge of the life and career of the American cult leader Charles Manson. The scratchy sound of an old vinyl copy of Manson's album *LIE: The Love and Terror Cult* formed the soundtrack to Strike's GCSE year.

Whittaker had been familiar with Leda's legend when he met her, and liked to hear about the parties she had been at, the men she had slept with. Through her, he became connected to the famous, and as Strike got to know him better he came to conclude that Whittaker craved celebrity above almost anything else. He made no moral distinction between his beloved Manson and the likes of Jonny Rokeby, rock star. Both had fixed themselves permanently in the popular consciousness. If anything, Manson had achieved it more successfully, because his myth would not fluctuate with fashion: evil was always fascinating.

However, Leda's fame was not all that attracted Whittaker. His lover had borne children to two wealthy rock stars who provided child support. Whittaker had entered the squat under the clear impression that it was part of Leda's style to dwell in impoverished bohemia, but that somewhere nearby was a vast pool of money into which Strike and Lucy's fathers—Jonny Rokeby and Rick Fantoni respectively—were pouring money. He did not seem to understand or believe the truth: that years of Leda's financial mismanagement and profligacy had led both men to tie up the money in such a way that Leda could not fritter it away. Gradually, over the months, Whittaker's spiteful asides and jibes on the subject of Leda's reluctance to spend money on him had become more frequent. There were grotesque tantrums when Leda would not fork out for the Fender Stratocaster on which he had set his heart, would not buy him the Jean Paul Gaultier velvet jacket for which, stinking and shabby though he was, he suddenly had a yen.

He increased the pressure, telling outrageous and easily disprovable lies: that he needed urgent medical treatment, that he was ten thousand pounds in debt to a man threatening to break his legs. Leda was alternately amused and upset.

"Darling, I haven't got any dough," she would say. "Really, darling, I haven't, or I'd give you some, wouldn't I?"

Leda had fallen pregnant in Strike's eighteenth year, while he was applying for university. He had been horrified, but even then he had not expected her to marry Whittaker. She had always told her son that she had hated being a wife. Her first teenage essay into matrimony had lasted two weeks before she had fled. Nor did marriage seem at all Whittaker's style.

Yet it had happened, undoubtedly because Whittaker thought it would be the only sure way to get his hands on those mysteriously hidden millions. The ceremony took place at the Marylebone registry office, where two Beatles had previously married. Perhaps Whittaker had imagined that he would be photographed in the doorway like Paul McCartney, but nobody had been interested. It would take the death of his beaming bride to bring the photographers swarming to the court steps.

Strike suddenly realized that he had walked all the way to Aldgate East station without meaning to. This whole trip, he castigated himself, had been a pointless detour. If he had got back on the train at Whitechapel he would have been well on the way to Nick and Ilsa's by now. Instead, he had careered off as fast as he could in the wrong direction, timing his arrival perfectly to hit the rush-hour crush on the Tube.

His size, to which was added the offense of a backpack, caused unexpressed disgruntlement in those commuters forced to share the space with him, but Strike barely noticed. A head taller than anyone near him, he held on to a hand strap and watched his swaying reflection in the darkened windows, remembering the last part, the worst part: Whittaker in court, arguing for his liberty, because the police had spotted anomalies in his story of where he had been on the day that the needle entered his wife's arm, inconsistencies in his account of where the heroin had come from and what Leda's history of drug use had been.

A raggle-taggle procession of fellow squat-dwellers had given evidence about Leda and Whittaker's turbulent, violent relationship, about Leda's eschewal of heroin in all its forms, about Whittaker's threats, his infidelities, his talk of murder and of money, his lack of noticeable grief after Leda's body had been found. They had insisted over and again, with unwise hysteria, that they were sure Whittaker had killed her. The defense found them pathetically easy to discredit.

An Oxford student in the dock had come as a refreshing change. The judge had eyed Strike with approval: he was clean, articulate and intelligent, however large and intimidating he might be if not suited and tied. The prosecution had wanted him there to answer questions on Whittaker's preoccupation with Leda's wealth. Strike told the silent court about his stepfather's previous attempts to get his hands on a fortune that existed largely in Whittaker's own head, and about his increasing pleas to Leda for her to put him in her will as proof of her love for him.

Whittaker watched out of his gold eyes, almost entirely impassive. In the last minute of his evidence, Strike and Whittaker's eyes had met across the room. The corner of Whittaker's mouth had lifted in a faint, derisive smile. He had raised his index finger half an inch from the place where it rested on the bench in front of him and made a tiny sideways swiping motion.

Strike had known exactly what he was doing. The micro-gesture had been made just for him, a miniature copy of one with which Strike was familiar: Whittaker's midair, horizontal slash of the hand, directed at the throat of the person who had offended him.

"You'll get yours," Whittaker used to say, the gold eyes wide and manic. "You'll get yours!"

He had brushed up well. Somebody in his moneyed family had stumped up for a decent defense lawyer. Scrubbed clean, soft-spoken and wearing a suit, he had denied everything in quiet, deferential tones. He had his story straight by the time he appeared in court.

Everything that the prosecution tried to pull in to draw a picture of the man he really was—Charles Manson on the ancient record player, the Satanic Bible on the bed, the stoned conversations about killing for pleasure—were batted away by a faintly incredulous Whittaker.

"What can I tell you... I'm a musician, your honor," he said at one point. "There's poetry in the darkness. *She* understood that better than anyone."

His voice had cracked melodramatically and he broke into dry sobs. Counsel for the defense hastened to ask whether he needed to take a moment.

It was then that Whittaker had shaken his head bravely and offered his gnomic pronouncement on Leda's death:

"She wanted to die. She was the quicklime girl."

Nobody else had understood the reference at the time, perhaps only Strike who had heard the song so many times through his childhood and adolescence. Whittaker was quoting from "Mistress of the Salmon Salt."

He had walked free. The medical evidence supported the view that Leda had not been a habitual heroin user, but her reputation was against her. She had done plenty of other drugs. She was an infamous party girl. To the men in curled wigs whose job it was to classify violent deaths, it seemed wholly in character that she would die on a dirty mattress in pursuit of pleasure her mundane life could not give her.

On the court steps, Whittaker announced that he intended to write a biography of his late wife, then vanished from view. The promised book had never appeared. Leda and Whittaker's son had been adopted by Whittaker's long-suffering grandparents and Strike had never seen him again. Strike had quietly left Oxford and joined the army; Lucy had gone off to college; life had carried on.

Whittaker's periodic reappearance in the newspapers, always connected with some criminal act, could never be a matter of indifference to Leda's children. Of course, Whittaker was never front-page news: he was a man who had married somebody famous for sleeping with the famous. Such limelight as he achieved was a weak reflection of a reflection.

"He's the turd that won't flush," as Strike put it to Lucy, who did not laugh. She was less inclined even than Robin to embrace rough humor as a means of dealing with unpalatable facts.

Tired and increasingly hungry, swaying with the train, his knee aching, Strike felt low and aggrieved, mainly at himself. For years he had turned his face resolutely towards the future. The past was unalterable: he did not deny what had happened, but there was no need to wallow in it, no need to go seeking out the squat of nearly two decades ago, to recall the rattling of that letter box, to relive the screams of the terrified cat, the sight of his mother in the undertaker's, pale and waxen in her bell-sleeved dress...

You're a fucking idiot, Strike told himself angrily as he scanned the Tube map, trying to work out how many changes he would have to make to get to Nick and Ilsa's. *Whittaker never sent the leg. You're just looking for an excuse to get at him.*

The sender of that leg was organized, calculating and efficient; the Whittaker he had known nearly two decades previously had been chaotic, hot-headed and volatile.

And yet...

You'll get yours...

She was the quicklime girl...

"*Fuck!*" said Strike loudly, causing consternation all around him. He had just realized that he had missed his connection.

11

Feeling easy on the outside,
But not so funny on the inside.

Blue Öyster Cult, "This Ain't the Summer of Love"

Strike and Robin took turns tailing Platinum over the next couple of days. Strike made excuses to meet during the working day and insisted that Robin leave for home during daylight hours, when the Tube was still busy. On Thursday evening, Strike followed Platinum until the Russian was safely back under the ever-suspicious gaze of Two-Times, then returned to Octavia Street in Wandsworth, where he was still living to avoid the press.

This was the second time in his detective career that Strike had been forced to take refuge with his friends Nick and Ilsa. Theirs was probably the only place he could have borne to stay, but Strike still felt strangely undomesticated within the orbit of a dual-career married couple. Whatever the drawbacks of the cramped attic space above his office, he had total freedom to come and go as he pleased, to eat at 2 a.m. when he had come in from a surveillance job, to move up and down the clanging metal stairs without fear of waking housemates. Now he felt unspoken pressure to be present for the occasional shared meal, feeling antisocial when he helped himself from the fridge in the small hours, even though he had been invited to do so.

On the other hand, Strike had not needed the army to teach him to be tidy and organized. The years of his youth that had been spent in chaos and filth had caused an opposite reaction. Ilsa had already remarked on the fact that Strike moved around the house without leaving any real mark on it, whereas her husband, a gastroenterologist, might be found by the trail of discarded belongings and imperfectly closed drawers.

Strike knew from acquaintances back in Denmark Street that press photographers were still hanging around the door to his office and he was resigned to spending the rest of the week in Nick and Ilsa's guest room, which had bare white walls and a melancholy sense of awaiting its true destiny. They had been trying unsuccessfully for years to have a child. Strike never inquired as to their progress and sensed that Nick, in particular, was grateful for his restraint.

He had known them both for a long time, Ilsa for most of his life. Fair-haired and bespectacled, she came from St. Mawes in Cornwall, which was the most constant home that Strike had ever known. He and Ilsa had been in the same primary school class. Whenever he had gone back to stay with Ted and Joan, as had happened regularly through his youth, they had resumed a friendship initially based on the fact that Joan and Ilsa's mother were themselves old schoolmates.

Nick, whose sandy hair had begun receding in his twenties, was a friend from the comprehensive in Hackney where Strike had finished his school career. Nick and Ilsa had met at Strike's eighteenth birthday party in London, dated for a year, then split up when they went off to separate universities. In their midtwenties they had met again, by which time Ilsa was engaged to another lawyer and Nick dating a fellow doctor. Within weeks both relationships were over; a year later, Nick and Ilsa had married, with Strike as best man.

Strike returned to their house at half past ten in the evening. As he closed the front door Nick and Ilsa greeted him from the sitting room and urged him to help himself to their still-plentiful takeaway curry.

"What's this?" he asked, looking around, disconcerted, at long lengths of Union Jack bunting, many sheets of scribbled notes and what looked like two hundred red, white and blue plastic cups in a large polythene bag.

"We're helping organize the street party for the royal wedding," said Ilsa.

"Jesus Christ almighty," said Strike darkly, heaping his plate with lukewarm Madras.

"It'll be fun! You should come."

Strike threw her a look that made her snigger.

"Good day?" asked Nick, passing Strike a can of Tennent's.

"No," said Strike, accepting the lager with gratitude. "Another job canceled. I'm down to two clients."

Nick and Ilsa made sympathetic noises, and there followed a comradely silence while he shoveled curry into his mouth. Tired and dispirited, Strike had spent most of the journey home contemplating the fact that the arrival of the severed leg was having, as he had feared, the effect of a wrecking ball on the business he had been working so hard to build up. His photograph was currently proliferating online and in the papers, in connection with a horrible, random act. It had been a pretext for the papers to remind the world that he was himself one-legged, a fact of which he was not ashamed, but which he was hardly likely to use in advertising; a whiff of something strange, something perverse, was attached to him now. He was tainted.

"Any news about the leg?" asked Ilsa, once Strike had demolished a considerable amount of curry and was halfway down the can of lager. "Have the police got anything?"

"I'm meeting Wardle tomorrow night to catch up, but it doesn't sound like they've got much. He's been concentrating on the gangster."

He had not given Nick and Ilsa details about three of the men he thought might be dangerous and vengeful enough to have sent him the leg, but he had mentioned that he had once run across a career criminal who had previously cut off and mailed a body part. Understandably, they had immediately taken Wardle's view that he was the likely culprit.

For the first time in years, sitting on their comfortable green sofa, Strike remembered that Nick and Ilsa had met Jeff Whittaker. Strike's eighteenth birthday party had taken place at the Bell pub in

Whitechapel; his mother was by this time six months pregnant. His aunt's face had been a mask of mingled disapproval and forced jollity and his Uncle Ted, usually the peacemaker, had been unable to disguise his anger and disgust as a patently high Whittaker had interrupted the disco to sing one of his self-penned songs. Strike remembered his own fury, his longing to be away, to be gone to Oxford, to be rid of it all, but perhaps Nick and Ilsa would not remember much about that: they had been engrossed in each other that night, dazed and amazed by their sudden, profound mutual attraction.

"You're worried about Robin," said Ilsa, more statement than question.

Strike grunted agreement, his mouth full of naan bread. He had had time to reflect on it over the last four days. In this extremity, and through no fault of her own, she had become a vulnerability, a weak spot, and he suspected that whoever had decided to re-address the leg to her had known it. If his employee had been male, he would not currently feel so worried.

Strike had not forgotten that Robin had hitherto been an almost unqualified asset. She was able to persuade recalcitrant witnesses to speak when his own size and naturally intimidating features inclined them to refuse. Her charm and ease of manner had allayed suspicion, opened doors, smoothed Strike's path a hundred times. He knew he owed her; he simply wished that, right now, she would bow out of the way, stay hidden until they had caught the sender of the severed leg.

"I like Robin," said Ilsa.

"Everyone likes Robin," said Strike thickly, through a second mouthful of naan. It was the truth: his sister Lucy, the friends who called in at the office, his clients—all made a point of telling Strike how much they liked the woman who worked with him. Nevertheless, he detected a note of faint inquiry in Ilsa's voice that made him keen to make any discussion of Robin impersonal, and he felt vindicated when Ilsa's next question was:

"How's it going with Elin?"

"All right," said Strike.

"Is she still trying to hide you from her ex?" asked Ilsa, a faint sting in the inquiry.

"Don't like Elin, do you?" said Strike, taking the discussion unexpectedly into the enemy camp for his own amusement. He had known Ilsa on and off for thirty years: her flustered denial was exactly what he had expected.

"I do like—I mean, I don't really know her, but she seems—anyway, you're happy, that's what counts."

He had thought that this would be sufficient to make Ilsa drop the subject of Robin—she was not the first of his friends to say that he and Robin got on so well, wasn't there a possibility...? Hadn't he ever considered...?—but Ilsa was a lawyer and not easily scared away from pursuing a line of questioning.

"Robin postponed her wedding, didn't she? Have they set a new—?"

"Yep," said Strike. "Second of July. She's taking a long weekend to go back to Yorkshire and—do whatever you do for weddings. Coming back on Tuesday."

He had been Matthew's unlikely ally in insisting that Robin take Friday and Monday off, relieved to think that she would be two hundred and fifty miles away in her family home. She had been deeply disappointed that she would not be able to come along to the Old Blue Last in Shoreditch and meet Wardle, but Strike thought he had detected a faint trace of relief at the idea of a break.

Ilsa looked slightly aggrieved at the news that Robin still intended to marry someone other than Strike, but before she could say anything else Strike's mobile buzzed in his pocket. It was Graham Hardacre, his old SIB colleague.

"Sorry," he told Nick and Ilsa, setting down his plate of curry and standing up, "got to take this, important—Hardy!"

"Can you talk, Oggy?" asked Hardacre, as Strike headed back to the front door.

"I can now," said Strike, reaching the end of the short garden path in three strides and stepping out into the dark street to walk and smoke. "What've you got for me?"

"To be honest," said Hardacre, who sounded stressed, "it'd be a big help if you came up here and had a look, mate. I've got a Warrant

Officer who's a real pain in the arse. We didn't get off on the right foot. If I start sending stuff out of here and she gets wind of it—"

"And if I come up?"

"Make it early in the morning and I could leave stuff open on the computer. Carelessly, y'know?"

Hardacre had previously shared information with Strike that, strictly speaking, he ought not to have done. He had only just moved to 35 Section: Strike was not surprised that he did not want to jeopardize his position.

The detective crossed the road, sat down on the low garden wall of the house opposite, lit a cigarette and asked: "Would it be worth coming up to Scotland for?"

"Depends what you want."

"Old addresses—family connections—medical and psychiatric records couldn't hurt. Brockbank was invalided out, what was it, 2003?"

"That's right," said Hardacre.

A noise behind Strike made him stand and turn: the owner of the wall on which he had been sitting was emptying rubbish into his dustbin. He was a small man of around sixty, and by the light of the streetlamp Strike saw his annoyed expression elide into a propitiatory smile as he took in Strike's height and breadth. The detective strolled away, past semidetached houses whose leafy trees and hedges were rippling in the spring breeze. There would be bunting, soon, to celebrate the union of yet another couple. Robin's wedding day would follow not long after.

"You won't have much on Laing, I s'pose," Strike said, his voice faintly interrogative. The Scot's army career had been shorter than Brockbank's.

"No—but Christ, he sounds a piece of work," said Hardacre.

"Where'd he go after the Glasshouse?"

The Glasshouse was the military jail in Colchester, where all convicted military personnel were transferred before being placed in a civilian prison.

"HMP Elmley. We've got nothing on him after that; you'd need the probation service."

"Yeah," said Strike, exhaling smoke at the starry sky. He and Hardacre both knew that as he was no longer any kind of policeman, he had no more right than any other member of the public to access the probation service's records. "Whereabouts in Scotland did he come from, Hardy?"

"Melrose. He put down his mother as next of kin when he joined up—I've looked him up."

"Melrose," repeated Strike thoughtfully.

He considered his two remaining clients: the moneyed idiot who got his kicks trying to prove he was a cuckold and the wealthy wife and mother who was paying Strike to gather evidence of the way her estranged husband was stalking their sons. The father was in Chicago and Platinum's movements could surely go uncharted for twenty-four hours.

There remained, of course, the possibility that none of the men he suspected had anything to do with the leg, that everything was in his mind.

A harvest of limbs . . .

"How far from Edinburgh is Melrose?"

"'Bout an hour, hour and a half's drive."

Strike ground out his cigarette in the gutter.

"Hardy, I could come up Sunday night on the sleeper, nip into the office early, then drive down to Melrose, see whether Laing's gone back to his family, or if they know where he is."

"Nice one. I'll pick you up at the station if you let me know when you're getting in, Oggy. In fact," Hardacre was gearing himself up for an act of generosity, "if it's only a day trip you're after, I'll lend you my car."

Strike did not immediately return to his curious friends and his cold curry. Smoking another cigarette, he strolled around the quiet street, thinking. Then he remembered that he was supposed to be attending a concert at the Southbank Centre with Elin on Sunday evening. She was keen to foster an interest in classical music that he had never pretended was more than lukewarm. He checked his watch. It was too late to ring and cancel now; he would need to remember to do so next day.

As he returned to the house, his thoughts drifted back to Robin. She spoke very little about the wedding that was now a mere two and a half months away. Hearing her tell Wardle about the disposable wedding cameras she had ordered had brought home to Strike how soon she would become Mrs. Matthew Cunliffe.

There's still time, he thought. For what, he did not specify, even to himself.

12

. . . the writings done in blood.

Blue Öyster Cult, "O.D.'d on Life Itself"

Many men might think it a pleasant interlude to receive cash for following a pneumatic blonde around London, but Strike was becoming thoroughly bored of trailing Platinum. After hours hanging around Houghton Street, where the LSE's glass and steel walkways occasionally revealed the part-time lap-dancer passing overhead on her way to the library, Strike followed her to Spearmint Rhino for her 4 p.m. shift. Here, he peeled away: Raven would call him if Platinum did anything that passed for untoward, and he was meeting Wardle at six.

He ate a sandwich in a shop near the pub chosen for their rendezvous. His mobile rang once, but on seeing that it was his sister, he let the call go to voicemail. He had a vague idea that it would soon be his nephew Jack's birthday and he had no intention of going to his party, not after the last time, which he remembered mainly for the nosiness of Lucy's fellow mothers and the ear-splitting screams of overexcited and tantrumming children.

The Old Blue Last stood at the top of Great Eastern Street in Shoreditch, a snub-nosed, imposing three-story brick building curved like the prow of a boat. Within Strike's memory, it had been a strip club and brothel: an old school friend of his and Nick's had allegedly lost his virginity there to a woman old enough to be his mother.

A sign just inside the doors announced the Old Blue Last's rebirth as a music venue. From eight o'clock that evening, Strike saw, he would be able to enjoy live performances from Islington Boys' Club, Red Drapes, In Golden Tears and Neon Index. There was a wry twist to his mouth as he pushed his way into a dark wood-floored bar, where an enormous antique mirror behind the bar bore gilded letters advertising the pale ales of a previous age. Spherical glass lamps hung from the high ceiling, illuminating a crowd of young men and women, many of whom looked like students and most dressed with a trendiness that was beyond Strike.

Although she was in her soul a lover of stadium bands, his mother had taken him to many such venues in his youth, where bands containing her friends might scrape a gig or two before splitting up acrimoniously, re-forming and appearing at a different pub three months later. Strike found the Old Blue Last a surprising choice of meeting place for Wardle, who had previously only drunk with Strike in the Feathers, which was right beside Scotland Yard. The reason became clear when Strike joined the policeman, who was standing alone with a pint at the bar.

"The wife likes Islington Boys' Club. She's meeting me here after work."

Strike had never met Wardle's wife, and while he had never given the matter much thought, he would have guessed her to be a hybrid of Platinum (because Wardle's eyes invariably followed fake tans and scanty clothing) and the only wife of a Met policeman that Strike knew, whose name was Helly and who was primarily interested in her children, her house and salacious gossip. The fact that Wardle's wife liked an indie band of whom Strike had never heard, notwithstanding the fact that he was already predisposed to despise that very band, made him think that she must be a more interesting person than the one he had expected.

"What've you got?" Strike asked Wardle, having secured himself a pint from an increasingly busy barman. By unspoken consent they left the bar and took the last free table for two in the place.

"Forensics are in on the leg," said Wardle as they sat down. "They reckon it came off a woman aged between midteens and midtwenties and that she was dead when it was cut off—but not long dead, looking at the clotting—and it was kept in a freezer in between cutting it off and handing it to your friend Robin."

Midteens to midtwenties: by Strike's calculations, Brittany Brockbank would be twenty-one now.

"Can't they be any more precise on the age?"

Wardle shook his head.

"That's as far as they're prepared to go. Why?"

"I told you why: Brockbank had a stepdaughter."

"Brockbank," repeated Wardle in the noncommittal tone that denotes lack of recall.

"One of the guys I thought might've sent the leg," said Strike, failing to conceal his impatience. "Ex–Desert Rat. Big dark guy, cauliflower ear—"

"Yeah, all right," said Wardle, immediately nettled. "I get passed names all the time, pal. Brockbank—he had the tattoo on his forearm—"

"That's Laing," said Strike. "He's the Scot I landed in jail for ten years. Brockbank was the one who reckoned I'd given him brain damage."

"Oh, yeah."

"His stepdaughter, Brittany, had old scarring on her leg. I told you that."

"Yeah, yeah, I remember."

Strike stifled a caustic retort by sipping his pint. He would have felt far more confident that his suspicions were being taken seriously had it been his old SIB colleague Graham Hardacre who sat opposite him, rather than Wardle. Strike's relationship with Wardle had been tinged from the first with wariness and, latterly, with a faint competitiveness. He rated Wardle's detective abilities higher than those of several other Met officers whom Strike had run across, but Wardle still regarded his own theories with paternal fondness that he never extended to Strike's.

"So have they said anything about the scarring on the calf?"

"Old. Long predated the death."

"Jesus fuck," said Strike.

The old scarring might be of no particular interest to forensics, but it was of vital importance to him. This was what he had dreaded. Even Wardle, whose habit it was to take the mickey out of Strike on every possible occasion, appeared to be experiencing something like empathy at the sign of the detective's concern.

"Mate," he said (and that, too, was new), "it's not Brockbank. It's Malley."

Strike had been afraid of this, afraid that the very mention of Malley would send Wardle careering after him to the exclusion of Strike's other suspects, excited at the thought of being the man who put away so notorious a gangster.

"Evidence?" Strike said bluntly.

"Harringay Crime Syndicate's been moving Eastern European prostitutes around London and up in Manchester. I've been talking to Vice. They bust into a brothel up the road last week and got two little Ukrainians out of there." Wardle dropped his voice still lower. "We've got female officers debriefing them. They had a friend who thought she was coming to the UK for a modeling job and never took kindly to the work, even when they beat the crap out of her. Digger dragged her out of the house by her hair two weeks ago and they haven't seen her since. They haven't seen Digger since, either."

"All in a day's work for Digger," said Strike. "That doesn't mean it's her leg. Has anyone ever heard him mention me?"

"Yes," said Wardle triumphantly.

Strike lowered the pint he had been about to sip. He had not expected an affirmative answer.

"They have?"

"One of the girls Vice got out of the house is clear she heard Digger talking about you not long ago."

"In what context?"

Wardle uttered a polysyllable: the surname of a wealthy Russian casino owner for whom Strike had indeed done some work at the end of the previous year. Strike frowned. As far as he could see, Digger knowing that he had worked for the casino owner made it no more likely that Digger had found out that he owed his previous stretch of incarceration to Strike's evidence. All Strike took from this fresh information was that his Russian client moved in extremely insalubrious circles, something of which he had already been aware.

"And how does me taking Arzamastsev's coin affect Digger?"

"Well, where d'you wanna start?" said Wardle, with what Strike felt was vagueness masquerading as the wide view. "The Syndicate's got fingers in a lot of pies. Basically, we've got a guy you've crossed with a history of sending people body parts, and he disappears with a young girl right before you get sent a young girl's leg."

"You put it like that, it sounds convincing," said Strike, who remained entirely unconvinced. "Have you done anything about looking at Laing, Brockbank and Whittaker?"

"Course," said Wardle. "Got people trying to locate all of them."

Strike hoped that was true, but refrained from questioning the statement on the basis that it would jeopardize his friendly relations with Wardle.

"We've got CCTV of the courier as well," said Wardle.

"And?"

"Your colleague's a good witness," said Wardle. "It *was* a Honda. Fake plates. Clothes exactly as she described. He drove off southwest—heading towards a real courier depot, as it goes. Last time we caught him on camera was in Wimbledon. No sign of him or the bike since, but like I say, fake plates. Could be anywhere."

"Fake plates," repeated Strike. "He did a hell of a lot of planning."

The pub was filling up all around them. Apparently the band was going to play upstairs: people were squeezing towards the door that led to the first floor and Strike could hear the familiar scream of microphone feedback.

"I've got something else for you," said Strike, without enthusiasm. "I promised Robin I'd give you copies."

He had returned to his office before daybreak that morning. The press had given up trying to catch him going in or out, though an acquaintance in the guitar shop opposite informed him that photographers had lingered until the previous evening.

Wardle took the two photocopied letters, looking mildly intrigued.

"They've both come in the last couple of months," said Strike.

"Robin thinks you should take a look. Want another?" he asked, gesturing to Wardle's almost empty glass.

Wardle read the letters while Strike bought two more pints. He was still holding the note signed RL when he returned. Strike picked up the other one and read, in clearly legible, rounded schoolgirlish writing:

> ...that I will only be truly me and truly complete when my leg is gone. Nobody gets that it isn't and never will be part of me. My need to be an amputee is very hard for my family to accept, they think it is all in my mind, but you understand...

You got that wrong, thought Strike, dropping the photocopy back onto the table top and noting as he did so that she had written her address in Shepherd's Bush as clearly and neatly as possible, so that his reply, advising her on how best to cut off her leg, would be in no danger of going astray. It was signed Kelsey, but with no surname.

Wardle, still deep in the second letter, let out a snort of mingled amusement and disgust.

"Fucking hell, have you *read* this?"

"No," said Strike.

More young people were squeezing into the bar. He and Wardle were not the only people in their midthirties, but they were definitely at the older end of the spectrum. He watched a pretty, pale young woman made up like a forties starlet, with narrow black eyebrows, crimson lipstick and powder-blue hair pinned into victory rolls, look around for her date. "Robin reads the nutter letters and gives me a précis if she thinks I need one."

" 'I want to massage your stump,' " read Wardle aloud. " 'I want you to use me as a living crutch. I want—' Holy shit. That's not even physically—"

He flipped over the letter.

" 'RL.' Can you read that address?"

"No," said Strike, squinting at it. The handwriting was dense and extremely difficult to read. The only legible word in the cramped address, on a first read, was "Walthamstow."

"What happened to 'I'll be by the bar,' Eric?"

The young woman with the pale blue hair and crimson lips had appeared at the table beside them, holding a drink. She wore a leather jacket over what looked like a forties summer dress.

"Sorry, babes, talking shop," said Wardle, unperturbed. "April, Cormoran Strike. My wife," he added.

"Hi," said Strike, extending a large hand. He would never have guessed Wardle's wife looked like this. For reasons he was too tired to analyze, it made him like Wardle better.

"Oh, it's *you!*" said April, beaming at Strike while Wardle slid the photocopied letters off the table, folded and pocketed them. "Cormoran Strike! I've heard loads about *you.* Are you staying for the band?"

"I doubt it," said Strike, though not unpleasantly. She was very pretty.

April seemed reluctant to let him go. They had friends joining them, she told him, and sure enough, within a few minutes of her arrival another six people turned up. There were two unattached women in the group. Strike allowed himself to be talked into moving upstairs with them, where there was a small stage and an already packed room. In response to his questions, April revealed that she was a stylist who had been working on a magazine shoot that very day, and—she said it casually—a part-time burlesque dancer.

"Burlesque?" repeated Strike at the top of his voice, as microphone feedback again screeched through the upper room, to shouts and groans of protest from the assembled drinkers. *Isn't that arty stripping?* he wondered, as April shared the information that her friend Coco—a girl with tomato-red hair who smiled at him and wiggled her fingers—was a burlesque dancer too.

They seemed a friendly group and none of the men were treating him with that tiresome chippiness that Matthew exhibited every time he came within Strike's orbit. He had not watched any live music in a long time. Petite Coco had already expressed a desire to be lifted up so she could see...

However, when Islington Boys' Club took to the stage Strike found himself forcibly transported back to times and people he strove not to think about. Stale sweat in the air, the familiar sound of guitars being tweaked and tuned, the humming of the open mic: he could have borne them all, had the lead singer's posture and his lithe androgyny not recalled Whittaker.

Four bars in and Strike knew he was leaving. There was nothing wrong with their brand of guitar-heavy indie rock: they played well and, in spite of his unfortunate resemblance to Whittaker, the lead singer had a decent voice. However, Strike had been in this environment too often and unable to leave: tonight, he was free to seek peace and clean air, and he intended to exercise that prerogative.

With a shouted farewell to Wardle and a wave and a smile to April, who winked and waved back, he left, large enough to carve an easy path through people already sweaty and breathless. He gained the door as the Islington Boys' Club finished their first song. The applause overhead sounded like muffled hail on a tin roof. A minute later, he was striding away, with relief, into the swishing sound of traffic.

13

In the presence of another world.

Blue Öyster Cult, "In the Presence of Another World"

On Saturday morning, Robin and her mother took the ancient family Land Rover from their small hometown of Masham to the dressmaker's in Harrogate where Robin's wedding dress was being altered. The design had been modified because it had initially been made for a wedding in January and was now to be worn in July.

"You've lost more weight," said the elderly dressmaker, sticking pins down the back of the bodice. "You don't want to go any thinner. This dress was meant for a bit of curve."

Robin had chosen the fabric and design of the dress over a year ago, loosely based on an Elie Saab model that her parents, who would also be forking out for half of her elder brother Stephen's wedding in six months' time, could never have afforded. Even this cut-price version would have been impossible on the salary Strike paid Robin.

The lighting in the changing room was flattering, yet Robin's reflection in the gilt-framed mirror looked too pale, her eyes heavy and tired. She was not sure that altering the dress to make it strapless had been successful. Part of what she had liked about the design in the first place had been the long sleeves. Perhaps, she thought, she was simply jaded from having lived with the idea of the dress for so long.

The changing room smelled of new carpet and polish. While Robin's mother Linda watched the dressmaker pin, tuck and twitch the yards of chiffon Robin, depressed by her own reflection, focused instead on the little corner stand carrying crystal tiaras and fake flowers.

"Remind me, have we fixed on a headdress?" asked the dressmaker, who had the habit of using the first person plural so often found in nursing staff. "We were leaning towards a tiara for the winter wedding, weren't we? I think it might be worth trying flowers with the strapless."

"Flowers would be nice," Linda agreed from the corner of the dressing room.

Mother and daughter closely resembled each other. Though her once slender waist had thickened and the faded red-gold hair piled untidily on top of her head was now laced with silver, Linda's blue-gray eyes were her daughter's and they rested now upon her second child with an expression of concern and shrewdness that would have been comically familiar to Strike.

Robin tried on an array of fake floral headdresses and liked none of them.

"Maybe I'll stick with the tiara," she said.

"Or fresh flowers?" suggested Linda.

"Yes," said Robin, suddenly keen to get away from the carpet smell and her pale, boxed-in reflection. "Let's go and see whether the florist could do something."

She was glad to have the changing room to herself for a few minutes. As she worked her way out of the dress and pulled her jeans and sweater back on, she tried to analyze her low mood. While she regretted that she had been forced to miss Strike's meeting with Wardle, she had been looking forward to putting a couple of hundred miles between her and the faceless man in black who had handed her a severed leg.

Yet she had no sense of escape. She and Matthew had rowed yet again on the train coming north. Even here, in the changing room in James Street, her multiplying anxieties haunted her: the agency's dwindling caseload, the fear of what would happen if Strike could no longer afford to employ her. Once dressed, she checked her mobile. No messages from Strike.

She was almost monosyllabic among the buckets of mimosa and lilies a quarter of an hour later. The florist fussed and fiddled, holding blooms against Robin's hair and accidentally letting drops of cold, greenish water fall from the long stem of a rose onto her cream sweater.

"Let's go to Bettys," suggested Linda when a floral headdress had at last been ordered.

Bettys of Harrogate was a local institution, the spa town's long-established tearoom. There were hanging flower baskets outside, where customers queued under a black, gold and glass canopy, and within were tea-canister lamps and ornamental teapots, squashy chairs and waitresses in broderie anglaise uniforms. It had been a treat to Robin, ever since she was small, to peer through the glass counter at rows of fat marzipan pigs, to watch her mother buying one of the luxurious fruitcakes laced with alcohol that came in its own special tin.

Today, sitting beside the window staring out at primary-colored flowerbeds resembling the geometric shapes cut out of plasticine by small children, Robin declined anything to eat, asked for a pot of tea and flipped over her mobile again. Nothing.

"Are you all right?" Linda asked her.

"Fine," said Robin. "I was just wondering if there was any news."

"What kind of news?"

"About the leg," said Robin. "Strike met Wardle last night—the Met officer."

"Oh," said Linda and silence fell between them until their tea arrived.

Linda had ordered a Fat Rascal, one of Bettys' large scones. She finished buttering it before she asked:

"You and Cormoran are going to try and find out who sent that leg yourselves, are you?"

Something in her mother's tone made Robin proceed warily.

"We're interested in what the police are doing, that's all."

"Ah," said Linda, chewing, watching Robin.

Robin felt guilty for being irritable. The wedding dress was expensive and she had not been appreciative.

"Sorry for being snappy."

"That's all right."

"It's just, Matthew's on my case all the time about working for Cormoran."

"Yes, we heard something about that last night."

"Oh God, Mum, I'm sorry!"

Robin had thought they'd kept the row quiet enough not to wake her parents. They had argued on the way up to Masham, suspended hostilities while having supper with her parents, then resumed the argument in the living room after Linda and Michael had gone to bed.

"Cormoran's name came up a lot, didn't it? I assume Matthew's—?"

"He's not *worried,*" said Robin.

Matthew determinedly treated Robin's work as a kind of joke, but when forced to take it seriously—when, for instance, somebody sent her a severed leg—he became angry rather than concerned.

"Well, if he's not worried, he should be," said Linda. "Somebody sent you part of a dead woman, Robin. It's not so long ago that Matt called us to say you were in hospital with concussion. I'm not telling you to resign!" she added, refusing to be cowed by Robin's reproachful expression. "I know this is what you want! Anyway"—she forced the larger half of her Fat Rascal into Robin's unresisting hand—"I wasn't going to ask whether Matt was worried. I was going to ask whether he was jealous."

Robin sipped her strong Bettys Blend tea. Vaguely she contemplated taking some of these tea bags back to the office. There was nothing as good as this in Ealing Waitrose. Strike liked his tea strong.

"Yes, Matt's jealous," she said at last.

"I'm assuming he's got no reason?"

"Of course not!" said Robin hotly. She felt betrayed. Her mother was always on her side, always—

"There's no need to get fired up," said Linda, unruffled. "I wasn't suggesting you'd done anything you shouldn't."

"Well, good," said Robin, eating the scone without noticing it. "Because I haven't. He's my boss, that's all."

"And your friend," suggested Linda, "judging by the way you talk about him."

"Yes," said Robin, but honesty compelled her to add, "it's not like a normal friendship, though."

"Why not?"

"He doesn't like talking about personal stuff. Blood out of a stone."

Except for one notorious evening—barely mentioned between them since—when Strike had got so drunk he could hardly stand, voluntary information about his private life had been virtually nonexistent.

"You get on well, though?"

"Yeah, really well."

"A lot of men find it hard to hear how well their other halves get on with other men."

"What am I supposed to do, only ever work with women?"

"No," said Linda. "I'm just saying: Matthew obviously feels threatened."

Robin sometimes suspected that her mother regretted the fact that her daughter had not had more boyfriends before committing herself to Matthew. She and Linda were close; she was Linda's only daughter. Now, with the tearoom clattering and tinkling around them, Robin realized that she was afraid that Linda might tell her it wasn't too late to back out of the wedding if she wanted to. Tired and low though she was, and in spite of the fact that they had had several rocky months, she knew that she loved Matthew. The dress was made, the church was booked, the reception almost paid for. She must plow on, now, and get to the finishing line.

"I don't fancy Strike. Anyway, he's in a relationship: he's seeing Elin Toft. She's a presenter on Radio Three."

She hoped that this information would distract her mother, an enthusiastic devourer of radio programs while cooking and gardening.

"Elin Toft? Is she that very beautiful blonde girl who was on the telly talking about Romantic composers the other night?" asked Linda.

"Probably," said Robin, with a pronounced lack of enthusiasm, and in spite of the fact that her diversionary tactic had been successful, she changed the subject. "So you're getting rid of the Land Rover?"

"Yes. We'll get nothing for it, obviously. Scrap, maybe... unless," said Linda, struck by a sudden thought, "you and Matthew want it? It's got a year's tax left on it and it always scrapes through its MOT somehow."

Robin chewed her scone, thinking. Matthew moaned constantly about their lack of car, a deficiency he attributed to her low salary. His sister's husband's A3 Cabriolet caused him almost physical pangs of envy. Robin knew he would feel very differently about a battered old Land Rover with its permanent smell of wet dog and Wellington boots, but at one o'clock that morning in the family sitting room, Matthew had listed his estimates of the salary of all their contemporaries, concluding with a flourish that Robin's pay lay right at the bottom of the league table. With a sudden spurt of malice, she imagined herself telling her fiancé, "But we've got the Land Rover, Matt, there's no point trying to save for an Audi now!"

"It could be really useful for work," she said aloud, "if we need to go outside London. Strike won't need to hire a car."

"Mm," said Linda, apparently absently, but with her eyes fixed on Robin's face.

They drove home to find Matthew laying the table with his future father-in-law. He was usually more helpful in the kitchen at her parents' house than at home with Robin.

"How's the dress looking?" he asked in what Robin supposed was an attempt at conciliation.

"All right," said Robin.

"Is it bad luck to tell me about it?" he said and then, when she did not smile, "I bet you look beautiful, anyway."

Softening, she reached out a hand and he winked, squeezing her fingers. Then Linda plonked a dish of mashed potato on the table between them and told him that she had given them the old Land Rover.

"What?" said Matthew, his face a study in dismay.

"You're always saying you want a car," said Robin, defensive on her mother's behalf.

"Yeah, but—the Land Rover, in London?"

"Why not?"

"It'll ruin his image," said her brother Martin, who had just entered the room with the newspaper in his hand; he had been examining the runners for that afternoon's Grand National. "Suit you down to the ground, though, Rob. I can just see you and Hopalong, off-roading to murder scenes."

Matthew's square jaw tightened.

"Shut up, Martin," snapped Robin, glaring at her younger brother as she sat down at the table. "And I'd love to see you call Strike Hopalong to his face," she added.

"He'd probably laugh," said Martin airily.

"Because you're peers?" said Robin, her tone brittle. "Both of you with your stunning war records, risking life and limb?"

Martin was the only one of the four Ellacott siblings who had not attended university, and the only one who still lived with their parents. He was always touchy at the slightest hint that he underachieved.

"The fuck's that supposed to mean—I should be in the army?" he demanded, firing up.

"Martin!" said Linda sharply. "Mind your language!"

"Does she have a go at you for still having both legs, Matt?" asked Martin.

Robin dropped her knife and fork and walked out of the kitchen.

The image of the severed leg was before her again, with its shining white tibia sticking out of the dead flesh, those slightly grubby toenails whose owner had meant, perhaps, to clean or paint before anybody else would see them…

And now she was crying, crying for the first time since she had taken the package. The pattern on the old stair carpet blurred and she had to grope for the doorknob of her bedroom. She crossed to the bed and dropped, face down, onto the clean duvet, her shoulders shaking and her chest heaving, her hands pressed over her wet face as she tried to muffle the sound of her sobs. She did not want any of them to come after her; she did not want to have to talk or explain; she simply wanted to be alone to release the emotion she had tamped down to get through the working week.

Her brother's glibness about Strike's amputation was an echo of

Strike's own jokes about the dismembered leg. A woman had died in what were likely to have been terrible, brutal circumstances, and nobody seemed to care as much as Robin did. Death and a hatchet had reduced the unknown female to a lump of meat, a problem to be solved and she, Robin, felt as though she was the only person to remember that a living, breathing human being had been using that leg, perhaps as recently as a week ago...

After ten minutes' solid weeping she rolled over onto her back, opened her streaming eyes and looked around her old bedroom as though it might give her succor.

This room had once seemed like the only safe place on earth. For the three months after she had dropped out of university she had barely left it, even to eat. The walls had been shocking pink back then, a mistaken decorating choice she had made when she was sixteen. She had dimly recognized that it did not work, but had not wanted to ask her father to repaint, so she had covered the garish glare with as many posters as possible. There had been a large picture of Destiny's Child facing her at the foot of the bed. Though there was nothing there now but the smooth eau de nil wallpaper Linda had put up when Robin left home to join Matthew in London, Robin could still visualize Beyoncé, Kelly Rowland and Michelle Williams staring at her out of the cover of their album *Survivor.* The image was indelibly connected with the worst time of her life.

The walls bore only two framed photographs these days: one of Robin with her old sixth form on their last day of school (Matthew at the back of the shot, the most handsome boy in the year, refusing to pull a face or wear a stupid hat) and the other of Robin, aged twelve, riding her old Highland pony Angus, a shaggy, strong and stubborn creature who had lived on her uncle's farm and on whom Robin had doted, his naughtiness notwithstanding.

Depleted and exhausted, she blinked away more tears and wiped her wet face with the heels of her hands. Muffled voices rose from the kitchen below her room. Her mother, she was sure, would be advising Matthew to leave her alone for a while. Robin hoped that he would listen. She felt as though she would like to sleep through the rest of the weekend.

An hour later she was still lying on the double bed, staring drowsily out of the window at the top of the lime tree in the garden, when Matthew knocked and entered with a mug of tea.

"Your mum thought you could use this."

"Thanks," said Robin.

"We're all going to watch the National together. Mart's put a big bet on Ballabriggs."

No mention of her distress or of Martin's crass comments; Matthew's manner implied that she had somehow embarrassed herself and he was offering her a way out. She knew at once that he had no conception of what the sight and feel of that woman's leg had stirred up in her. No, he was simply annoyed that Strike, whom none of the Ellacotts had ever met, was once again taking up space in weekend conversation. It was Sarah Shadlock at the rugby all over again.

"I don't like watching horses break their necks," said Robin. "Anyway, I've got some work to do."

He stood looking down at her, then walked out, closing the door with a little too much force, so that it jumped open again behind him.

Robin sat up, smoothed her hair, took a deep breath and then went to fetch her laptop case from on top of the dressing table. She had felt guilty bringing it along on their trip home, guilty for hoping that she might find time for what she was privately calling her lines of inquiry. Matthew's air of generous forgiveness had put paid to that. Let him watch the National. She had better things to do.

Returning to the bed, she made a pile of pillows behind her, opened the laptop and navigated to certain bookmarked webpages that she had talked to nobody about, not even Strike, who would no doubt think she was wasting her time.

She had already spent several hours pursuing two separate but related lines of inquiry suggested by the letters that she had insisted Strike should take to Wardle: the communication from the young woman who wished to remove her own leg, and the missive from the person who wished to do things to Strike's stump that had made Robin feel faintly queasy.

Robin had always been fascinated by the workings of the human mind. Her university career, though cut short, had been dedicated to the study of psychology. The young woman who had written to Strike seemed to be suffering from body integrity identity disorder, or BIID: the irrational desire for the removal of a healthy body part.

Having read several scientific papers online, Robin now knew that sufferers of BIID were rare and that the precise cause of their condition was unknown. Visits to support sites had already shown her how much people seemed to dislike sufferers of the condition. Angry comments peppered the message boards, accusing BIID sufferers of coveting a status that others had had thrust upon them by bad luck and illness, of wanting to court attention in a grotesque and offensive manner. Equally angry retorts followed the attacks: did the writer really think the sufferer *wanted* to have BIID? Did they not understand how difficult it was to be transabled—wanting, needing, to be paralyzed or amputated? Robin wondered what Strike would think of the BIID sufferers' stories, were he to read them. She suspected that his reaction would not be sympathetic.

Downstairs, the sitting room door opened and she heard a brief snatch of a commentator's voice, her father telling their old chocolate Labrador to get out because it had farted and Martin's laughter.

To her own frustration, the exhausted Robin could not remember the name of the young girl who had written to Strike, asking for advice on cutting off her leg, but she thought it had been Kylie or something similar. Scrolling slowly down the most densely populated support site she had found, she kept an eye out for usernames that might in any way connect to her, because where else would a teenager with an unusual fixation go to share her fantasy, if not cyberspace?

The bedroom door, still ajar since Matthew's exit, swung open as the banished Labrador, Rowntree, came waddling into the bedroom. He reported to Robin for an absentminded rub of his ears, then flopped down beside the bed. His tail bumped against the floor for a while and then he fell wheezily asleep. To the accompaniment of his snuffling snores, Robin continued to comb the message boards.

Quite suddenly, she experienced one of those jolts of excitement with which she had become familiar since starting work for Strike, and which were the immediate reward of looking for a tiny piece of information that might mean something, nothing or, occasionally, everything.

Nowheretoturn: Does anyone know anything about Cameron Strike?

Holding her breath, Robin opened the thread.

W@nBee: that detective with one leg? yeah, hes a veteran.
Nowheretoturn: I heard he might of done it himself.
W@nBee: No, if you look up he's was in Afganistan.

That was all. Robin combed more threads on the forum, but Nowheretoturn had not pursued their inquiry, nor did they appear again. That meant nothing; they might have changed their username. Robin searched until satisfied that she had probed every corner of the site, but Strike's name did not recur.

Her excitement ebbed away. Even assuming that the letter-writer and Nowheretoturn were the same person, her belief that Strike's amputation had been self-inflicted had been clear in the letter. There weren't many famous amputees on whom you might be able to pin the hope that their condition was voluntary.

Shouts of encouragement were now emanating from the sitting room below. Abandoning the BIID boards, Robin turned to her second line of inquiry.

She liked to think that she had developed a tougher skin since working at the detective agency. Nevertheless, her first forays into the fantasies of acrotomophiliacs—those who were sexually attracted to amputees—which had been accessed with only a few clicks of the mouse, had left her with a cringing feeling in her stomach that lingered long after she had left the internet. Now she found herself reading the outpourings of a man (she assumed he was a man) whose most exciting sexual fantasy was a woman with all four limbs amputated above the elbow and knee joints. The precise point at which limbs were cut seemed to be a particular preoccupation. A second man (they could not be women, surely) had masturbated since early youth over the idea of accidentally guillotining off his own and his best friend's legs. Everywhere was discussion of the fascination of the stumps themselves, of the restricted movement of amputees, of what Robin assumed was disability as an extreme manifestation of bondage.

While the distinctive nasal voice of the commentator on the Grand National gabbled incomprehensibly from below, and her brother's shouts of encouragement became louder, Robin scanned more message boards, seeking any mention of Strike and also searching for a connecting line between this paraphilia and violence.

Robin found it notable that none of the people pouring their amputee and amputation fantasies onto this forum seemed to be aroused by violence or pain. Even the man whose sexual fantasy involved him and his friend cutting off their own legs together was clear and articulate on that subject: the guillotining was merely the necessary precursor to the achievement of stumps.

Would a person aroused by Strike-as-amputee cut off a woman's leg and send it to him? That was the sort of thing Matthew might think would happen, Robin thought scornfully, because Matthew would assume that anyone odd enough to find stumps attractive would be crazy enough to dismember somebody else: indeed, he would think it likely. However, from what Robin remembered of the letter from RL, and after perusing the online outpourings of his fellow acrotomophiliacs, she thought it much more likely that what RL meant by "making it up" to Strike was likely to mean practices that Strike would probably find a lot less appetizing than the original amputation.

Of course, RL might be both an acrotomophiliac and a psychopath...

"YES! FUCKING YES! FIVE HUNDRED QUID!" screamed Martin. From the rhythmic thumping emanating from the hall, it sounded as though Martin had found the sitting room inadequate for the full performance of a victory dance. Rowntree woke, jumped to his feet and let out a groggy bark. The noise was such that Robin did not hear Matthew approaching until he pushed the door open. Automatically, she clicked the mouse repeatedly, backtracking through the sites devoted to the sexual fetishization of amputees.

"Hi," she said. "I take it Ballabriggs won."

"Yeah," said Matthew.

For the second time that day, he held out a hand. Robin slid the laptop aside and Matthew pulled her to her feet and hugged her. With the warmth of his body came relief, seeping through her, calming her. She could not stand another night's bickering.

Then he pulled away, his eyes fixed on something over her shoulder.

"What?"

She looked down at the laptop. There in the middle of a glowing white screen of text was a large boxed definition:

> **Acrotomophilia** *noun*
> A paraphilia in which sexual gratification is derived from fantasies or acts involving an amputee.

There was a brief silence.

"How many horses died?" asked Robin in a brittle voice.

"Two," Matthew answered, and walked out of the room.

14

...you ain't seen the last of me yet,
I'll find you, baby, on that you can bet.

Blue Öyster Cult, "Showtime"

Half past eight on Sunday evening found Strike standing outside Euston station, smoking what would be his last cigarette until he arrived in Edinburgh in nine hours' time.

Elin had been disappointed that he was going to miss the evening concert, and instead they had spent most of the afternoon in bed, an alternative that Strike had been more than happy to accept. Beautiful, collected and rather cool outside the bedroom, Elin was considerably more demonstrative inside it. The memory of certain erotic sights and sounds—her alabaster skin faintly damp under his mouth, her pale lips wide in a moan—added savor to the tang of nicotine. Smoking was not permitted in Elin's spectacular flat on Clarence Terrace, because her young daughter had asthma. Strike's post-coital treat had instead been to fight off sleep while she showed him a recording of herself talking about the Romantic composers on the bedroom television.

"You know, you look like Beethoven," she told him thoughtfully, as the camera closed in on a marble bust of the composer.

"With a buggered nose," said Strike. He had been told it before.

"And *why* are you going to Scotland?" Elin had asked as he re-attached his prosthetic leg while sitting on the bed in her bedroom, which was decorated in creams and whites and yet had none of the depressing austerity of Ilsa and Nick's spare room.

"Following a lead," said Strike, fully aware that he was overstating the case. There was nothing except his own suspicions to connect Donald Laing and Noel Brockbank to the severed leg. Nevertheless, and much though he might silently lament the nearly three hundred quid the round-trip was costing him, he did not regret the decision to go.

Grinding the stub of his cigarette under the heel of his prosthetic foot, he proceeded into the station, bought himself a bag of food at the supermarket and clambered onto the overnight train.

The single berth, with its fold-down sink and its narrow bunk, might be tiny, but his army career had taken him to far more uncomfortable places. He was pleased to find that the bed could just accommodate his six foot three and after all, a small space was always easier to navigate once his prosthesis had been removed. Strike's only gripe was that the compartment was overheated: he kept his attic flat at a temperature every woman he knew would have deplored as icy, not that any woman had ever slept in his attic flat. Elin had never even seen the place; Lucy, his sister, had never been invited over lest it shatter her delusion that he was making plenty of money these days. In fact, now he came to think about it, Robin was the only woman who had ever been in there.

The train jolted into motion. Benches and pillars flickered past the window. Strike sank down on the bunk, unwrapped the first of his bacon baguettes and took a large mouthful, remembering as he did so Robin sitting at his kitchen table, white-faced and shaken. He was glad to think of her at home in Masham, safely out of the way of possible harm: at least he could stow one nagging worry.

The situation in which he now found himself was deeply familiar. He might have been back in the army, traveling the length of the UK as cheaply as possible, to report to the SIB station in Edinburgh. He had never been stationed there. The offices, he knew, were in the castle that stood on top of a jagged rock outcrop in the middle of the city.

Later, after swaying along the rattling corridor to pee, he undressed to his boxer shorts and lay on top of the thin blankets to sleep, or rather to doze. The side-to-side rocking motion was soothing, but the heat and the changing pace of the train kept jarring him out of sleep. Ever since the Viking in which he was being driven had blown up around him in Afghanistan, taking half his leg and two colleagues with it, Strike had found it difficult to be driven by other people. Now he discovered that this mild phobia extended to trains. The whistle of an engine speeding past his carriage in the opposite direction woke him like an alarm three times; the slight sway as the train cornered made him imagine the terror of the great metal monster overbalancing, rolling, crashing and smashing apart...

The train pulled into Edinburgh Waverley at a quarter past five, but breakfast was not served until six. Strike woke to the sound of a porter moving down the carriage, delivering trays. When Strike opened his door, balancing on one leg, the uniformed youth let out an uncontrolled yelp of dismay, his eyes on the prosthesis which lay on the floor behind Strike.

"Sorry, pal," he said in a thick Glaswegian accent as he looked from the prosthesis to Strike's leg, realizing that the passenger had not, after all, hacked off his own leg. "Whit a reddy!"

Amused, Strike took the tray and closed the door. After a wakeful night he wanted a cigarette much more than a reheated, rubbery croissant, so he set about reattaching the leg and getting dressed, gulping black coffee as he did so, and was among the first to step out into the chilly Scottish early morning.

The station's situation gave the odd feeling of being at the bottom of an abyss. Through the concertinaed glass ceiling Strike could make out the shapes of dark Gothic buildings towering above him on higher ground. He found the place near the taxi rank where Hardacre had said he would pick him up, sat down on a cold metal bench and lit up, his backpack at his feet.

Hardacre did not appear for twenty minutes, and when he did so, Strike felt a profound sense of misgiving. He had been so grateful to escape the expense of hiring a car that he had felt it would be churlish to ask Hardacre what he drove.

A Mini. A fucking Mini...

"Oggy!"

They performed the American half-hug, half-handshake that had permeated even the armed forces. Hardacre was barely five foot eight, an amiable-looking investigator with thinning, mouse-colored hair. Strike knew his nondescript appearance hid a sharp investigative brain. They had been together for the Brockbank arrest, and that alone had been enough to bond them, with the mess it had landed them in afterwards.

Only when he watched his old friend folding himself into the Mini did it seem to occur to Hardacre that he ought to have mentioned the make of car he drove.

"I forgot you're such a big bastard," he commented. "You gonna be all right to drive this?"

"Oh yeah," said Strike, sliding the passenger seat as far back as it could go. "Grateful for the lend, Hardy."

At least it was an automatic.

The little car wound its way out of the station and up the hill to the soot-black buildings that had peered down at Strike through the glass roof. The early morning was a cool gray.

"S'posed to be nice later," muttered Hardacre as they drove up the steep, cobbled Royal Mile, past shops selling tartan and flags of the lion rampant, restaurants and cafés, boards advertising ghost tours and narrow alleyways affording fleeting glimpses of the city stretched out below to their right.

At the top of the hill the castle came into view: darkly forbidding against the sky, surrounded by high, curved stone walls. Hardacre took a right, away from the crested gates where tourists keen to beat the queues were already lurking. At a wooden booth he gave his name, flashed his pass and drove on, aiming for the entrance cut in the volcanic rock, which led to a floodlit tunnel lined with thick power cables. Leaving the tunnel, they found themselves high above the city, cannons ranged on the battlements beside them, giving on to a misty view of the spires and rooftops of the black and gold city stretching out to the Firth of Forth in the distance.

"Nice," said Strike, moving to the cannons for a better look.

"Not bad," agreed Hardacre, with a matter-of-fact glance down at the Scottish capital. "Over here, Oggy."

They entered the castle through a wooden side door. Strike followed Hardacre along a chilly, narrow stone-flagged corridor and up a couple of flights of stairs that were not easy on the knee joint of Strike's right leg. Prints of Victorian military men in dress uniforms hung at unequal intervals on the walls.

A door on the first landing led into a corridor lined with offices, carpeted in shabby dark pink, with hospital-green walls. Though Strike had never been there before, it felt instantly familiar in a way that the old squat in Fulbourne Street could not touch. This had been his life: he could have settled down at an unoccupied desk and been back at work within ten minutes.

The walls bore posters, one reminding investigators of the importance of and procedures relating to the Golden Hour—that short period of time after an offense when clues and information were most plentiful and easiest to gather—another showing photographs of Drugs of Abuse. There were whiteboards covered with updates and deadlines for various live cases—"awaiting phone & DNA analysis," "SPA Form 3 required"—and metal file cases carrying mobile fingerprint kits. The door to the lab stood open. On a high metal table sat a pillow in a plastic evidence bag; it was covered in dark brown bloodstains. A cardboard box next to it contained bottles of spirits. Where there was bloodshed, there was always alcohol. An empty bottle of Bell's stood in the corner, supporting a red military cap, the very item of clothing after which the corps was nicknamed.

A short-haired blonde in a pin-striped suit approached, going in the opposite direction:

"Strike."

He did not recognize her immediately.

"Emma Daniels. Catterick, 2002," she said with a grin. "You called our Staff Sergeant a negligent twat."

"Oh yeah," he said, while Hardacre sniggered. "He was. You've had your hair cut."

"And you've got famous."

"I wouldn't go that far," said Strike.

A pale young man in shirtsleeves put his head out of an office further down the corridor, interested in the conversation.

"Gotta get on, Emma," said Hardacre briskly. "Knew they'd be interested if they saw you," he told Strike, once he had ushered the private detective into his office and closed the door behind them.

The room was rather dark, due largely to the fact that the window looked directly out onto a bare face of craggy rock. Photographs of Hardacre's kids and a sizable collection of beer steins enlivened the decor, which comprised the same shabby pink carpet and pale green walls as the corridor outside.

"All right, Oggy," said Hardacre, tapping at his keyboard, then standing back to let Strike sit down at his desk. "Here he is."

The SIB was able to access records across all three services. There on the computer monitor was a headshot of Noel Campbell Brockbank. It had been taken before Strike met him, before Brockbank had taken the hits to the face that had permanently sunken one of his eye sockets and enlarged one of his ears. A dark crew cut, a long, narrow face, tinged blue around the jaw and with an unusually high forehead: Strike had thought when they had first met that his elongated head and slightly lopsided features made it look as though Brockbank's head had been squeezed in a vice.

"I can't let you print anything out, Oggy," said Hardacre as Strike sat down on the wheeled computer chair, "but you could take a picture of the screen. Coffee?"

"Tea, if you've got any. Cheers."

Hardacre left the room, closing the door carefully behind him, and Strike took out his mobile to take pictures of the screen. When he was confident he had a decent likeness he scrolled down to see Brockbank's full record, making a note of his date of birth and other personal details.

Brockbank had been born on Christmas Day in the year of Strike's own birth. He had given a home address in Barrow-in-Furness when he had joined the army. Shortly before serving in Operation Granby—better known to the public as the first Gulf war—he had married a military widow with two daughters, one of them Brittany. His son had been born while he was serving in Bosnia.

Strike went through the record, making notes as he did so, all the way down to the life-changing injury that had put paid to Brockbank's career. Hardacre reentered the room with two mugs and Strike muttered thanks as he continued to peruse the digital file. There was no mention in here of the crime of which Brockbank had been accused, which Strike and Hardacre had investigated and of which they both remained convinced that Brockbank was guilty. The fact that he had eluded justice was one of the biggest regrets of Strike's military career. His most vivid memory of the man was Brockbank's expression, feral in its wildness, as he launched himself at Strike bearing a broken beer bottle. He had been around Strike's own size, perhaps even taller. The sound of Brockbank hitting the wall when Strike punched him had been, Hardacre said later, like a car ramming the side of the flimsy army accommodation.

"He's drawing a nice fat military pension, I see," muttered Strike, scribbling down the various locations to which it had been sent since Brockbank had left the military. He had gone home first: Barrow-in-Furness. Then Manchester, for a little under a year.

"Ha," said Strike quietly. "So it *was* you, you bastard."

Brockbank had left Manchester for Market Harborough, then returned to Barrow-in-Furness.

"What's this here, Hardy?"

"Psych report," said Hardacre, who had sat down on a low chair by the wall and was perusing a file of his own. "You shouldn't be looking at that at all. Very careless of me to have left it up there."

"Very," agreed Strike, opening it.

However, the psychiatric report did not tell Strike much that he did not already know. Only once he had been hospitalized had it become clear that Brockbank was an alcoholic. There had been much debate among his doctors as to which of his symptoms could be attributed to alcohol, which to PTSD and which to his traumatic brain injuries. Strike had to Google some of the words as he went: aphasia—difficulty finding the right word; dysarthria—disordered speech; alexithymia—difficulty understanding or identifying one's own emotions.

Forgetfulness had been very convenient to Brockbank around that time. How difficult would it have been for him to fake some of these classic symptoms?

"What they didn't take into account," said Strike, who had known and liked several other men with traumatic brain injury, "was that he was a cunt to start with."

"True that," said Hardacre, sipping his coffee while he worked.

Strike closed down Brockbank's files and opened Laing's. His photograph tallied exactly with Strike's memories of the Borderer, who had been only twenty when they had first met: broad and pale, his hair growing low on his forehead, with the small, dark eyes of a ferret.

Strike had good recall of the details of Laing's brief army career, which he himself had ended. Having taken a note of Laing's mother's address in Melrose, he skim-read the rest of the document and then opened the attached psychiatric report.

Strong indications of antisocial and borderline personality disorders... likely to present continuing risk of harm to others...

A loud knock on the office door caused Strike to close down the records on screen and get to his feet. Hardacre had barely reached the door when a severe-looking woman in a skirt suit appeared.

"Got anything for me on Timpson?" she barked at Hardacre, but she gave Strike a suspicious glare and he guessed that she had already been well aware of his presence.

"I'll cut away now, Hardy," he said at once. "Great to catch up."

Hardacre introduced him briefly to the Warrant Officer, gave a potted version of his and Strike's previous association and walked Strike out.

"I'll be here late," he said as they shook hands at the door. "Ring me when you know what time you'll have the car back. Happy travels."

As Strike made his way carefully down the stone stairs, it was impossible not to reflect that he could have been here, working alongside Hardacre, subject to the familiar routines and demands of the Special Investigation Branch. The army had wanted to keep him, even with his lower leg gone. He had never regretted his decision to leave, but this sudden, brief re-immersion in his old life gave rise to an inevitable nostalgia.

As he stepped out into the weak sunshine that was gleaming through a rupture in the thick clouds, he had never been more conscious of the change in his status. He was free, now, to walk away from the demands of unreasonable superiors and the confinement of a rock-bound office, but he had also been stripped of the might and status of the British Army. He was completely alone as he resumed what might well prove a wild goose chase, armed only with a few addresses, in pursuit of the man who had sent Robin a woman's leg.

15

Where's the man with the golden tattoo?

Blue Öyster Cult, "Power Underneath Despair"

As Strike had expected, driving the Mini, even once he had made every possible adjustment to the seat, was extremely uncomfortable. The loss of his right foot meant that he operated the accelerator with his left. This required a tricky and uncomfortable angling of his body in such a cramped space. Not until he was out of the Scottish capital and safely on the quiet and straight A7 to Melrose did he feel able to turn his thoughts from the mechanics of driving the borrowed car to Private Donald Laing of the King's Own Royal Borderers, whom he had first met eleven years previously in a boxing ring.

The encounter had happened by evening in a stark, dark sports hall that rang with the raucous cries of five hundred baying squaddies. He had been Corporal Cormoran Strike of the Royal Military Police then, fully fit, toned and muscled with two strong legs, ready to show what he could do in the Inter-Regimental Boxing Tournament. Laing's supporters had outnumbered Strike's by at least three to one. It was nothing personal. The military police were unpopular on principle. Watching a Red Cap being knocked senseless would be a satisfying end to a good night's boxing. They were two big men and this would be the last bout of the night. The roar of the crowd had thundered through both fighters' veins like a second pulse.

Strike remembered his opponent's small black eyes and his bristle cut, which was the dark red of fox fur. A tattoo of a yellow rose spanned the length of his left forearm. His neck was thicker by far than his narrow jaw and his pale, hairless chest was muscled like a marble statue of Atlas, the freckles that peppered his arms and shoulders standing out like gnat bites on his white skin.

Four rounds and they were evenly matched, the younger man perhaps faster on his feet, Strike superior in technique.

In the fifth, Strike parried, feinted to the face then struck Laing with a blow to the kidneys that floored him. The anti-Strike faction fell silent as his opponent hit the canvas, then boos echoed throughout the hall like the bellowing of elephants.

Laing was back on his feet by the count of six, but he had left some of his discipline behind him on the canvas. Wild punches; a temporary refusal to break that earned a stern reproof from the ref; an extra jab after the bell: a second warning.

One minute into the sixth round, Strike managed to capitalize on his opponent's disintegrating technique and forced Laing, whose nose was now pouring blood, onto the ropes. When the referee separated them, then signaled to continue, Laing shed the last thin membrane of civilized behavior and attempted to land a headbutt. The referee tried to intervene and Laing became crazed. Strike narrowly avoided a kick to the crotch, then found himself locked in Laing's arms, with the other's teeth digging into his face. Indistinctly Strike heard the ref's shouts, the sudden drop in noise from the crowd as enthusiasm turned to unease at the ugly force emanating from Laing. The referee forced the boxers apart, bellowing at Laing, but he seemed to hear none of it, merely gathering himself again then swinging at Strike who sidestepped and landed a hard punch to Laing's gut. Laing doubled over, winded, and hit the floor on his knees. Strike left the ring to weak applause, blood trickling from the stinging bite on his cheekbone.

Strike, who finished the tournament as runner-up to a Sergeant from 3 Para, was rotated out of Aldershot two weeks later, but not before word had reached him that Laing had been confined to barracks for his display of ill discipline and violence in the ring. The punishment might have been worse, but Strike heard that his senior officer had accepted Laing's plea of mitigating circumstances. His story was that he had entered the ring deeply distressed by news of his fiancée's miscarriage.

Even then, years before he had gained the additional knowledge of Laing that had led Strike to this country road in a borrowed Mini, he had not believed that a dead fetus meant anything to the animal he had sensed seething beneath Laing's hairless, milk-white skin. Laing's incisor marks had still been visible on his face as he left the country.

Three years later, Strike had arrived in Cyprus to investigate an alleged rape. On entering the interrogation room he came face to face for the second time with Donald Laing, who was now carrying a little more weight and sporting a few new tattoos, his face heavily freckled from the Cyprus sun and creases etched around the deep-set eyes.

Unsurprisingly, Laing's lawyer objected to the investigation being undertaken by a man whom his client had once bitten, so Strike swapped cases with a colleague who was in Cyprus investigating a drugs ring. When he met this colleague for a drink a week later Strike found, to his surprise, that he was inclined to believe Laing's story, which was that he and the alleged victim, a local waitress, had had clumsy, drunken, consensual sex which she now regretted because her boyfriend had heard rumors that she had left her place of work with Laing. There were no witnesses to the alleged attack, which the waitress claimed had taken place at knifepoint.

"Real party girl," was his fellow SIB man's assessment of the alleged victim.

Strike was in no position to contradict him, but he had not forgotten that Laing had once managed to gain the sympathy of a senior officer after a display of violence and insubordination witnessed by hundreds. When Strike asked for details of Laing's story and demeanor, his colleague had described a sharp, likable man with a wry sense of humor.

"Discipline could be better," the investigator admitted, having reviewed Laing's file, "but I don't see him as a rapist. Married to a girl from home; she's out here with him."

Strike returned to his drug case in the sweltering sun. A couple of weeks later, by now sporting the full beard that grew conveniently fast when he wished to look "less army," as the military phrase had it, he was to be found lying on the floorboards of a smoke-filled loft, listening to an odd story. Given Strike's unkempt appearance, his Jesus sandals, baggy shorts and the sundry bracelets tied around his thick wrist, the stoned young Cypriot dealer beside him was perhaps justified in not suspecting that he was talking to a British military policeman. As they lounged side by side with spliffs in their hands, his companion confided the names of several soldiers dealing on the island, and not merely in cannabis. The youth's accent was thick and Strike was so busy memorizing approximations of the real names, or indeed pseudonyms, that the new name of "Dunnullung" did not immediately suggest anyone he knew. Only when his companion began to tell him how "Dunnullung" tied up and tortured his wife did Strike connect Dunnullung with Laing. "Crazy man," said the ox-eyed boy in a detached voice. "Because she try and leave." Upon careful, casual questioning, the Cypriot confided that he had had the story from Laing himself. It seemed to have been told partly to amuse, partly to warn the young man with whom he was dealing.

The Seaforth Estate had been baking in the midday sun when Strike visited it the following day. The houses here were the oldest of the island's military accommodation, white-painted and a little shabby. He had chosen to visit while Laing, who had successfully eluded his charge of rape, was busy at work. When he rang the doorbell, he heard only a baby's distant cries.

"We think she's agoraphobic," confided a gossipy female neighbor who had rushed outside to share her views. "There's something a bit off there. She's really shy."

"What about her husband?" asked Strike.

"Donnie? Oh, he's the life and soul, Donnie," said the neighbor brightly. "You should hear him imitating Corporal Oakley! Oh, it's spot on. So funny."

There were rules, many of them, about entering another soldier's house without his express permission. Strike pounded on the door, but there was no answer. He could still hear the baby crying. He moved around to the rear of the house. The curtains were all closed. He knocked on the back door. Nothing.

His only justification, if he had to defend his actions, would be the sound of that baby crying. It might not be considered sufficient reason for forcing entry without a warrant. Strike mistrusted anyone who was overreliant on instinct or intuition, but he was convinced that there was something wrong. He possessed a finely honed sense for the strange and the wicked. He had seen things all through his childhood that other people preferred to imagine happened only in films.

The door buckled and gave the second time he shouldered it. The kitchen smelled bad. Nobody had emptied the bin for days. He moved into the house.

"Mrs. Laing?"

Nobody answered. The baby's feeble cries were coming from the upper floor. He climbed the stairs, calling out as he went.

The door to the main bedroom stood open. The room was in semidarkness. It smelled horrible.

"Mrs. Laing?"

She was naked, tied by one wrist to the headboard, partially covered by a heavily bloodstained sheet. The baby lay beside her on the mattress, wearing only a nappy. Strike could see that it looked shrunken, unhealthy.

As he bounded across the room to free her, his other hand already scrambling for the mobile to call an ambulance, she spoke in a cracked voice:

"No . . . go away . . . get out . . ."

Strike had rarely seen terror like it. In his inhumanity, her husband had come to seem almost supernatural. Even as Strike worked to release her wrist, which was bloody and swollen, she begged him to leave her there. Laing had told her that he would kill her if the baby was not happier when he returned. She did not seem able to conceive of a future where Laing was not omnipotent.

Donald Laing had been sentenced to sixteen years' imprisonment for what he had done to his wife, and Strike's evidence had put him away. To the last, Laing had denied everything, saying that his wife had tied herself up, that she liked it, that she was kinky that way, that she had neglected the baby, that she had tried to frame him, that it was all a put-up job.

The memories were as filthy as any he had. Strange to relive them while the Mini moved past sweeping slopes of green, sparkling in the strengthening sun. This scenery was of a kind that was not familiar to Strike. The sweeping masses of granite, these rolling hills, had an alien grandeur in their bareness, in their calm spaciousness. He had spent much of his childhood perched on the coast, with the taste of salt in the air: this was a place of woodland and river, mysterious and secretive in a different way from St. Mawes, the little town with its long smuggling history, where colorful houses tumbled down to the beach.

As he passed a spectacular viaduct to his right, he thought about psychopaths, and how they were to be found everywhere, not only in run-down tenements and slums and squats, but even here, in this place of serene beauty. The likes of Laing resembled rats: you knew they were there, but you never gave them much thought until you came face to face with one.

A pair of miniature stone castles stood sentinel on either side of the road. As Strike drove into Donald Laing's hometown, the sun broke through, dazzlingly bright.

16

So grab your rose and ringside seat,
We're back home at Conry's bar.

Blue Öyster Cult, "Before the Kiss, A Redcap"

Behind the glass door of a shop on the high street hung a tea towel. It was decorated with black line drawings of local landmarks, but what attracted Strike's attention were a number of stylized yellow roses exactly like the tattoo he remembered on Donald Laing's powerful forearm. He paused to read the verse in the middle:

It's oor ain toon
It's the best toon
That ever there be:
Here's tae Melrose,
Gem o' Scotland,
The toon o' the free.

He had deposited the Mini in a car park beside the abbey, with its dark red arches rising against a pale blue sky. Beyond, to the southeast, was the triple peak of Eildon Hill, which Strike had noted on the map and which added drama and distinction to the skyline. After a bacon roll purchased at a nearby coffee shop and eaten at an outside table, followed by a cigarette and his second strong tea of the day, Strike had set out on foot in search of the Wynd, the home address Laing had given sixteen years previously when he joined the army and which Strike was not entirely sure how to pronounce. Was it "wind" as in breeze, or "wind" as in clock?

The small town looked prosperous in the sunshine as Strike strolled up the sloping high street to the central square, where a unicorn-topped pillar stood in a basin of flowers. A round stone in the pavement bore the town's old Roman name, Trimontium, which Strike knew must refer to the triple-peaked hill nearby.

He seemed to have missed the Wynd, which according to the map on his phone led off the high street. He doubled back and found a narrow entrance in the walls to his right, only large enough for a pedestrian, which led to a dim inner courtyard. Laing's old family home had a bright blue front door and was reached by a short flight of steps.

Strike's knock was answered almost at once by a pretty, dark-haired woman far too young to be Laing's mother. When Strike explained his mission, she responded in a soft accent he found attractive:

"Mrs. Laing? She's no been here for ten years or more."

Before his spirits had time to sink, she added:

"She stays up in Dingleton Road."

"Dingleton Road? Is that far?"

"Just up the way." She pointed behind her, to the right. "I dinnae ken the number, sorry."

"No problem. Thanks for your help."

It occurred to him as he walked back along the dingy passageway to the sunlit square that, barring the obscenities the young soldier had muttered into Strike's ear in the boxing ring, he had never heard Donald Laing speak. Still working undercover on his drugs case, it had been imperative that Strike was not seen wandering in and out of HQ in his beard, so the interrogation of Laing after his arrest had been undertaken by others. Later, when he had successfully concluded the drugs case and was again clean-shaven, Strike had given evidence against Laing in court, but he had been on a plane out of Cyprus by the time that Laing had stood up to deny that he had tied up or tortured his wife. As he crossed Market Square, Strike wondered whether his Borders accent might have been one reason that people had been so willing to believe in Donnie Laing, to forgive him, to like him. The detective seemed to remember reading that advertisers used Scottish accents to suggest integrity and honesty.

The only pub he had spotted so far stood a short distance along a street Strike passed on the way to Dingleton Road. Melrose appeared to be fond of yellow: though the walls were white, the pub's doors and window were picked out in acid-bright lemon and black. To the Cornish-born Strike's amusement, given the landlocked situation of the town, the pub was called the Ship Inn. He walked on into Dingleton Road, which snaked under a bridge, became a steep hill and disappeared out of sight.

The term "not far" was a relative one, as Strike had often had occasion to observe since losing his calf and foot. After ten minutes' walk up the hill he was beginning to regret that he had not returned to the abbey car park for the Mini. Twice he asked women in the street whether they knew where Mrs. Laing lived, but though polite and friendly, neither could tell him. He trudged on, sweating slightly, past a stretch of white bungalows, until he met an elderly man coming the other way, wearing a tweed flat cap and walking a black and white Border collie.

"Excuse me," said Strike. "Do you happen to know where Mrs. Laing lives? I've forgotten the number."

"Messus Laing?" replied the dog walker, surveying Strike from beneath thick salt and pepper eyebrows. "Aye, she's my next-door neighbor."

Thank Christ.

"Three along," said the man, pointing, "wi' the stone wishing well oot front."

"Thanks very much," said Strike.

As he turned up Mrs. Laing's drive he noticed, out of the corner of his eye, that the old man was still standing on the spot, watching him, in spite of the collie trying to tug him downhill.

Mrs. Laing's bungalow looked clean and respectable. Stone animals of Disneyesque cuteness littered her lawn and peeped out from her flowerbeds. The front door lay at the side of the building, in shadow. Only as he raised his hand to the doorknocker did it occur to Strike that he might, within seconds, come face to face with Donald Laing.

For a whole minute after he knocked, nothing happened except that the elderly dog walker retraced his steps and stood at Mrs. Laing's gate, unabashedly staring. Strike suspected that the man regretted giving out his neighbor's address and was checking that the large stranger meant the woman no harm, but he was wrong.

"She's in," he called to Strike, who was deliberating as to whether to try again. "But she's wud."

"She's what?" Strike called back as he knocked for a second time.

"Wud. Doolally."

The dog walker took a few steps down the drive towards Strike.

"Demented," he translated for the Englishman.

"Ah," said Strike.

The door opened, revealing a tiny, wizened, sallow-faced old woman wearing a deep blue dressing gown. She glared up at Strike with a kind of unfocused malevolence. There were several stiff whiskers growing out of her chin.

"Mrs. Laing?"

She said nothing, but peered at him out of eyes that he knew, bloodshot and faded though they were, must have been beady and ferret-like in their day.

"Mrs. Laing, I'm looking for your son Donald."

"No," she said, with surprising vehemence. "No."

She retreated and slammed the door.

"Bugger," said Strike under his breath, which made him think of Robin. She would almost certainly have been better than him at charming the little old woman. Slowly he turned, wondering whether there was anyone else in Melrose who might help—he had definitely seen other Laings listed on 192.com—and found himself face to face with the dog walker, who had proceeded all the way down the drive to meet him and was looking cautiously excited.

"You're the detective," he said. "You're the detective that put her son away."

Strike was astonished. He could not imagine how he was recognizable to an elderly Scottish man whom he had never met before.

His so-called fame was of a very low order when it came to being identified by strangers. He walked the streets of London daily without anyone caring who he was, and unless somebody met him or heard his name in the context of an investigation, was rarely associated with the newspaper stories about his successful cases.

"Aye, you did!" said the elderly man, his excitement rising. "My wife and I are friends of Margaret Bunyan's." And in the face of Strike's mystification he elaborated: "Rhona's mother."

It took a few seconds for Strike's capacious memory to render up the information that Laing's wife, the young woman whom he had discovered tied to the bed beneath the bloodstained sheet, had been called Rhona.

"When Margaret seen you in the papers she said to us, 'That's him, that's the lad that rescued our Rhona!' You've done very well for yourself, haven't you? Stop it, Wullie!" he added in a loud aside to the eager collie, which was still pulling on its lead, trying to regain the road. "Oh, aye, Margaret follows everything you do, all the stories in the papers. You found out who killed that model girl—and that writer! Margaret's never forgot what you did for her girl, never."

Strike muttered something indistinct, something he hoped sounded grateful for Margaret's appreciation.

"Wha' for are you wanting to talk to auld Mrs. Laing? He's nae done something else, has he, Donnie?"

"I'm trying to find him," said Strike evasively. "D'you know if he's back in Melrose?"

"Och, no, I wouldnae think so. He came back to see his mother a few years back, but I dinnae know that he's been here since. It's a small toon: Donnie Laing back—we'd hear, ken?"

"D'you think Mrs.—Bunyan, did you say?—might have any—?"

"She'd love tae meet you," said the old man excitedly. "*No,* Wullie," he added to the whining Border collie, which was trying to tug him to the gate. "I'll ring her, will I? She's only over in Darnick. Next village. Will I ring?"

"That'd be very helpful."

So Strike accompanied the old man next door and waited in a

small, spotless sitting room while he gabbled excitedly into the phone over his dog's increasingly furious whines.

"She'll come over," said the old man, with his hand over the receiver. "D'ye want to meet her here? You're welcome. The wife'll make tea—"

"Thanks, but I've got a couple of things to do," lied Strike, who doubted the possibility of a successful interview in the presence of this garrulous witness. "Could you see whether she'd be free for lunch at the Ship Inn? In an hour?"

The collie's determination for its walk tipped the balance in Strike's favor. The two men left the house and walked back down the hill together, the collie tugging all the way so that Strike was forced into a faster gait than suited him on a steep downward slope. He said good-bye with relief to his helpful acquaintance in Market Square. With a cheery wave, the old man headed off in the direction of the River Tweed and Strike, now limping slightly, walked down the high street, killing time until he needed to return to the Ship.

At the bottom of the road he encountered another explosion of black and acid yellow which, Strike realized, explained the Ship Inn's colors. Here again was the yellow rose, on a sign announcing MELROSE RUGBY FOOTBALL CLUB. Strike paused, hands in pockets, looking over the low wall at a smooth, level expanse of viridian velvet surrounded by trees, the yellow rugby posts shining in the sun, stands to the right and softly undulating hills beyond. The pitch was as well maintained as any place of worship, and an extraordinarily well-appointed facility for such a small town.

Staring out across the expanse of velvety grass, Strike remembered Whittaker, stinking and smoking in the corner of the squat while Leda lay beside him, listening open-mouthed to the tales of his hard life—credulous and greedy as a baby bird, as Strike now saw it, for the yarns Whittaker spun her. From Leda's point of view, Gordonstoun might as well have been Alcatraz: it was nothing short of outrageous that her slender poet had been forced out into the harsh Scottish winter to be pummeled and knocked about in the mud and the rain.

"Not rugby, darling. Oh, poor baby... *you* playing rugby!"

And when the seventeen-year-old Strike (sporting a fat lip from the boxing club at the time) had laughed, softly, into his homework, Whittaker had staggered to his feet, shouting in his obnoxious mockney:

"What are you facking laughing about, meathead?"

Whittaker could not stand laughter at his expense. He needed, craved adulation; in its absence, he would take fear or even loathing as evidence of his power, but ridicule was evidence of another's assumed superiority and consequently unbearable.

"You'd facking love it, wouldn't you, you stupid little tit? Think you're facking officer class already, dontcha, out with the rugger buggers. Get his rich daddy to send him to facking Gordonstoun!" Whittaker had yelled at Leda.

"Calm down, darling!" she had said, and then, in slightly more peremptory terms: "No, Corm!"

Strike had stood up, braced, ready and eager to hit Whittaker. That had been the closest he had ever come to doing it, but his mother had staggered between them, a thin, beringed hand on each heaving chest.

Strike blinked and the bright sunlit pitch, a place of innocent endeavor and excitement, seemed to come back into focus. He could smell leaves, grass and the warm rubber from the road beside him. Slowly he turned and headed back towards the Ship Inn, craving a drink, but his treacherous subconscious was not done with him yet.

The sight of that smooth rugby pitch had unleashed another memory: black-haired, dark-eyed Noel Brockbank, running at him with the broken beer bottle in his hand. Brockbank had been massive, powerful and fast: a flanker. Strike remembered his own fist rising around the side of that broken bottle, connecting just as the glass touched his own neck—

A basal skull fracture, that's what they had called it. Bleeding from the ear. A massive brain injury.

"Fuck, fuck, fuck," mumbled Strike under his breath, in time with his own footsteps.

Laing, that's what you're here for. Laing.

He passed under the metal galleon with bright yellow sails that hung over the Ship Inn's door. A sign just inside read MELROSE'S ONLY PUB.

He found the place instantly calming: a glow of warm color, shining glass and brass; a carpet that resembled a patchwork of faded browns, reds and greens; walls of warm peach and exposed stone. Everywhere were more indications of Melrose's sporting obsession: blackboards announcing upcoming matches, several enormous plasma screens and, above the urinal (it had been hours since Strike had last peed), a small wall-mounted television, just in case a try was pending at the point a full bladder could no longer be ignored.

Mindful of the journey back to Edinburgh in Hardacre's car, he bought himself half a pint of John Smith's and sat down on a leather-covered sofa facing the bar, perusing the laminated menu and hoping that Margaret Bunyan would be punctual, because he had just realized that he was hungry.

She appeared a mere five minutes later. Although he could barely remember what her daughter looked like and had never met Mrs. Bunyan before, her expression of mingled apprehension and anticipation gave her away as she paused, staring at him, on the doormat.

Strike got up and she stumbled forwards, both hands gripping the strap of a large black handbag.

"It *is* you," she said breathlessly.

She was around sixty, small and fragile-looking, wearing metal-framed glasses, her expression anxious beneath tightly permed fair hair.

Strike held out a large hand and shook hers, which trembled slightly, cold and fine-boned.

"Her dad's over in Hawick today, he can't come, I rang him, he said to tell you we'll never forget what you did for Rhona," she said on a single breath. She sank down beside Strike on the sofa, continuing to observe him with mingled awe and nerves. "We've never forgot. We read about you in the papers. We were so sorry about your leg. What you did for Rhona! What you did—"

Her eyes were suddenly brimful of tears.

"—we were so..."

"I'm glad I was able to—"

Find her child tied naked and bloodstained on a bed? Talking to relatives about what the people they loved had endured was one of the worst parts of the job.

"—able to help her."

Mrs. Bunyan blew her nose on a handkerchief retrieved from the bottom of her black handbag. He could tell that she was of the generation of women who would never usually enter a pub alone and certainly not buy drinks at a bar if a man were there to undertake the ordeal for them.

"Let me get you something."

"Just an orange juice," she said breathlessly, dabbing at her eyes.

"And something to eat," Strike urged, keen to order the beer-battered haddock and chips for himself.

When he had placed their order at the bar and returned to her, she asked what he was doing in Melrose and the source of her nervousness became apparent at once.

"He's not come back, has he? Donnie? Is he back?"

"Not as far as I know," said Strike. "I don't know where he is."

"D'you think he's got something to do...?"

Her voice had dropped to a whisper.

"We read in the paper...we saw that someone sent you a—a—"

"Yes," said Strike. "I don't know whether he's got anything to do with it, but I'd like to find him. Apparently he's been back here to see his mother since leaving jail."

"Och, four or five years ago, that would've been," said Margaret Bunyan. "He turned up on her doorstep, forced his way into the bungalow. She's got Alzheimer's now. She couldn't stop him, but the neighbors called his brothers and they came and threw him out."

"They did, did they?"

"Donnie's the youngest. He's got four older brothers. They're hard men," said Mrs. Bunyan, "all of them. Jamie stays in Selkirk—he came tearing through to get Donnie out of his mother's house. They say he knocked him senseless."

She took a tremulous sip of her orange juice and continued:

"We heard all about it. Our friend Brian, who you just met, he saw the fight happening out on the street. Four of them onto one, all of them shouting and yelling. Someone called the police. Jamie got a caution. He didn't care," said Mrs. Bunyan. "They didn't want him anywhere near them, or their mother. They ran him out of town.

"I was terrified," she continued. "For Rhona. He'd always said he'd find her when he got out."

"And did he?" asked Strike.

"Och, yes," said Margaret Bunyan miserably. "We knew he would. She'd moved tae Glasgow, got a job in a travel agent's. He still found her. Six months she lived in fear of him turning up and then one day he did. Came to her flat one night, but he'd been ill. He wasn't the same."

"Ill?" repeated Strike sharply.

"I can't remember what it was he'd got, some kind of arthritis, I think, and Rhona said he'd put on a lot of weight. He turned up at her flat at night, he'd tracked her down, but thanks be to God," said Mrs. Bunyan fervently, "her fiancé was staying over. His name's Ben," she added, with a triumphal flourish, the color high in her faded cheeks, "and he's a *policeman*."

She said it as though she thought Strike would be especially glad to hear this, as though he and Ben were comembers of some great investigative brotherhood.

"They're married now," said Mrs. Bunyan. "No kids, because—well, you know why—"

And without warning, a torrent of tears burst forth, streaming down Mrs. Bunyan's face behind her glasses. The horror of what had happened a decade ago was suddenly fresh and raw, as though a pile of offal had been dumped on the table in front of them.

"—Laing stuck a knife up inside her," whispered Mrs. Bunyan.

She confided in him as though Strike were a doctor or a priest, telling him the secrets that weighed on her, but which she could not tell her friends: he already knew the worst. As she groped again for the handkerchief in her square black bag, Strike remembered the wide patch of blood on the sheets, the excoriated skin on her wrist where Rhona had tried to free herself. Thank God her mother could not see inside his head.

"He stuck a knife inside—and they tried to—you know—repair—"

Mrs. Bunyan took a deep, shuddering breath as two plates of food appeared in front of them.

"But she and Ben have lovely holidays," she whispered frantically, dabbing repeatedly at her hollow cheeks, lifting her glasses to reach her eyes. "And they breed—they breed German—German Shepherds."

Hungry though he was, Strike could not eat in the immediate aftermath of discussing what had been done to Rhona Laing.

"She and Laing had a baby, didn't they?" he asked, remembering its feeble whimpering from beside its bloodstained, dehydrated mother. "The kid must be, what, ten by now?"

"He d-died," she whispered, tears dripping off the end of her chin. "C-cot death. He was always sickly, the bairn. It happened two d-days after they put D-Donnie away. And h-he—Donnie—he telephoned her out of the jail and told her he knew she'd killed—killed—the baby—and that he'd kill her when he got out—"

Strike laid a large hand briefly on the sobbing woman's shoulder, then hoisted himself to his feet and approached the young barmaid who was watching them with her mouth open. Brandy seemed too strong for the sparrow-like creature behind him. Strike's Aunt Joan, who was only a little older than Mrs. Bunyan, always regarded port as medicinal. He ordered a glass and took it back to her.

"Here. Drink this."

His reward was a recrudescence of tears, but after much more dabbing with the sodden handkerchief she said shakily, "You're very kind," sipped it, gave a little gasping sigh and blinked at him, her fair-lashed eyes pink like a piglet's.

"Have you got any idea where Laing went after turning up at Rhona's?"

"Yes," she whispered. "Ben put out feelers through work, through the probation office. Apparently he went to Gateshead, but I don't know whether he's still there."

Gateshead. Strike remembered the Donald Laing he had found online. Had he moved from Gateshead to Corby? Or were they different men?

"Anyway," said Mrs. Bunyan, "he's never bothered Rhona and Ben again."

"I'll bet he hasn't," said Strike, picking up his knife and fork. "A copper and German Shepherds, eh? He's not stupid."

She seemed to take courage and comfort from his words, and with a timid, tearful smile began to pick at her macaroni cheese.

"They married young," commented Strike, who was keen to hear anything he could about Laing, anything that might give a lead on his associations or habits.

She nodded, swallowed and said:

"Far too young. She started seeing him when she was only fifteen and we didn't like it. We'd heard things about Donnie Laing. There was a young girl who said he'd forced himself on her at the Young Farmers' disco. It never came to anything: the police said there wasn't enough evidence. We tried to warn Rhona he was trouble," she sighed, "but that made her more determined. She was always headstrong, our Rhona."

"He'd already been accused of rape?" asked Strike. His fish and chips were excellent. The pub was filling up, for which he was grateful: the barmaid's attention was diverted from them.

"Oh yes. They're a rough family," said Mrs. Bunyan, with the sort of prim small-town snobbery that Strike knew well from his own upbringing. "All those brothers, they were always fighting, in trouble with the police, but he was the worst of them. His own brothers didn't like him. I don't think his mother liked him much, tae tell the truth. There was a rumor," she said in a burst of confidence, "that he wasnae the father's. The parents were always fighting and they separated round about the time she got pregnant with Donnie. They say she had a run-around with one of the local policemen, as a matter of fact. I don't know whether it's true. The policeman moved on and Mr. Laing moved back in, but Mr. Laing never liked Donnie, I know that. Never liked him at all. People said it was because he knew Donnie wasn't his.

"He was the wildest of all of them. A big lad. He got into the junior sevens—"

"Sevens?"

"The rugby sevens," she said, and even this small, genteel lady was surprised that Strike did not immediately understand what, to Melrose, seemed more religion than sport. "But they kicked him out. No discipline. *Someone* carved up Greenyards the week after they kicked him out. The pitch," she added, in response to the Englishman's mystifying ignorance.

The port was making her talkative. Words were tumbling out of her now.

"He took up boxing instead. He had the gift of the gab, though, oh aye. When Rhona first took up with him—she was fifteen and he was seventeen—I had some folk telling me he wasn't a bad lad really. Oh, aye," she repeated, nodding at Strike's look of disbelief. "Folk that didn't know him so well were took in by him. He could be charming when he wanted to, Donnie Laing.

"But you just ask Walter Gilchrist whether he was charming. Walter sacked him off the farm—he was always being late—and *someone* set fire to his barn after. Oh, they never proved it was Donnie. They never proved it was him who wrecked the pitch, neither, but I know what I believe.

"Rhona wouldn't listen. She thought she knew him. He was misunderstood and I don't know what else. We were prejudiced, narrow-minded. He wanted tae join the army. Good riddance, I thought. I hoped she'd forget him if he left.

"Then he came back. He got her pregnant but she lost it. She was angry with me because I said—"

She did not want to tell him what she had said, but Strike could imagine.

"—and then she wouldn't talk to me anymore, and she went and married him on his next leave. Her dad and I weren't invited," she said. "Off to Cyprus together. But I know he killed our cat."

"What?" said Strike, thrown.

"I know it was him. We'd told Rhona she was making an awful mistake, last time we saw her before she married him. That night we couldn't find Purdy. Next day she was on the back lawn, dead. The vet said she'd been strangled."

On the plasma screen over her shoulder a scarlet-clad Dimitar Berbatov was celebrating a goal against Fulham. The air was full of Borders voices. Glasses clinked and cutlery tinkled as Strike's companion talked of death and mutilation.

"I know he did it, I know he killed Purdy," she said feverishly. "Look at what he did to Rhona and the baby. He's evil."

Her hands fumbled with the catch on her bag and pulled out a small wad of photographs.

"My husband always says, 'Why are you keeping them? Burn them.' But I always thought we might need pictures of him one day. There," she said, thrusting them into Strike's eager hands. "You have them, you keep them. Gateshead. That's where he went next."

Later, after she had left with renewed tears and thanks, after he had paid the bill, Strike walked to Millers of Melrose, a family butcher he had noticed on his stroll around the town. There he treated himself to some venison pies that he suspected would be far tastier than anything he would be able to purchase at the station before boarding the sleeper back to London.

Returning to the car park via a short street where golden roses bloomed, Strike thought again about the tattoo on that powerful forearm.

Once, years ago, it had meant something to Donnie Laing to belong to this lovely town, surrounded by farmland and overlooked by the triple peaks of Eildon Hill. Yet he had been no straightforward worker of the soil, no team player, no asset to a place that seemed to pride itself on discipline and honest endeavor. Melrose had spat out the burner of barns, the strangler of cats, the carver-up of rugby fields, so Laing had taken refuge in a place where many men had found either their salvation or their inevitable comeuppance: the British Army. When that had led to jail, and jail disgorged him, he had tried to come home, but nobody had wanted him.

Had Donald Laing found a warmer welcome in Gateshead? Had he moved from there to Corby? Or, Strike wondered, as he folded himself back into Hardacre's Mini, had these been mere stopping posts on his way to London and Strike?

17

The Girl That Love Made Blind

Tuesday morning. It was asleep after what It said had been a long, hard night. Like he fucking cared, although he had to act like he did. He had persuaded It to go and lie down, and when It began to breathe deeply and evenly he watched It for a while, imagining choking the fucking life out of It, seeing Its eyes open and Its struggle for breath, Its face slowly turning purple...

When he had been sure that he would not wake It, he had left the bedroom quietly, pulled on a jacket and slipped out into the early morning air to find The Secretary. This was his first chance of following her in days and he was too late to pick up the trail at her home station. The best he could do was to lurk around the mouth of Denmark Street.

He spotted her from a distance: that bright, wavy strawberry-blonde head was unmistakable. The vain bitch must like standing out in the crowd or she'd cover it or cut it or dye it. They all wanted attention, he knew that for a fact: all of them.

As she moved closer, his infallible instinct for other people's moods told him something had changed. She was looking down as she walked, hunch-shouldered, oblivious to the other workers swarming around her, clutching bags, coffees and phones.

He passed right by her in the opposite direction, drawing so close that he could have smelled her perfume if they had not been in that bustling street full of car fumes and dust. He might have been a traffic bollard. That annoyed him a little, even though it had been his intention to pass by her unnoticed. He had singled her out, but she treated him with indifference.

On the other hand, he had made a discovery: she had been crying for hours. He knew what it looked like when women did that; he had seen it plenty of times. Puffy and reddened and flabby-faced, leaking and whining: they all did it. They liked playing the victim. You'd kill them just to make them shut up.

He turned and followed her the short distance to Denmark Street. When women were in her state, they were often malleable in ways they would not be when less distressed or frightened. They forgot to do all the things that bitches did routinely to keep the likes of him at bay: keys between their knuckles, phones in their hands, rape alarms in their pockets, walking in packs. They became needy, grateful for a kind word, a friendly ear. That was how he had landed It.

His pace quickened as she turned into Denmark Street, which the press had at last given up as a bad job after eight days. She opened the black door of the office and went inside.

Would she come out again, or was she going to spend the day with Strike? He really hoped they were screwing each other. They probably were. Just the two of them in the office all the time—bound to be.

He withdrew into a doorway and pulled out his phone, keeping one eye on the second-floor window of number twenty-four.

18

I've been stripped, the insulation's gone.

Blue Öyster Cult, "Lips in the Hills"

The first time that Robin had ever entered Strike's office had been on her first morning as an engaged woman. Unlocking the glass door today, she remembered watching the new sapphire on her finger darken, shortly before Strike had come hurtling out of the office and nearly knocked her down the metal staircase to her death.

There was no ring on her finger anymore. The place where it had sat all these months felt hypersensitive, as though it had left her branded. She was carrying a small holdall that contained a change of outfit and a few toiletries.

You can't cry here. You mustn't cry here.

Automatically she performed the usual start-of-the-working-day tasks: took off her coat, hung it up with her handbag on a peg beside the door, filled and switched on the kettle, and stowed the holdall under her desk, where Strike would not see it. She kept turning back to check that she'd done what she had meant to do, feeling disembodied, like a ghost whose chilly fingers might slip through the handles of handbags and kettles.

It had taken four days to dismantle a relationship that had lasted nine years. Four days of mounting animosity, of grudges aired and accusations hurled. Some of it seemed so trivial, looking back. The Land Rover, the Grand National, her decision to take her laptop home. On Sunday there had been a petty squabble about whose parents were paying for the wedding cars, which had led yet again to an argument about her pitiful pay packet. By the time they had got into the Land Rover on Monday morning to drive back home, they had barely been speaking.

Then last night, at home in West Ealing, had come the explosive argument that had rendered all the squabbling that had gone before trivial, mere warning tremors of the seismic disaster that would lay waste to everything.

Strike would be down shortly. She could hear him moving around in the flat upstairs. Robin knew that she must not look shaky or unable to cope. Work was all she had now. She would have to find a room in somebody else's flat, which would be all she would be able to afford on the pittance Strike paid her. She tried to imagine future housemates. It would be like being back in halls of residence.

Don't think about that now.

As she made tea she realized that she had forgotten to bring in the tin of Bettys tea bags she had bought shortly after trying on her wedding dress for the last time. The thought almost overset her, but by a powerful effort of will she restrained the urge to cry and took her mug to the computer, ready to trawl through the emails she had not been able to answer during their week of exile from the office.

Strike, she knew, had only just got back from Scotland: he had returned on the overnight train. She would make conversation about that when he appeared, so as to keep attention away from her red, swollen eyes. Before leaving the flat this morning she had tried to improve their appearance with ice and cold water, but with limited success.

Matthew had tried to block her path as she headed out of the flat. He had looked ghastly too.

"Look, we've got to talk. We've got to."

Not anymore, thought Robin, whose hands shook as she lifted the hot tea to her lips. *I haven't got to do anything I don't want to do anymore.*

The brave thought was undermined by a single hot tear that leaked without warning down her cheek. Horrified, she brushed it away; she had not thought that she had any tears left to cry. Turning to her monitor she began typing a reply to a client who had queried his invoice, hardly knowing what she wrote.

Clanging footsteps on the stairs outside made her brace herself. The door opened. Robin looked up. The man who stood there was not Strike.

Primal, instinctive fear ripped through her. There was no time to analyze why the stranger had such an effect on her; she only knew that he was dangerous. In an instant she had calculated that she would not be able to reach the door in time, that her rape alarm was in her coat pocket and that her best weapon was the sharp letter-opener lying inches from her left hand.

He was gaunt and pale, his head was shaven, a few freckles were scattered across a broad nose and his mouth was wide and thick lipped. Tattoos covered his wrists, knuckles and neck. A gold tooth glinted on one side of his grinning mouth. A deep scar ran from the middle of his upper lip towards his cheekbone, dragging his mouth upwards in a permanent Elvis-style sneer. He wore baggy jeans and a tracksuit top and he smelled strongly of stale tobacco and cannabis.

"'S'up?" he said. He repeatedly clicked the fingers of both hands hanging at his sides as he moved into the room. *Click, click, click.* "You all alone, yeah?"

"No," she said, her mouth completely dry. She wanted to grab the letter-opener before he came any closer. *Click, click, click.* "My boss is just—"

"Shanker!" said Strike's voice from the doorway.

The stranger turned.

"Bunsen," he said and stopped clicking his fingers, held out a hand and gave Strike a dap greeting. "'Ow you doin', bruv?"

Dear God, thought Robin, limp with relief. Why hadn't Strike told her that the man was coming? She turned away, busying herself with email so that Strike would not see her face. As Strike led Shanker into the inner office and closed the door behind them, she caught the word "Whittaker."

Ordinarily she would have wished that she could be in there, listening. She finished her email and supposed that she ought to offer them coffee. First she went to splash more cold water on her face in the tiny bathroom on the landing, which retained a strong smell of drains no matter how many air-fresheners she bought out of petty cash.

Strike, meanwhile, had seen just enough of Robin to be shocked by her appearance. He had never seen her face so pale, nor her eyes so puffy and bloodshot. Even as he sat down at his desk, eager to hear what information on Whittaker Shanker had brought to his office, the thought crossed his mind: *What's the bastard done to her?* And for a fraction of a second, before fixing all his attention on Shanker, Strike imagined punching Matthew and enjoying it.

"Why you lookin' so ugly, Bunsen?" asked Shanker, stretching himself out in the chair opposite and clicking his fingers enthusiastically. He had had the tic since his teens and Strike pitied the person who would try to make him stop.

"Knackered," said Strike. "Got back from Scotland a couple of hours ago."

"Never been to Scotland," said Shanker.

Strike was not aware that Shanker had ever been out of London in his life.

"So what've you got for me?"

"'E's still around," said Shanker, ceasing his finger-clicking to pull a pack of Mayfairs out of his pocket. He lit one with a cheap lighter without asking whether Strike minded. With a mental shrug, Strike took out his own Benson & Hedges and borrowed the lighter. "Seen 'is dealer. Geezer says 'e's in Catford."

"He's left Hackney?"

"Unless 'e's left a clone of 'imself behind 'e musta done, Bunsen. I didn't check for clones. Gimme another ton an' I'll go see."

Strike gave a short snort of amusement. People underestimated Shanker at their peril. Given that he looked as though he had done every kind of illegal substance in his time, his restlessness often misled acquaintances into assuming he was on something. In fact, he was sharper and soberer than many a businessman at the end of their working day, if incurably criminal.

"Got an address?" said Strike, pulling a notebook towards him.

"Not yet," said Shanker.

"Is he working?"

" 'E tells ev'ryone 'e's a road manager for some metal band."

"But?"

" 'E's pimping," said Shanker matter-of-factly.

There was a knock on the door.

"Anyone want coffee?" asked Robin. Strike could tell that she was deliberately keeping her face out of the light. His eyes found her left hand: the engagement ring was missing.

"Cheers," said Shanker. "Two sugars."

"Tea would be great, thanks," said Strike, watching her move away as he reached into his desk for the old tin ashtray he had swiped from a bar in Germany. He pushed it across to Shanker before the latter could tap his lengthening ash on the floor.

"How d'you know he's pimping?"

"I know this uvver geezer who met 'im with the brass," said Shanker. Strike was familiar with the cockney slang: brass nail—"tail." "Says Whittaker lives with 'er. Very young. Just legal."

"Right," said Strike.

He had dealt with prostitution in its various aspects ever since he had become an investigator, but this was different: this was his ex-stepfather, a man whom his mother had loved and romanticized, to whom she had borne a child. He could almost smell Whittaker in the room again: his filthy clothes, his animal stink.

"Catford," he repeated.

"Yeah. I'll keep looking if you want," said Shanker, disregarding the ashtray and flicking his ash onto the floor. " 'Ow much is it wurf to you, Bunsen?"

While they were still negotiating Shanker's fee, a discussion that proceeded with good humor but the underlying seriousness of two men who knew perfectly well that he would do nothing without payment, Robin brought in the coffee. With the light full on her face, she looked ghastly.

"I've done the most important emails," she told Strike, pretending not to notice his inquiring look. "I'll head off and do Platinum now."

Shanker looked thoroughly intrigued by this announcement, but nobody explained.

"You OK?" Strike asked her, wishing that Shanker were not present.

"Fine," said Robin, with a pathetic attempt at a smile. "I'll catch up with you later."

"''Ead off and do platinum'?" repeated Shanker curiously over the sound of the outer door closing.

"It's not as good as it sounds," said Strike, leaning back in his seat to look out of the window. Robin left the building in her trench coat and headed off up Denmark Street and out of sight. A large man in a beanie hat came out of the guitar shop opposite and set off in the same direction, but Strike's attention had already been recalled by Shanker, who said:

"Someone really sent you a fucking leg, Bunsen?"

"Yep," said Strike. "Cut it off, boxed it up and delivered it by hand."

"Fuck me backwards," said Shanker, whom it took a great deal to shock.

After Shanker had left in possession of a wad of cash for services already rendered, and the promise of the same again for further details on Whittaker, Strike phoned Robin. She did not pick up, but that wasn't unusual if she was somewhere she couldn't easily talk. He texted her:

Let me know when you're somewhere I can meet you

then sat down in her vacated chair, ready to do his fair share of answering inquiries and paying invoices.

However, he found it hard to focus after the second night on a sleeper. Five minutes later he checked his mobile but Robin had not responded, so he got up to make himself another mug of tea. As he raised the mug to his lips he caught a faint whiff of cannabis, transferred from hand to hand as he and Shanker said farewell.

Shanker came originally from Canning Town but had cousins in Whitechapel who, twenty years previously, had become involved in a feud with a rival gang. Shanker's willingness to help out his cousins had resulted in him lying alone in the gutter at the end of Fulbourne Street, bleeding copiously from the deep gash to his mouth and cheek that disfigured him to this day. It was there that Leda Strike, returning from a late-evening excursion to purchase Rizlas, had found him.

To walk past a boy of her own son's age while he lay bleeding in the gutter would have been impossible for Leda. The fact that the boy was clutching a bloody knife, that he was screaming imprecations and clearly in the grip of some kind of drug made no difference at all. Shanker found himself being mopped up and talked to as he had not been talked to since his own mother had died when he was eight. When he refused point blank to let the strange woman call an ambulance, for fear of what the police would do to him (Shanker had just stuck his knife through the thigh of his attacker), Leda took what, to her, was the only possible course: she helped him home to the squat and looked after him personally. After cutting up Band Aids and sticking them clumsily over the deep cut in a semblance of stitches, she cooked him a sloppy mess full of cigarette ash and told her bemused son to find a mattress where Shanker could sleep.

Leda treated Shanker from the first as though he were a long-lost nephew, and in return he had worshipped her in the way that only a broken boy clinging to the memory of a loving mother could. Once healed, he availed himself of her sincere invitation to drop round whenever he felt like it. Shanker talked to Leda as he could talk to no other human being and was perhaps the only person who could see no flaw in her. To Strike, he extended the respect he felt for his mother. The two boys, who in almost every other regard were as different as it was possible to be, were further bonded by a silent but powerful hatred of Whittaker, who had been insanely jealous of the new element in Leda's life but wary of treating him with the disdain he showed Strike.

Strike was sure that Whittaker had recognized in Shanker the same deficit from which he himself suffered: a lack of normal boundaries. Whittaker had concluded, rightly, that his teenage stepson might well wish him dead, but that he was restrained by a desire not to distress his mother, a respect for the law and a determination not to make an irrevocable move that would forever blight his own prospects. Shanker, however, knew no such restraints and his long periods of cohabitation with the fractured family kept a precarious curb on Whittaker's growing tendency towards violence.

In fact, it had been the regular presence of Shanker in the squat that had made Strike feel he could safely leave for university. He had not felt equal to putting into words what he most feared when he took leave of Shanker, but Shanker had understood.

"No worries, Bunsen, mate. No worries."

Nevertheless, he could not always be there. On the day that Leda had died, Shanker had been away on one of his regular, drug-related business trips. Strike would never forget Shanker's grief, his guilt, his uncontrollable tears when they next met. While Shanker had been negotiating a good price for a kilo of premium Bolivian cocaine in Kentish Town, Leda Strike had been slowly stiffening on a filthy mattress. The finding of the post-mortem was that she had ceased to breathe a full six hours before any of the other squat dwellers tried to rouse her from what they had thought was a profound slumber.

Like Strike, Shanker had been convinced from the first that Whittaker had killed her, and such was the violence of his grief and his desire for instant retribution that Whittaker might well have been glad he was taken into custody before Shanker could get his hands on him. Inadvisably allowed into the witness box to describe a maternal woman who had never touched heroin in her life, Shanker had screamed "That fucker done it!," attempted to clamber over the barrier towards Whittaker and been bundled unceremoniously out of court.

Consciously pushing away these memories of the long-buried past, which smelled no better for being dug up again, Strike took a swig of hot tea and checked his mobile again. There was still no word from Robin.

19

Workshop of the Telescopes

He had known the second he laid eyes on The Secretary that morning that she was out of kilter, off-balance. Look at her, sitting in the window of the Garrick, the large students' restaurant serving the LSE. She was plain today. Puffy, red-eyed, pale. He could probably take the seat next to her and the stupid bitch wouldn't notice. Concentrating on the tart with the silver hair, who was working on a laptop a few tables away, she had no attention to spare for men. Suited him. She'd be noticing him before long. He'd be her last sight on earth.

He didn't need to look like Pretty Boy today; he never approached them sexually if they were upset. That was when he became the friend in need, the avuncular stranger. *Not all men are like that, darling. You deserve better. Let me walk you home. Come on, I'll give you a lift.* You could do almost anything with them if you made them forget you had a dick.

He entered the crowded restaurant, skulking around the counter, buying a coffee and finding himself a corner where he could watch her from behind.

Her engagement ring was missing. That was interesting. It shone a new light on the holdall she had been alternately carrying over her shoulder and hiding under tables. Was she planning to sleep somewhere other than the flat in Ealing? Might she be heading down a deserted street for once, a shortcut with poor lighting, a lonely underpass?

The very first time he'd killed had been like that: a simple question of seizing the moment. He remembered it in snapshots, like a slide-show, because it had been thrilling and new. That was before he had honed it to an art, before he had started playing it like the game it was.

She'd been plump and dark. Her mate had just left, got into a punter's car and disappeared. The bloke in the car had not known that he was choosing which of them would survive the night.

He, meanwhile, had been driving up and down the street with his knife in his pocket. When he had been sure that she was alone, completely alone, he had drawn up and leaned across the passenger seat to talk to her through the window. His mouth had been dry as he asked for it. She had agreed a price and got in the car. They had driven down a nearby dead end where neither streetlights nor passersby would trouble them.

He got what he'd asked for, then, as she was straightening up, before he had even zipped up his flies, he had punched her, knocking her back into the car door, the back of her head banging off the window. Before she could make a sound he'd pulled out the knife.

The meaty thump of the blade in her flesh—the heat of her blood gushing over his hands—she did not even scream but gasped, moaned, sinking down in the seat as he pounded the blade into her again and again. He had torn the gold pendant from around her neck. He had not thought, then, about taking the ultimate trophy: a bit of her, but instead wiped his hands on her dress while she sat slumped beside him, twitching in her death throes. He had reversed out of the alleyway, trembling with fear and elation, and driven out of town with the body beside him, keeping carefully to the speed limit, looking in his rearview mirror every few seconds. There was a place he had checked out just a few days previously, a stretch of deserted countryside and an overgrown ditch. She had made a heavy, wet thump when he rolled her into it.

He had her pendant still, along with a few other souvenirs. They were his treasure. What, he wondered, would he take from The Secretary?

A Chinese boy near him was reading something on a tablet. *Behavioral Economics*. Dumb psychological crap. *He* had seen a psychologist once, been forced to.

"Tell me about your mother."

The little bald man had literally said it, the joke line, the cliché. They were supposed to be smart, psychologists. He'd played along for the fun of it, telling the idiot about his mother: that she was a cold, mean, screwed-up bitch. His birth had been an inconvenience, an embarrassment to her, and she wouldn't have cared if he'd lived or died.

"And your father?"

"I haven't got a father," he'd said.

"You mean you never see him?"

Silence.

"You don't know who he is?"

Silence.

"Or you simply don't like him?"

He said nothing. He was tired of playing along. People were brain dead if they fell for this kind of crap, but he had long since realized that other people *were* brain dead.

In any case, he'd told the truth: he had no father. The man who had filled that role, if you wanted to call it that—the one who had knocked him around day in, day out ("a hard man, but a fair man")—had not fathered him. Violence and rejection, that was what family meant to him. At the same time, home was where he had learned to survive, to box clever. He had always known that he was superior, even when he'd been cowering under the kitchen table as a child. Yes, even then he'd known that he was made of better stuff than the bastard coming at him with his big fist and his clenched face...

The Secretary stood up, imitating the tart with the silver hair, who was just leaving with her laptop in a case. He downed his coffee in one and followed.

She was so easy today, so easy! She'd lost all her wariness; she barely had attention to spare for the platinum whore. He boarded the same Tube train as the pair of them, keeping his back to The Secretary but watching her reflection from between the reaching arms of a bunch of Kiwi tourists. He found it easy to slip into the crowd behind her when she left the train.

The three of them moved in procession, the silver-haired tart, The Secretary and him, up the stairs, onto the pavement, along the road to Spearmint Rhino... he was already late home, but he could not resist this. She had not stayed out after dark before and the hold-all and the lack of engagement ring all added up to an irresistible opportunity. He would simply have to make up some story for It.

The silver-haired tart disappeared into the club. The Secretary slowed down and stood irresolute on the pavement. He slid out his mobile and pulled back into a shadowy doorway, watching her.

20

I never realized she was so undone.

Blue Öyster Cult, "Debbie Denise"
Lyrics by Patti Smith

Robin had forgotten her promise to Strike that she would not stay out after dark. In fact, she had hardly registered the fact that the sun had gone down until she realized that headlights were swooping past her and that the shop windows were lit up. Platinum had changed her routine today. She would usually have been inside Spearmint Rhino for several hours already, gyrating half naked for the benefit of strange men, not striding along the road, fully dressed in jeans, high-heeled boots and a fringed suede jacket. Presumably she had changed her shift, but she would soon be safely gyrating around a pole, which left the question of where Robin was going to spend the night.

Her mobile had been vibrating inside the pocket of her coat all day. Matthew had sent more than thirty texts.

We've got to talk.
Ring me, please.
Robin, we can't sort anything out if you don't talk to me.

As the day had worn on and her silence had not broken, he had started trying to call. Then the tone of his texts had changed.

Robin, you know I love you.

I wish it hadn't happened. I wish I could change it, but I can't. It's you I love, Robin. I always have and I always will.

She had not texted back, or picked up his calls, or rung him. All she knew was that she could not bear to go back to the flat, not tonight. What would happen tomorrow, or the next day, she had no idea. She was hungry, exhausted and numb.

Strike had become almost as importuning towards late afternoon.

Where are you? Ring me pls.

She had texted him back, because she could not face talking to him either.

Can't speak. Platinum's not at work.

She and Strike maintained a certain emotional distance, always, and she was afraid that if he were kind to her she would cry, revealing the sort of weakness that he would deplore in an assistant. With virtually no cases left, with the threat of the man who had sent the leg hanging over her, she must not give Strike another reason to tell her to stay at home.

He had not been satisfied with her response.

Call me asap.

She had ignored that one on the basis that she might easily have failed to receive it, being close to the Tube when he sent it and shortly afterwards having no reception as she and Platinum rode the Tube back to Tottenham Court Road. On emerging from the station Robin found another missed call from Strike on her phone, as well as a new text from Matthew.

I need to know whether you're coming home tonight. I'm worried sick about you. Just text to tell me you're alive, that's all I'm asking.

"Oh, don't flatter yourself," muttered Robin. "Like I'd kill myself over you."

A strangely familiar paunchy man in a suit walked past Robin, illuminated by the glow of Spearmint Rhino's canopy. It was Two-Times. Robin wondered whether she imagined the self-satisfied smirk he gave her.

Was he going inside to watch his girlfriend gyrate for other men? Did he get a thrill out of having his sex life documented? Precisely what kind of weirdo was he?

Robin turned away. She needed to make a decision as to what to do tonight. A large man in a beanie hat appeared to be arguing into his mobile phone in a dark doorway a hundred yards away.

The disappearance of Platinum had robbed Robin of purpose. Where was she going to sleep? As she stood there, irresolute, a group of young men walked past her, deliberately close, one of them brushing against her holdall. She could smell Lynx and lager.

"Got your costume in there, darling?"

She became aware of the fact that she was standing outside a lap-dancing club. As she turned automatically in the direction of Strike's office, her mobile rang. Without thinking, she answered it.

"Where the hell have you been?" said Strike's angry voice in her ear.

She barely had time to be glad that he wasn't Matthew before he said:

"I've been trying to get hold of you all day! Where *are* you?"

"On Tottenham Court Road," she said, walking fast away from the still-jeering men. "Platinum's only just gone inside and Two—"

"What did I tell you about not staying out after dark?"

"It's well-lit," said Robin.

She was trying to remember whether she had ever noticed a Travelodge near here. She needed somewhere clean and cheap. It must be cheap, because she was drawing on the joint account; she was determined not to spend more than she had put in.

"Are you all right?" asked Strike, slightly less aggressively.

A lump rose in her throat.

"Fine," she said, as forcefully as she could. She was trying to be professional, to be what Strike wanted.

"I'm still at the office," he said. "Did you say you're on Tottenham Court Road?"

"I've got to go, sorry," she said, in a tight, cold voice and hung up.

The fear of crying had become so overwhelming that she had to end the call. She thought he had been on the verge of offering to meet her, and if they met she would tell him everything, and she must not do that.

Tears were suddenly pouring down her face. She had no one else. There! She had admitted it to herself at last. The people they had meals with at weekends, the ones they went to watch rugby with: they were all Matthew's friends, Matthew's work colleagues, Matthew's old university friends. She had nobody of her own but Strike.

"Oh God," she said, wiping her eyes and nose on the sleeve of her coat.

"You all right, sweetheart?" called a toothless tramp from a doorway.

She was not sure why she ended up in the Tottenham, except that the bar staff knew her, she was familiar with where the Ladies was, and it was somewhere that Matthew had never been. All she wanted was a quiet corner in which she could look up cheap places to stay. She was also craving a drink, which was most unlike her. After splashing her face with cold water in the bathroom she bought herself a glass of red wine, took it to a table and pulled out her phone again. She had missed another call from Strike.

Men at the bar were looking over at her. She knew what she must look like, tear-stained and alone, her holdall beside her. Well, she couldn't help that. She typed into her mobile: **Travelodges near Tottenham Court Road,** and waited for the slow response, drinking her wine faster than perhaps she ought to have done on a virtually empty stomach. No breakfast, no lunch: a bag of crisps and an apple consumed at the student café where Platinum had been studying were all she had eaten that day.

There was a Travelodge in High Holborn. That would have to do.

She felt slightly calmer for knowing where she was going to spend the night. Careful not to make eye contact with any of the men at the bar, she went up to get a second glass of wine. Perhaps she ought to call her mother, she thought suddenly, but the prospect made her feel tearful all over again. She could not face Linda's love and disappointment, not yet.

A large figure in a beanie hat entered the pub, but Robin was keeping her attention determinedly on her change and her wine, giving none of the hopeful men lurking at the bar the slightest reason to suppose that she wanted any of them to join her.

The second glass of wine made her feel much more relaxed. She remembered how Strike had got so drunk here, in this very pub, that he could barely walk. That had been the only night that he had ever shared personal information. Maybe that was the real reason she had been drawn here, she thought, raising her eyes to the colorful glass cupola overhead. This was the bar where you went to drink when you found out that the person you loved was unfaithful.

"You alone?" said a man's voice.

"Waiting for someone," she said.

He was slightly blurred when she looked up at him, a wiry blond man with bleached blue eyes, and she could tell that he did not believe her.

"Can I wait with you?"

"No, you fucking can't," said another, familiar voice.

Strike had arrived, massive, scowling, glaring at the stranger, who retreated with ill grace to a couple of friends at the bar.

"What are you doing here?" asked Robin, surprised to find that her tongue felt numb and thick after two glasses of wine.

"Looking for you," said Strike.

"How did you know I was—?"

"I'm a detective. How many of those have you had?" he asked, looking down at her wineglass.

"Only one," she lied, so he went to the bar for another, and a pint of Doom Bar for himself. As he ordered, a large man in a beanie hat ducked out of the door, but Strike was more interested in keeping an eye on the blond man who was still staring over at Robin and only seemed to give up on her once Strike reappeared, glowering, with two drinks and sat down opposite her.

"What's going on?"

"Nothing."

"Don't give me that. You look like bloody death."

"Well," said Robin, taking a large slurp of wine, "consider my morale boosted."

Strike gave a short laugh.

"Why have you got a holdall with you?" When she did not answer, he said, "Where's your engagement ring?"

She opened her mouth to answer but a treacherous desire to cry rose to drown the words. After a short inner struggle and another gulp of wine she said:

"I'm not engaged anymore."

"Why not?"

"This is rich, coming from you."

I'm drunk, she thought, as though watching herself from outside her own body. *Look at me. I'm drunk on two and a half glasses of wine, no food and no sleep.*

"What's rich?" asked Strike, confused.

"We don't talk about personal...you don't talk about personal stuff."

"I seem to remember spilling my guts all over you in this very pub."

"Once," said Robin.

Strike deduced from her pink cheeks and her thickened speech that she was not on her second glass of wine. Both amused and concerned, he said:

"I think you need something to eat."

"That's 'zacktly what I said to you," Robin replied, "that night when you were...and we ended up having a kebab—and I do not," she said with dignity, "want a kebab."

"Well," said Strike, "y'know, it's London. We can probably find you something that isn't a kebab."

"I like crisps," said Robin, so he bought her some.

"What's going on?" he repeated on his return. After a few seconds of watching her attempting to open the crisps he took them from her to do it himself.

"Nothing. I'm going to sleep in a Travelodge tonight, that's all."

"A Travelodge."

"Yeah. There's one in...there's one..."

She looked down at her dead mobile and realized that she had forgotten to charge it the previous night.

"I can't remember where it is," she said. "Just leave me, I'm fine," she added, groping in her holdall for something to blow her nose on.

"Yeah," he said heavily, "I'm totally reassured now I've seen you."

"I *am* fine," she said fiercely. "I'll be at work as usual tomorrow, you wait and see."

"You think I came to find you because I'm worried about work?"

"Don't be nice!" she groaned, burying her face in her tissues. "I can't take it! Be normal!"

"What's normal?" he asked, confused.

"G-grumpy and uncommunic—uncommunica—"

"What do you want to communicate about?"

"Nothing in particular," she lied. "I just thought...keep things profess'nal."

"What's happened between you and Matthew?"

"What's happening b'tween you and Elin?" she countered.

"How's that important?" he asked, nonplussed.

"Same thing," she said vaguely, draining her third glass. "I'd like 'nother—"

"You're having a soft drink this time."

She examined the ceiling while waiting for him. There were theatrical scenes painted up there: Bottom cavorted with Titania amid a group of fairies.

"Things are going OK with Elin," he told her when he sat back down, having decided that an exchange of information was the easiest way to make her talk about her own problems. "It suits me, keeping it low key. She's got a daughter she doesn't want me getting too close to. Messy divorce."

"Oh," said Robin, blinking at him over her glass of Coke. "How did you meet her?"

"Through Nick and Ilsa."

"How do they know her?"

"They don't. They had a party and she came along with her brother. He's a doctor, works with Nick. They hadn't ever met her before."

"Oh," said Robin again.

She had briefly forgotten her own troubles, diverted by this glimpse into Strike's private world. So normal, so unremarkable! A party and he had gone along and got talking to the beautiful blonde. Women liked Strike—she had come to realize that over the months they had worked together. She had not understood the appeal when she had started working for him. He was so very different from Matthew.

"Does Ilsa like Elin?" asked Robin.

Strike was startled by this flash of perception.

"Er—yeah, I think so," he lied.

Robin sipped her Coke.

"OK," said Strike, restraining his impatience with difficulty, "your turn."

"We've split up," she said.

Interrogation technique told him to remain silent, and after a minute or so the decision was vindicated.

"He . . . told me something," she said. "Last night."

Strike waited.

"And we can't go back from that. Not that."

She was pale and composed but he could almost feel the anguish behind the words. Still he waited.

"He slept with someone else," she said in a small, tight voice.

There was a pause. She picked up her crisp packet, found that she had finished the contents and dropped it on the table.

"Shit," said Strike.

He was surprised: not that Matthew had slept with another woman, but that he had admitted it. His impression of the handsome young accountant was of a man who knew how to run his life to suit himself, to compartmentalize and categorize where necessary.

"And not just once," said Robin, in that same tight voice. "He was doing it for months. With someone we both know. Sarah Shadlock. She's an old friend of his from university."

"Christ," said Strike. "I'm sorry."

He *was* sorry, genuinely sorry, for the pain she was in. Yet the revelation had caused certain other feelings—feelings he usually kept under tight rein, considering them both misguided and dangerous—to flex inside him, to test their strength against their restraining bonds.

Don't be a stupid fucker, he told himself. *That's one thing that can never happen. It'd screw everything up royally.*

"What made him tell you?" Strike asked.

She did not answer, but the question brought back the scene in awful clarity.

Their magnolia sitting room was far too tiny to accommodate a couple in such a state of fury. They had driven all the way home from Yorkshire in the Land Rover that Matthew had not wanted. Somewhere along the way, an incensed Matthew had asserted that it was a matter of time before Strike made a pass at Robin and what was more, he suspected that she would welcome the advance.

"He's my friend, that's all!" she had bellowed at Matthew from beside their cheap sofa, their weekend bags still in the hall. "For you to suggest I'm *turned on* by the fact he's had his leg—"

"You're so bloody naive!" he had bellowed. "He's your friend until he tries to get you into bed, Robin—"

"Who are you judging him by? Are you biding your time before you jump on your coworkers?"

"Of course I'm bloody not, but you're so frigging starry-eyed about him—he's a man, it's just the two of you in the office—"

"He's my *friend,* like you're *friends* with Sarah Shadlock but you've never—"

She had seen it in his face. An expression she had never noticed before passed across it like a shadow. Guilt seemed to slide physically over the high cheekbones, the clean jaw, the hazel eyes she had adored for years.

"—have you?" she said, her tone suddenly wondering. "*Have* you?"

He hesitated too long.

"No," he had said forcefully, like a paused film jerking back into action. "Of course n—"

"You have," she said. "You've slept with her."

She could see it in his face. He did not believe in male-female friendships because he had never had one. He and Sarah had been sleeping together.

"When?" she had asked. "Not... was it *then?*"

"I didn't—"

She heard the feeble protestation of a man who knows he has lost, who had even wanted to lose. That had haunted her all night and all day: on some level, he had wanted Robin to know.

Her strange calm, more stunned than accusatory, had led him on to tell her everything. Yes, it had been *then*. He felt terrible about it, he always had—but he and Robin hadn't been sleeping together at the time and, one night, Sarah had been comforting him, and, well, things had got out of hand—

"She was *comforting* you?" Robin had repeated. Rage had come then, at last, unfreezing her from her state of stunned disbelief. "She was comforting *you?*"

"It was a difficult time for me too, you know!" he had shouted.

Strike watched as Robin shook her head unconsciously, trying to clear it, but the recollections had turned her pink and her eyes were sparkling again.

"What did you say?" she asked Strike, confused.

"I asked what made him tell you."

"I don't know. We were in the middle of a row. He thinks..." She took a deep breath. Two-thirds of a bottle of wine on an empty stomach was leading her to emulate Matthew's honesty. "He doesn't believe you and I are just friends."

This was no surprise to Strike. He had read suspicion in every look Matthew had ever given him, heard insecurity in every chippy comment thrown his way.

"So," Robin went on unsteadily, "I pointed out that we *are* just friends, and that he's got a platonic friend himself, dear old Sarah Shadlock. So then it all came out. He and Sarah had an affair at university while I was... while I was at home."

"That long ago?" Strike said.

"You think I shouldn't mind if it was seven years ago?" she demanded. "If he's lied about it ever since and we constantly see her?"

"I was just surprised," said Strike evenly, refusing to be drawn into a fight, "that he's owned up to it after all this time."

"Oh," said Robin. "Well, he was ashamed. Because of when it happened."

"At university?" said Strike, confused.

"It was right after I dropped out," said Robin.

"Ah," said Strike.

They had never discussed what had made her leave her psychology degree and return to Masham.

Robin had not intended to tell Strike the story, but all resolutions were adrift tonight on the little sea of alcohol with which she had filled her hungry and exhausted body. What did it matter if she told him? Without that information he would not have the full picture or be able to advise her what to do next. She was relying on him, she realized dimly, to help her. Whether she liked it or not—whether *he* liked it or not—Strike was her best friend in London. She had never looked that fact squarely in the face before. Alcohol buoyed you up and it washed your eyes clean. *In vino veritas,* they said, didn't they? Strike would know. He had an odd, occasional habit of quoting Latin.

"I didn't *want* to leave uni," said Robin slowly, her head swimming, "but something happened and afterwards I had problems..."

That was no good. That didn't explain it.

"I was coming home from a friend's, in another hall of residence," she said. "It wasn't that late... only eight o'clock or something... but there had been a warning out about him—on the local news—"

That was no good either. Far too much detail. What she needed was a bald statement of fact, not to talk him through every little bit of it, the way she'd had to in court.

She took a deep breath, looked into Strike's face and read dawning comprehension there. Relieved not to have to spell it out, she asked:

"Please could I have some more crisps?"

When he returned from the bar he handed them to her in silence. She did not like the look on his face.

"Don't go thinking—it doesn't make any difference!" she said desperately. "It was twenty minutes of my life. It was something that happened to me. It isn't me. It doesn't *define* me."

Strike guessed that they were phrases she had been led to embrace in some kind of therapy. He had interviewed rape victims. He knew the forms of words they were given to make sense of what, to a woman, was incomprehensible. A lot of things about Robin were explained now. The long allegiance to Matthew, for instance: the safe boy from home.

However, the drunken Robin read in Strike's silence the thing she had most feared: a shift in the way he saw her, from equal to victim.

"It doesn't make any difference!" she repeated furiously. "I'm still the same!"

"I know that," he said, "but it's still one fucking horrible thing to have happened to you."

"Well, yes... it was..." she muttered, mollified. Then, firing up again: "My evidence got him. I noticed things about him while... He had this patch of white skin under his ear—they call it vitiligo—and one of his pupils was fixed, dilated."

She was gabbling slightly now, wolfing down her third packet of crisps.

"He tried to strangle me; I went limp and played dead and he ran for it. He'd attacked two other girls wearing the mask and neither of them could tell the police anything about him. My evidence got him put away."

"That doesn't surprise me," said Strike.

She found this response satisfactory. They sat in silence for a minute while she finished the crisps.

"Only, afterwards, I couldn't leave my room," she said, as though there had been no pause. "In the end, the university sent me home. I was only supposed to take a term off, but I—I never went back."

Robin contemplated this fact, staring into space. Matthew had urged her to stay at home. When her agoraphobia had resolved, which had taken more than a year, she had begun visiting him at his university in Bath, wandering hand in hand among dwellings of soft Cotswold stone, down sweeping Regency crescents, along the tree-lined banks of the River Avon. Every time they had gone out with his friends Sarah Shadlock had been there, braying at Matthew's jokes, touching his arm, leading the conversation constantly to the good times they all enjoyed when Robin, the tedious girlfriend from home, was not present...

She was comforting me. It was a difficult time for me too, you know!

"Right," said Strike, "we've got to get you a place to spend tonight."

"I'm going to the Travel—"

"No, you're not."

He did not want her staying in a place where anonymous people might wander the corridors unchallenged, or could walk in off the street. Perhaps he was being paranoid, but he wanted her somewhere that a scream would not be lost in the raucous cries of hen parties.

"I could sleep in the office," said Robin, swaying as she tried to stand; he grabbed her by the arm. "If you've still got that camp—"

"You're not sleeping in the office," he said. "I know a good place. My aunt and uncle stayed there when they came up to see *The Mousetrap.* C'mon, give me the holdall."

He had once before put his arm around Robin's shoulders but that had been quite different: he had been using her as a walking stick. This time it was she who could barely move in a straight line. He found her waist and held her steady as they left the pub.

"Matthew," she said, as they moved off, "would *not* like this."

Strike said nothing. In spite of everything he had heard, he was not as sure as Robin was that the relationship was over. They had been together nine years and there was a wedding dress ready and waiting in Masham. He had been careful to offer no criticism of Matthew that might be repeated to her ex-fiancé in the renewal of hostilities that was surely coming, because the accumulated ties of nine years could not be severed in a single night. His reticence was for Robin's sake rather than his own. He had no fear of Matthew.

"Who *was* that man?" asked Robin sleepily, after they had walked a hundred yards in silence.

"Which man?"

"That man this morning...I thought he might be the leg man... he scared the hell out of me."

"Ah...that's Shanker. He's an old friend."

"He's terrifying."

"Shanker wouldn't hurt you," Strike assured her. Then, as an afterthought: "But don't ever leave him alone in the office."

"Why not?"

"He'll nick anything that's not nailed down. He does nothing for nothing."

"Where did you meet him?"

The story of Shanker and Leda took them all the way to Frith Street, where quiet town houses looked down upon them, exuding dignity and order.

"Here?" said Robin, gazing open-mouthed up at Hazlitt's Hotel. "I can't stay here—this'll be expensive!"

"I'm paying," said Strike. "Think of it as this year's bonus. No arguments," he added, as the door opened and a smiling young man stood back to let them in. "It's my fault you need somewhere safe."

The wood-paneled hall was cozy, with the feeling of a private house. There was only one way in and nobody could open the front door from outside.

When he had given the young man his credit card Strike saw the unsteady Robin to the foot of the stairs.

"You can take tomorrow morning off if you—"

"I'll be there at nine," she said. "Cormoran, thanks for—for—"

"Not a problem. Sleep well."

Frith Street was quiet as he closed the Hazlitt's door behind him. Strike set off, his hands deep in his pockets, lost in thought.

She had been raped and left for dead. *Holy shit.*

Eight days previously some bastard had handed her a woman's severed leg and she had not breathed a word of her past, not asked for special dispensation to take time off, nor deviated in any respect from the total professionalism she brought to work every morning. It was he, without even knowing her history, who had insisted on the best rape alarm, on nothing after dark, on checking in with her regularly through the working day...

At the precise moment Strike became aware that he was walking away from Denmark Street rather than towards it, he spotted a man in a beanie hat twenty yards away, skulking on the corner of Soho

Square. The amber tip of the cigarette swiftly vanished as the man turned and began to walk hurriedly away.

"'Scuse me, mate!"

Strike's voice echoed through the quiet square as he sped up. The man in the hat did not look back, but broke into a run.

"Oi! Mate!"

Strike, too, began to run, his knee protesting with every jolting step. His quarry looked back once then took a sharp left, Strike moving as fast as he could in pursuit. Entering Carlisle Street, Strike squinted ahead at the crowd clustered around the entrance of the Toucan, wondering whether his man had joined it. Panting, he ran on past the pub drinkers, drawing up at the junction with Dean Street and revolving on the spot, looking for his quarry. He had a choice of taking a left, a right or continuing along Carlisle Street, and each offered a multitude of doorways and basement spaces in which the man in the beanie hat could have hidden, assuming he had not hailed a passing cab.

"Bollocks," Strike muttered. His stump was sore against the end of his prosthesis. All he had was an impression of ample height and breadth, a dark coat and hat and the suspicious fact that he had run when called, run before Strike could ask him for the time, or a light, or directions.

He took a guess and headed right, up Dean Street. The traffic swooshed past him in either direction. For nearly an hour Strike continued to prowl the area, probing into dark doorways and basement cavities. He knew this was almost certainly a fool's errand, but if—if—they had been followed by the man who had sent the leg, he was clearly a reckless bastard who might not have been scared away from Robin's vicinity by Strike's ungainly pursuit.

Men in sleeping bags glared at him as he moved far closer than members of the public usually dared; twice he startled cats out from behind dustbins, but the man in the beanie hat was nowhere to be seen.

21

...the damn call came,
And I knew what I knew and didn't want to know.

Blue Öyster Cult, "Live for Me"

Robin woke next day to a sore head and a weight in the pit of her stomach. In the time it took to roll over on unfamiliar, crisp white pillows, the events of the previous evening seemed to come crashing down on her. Shaking her hair out of her face she sat up and looked around. Between the carved posts of her wooden four-poster she made out the dim outlines of a room barely illuminated by the line of brilliant light between brocade curtains. As her eyes became accustomed to the gilded gloom she made out the portrait of a fat gentleman with mutton-chop whiskers, framed in gilt. This was the kind of hotel in which you took an expensive city break, not where you slept off a hangover with a few hastily snatched clothes in a holdall.

Had Strike deposited her here in elegant, old-fashioned luxury as preemptive compensation for the serious talk he would initiate today? *You're obviously in a very emotional place... I think it would be good if you took a break from work.*

Two-thirds of a bottle of bad wine and she had told him everything. With a weak groan, Robin sank back on the pillows, covered her face with her arms and succumbed to the memories that had regained all their power now that she was weak and miserable.

The rapist had worn a rubber gorilla mask. He had held her down with one hand and the weight of a whole arm on her throat, telling her she was about to die as he raped her, telling her he was going to choke the fucking life out of her. Her brain a scarlet cavity of screaming panic, his hands tightening like a noose around her neck, her survival had hung on her ability to pretend that she was already dead.

Later there had been days and weeks when she had felt as though she had in fact died, and was trapped in the body from which she felt entirely disconnected. The only way to protect herself, it had seemed, was to separate herself from her own flesh, to deny their connection. It had been a long time before she had felt able to take possession again.

He had been soft-spoken in court, meek, "yes, your honor," "no, your honor," a nondescript middle-aged white man, florid in complexion except for that white patch under his ear. His pale, washed-out eyes blinked too often, eyes that had been slits viewed through the holes in his mask.

What he had done to her shattered her view of her place in the world, ended her university career and drove her back to Masham. It forced her through a grueling court case in which the cross-examination had been almost as traumatic as the original attack, for his defense was that she had invited him into the stairwell for sex. Months after his gloved hands had reached out of the shadows and dragged her, gagging, into the cavity behind the stairs, she had not been able to stand physical contact, not even a gentle hug from a family member. He had polluted her first and only sexual relationship, so that she and Matthew had had to start again, with fear and guilt attending them every step of the way.

Robin pressed her arms down over her eyes as though she might obliterate it all from her mind by force. Now, of course, she knew that the young Matthew, whom she had considered a selfless paragon of kindness and understanding, had in fact been cavorting with a naked Sarah in his student house in Bath while Robin lay on her lonely bed in Masham for hours at a stretch, staring blankly at Destiny's Child. Alone in the sumptuous quiet of Hazlitt's, Robin contemplated for the first time the question of whether Matthew would have left her for Sarah, had she been happy and unharmed, or even whether she and Matthew might have grown naturally apart if she had completed her degree.

She lowered her arms and opened her eyes. They were dry today; she felt as though she had no tears left to weep. The pain of Matthew's confession no longer pierced her. She felt it as a dull ache underlying the more urgent panic about the damage she feared she might have done to her work prospects. How could she have been so stupid as to tell Strike what had happened to her? Hadn't she already learned what happened when she was honest?

A year after the rape, when the agoraphobia had been overcome, when her weight was nearly back to normal, when she was itching to get back out into the world and make up the time she had lost, she had expressed a vague interest in "something related" to criminal investigative work. Without her degree and with her confidence so recently shredded, she had not dared voice aloud her true desire to be some kind of investigator. A good thing too, because every single person she knew had tried to dissuade her even from her tentatively expressed desire to explore the outer reaches of police work, even her mother, usually the most understanding of creatures. They had all taken what they thought a strange new interest as a sign of continuing sickness, a symptom of her inability to throw off what had happened to her.

It was not true: the desire had long predated the rape. At the age of eight she had informed her brothers that she was going to catch robbers and had been roundly mocked, for no better reason than that she ought to be laughed at, given that she was a girl and their sister. Though Robin hoped that their response was not a true reflection of their estimate of her abilities, but based on a kind of collegiate male reflex, it had left her diffident about expressing her interest in detective work to three loud, opinionated brothers. She had never told anyone that she had chosen to study psychology with a secret eye towards investigative profiling.

Her pursuit of that goal had been utterly thwarted by the rapist. That was another thing he had taken from her. Asserting her ambition while recuperating from a state of intense fragility, at a time when everyone around her appeared to be waiting for her to fall apart again, had proved too difficult. Out of exhaustion and a feeling of obligation to the family that had been so protective and loving in her time of greatest need she had let a lifelong ambition fall by the wayside, and everyone else had been satisfied to see it go.

Then a temping agency had sent her by mistake to a private detective. She should have been there a week, but she had never left. It had felt like a miracle. Somehow, by luck, then through talent and tenacity, she had made herself valuable to the struggling Strike and ended up almost exactly where she had fantasized being before a total stranger had used her for his perverse enjoyment like a disposable, inanimate object, then beaten and throttled her.

Why, *why,* had she told Strike what had happened to her? He had been worried about her before she revealed her history: now what? He would decide she was too fragile to work, Robin was sure of it, and from there it would be a swift, short step to the sidelines, because she was unable to take on all the responsibilities he needed a workmate to shoulder.

The calm Georgian room's silence and solidity was oppressive.

Robin struggled out from under the heavy covers and crossed the sloping wooden floorboards to a bathroom with a claw-footed bath and no shower. Fifteen minutes later, as she was dressing, her mobile, which she had mercifully remembered to charge the previous night, rang on the dressing table.

"Hi," said Strike. "How are you?"

"Fine," she said, her voice brittle.

He had called to tell her not to come in, she knew it.

"Wardle's just phoned. They've found the rest of the body."

Robin sat down hard on the needlepoint stool, both hands clutching the mobile to her ear.

"What? Where? Who is she?"

"Tell you when I pick you up. They want to talk to us. I'll be outside at nine. Make sure you eat something," he added.

"Cormoran!" she said, to stop him hanging up.

"What?"

"I'm still...I've still got a job, then?"

There was a slight pause.

"What're you talking about? Of course you've still got a job."

"You don't... I'm still... nothing's changed?" she said.

"Are you going to do as you're told?" he asked. "When I say nothing after dark, you're going to listen from now on?"

"Yes," she said, a little shakily.

"Good. I'll see you at nine."

Robin breathed a deep, shuddering sigh of relief. She was not finished: he still wanted her. As she went to replace the mobile on the dressing table she noticed that the longest text message that she had ever received had arrived overnight.

> Robin, I can't sleep for thinking about you. You don't know how much I wish it hadn't happened. It was a shitty thing to do and there's no defense. I was 21 and I didn't know then what I know now: that there's nobody like you and that I could never love anyone else as much as I love you. There's never been anyone apart from you since then. I've been jealous of you and Strike and you might say I don't have the right to feel jealous because of what I did but maybe on some level I think you deserve better than me and that's what's been getting to me. I only know I love you and I want to marry you and if that's not what you want now then I'll have to accept that but please Robin just text me and let me know you're OK, please. Matt xxxxxxx

Robin put the mobile back on the dressing table and continued dressing. She ordered a croissant and coffee from room service and was surprised how much better food and drink made her feel when they arrived. Only then did she read Matthew's text again.

> ... maybe on some level I think you deserve better than me and that's what's been getting to me...

This was touching, and most unlike Matthew, who frequently expressed the view that citing subconscious motivation was no more than chicanery. Hard on the heels of that thought, though, came the reflection that Matthew had never cut Sarah out of his life. She was one of his best friends from university: embracing him tenderly at his mother's funeral, dining out with them as part of a cozy foursome, still flirting with Matthew, still stirring between him and Robin.

After a brief inner deliberation, Robin texted back:

I'm fine.

She was waiting for Strike on the doorstep of Hazlitt's, neat as ever, when the black cab drew up at five to nine.

Strike had not shaved, and as his beard grew with vigor his jaw looked grimy.

"Have you seen the news?" he asked as soon as she had got into the cab.

"No."

"Media have just got it. Saw it on the telly as I left."

He leaned forward to slide shut the plastic divider between themselves and the driver.

"Who is she?" asked Robin.

"They haven't formally ID'd her yet, but they think she's a twenty-four-year-old Ukrainian woman."

"Ukrainian?" said Robin, startled.

"Yeah." He hesitated, then said, "Her landlady found her dismembered in a fridge-freezer in what looks like her own flat. The right leg's missing. It's definitely her."

The taste of Robin's toothpaste in her mouth turned chemical; croissant and coffee churned in her stomach.

"Where's the flat?"

"Coningham Road, Shepherd's Bush. Ring any bells?"

"No, I—oh God. *Oh God.* The girl who wanted to cut off her leg?"

"Apparently."

"But she didn't have a Ukrainian name, did she?"

"Wardle thinks she might've been using a fake one. You know—hooker name."

The taxi bore them down Pall Mall towards New Scotland Yard. White neoclassical buildings slid past the windows on both sides: august, haughty and impervious to the shocks of frail humanity.

"It's what Wardle expected," said Strike after a long pause. "His theory was that the leg belonged to a Ukrainian prostitute last seen with Digger Malley."

Robin could tell that there was more. She looked at him anxiously.

"There were letters from me in her flat," said Strike. "Two letters, signed with my name."

"But you didn't write back!"

"Wardle knows they're fake. Apparently they've spelled my name wrong—Cameron—but he's still got to get me in."

"What do the letters say?"

"He wouldn't tell me over the phone. He's being pretty decent," said Strike. "Not being a dick about it."

Buckingham Palace rose up ahead of them. The gigantic marble statue of Queen Victoria frowned down on Robin's confusion and her hangover, then slid out of view.

"They're probably going to ask us to look at pictures of the body to see whether we can ID her."

"OK," said Robin, more stoutly than she felt.

"How are you?" Strike asked.

"I'm fine," she said. "Don't worry about me."

"I was going to call Wardle this morning anyway."

"Why?"

"Last night, walking away from Hazlitt's, I saw a big guy in a black beanie hat lurking down a side street. There was something about his body language I didn't like. I called out to him—I was going to ask him for a light—and he scarpered. *Don't,*" said Strike, though Robin had not made a sound, "tell me I'm jumpy or imagining things. I think he followed us, and I'll tell you something else—I think he was in the pub when I arrived. I didn't see his face, just the back of his head as he left."

To his surprise, Robin did not dismiss him. Instead she frowned in concentration, trying to recall a vague impression.

"You know...I saw a big bloke in a beanie hat somewhere yesterday, too...yeah, he was in a doorway on Tottenham Court Road. His face was in shadow, though."

Strike muttered another oath under his breath.

"Please don't tell me to stop working," said Robin in a more high-pitched voice than usual. "*Please.* I love this job."

"And if the fucker's stalking you?"

She could not repress a frisson of fear, but determination overrode it. To help catch this animal, whoever he was, would be worth almost anything...

"I'll be vigilant. I've got two rape alarms."

Strike did not look reassured.

They disembarked at New Scotland Yard and were shown upstairs at once, into an open-plan office where Wardle stood in his shirtsleeves, talking to a group of subordinates. When he saw Strike and Robin he left his colleagues at once and led the detective and his partner into a small meeting room.

"Vanessa!" he called through the door as Strike and Robin took seats at an oval table, "have you got the letters?"

Detective Sergeant Ekwensi appeared shortly afterwards with two typewritten sheets protected in plastic slips and a copy of what Strike recognized as one of the handwritten letters that he had given Wardle in the Old Blue Last. Detective Sergeant Ekwensi, who greeted Robin with a smile that the latter again found disproportionately reassuring, sat down beside Wardle with a notebook.

"You want coffee or anything?" Wardle asked. Strike and Robin shook their heads. Wardle slid the letters across the table to Strike. He read both before pushing them sideways to Robin.

"I didn't write either of them," Strike told Wardle.

"I didn't think so," said Wardle. "You didn't answer on Strike's behalf, Miss Ellacott?"

Robin shook her head.

The first letter admitted that Strike had indeed arranged the removal of his own leg because he wished to be rid of it, confessing that the story of an Afghan IED was an elaborate cover-up, and that he did not know how Kelsey had found this out, but implored her not to tell anybody else. The fake Strike then agreed to help her with her own "encumbrance" and asked where and when they could meet face to face.

The second letter was brief, confirming that Strike would come and visit her on the third of April at 7 p.m.

Both of the letters were signed *Cameron Strike* in thick black ink.

"That," said Strike, who had pulled the second letter back towards him after Robin had finished reading it, "reads as though she wrote back to me suggesting a time and place."

"That was going to be my next question," said Wardle. "Did you get a second letter?"

Strike looked towards Robin, who shook her head.

"OK," said Wardle, "for the record: when did the original letter from—" He checked the photocopy. "Kelsey, she's signed herself—come in?"

Robin answered.

"I've got the envelope back in the nut—" The ghost of a smile passed over Strike's face. "—in the drawer where we keep unsolicited letters. We can check the postcode, but as far as I can remember it was early this year. Maybe February."

"OK, excellent," said Wardle, "we'll be sending someone over to retrieve that envelope." He smiled at Robin, who was looking anxious. "Calm down: I believe you. Some total nutter's trying to frame Strike. None of it hangs together. Why would he stab a woman, dismember her and then mail her leg to his own office? Why would he leave letters from himself in the flat?"

Robin tried to smile back.

"She was stabbed?" interposed Strike.

"They're working on what actually killed her," said Wardle, "but there are two deep wounds to the torso they're pretty sure would have done it before he started cutting her up."

Beneath the table top, Robin made fists, her nails digging deep into her palms.

"Now," said Wardle, and Detective Sergeant Ekwensi clicked out the nib of her pen and prepared to write, "does the name Oxana Voloshina mean anything to either of you?"

"No," said Strike and Robin shook her head.

"It looks like that was the victim's real name," Wardle explained. "That's how she signed her tenancy agreement and the landlady says she provided ID. She was claiming to be a student."

"Claiming?" said Robin.

"We're looking into who she really was," said Wardle.

Of course, thought Robin, *he's expecting her to be a prostitute.*

"Her English was good, judging by her letter," commented Strike. "That's if she genuinely wrote it."

Robin looked at him, confused.

"If someone's faking letters from me, why couldn't they have faked the letter from her?" Strike asked her.

"To try and get you to genuinely communicate with her, you mean?"

"Yeah—lure me to a rendezvous or lay some kind of paper trail between us that would look incriminating once she was dead."

"Van, go see if the photos of the body are viewable," said Wardle.

Detective Sergeant Ekwensi left the room. Her posture was that of a model. Robin's insides began to crawl with panic. As though Wardle had sensed it, he turned to her and said:

"I don't think you'll need to look at them if Strike—"

"She should look," said Strike.

Wardle looked taken aback and Robin, though she tried not to show it, found herself wondering whether Strike was trying to scare her into compliance with his nothing-after-dark rule.

"Yes," she said, with a decent show of calm. "I think I should."

"They're—not nice," said Wardle, with uncharacteristic understatement.

"The leg was sent to Robin," Strike reminded him. "There's as much chance that she's seen this woman previously as I have. She's my partner. We work the same jobs."

Robin glanced sideways at Strike. He had never before described her as his partner to somebody else, or not within Robin's hearing. He was not looking at her. Robin switched her attention back to Wardle. Apprehensive though she was, after hearing Strike put her on equal professional footing with himself she knew that, whatever she was about to see, she would not let herself, or him, down. When

Detective Sergeant Ekwensi returned holding a sheaf of photographs in her hand Robin swallowed hard and straightened her back.

Strike took them first and his reaction was not reassuring.

"Holy fucking shit."

"The head's best preserved," said Wardle quietly, "because he put it in the freezer."

Just as she would have withdrawn her hand instinctively from something red hot, Robin now had to fight a powerful urge to turn away, to close her eyes, to flip the photograph over. Instead she took it from Strike and looked down; her intestines became liquid.

The severed head sat on what remained of its neck, staring blindly into the camera, its eyes so frosted their color was invisible. The mouth gaped darkly. Her brown hair was stiff, flecked with ice. The cheeks were full and chubby, the chin and forehead covered in acne. She looked younger than twenty-four.

"Do you recognize her?"

Wardle's voice sounded startlingly close to Robin. She had felt as though she had traveled a long distance as she stared at the severed head.

"No," said Robin.

She put the picture down and took the next from Strike. A left leg and two arms had been rammed into the fridge, where they had begun to decompose. Having steeled herself for the head she had not thought anything else could be as bad and she was ashamed of the small bleat of distress that escaped her.

"Yeah, it's bad," said Detective Sergeant Ekwensi quietly. Robin met her eyes with gratitude.

"There's a tattoo on the wrist of the left arm," Wardle pointed out, handing them a third picture in which the relevant arm lay outstretched on a table. Now feeling definitely nauseated, Robin looked and made out "1D" in black ink.

"You don't need to see the torso," said Wardle, shuffling the photographs and handing them back to Detective Sergeant Ekwensi.

"Where was it?" asked Strike.

"In the bath," said Wardle. "That's where he killed her, the bathroom. It looked like an abattoir in there." He hesitated. "The leg wasn't the only thing he cut off her."

Robin was glad that Strike did not ask what else had gone. She did not think she could stand to hear.

"Who found her?" asked Strike.

"The landlady," said Wardle. "She's elderly and she collapsed right after we got there. Looks like a heart attack. They took her to Hammersmith Hospital."

"What made her go round?"

"Smell," said Wardle. "Downstairs had rung her. She decided to pop in early before doing her shopping, try and catch this Oxana at home. When she didn't answer the landlady let herself in."

"Downstairs hadn't heard anything—screams—anything?"

"It's a converted house full of students. Less than bloody useless," said Wardle. "Loud music, mates coming and going all hours, they gaped like sheep when we asked them if they'd heard anything from upstairs. The girl who'd rung the landlady had total hysterics. She said she'd never forgive herself for not phoning up when she first smelled something bad."

"Yeah, that would've changed everything," said Strike. "You could've stuck her head back on and she'd have been fine."

Wardle laughed. Even Detective Sergeant Ekwensi smiled.

Robin stood up abruptly. Last night's wine and this morning's croissant were churning horribly in her guts. Excusing herself in a small voice, she moved briskly towards the door.

22

I don't give up but I ain't a stalker,
I guess I'm just an easy talker.

Blue Öyster Cult, "I Just Like to Be Bad"

"Thank you, I *get* the concept of gallows humor," said Robin an hour later, part exasperated, part amused. "Can we move on?"

Strike regretted his witticism in the meeting room, because Robin had returned from a twenty-minute bathroom trip looking white and slightly clammy, a whiff of peppermint revealing that she had cleaned her teeth again. Instead of taking a taxi he had suggested they take a short walk in the fresh air along Broadway to the Feathers, the closest pub, where he ordered them a pot of tea. Personally, he was ready for a beer, but Robin had not been trained up to consider alcohol and bloodshed natural fellows and he felt a pint might reinforce her impression of his callousness.

The Feathers was quiet at half past eleven on a Wednesday morning. They took a table at the back of the large pub, away from a couple of plainclothes officers who were talking in soft voices near the window.

"I told Wardle about our friend in the beanie while you were in the bathroom," Strike told Robin. "He says he's going to put a plainclothes man around Denmark Street to keep an eye out for a few days."

"D'you think the press are going to come back?" asked Robin, who had not yet had time to worry about this.

"I hope not. Wardle's going to keep the fake letters under wraps. He says it's playing into this nutter's hands to release them. He inclines to the view that the killer's genuinely trying to frame me."

"You don't?"

"No," said Strike. "He's not that unhinged. There's something weirder going on here."

He fell silent and Robin, respecting his thought process, maintained her own silence.

"Terrorism, that's what this is," said Strike slowly, scratching his unshaven chin. "He's trying to put the wind up us, disrupt our lives as much as possible; and let's face it, he's succeeding. We've got police crawling over the office and calling us into the Yard, we've lost most of our clients, you're—"

"Don't worry about me!" said Robin at once, "I don't want you to worry—"

"For fuck's sake, Robin," said Strike on a flash of temper, "both of us saw that guy yesterday. Wardle thinks I should tell you to stay home and I—"

"Please," she said, her early-morning fears swarming back upon her, "don't make me stop work—"

"It's not worth being murdered to escape your home life!"

He regretted saying it immediately, as he saw her wince.

"I'm not using it as an escape," she muttered. "I love this job. I woke up this morning feeling sick about what I told you last night. I was worried you—might not think I'm tough enough anymore."

"This hasn't got anything to do with what you told me last night and nothing to do with being tough. It's about a psycho who might be following you, who's already hacked a woman to bits."

Robin drank her lukewarm tea and said nothing. She was ravenous. However, the thought of eating pub food containing any form of meat made sweat break out over her scalp.

"It can't have been a first murder, can it?" Strike asked rhetorically, his dark eyes fixed on the hand-painted names of beers over the bar. "Beheading her, cutting off her limbs, taking bits of her away? Wouldn't you work up to that?"

"You'd think so," Robin agreed.

"That was done for the pleasure of doing it. He had a one-man orgy in that bathroom."

Robin was now unsure whether she was experiencing hunger or nausea.

"A sadistic maniac who's got a grudge against me and has decided to unite his hobbies," Strike mused aloud.

"Does that fit any of the men you suspect?" Robin asked. "Have any of them killed before, that you know of?"

"Yeah," said Strike. "Whittaker. He killed my mother."

But in a very different way, thought Robin. It had been a needle, not knives, that had dispatched Leda Strike. Out of respect for Strike, who was looking grim, she did not voice the thought. Then she remembered something else.

"I suppose you know," she said cautiously, "that Whittaker kept another woman's dead body in his flat for a month?"

"Yeah," said Strike. "I heard."

The news had filtered through to him while he was out in the Balkans, passed on by his sister Lucy. He had found a picture online of Whittaker walking into court. His ex-stepfather had been almost unrecognizable, crew-cutted and bearded, but still with those staring gold eyes. Whittaker's story, if Strike remembered correctly, had been that he had been afraid of "another false accusation" of murder, so he had attempted to mummify the dead woman's body, binding it up in bin bags and hiding it under floorboards. The defense had claimed to an unsympathetic judge that their client's novel approach to his problem was due to heavy drug use.

"He hadn't murdered her, though, had he?" Robin asked, trying to remember exactly what Wikipedia had said.

"She'd been dead a month, so I doubt it was an easy post-mortem," said Strike. The look that Shanker had described as ugly had returned. "Personally, I'd lay odds he killed her. How unlucky does a man get, two of his girlfriends dropping dead at home while he's sitting there doing nothing?

"He liked death, Whittaker; he liked bodies. He claimed he'd been a gravedigger when he was a teenager. He had a thing about corpses. People took him for a hardcore goth or some ten-a-penny poseur—the necrophiliac lyrics, the Satanic Bible, Aleister Crowley, all that crap—but he was an evil, amoral bastard who told everyone he met he was an evil, amoral bastard and what happened? Women fell over themselves to get at him.

"I need a drink," said Strike. He got up and headed for the bar.

Robin watched him go, slightly taken aback by his sudden rush of anger. His opinion that Whittaker had murdered twice was unsupported by either the courts or, as far as she knew, police evidence. She had become used to Strike's insistence on the meticulous collection and documentation of facts, his oft-repeated reminders that hunches and personal antipathies might inform, but must never be allowed to dictate, the direction of an investigation. Of course, when it was a case of Strike's own mother…

Strike returned with a pint of Nicholson's Pale Ale and a couple of menus.

"Sorry," he muttered when he had sat back down and taken a long pull on the pint. "Thinking about stuff I haven't thought about for a long time. Those bloody lyrics."

"Yes," said Robin.

"For fuck's sake, it *can't* be Digger," said Strike in frustration, running a hand through his dense, curly hair and leaving it entirely unchanged. "He's a professional gangster! If he'd found out I gave evidence against him and wanted retribution he'd have bloody shot me. He wouldn't fanny about with severed legs and song lyrics, knowing it'd bring the police down on him. He's a businessman."

"Does Wardle still think it's him?"

"Yeah," said Strike, "but he should know as well as anyone the procedures on anonymous evidence are watertight. You'd have coppers lying dead all over town if they weren't."

He refrained from further criticism of Wardle, though it cost him an effort. The man was being considerate and helpful when he could be causing Strike difficulties. Strike had not forgotten that the last time he had tangled with the Met they had kept him in an interrogation room for five solid hours on what appeared to be the whim of resentful officers.

"What about the two men you knew in the army?" asked Robin, dropping her voice because a group of female office workers were settling themselves at a table nearby. "Brockbank and Laing. Had either of them killed anyone? I mean," she added, "I know they were soldiers, but outside combat?"

"It wouldn't surprise me to hear Laing had done someone in," said Strike, "but he hadn't, as far as I know, before he went down. He used a knife on his ex-wife, I know that—tied her up and cut her. He spent a decade inside and I doubt they managed to rehabilitate him. He's been out over four years: plenty of time to commit murder.

"I haven't told you—I met his ex-mother-in-law in Melrose. She reckons he went to Gateshead when he got out of the nick and we know he might have been in Corby in 2008...but," said Strike, "she also told me he was ill."

"What kind of ill?"

"Some form of arthritis. She didn't know the details. Could an unfit man have done what we saw in those photos?" Strike picked up the menu. "Right. I'm bloody starving and you haven't eaten anything except crisps for two days."

When Strike had ordered pollock and chips and Robin a plowman's, he made another conversational swerve.

"Did the victim look twenty-four to you?"

"I—I couldn't tell," said Robin, trying and failing to block the image of the head with its smooth chubby cheeks, its frosted-white eyes. "No," she said, after a brief pause. "I thought it—she—looked younger."

"Me too."

"I might...bathroom," said Robin, standing up.

"You OK?"

"I just need a pee—too much tea."

He watched her go, then finished his pint, following a train of thought he had not yet confided to Robin, or indeed anyone else.

The child's essay had been shown to him by a female investigator in Germany. Strike could still remember the last line, written in neat girlish handwriting on a sheet of pale pink paper.

The lady changed her name to Anastassia and died her hair and nobody ever found out were she went, she vanished.

"Is that what you'd like to do, Brittany?" the investigator had asked quietly on the tape Strike had watched later. "You'd like to run away and vanish?"

"It's just a story!" Brittany had insisted, trying for a scornful laugh, her little fingers twisting together, one leg almost wrapped around the other. Her thin blonde hair had hung lank around her pale, freckly face. Her spectacles had been wonky. She had reminded Strike of a yellow budgerigar. "I only made it up!"

DNA testing would find out soon enough who the woman in the fridge had been, and then the police would trawl backwards to see who Oxana Voloshina—if that was her name—really was. Strike could not tell whether he was being paranoid or not in continuing to worry that the body belonged to Brittany Brockbank. Why had the name Kelsey been used on the first letter to him? Why did the head look so young, still smooth with puppy fat?

"I should be on Platinum by now," said Robin sadly, checking her watch as she sat back down at the table. One of the office workers beside them seemed to be celebrating her birthday: with much raucous laughter from her colleagues she had just unwrapped a red and black basque.

"I wouldn't worry about it," Strike said absently, as his fish and chips and Robin's plowman's descended in front of them. He ate silently for a couple of minutes, then set down his knife and fork, pulled out his notebook, looked something up in the notes he had made back in Hardacre's Edinburgh office and picked up his phone. Robin watched him key in words, wondering what he was doing.

"Right," said Strike, after reading the results, "I'm going to Barrow-in-Furness tomorrow."

"You're—what?" asked Robin, bewildered. "Why?"

"Brockbank's there—or he's supposed to be."

"How do you know?"

"I found out in Edinburgh that his pension's being sent there and I've just looked up the old family address. Someone called Holly

Brockbank's living in the house now. Obviously a relative. She should know where he is. If I can establish that he's been in Cumbria for the last few weeks, we'll know he hasn't been delivering legs or stalking you in London, won't we?"

"What aren't you telling me about Brockbank?" Robin asked, her blue-gray eyes narrowing.

Strike ignored the question.

"I want you to stay at home while I'm out of town. Sod Two-Times, he's got only himself to blame if Platinum cops off with another punter. We can live without his money."

"That'll leave us with a single client," Robin pointed out.

"I've got a feeling we'll have none at all unless this nutter's caught," said Strike. "People aren't going to want to come near us."

"How are you going to get to Barrow?" asked Robin.

A plan was dawning. Hadn't she foreseen this very eventuality?

"Train," he said, "you know I can't afford a hire car right now."

"How about," said Robin triumphantly, "I drive you in my new—well, it's ancient, but it goes fine—Land Rover!"

"Since when have you had a Land Rover?"

"Since Sunday. It's my parents' old car."

"Ah," he said. "Well, that sounds great—"

"But?"

"No, it'd be a real help—"

"*But?*" repeated Robin, who could tell that he had some reservations.

"I don't know how long I'll be up there."

"That doesn't matter. You've just told me I'll be moldering at home in any case."

Strike hesitated. How much of her desire to drive him was rooted in the hope of wounding Matthew, he wondered. He could well imagine how the accountant would view an open-ended trip north, the two of them alone, staying overnight. A clean and professional relationship ought not to include using each other to make partners jealous.

"Oh shit," he said suddenly, plunging his hand into his pocket for his mobile.

"What's the matter?" asked Robin, alarmed.

"I've just remembered—I was supposed to be meeting Elin last night. Fuck—totally forgot. Wait there."

He walked out into the street, leaving Robin to her lunch. Why, she wondered, her eyes on Strike's large figure as he paced up and down outside the floor-to-ceiling windows, phone pressed to his ear, hadn't Elin called or texted to ask where Strike was? From there it was an easy step to wondering—for the first time, no matter what Strike had suspected—what Matthew was going to say if she returned home only to pick up the Land Rover and disappeared with several days' worth of clothes in a bag.

He can't complain, she thought, with a bold attempt at defiance. *It's nothing to do with him anymore.*

Yet the thought of having to see Matthew, even briefly, was unnerving.

Strike returned, rolling his eyes.

"Doghouse," he said succinctly. "I'll meet her tonight instead."

Robin did not know why the announcement that Strike was off to meet Elin should lower her spirits. She supposed that she was tired. The various strains and emotional shocks of the last thirty-six hours were not to be overcome in one pub lunch. The office workers nearby were now screeching with laughter as a pair of fluffy handcuffs fell out of another package.

It isn't her birthday, Robin realized. *She's getting married.*

"Well, am I driving you, or what?" she asked curtly.

"Yeah," said Strike, who appeared to be warming to the idea (or was he merely cheered by the thought of his date with Elin?). "You know what, that'd be great. Thanks."

23

Moments of pleasure, in a world of pain.

Blue Öyster Cult, "Make Rock Not War"

Mist lay in thick, soft layers like cobweb over the treetops of Regent's Park next morning. Strike, who had swiftly silenced his alarm so as not to wake Elin, stood balancing on his single foot at the window, the curtain behind him to block out the light. For a minute he looked out upon the ghostly park and was transfixed by the effect of the rising sun on leafy branches rising from the sea of vapor. You could find beauty nearly anywhere if you stopped to look for it, but the battle to get through the days made it easy to forget that this totally cost-free luxury existed. He carried memories like this from his childhood, especially those parts of it that he had spent in Cornwall: the glitter of the sea as you first saw it on a morning as blue as a butterfly's wing; the mysterious emerald-and-shadow world of the Gunnera Passage at Trebah Garden; distant white sails bobbing like seabirds on blustery gunmetal waves.

Behind him in the dark bed, Elin shifted and sighed. Strike moved carefully out from behind the curtain, took the prosthesis leaning against the wall and sat down on one of her bedroom chairs to attach it. Then, still moving as quietly as possible, he headed for the bathroom with the day's clothes in his arms.

They'd had their first row the previous evening: a landmark in every relationship. The total absence of communication when he failed to turn up for their date on Tuesday ought to have been a warning, but he had been too busy with Robin and a dismembered body to give it much thought. True, she had been frosty when he had phoned to apologize, but the fact that she had so readily agreed to a rescheduled date had not prepared him for a near-glacial reception when he had turned up in person twenty-four hours later. After a dinner eaten to the accompaniment of painful, stilted conversation he had offered to clear out and leave her to her resentment. She had become briefly angry as he reached for his coat, but it was the feeble spurt of a damp match; she had then crumbled into a tearful, semi-apologetic tirade in which he learned, firstly, that she was in therapy, secondly, that her therapist had identified a tendency towards passive aggression and, thirdly, that she had been so deeply wounded by his failure to turn up on Tuesday that she had drunk an entire bottle of wine alone in front of the television.

Strike had apologized again, offering in extenuation a difficult case, a tricky and unexpected development, expressing sincere remorse for having forgotten their date, but added that if she could not forgive, he had better clear out.

She had flung herself into his arms; they had gone straight to bed and had the best sex of their brief relationship.

Shaving in Elin's immaculate bathroom with its sunken lights and snow-white towels, Strike reflected that he had got off pretty lightly. If he had forgotten to turn up to a date with Charlotte, the woman with whom he had been involved, on and off, for sixteen years, he would have been carrying physical wounds right now, searching for her in the cold dawn, or perhaps trying to restrain her from throwing herself from the high balcony.

He had called what he felt for Charlotte love and it remained the most profound feeling he had had for any woman. In the pain it had caused him and its lasting after-effects it had more resembled a virus that, even now, he was not sure he had overcome. Not seeing her, never calling her, never using the new email address she had set up to show him her distraught face on the day of her wedding to an old boyfriend: this was his self-prescribed treatment, which was keeping the symptoms at bay. Yet he knew he had been left impaired, that he no longer had the capacity to feel in the way that he had once felt. Elin's distress of the previous evening had not touched him at his core in the way Charlotte's had once done. He felt as though his capacity for loving had been blunted, the nerve endings severed. He had not intended to wound Elin; he did not enjoy seeing her cry; yet the ability to feel empathetic pain seemed to have closed down. A small part of him, in truth, had been mentally planning his route home as she sobbed.

Strike dressed in the bathroom then moved quietly back into the dimly lit hall, where he stowed his shaving things in the holdall he had packed for Barrow-in-Furness. A door stood ajar to his right. On a whim, he pushed it wider.

The little girl whom he had never met slept here when not at her father's. The pink and white room was immaculate, with a ceiling mural of fairies around the cornice. Barbies sat in a neat line on a shelf, their smiles vacant, their pointy breasts covered in a rainbow of gaudy dresses. A fake-fur rug with a polar bear's head lay on the floor beside a tiny white four-poster.

Strike knew hardly any little girls. He had two godsons, neither of whom he had particularly wanted, and three nephews. His oldest friend back in Cornwall had daughters, but Strike had virtually nothing to do with them; they rushed past him in a blur of ponytails and casual waves: "Hi Uncle Corm, bye Uncle Corm." He had grown up, of course, with a sister, although Lucy had never been indulged with sugar-pink-canopied four-posters, much as she might have wanted them.

Brittany Brockbank had had a cuddly lion. It came back to him suddenly, out of nowhere, looking at the polar bear on the floor: a cuddly lion with a comical face. She had dressed it in a pink tutu and it had been lying on the sofa when her stepfather came running at Strike, a broken beer bottle in his hand.

Strike turned back to the hall, feeling in his pocket. He always carried a notebook and pen on him. He scribbled a brief note to Elin, alluding to the best part of the previous night, and left it on the hall table so as not to risk waking her. Then, as quietly as he had done everything else, he hoisted his holdall onto his shoulder and let himself out of the flat. He was meeting Robin at West Ealing station at eight.

The last traces of mist were lifting from Hastings Road when Robin left her house, flustered and heavy-eyed, a carrier bag of food in one hand and a holdall full of clean clothes in the other. She unlocked the rear of the old gray Land Rover, swung the clothes into it and hurried around to the driver's seat with the food.

Matthew had just tried to hug her in the hall and she had forcibly resisted, two hands on his smooth warm chest, pushing him away, shouting at him to get off. He had been wearing only boxer shorts. Now she was afraid that he might be struggling into some clothes, ready to give chase. She slammed the car door and dragged on her seatbelt, eager to be gone, but as she turned the key in the ignition Matthew burst out of the house, barefoot, in T-shirt and tracksuit bottoms. She had never seen his expression so naked, so vulnerable.

"Robin," he called as she stepped on the accelerator and pulled away from the curb. "I love you. *I love you!*"

She spun the wheel and moved precariously out of the parking space, missing their neighbor's Honda by inches. She could see Matthew shrinking in the rearview mirror; he, whose self-possession was usually total, was proclaiming his love at the top of his voice, risking the neighbors' curiosity, their scorn and their laughter.

Robin's heart thumped painfully in her chest. A quarter past seven; Strike would not be at the station yet. She turned left at the end of the road, intent only on putting distance between herself and Matthew.

He had risen at dawn, while she was trying to pack without waking him.

"Where are you going?"

"To help Strike with the investigation."

"You're going away overnight?"

"I expect so."

"Where?"

"I don't know exactly."

She was afraid to tell him their destination in case he came after them. Matthew's behavior when she had arrived home the previous evening had left her shaken. He had cried and begged. She had never seen him like that, not even after his mother's death.

"Robin, we've got to talk."

"We've talked enough."

"Does your mother know where you're going?"

"Yes."

She was lying. Robin had not told her mother about the ruptured engagement yet, nor that she was heading off north with Strike. After all, she was twenty-six; it was none of her mother's business. She knew, though, that Matthew was really asking whether she had told her mother that the wedding was off, because they were both aware that she would not have been getting in the Land Rover to drive off to an undisclosed location with Strike if their engagement had still been intact. The sapphire ring was lying exactly where she had left it, on a bookshelf loaded with his old accountancy textbooks.

"Oh shit," Robin whispered, blinking away tears as she turned at random through the quiet streets, trying not to focus on her naked finger, or on the memory of Matthew's anguished face.

One short walk took Strike much further than simple physical distance. This, he thought as he smoked his first cigarette of the day, was London: you started in a quiet, symmetrical Nash terrace that resembled a sculpture in vanilla ice-cream. Elin's pin-striped Russian neighbor had been getting into his Audi, and Strike had received a curt nod in response to his "Morning." A short walk past the silhouettes of Sherlock Holmes at Baker Street station and he was sitting on a grimy Tube train surrounded by chattering Polish workmen, fresh and businesslike at 7 a.m. Then bustling Paddington, forcing a path through commuters and coffee shops, holdall over shoulder. Finally a few stops on the Heathrow Connect, accompanied by a large West Country family who were already dressed for Florida in spite of the early morning chill. They watched the station signs like nervous meerkats, their hands gripping their suitcase handles as though expecting an imminent mugging.

Strike arrived at West Ealing station fifteen minutes early and desperate for a cigarette. Dropping the holdall by his feet he lit up, hoping that Robin would not be too prompt, because he doubted that she would want him smoking in the Land Rover. He had only taken a couple of satisfying drags, however, when the box-like car rounded the corner, Robin's bright red-gold head clearly visible through the windscreen.

"I don't mind," she called over the running engine as he hoisted his holdall back onto his shoulder and made to extinguish the cigarette, "as long as you keep the window open."

He climbed inside, shoved his bag into the back and slammed the door.

"You can't make it smell worse than it already does," said Robin, managing the stiff gears with her usual expertise. "It's pure dog in here."

Strike pulled on a seatbelt as they accelerated away from the pavement, looking around at the interior of the car. Shabby and scuffed, a pungent fug of Wellington boot and Labrador certainly pervaded. It reminded Strike of military vehicles that he had driven across all terrains in Bosnia and Afghanistan, but at the same time it added something to his picture of Robin's background. This Land Rover spoke of muddy tracks and plowed fields. He remembered her saying that an uncle had a farm.

"Did you ever have a pony?"

She glanced at him, surprised. In that fleeting full-face look he noted the heaviness of her eyes, her pallor. She had clearly not slept much.

"What on earth do you want to know that for?"

"This feels like the kind of car you'd take to the gymkhana."

Her reply had a touch of defensiveness:

"Yes, I did."

He laughed, pushing the window down as far as it would go and resting his left hand there with the cigarette.

"Why is that funny?"

"I don't know. What was it called?"

"Angus," she said, turning left. "He was a bugger. Always carting me off."

"I don't trust horses," said Strike, smoking.

"Have you ever been on one?"

It was Robin's turn to smile. She thought it might be one of the few places where she would see Strike truly discomforted, on the back of a horse.

"No," said Strike. "And I intend to keep it that way."

"My uncle's got something that'd carry you," said Robin. "Clydesdale. It's massive."

"Point taken," said Strike drily, and she laughed.

Smoking in silence as she concentrated on navigating through the increasingly heavy morning traffic, Strike noted how much he liked making her laugh. He also recognized that he felt much happier, much more comfortable, sitting here in this ramshackle Land Rover talking inconsequential nonsense with Robin than he had felt last night at dinner with Elin.

He was not a man who told himself comfortable lies. He might have argued that Robin represented the ease of friendship; Elin, the pitfalls and pleasures of a sexual relationship. He knew that the truth was more complicated, and certainly made more so by the fact that the sapphire ring had vanished from Robin's finger. He had known, almost from the moment they had met, that Robin represented a threat to his peace of mind, but endangering the best working relationship of his life would be an act of willful self-sabotage that he, after years of a destructive on-off relationship, after the hard graft and sacrifice that had gone into building his business, could not and would not let happen.

"Are you ignoring me on purpose?"

"What?"

It was just plausible that he had not heard her, so noisy was the old Land Rover's engine.

"I said, how are things with Elin?"

She had never asked him outright about a relationship before. Strike supposed the confidences of two nights ago had moved them onto a different level of intimacy. He would have avoided this, if he could.

"All right," he said repressively, throwing away his cigarette butt and pulling up the window, which marginally reduced the noise.

"She forgave you, then?"

"What for?"

"For completely forgetting that you had a date!" said Robin.

"Oh, that. Yeah. Well, no—then, yeah."

As she turned onto the A40, Strike's ambiguous utterance brought to Robin a sudden, vivid mental image: of Strike, with his hairy bulk and his one and a half legs, entangled with Elin, blonde and alabaster against pure white sheets…she was sure that Elin's sheets would be white and Nordic and clean. She probably had somebody to do her laundry. Elin was too upper middle class, too wealthy, to iron her own duvet covers in front of the TV in a cramped sitting room in Ealing.

"How about Matthew?" Strike asked her as they moved out onto the motorway. "How'd that go?"

"Fine," said Robin.

"Bollocks," said Strike.

Though another laugh escaped her, Robin was half inclined to resent his demand for more information when she was given so little about Elin.

"Well, he wants to get back together."

"Course he does," said Strike.

"Why 'of course'?"

"If I'm not allowed to fish, you aren't."

Robin was not sure what to say to that, though it gave her a small glow of pleasure. She thought it might be the very first time that Strike had ever given any indication that he saw her as a woman, and she silently filed away the exchange to pore over later, in solitude.

"He apologized and kept asking me to put my ring back on," Robin said. Residual loyalty to Matthew prevented her mentioning the crying, the begging. "But I…"

Her voice trailed away, and although Strike wanted to hear more, he asked no further questions, but pulled down the window and smoked another cigarette.

They stopped for a coffee at Hilton Park Services. Robin went to the bathroom while Strike queued for coffees in Burger King. In front of the mirror she checked her mobile. As she had expected, a message from Matthew was waiting, but the tone was no longer pleading and conciliatory.

> **If you sleep with him, we're over for good. You might think it'll make things even but it's not like for like. Sarah was a long time ago, we were kids and I didn't do it to hurt you. Think about what you're throwing away, Robin. I love you.**

"Sorry," Robin muttered, moving aside to allow an impatient girl access to the hand-dryer.

She read Matthew's text again. A satisfying gush of anger obliterated the mingled pity and pain engendered by that morning's pursuit. Here, she thought, was the authentic Matthew: **if you sleep with him, we're over for good**. So he did not really believe that she had meant it when she took off her ring and told him she no longer wished to marry him? It would be over "for good" only when he, Matthew, said so? **It's not like for like**. Her infidelity would be worse than his by definition. To him, her journey north was simply an exercise in retaliation: a dead woman and a killer loose mere pretext for feminine spite.

Screw you, she thought, ramming the mobile back into her pocket as she returned to the café, where Strike sat eating a double Croissan'Wich with sausage and bacon.

Strike noted her flushed face, her tense jaw, and guessed that Matthew had been in touch.

"Everything all right?"

"Fine," said Robin and then, before he could ask anything else, "So are you going to tell me about Brockbank?"

The question came out a little more aggressively than she had intended. The tone of Matthew's text had riled her, as had the fact that it had raised in her mind the question of where she and Strike were actually going to sleep that night.

"If you want," said Strike mildly.

He drew his phone out of his pocket, brought up the picture of Brockbank that he had taken from Hardacre's computer and passed it across the table to Robin.

Robin contemplated the long, swarthy face beneath its dense dark hair, which was unusual, but not unattractive. As though he had read her mind, Strike said:

"He's uglier now. That was taken when he'd just joined up. One of his eye sockets is caved in and he's got a cauliflower ear."

"How tall is he?" asked Robin, remembering the courier standing over her in his leathers, his mirrored visor.

"My height or bigger."

"You said you met him in the army?"

"Yep," said Strike.

She thought for a few seconds that he was not going to tell her anything more, until she realized that he was merely waiting for an elderly couple, who were dithering about where to sit, to pass out of earshot. When they had gone Strike said:

"He was a major, Seventh Armoured Brigade. He married a dead colleague's widow. She had two small daughters. Then they had one of their own, a boy."

The facts flowed, having just reread Brockbank's file, but in truth Strike had never forgotten them. It had been one of those cases that stayed with you.

"The eldest stepdaughter was called Brittany. When she was twelve, Brittany disclosed sexual abuse to a school friend in Germany. The friend told her mother, who reported it. We were called in—I didn't interview her personally, that was a female officer. I just saw the tape."

What had crucified him was how grown-up she had tried to be, how together. She was terrified of what would happen to the family now she had blabbed, and was trying to take it back.

No, of course she hadn't told Sophie that he had threatened to kill her little sister if she told on him! No, Sophie wasn't lying, exactly—it had been a joke, that was all. She'd asked Sophie how to stop yourself having a baby because—because she'd been curious, everyone wanted to know stuff like that. Of course he hadn't said he'd carve up her mum in little pieces if she told—the thing about her leg? Oh, that—well, that was a joke, too—it was all joking—he told her she had scars on her leg because he'd nearly cut her leg off when she was little, but her mum had walked in and seen him. He'd said he did it because she'd trodden on his flowerbeds when she was a toddler, but of course it was a joke—ask her mum. She'd got stuck in some barbed wire, that was all, and badly cut trying to pull herself free. They could ask her mum. He hadn't cut her. He'd never cut her, not Daddy.

The involuntary expression she had made when forcing herself to say "Daddy" was with Strike still: she had looked like a child trying to swallow cold tripe, under threat of punishment. Twelve years old and she had learned life was only bearable for her family if she shut up and took whatever he wanted to do without complaint.

Strike had taken against Mrs. Brockbank from their first interview. She had been thin and over made-up, a victim, no doubt, in her way, but it seemed to Strike that she had voluntarily jettisoned Brittany to save the other two children, that she turned two blind eyes to the long absences from the house of her husband and eldest child, that her determination not to know was tantamount to collaboration. Brockbank had told Brittany that he would strangle both her mother and her sister if she ever spoke about what he did to her in the car when he took her on lengthy excursions into nearby woods, into dark alleyways. He would cut all of them up into little bits and bury them in the garden. Then he'd take Ryan—Brockbank's small son, the only family member whom he seemed to value—and go where no one would ever find them.

"It was a joke, just a joke. I didn't mean any of it."

Thin fingers twisting, her glasses lopsided, her legs not long enough for her feet to reach the floor. She was still refusing point blank to be physically examined when Strike and Hardacre went to Brockbank's house to bring him in.

"He was pissed when we got there. I told him why we'd come and he came at me with a broken bottle.

"I knocked him out," said Strike without bravado, "but I shouldn't've touched him. I didn't need to."

He had never admitted this out loud before, even though Hardacre (who had backed him to the hilt in the subsequent inquiry) had known it as well.

"If he came at you with a bottle—"

"I could've got the bottle off him without decking him."

"You said he was big—"

"He was pretty pissed. I could've managed him without punching him. Hardacre was there, it was two on one.

"Truth is, I was glad he came at me. I wanted to punch him. Right hook, literally knocked him senseless—which is how he got away with it."

"Got away with—"

"Got off," said Strike. "Got clean away."

"How?"

Strike drank more coffee, his eyes unfocused, remembering.

"He was hospitalized after I hit him because he had a massive epileptic seizure when he came out of the concussion. Traumatic brain injury."

"Oh God," said Robin.

"He needed emergency surgery to stop the bleeding from his brain. He kept having fits. They diagnosed TBI, PTSD and alcoholism. Unfit to stand trial. Lawyers came stampeding in. I was put on an assault charge.

"Luckily, my legal team found out that, the weekend before I hit him, he'd played rugby. They dug around a bit and found out he'd taken a knee to the head from an eighteen-stone Welshman and been stretchered off the field. A junior medic had missed the bleeding from his ear because he was covered in mud and bruises, and just told him to go home and take it easy. As it turned out, they'd missed a basal skull fracture, which my legal team found out when they got doctors to look at the post-match X-ray. The skull fracture had been done by a Welsh forward, not me.

"Even so, if I hadn't had Hardy as a witness to the fact that he'd come at me with the bottle, I'd have been in it up to my neck. In the end, they accepted that I'd acted in self-defense. I couldn't have known his skull was already cracked, or how much damage I'd do by punching him.

"Meanwhile, they found child porn on his computer. Brittany's story tallied with frequent sightings of her being driven out, alone, by her stepfather. Her teacher was interviewed and said she was getting more and more withdrawn at school.

"Two years he'd been assaulting her and warning her he'd kill her, her mother and her sister if she told anyone. He had her convinced that he'd already tried to cut her leg off once. She had scarring all around her shin. He'd told her he was just sawing it off when the mother came in and stopped him. In her interview, the mother said the scarring was from an accident when she was a toddler."

Robin said nothing. Both hands were over her mouth and her eyes were wide. Strike's expression was frightening.

"He lay in hospital while they tried to get his fits under control, and whenever anyone tried to interview him he faked confusion and amnesia. He had lawyers swarming all over him, smelling a big fat payout: medical neglect, assault. He claimed he'd been a victim of abuse himself, that the child porn was just a symptom of his mental issues, his alcoholism. Brittany was insisting she'd made everything up, the mother was screaming to everyone that Brockbank had never laid a finger on any of the kids, that he was a perfect father, that she'd lost one husband and now she was going to lose another. Top brass just wanted the accusation to go away.

"He was invalided out," said Strike, his dark eyes meeting Robin's blue-gray ones. "He got off scot-free, with a payout and pension to boot, and off he went, Brittany in tow."

24

Step into a world of strangers
Into a sea of unknowns…

Blue Öyster Cult, "Hammer Back"

The rattling Land Rover devoured the miles with stoic competence, but the journey north had begun to seem interminably long before the first signs to Barrow-in-Furness appeared. The map had not adequately conveyed how far away the seaport was, how isolated. Barrow-in-Furness was not destined to be passed through, or visited incidentally; an end unto itself, it constituted a geographical cul-de-sac.

Through the southernmost reaches of the Lake District they traveled, past rolling fields of sheep, dry stone walls and picturesque hamlets that reminded Robin of her Yorkshire home, through Ulverston ("Birthplace of Stan Laurel"), until they achieved their first glimpse of a wide estuary that hinted at their approach to the coast. At last, past midday, they found themselves in an unlovely industrial estate, the road flanked by warehouses and factories, which marked the periphery of the town.

"We'll grab something to eat before we go to Brockbank's," said Strike, who had been examining a map of Barrow for the past five minutes. He disdained using electronic devices to navigate on the basis that you did not need to wait for paper to download, nor did the information disappear under adverse conditions. "There's a car park up here. Take a left at the roundabout."

They passed a battered side entrance to Craven Park, home ground of the Barrow Raiders. Strike, whose eyes were peeled for a sighting of Brockbank, drank in the distinct character of the place. He had expected, Cornish-born as he was, to be able to see the sea, to taste it, but they might have been miles inland for all he could tell. The initial impression was of a gigantic out-of-town retail center, where the garish façades of high-street outlets confronted them on all sides, except that here and there, standing proud and incongruous between the DIY stores and pizza restaurants, were architectural gems that spoke of a prosperous industrial past. The art deco customs house had been turned into a restaurant. A Victorian technical college embellished with classical figures bore the legend *Labor Omnia Vincit*. A little further and they came across rows and rows of terraced housing, the kind of cityscape Lowry painted, the hive where workers lived.

"Never seen so many pubs," said Strike as Robin turned into the car park. He fancied a beer, but with *Labor Omnia Vincit* in mind, agreed to Robin's suggestion of a quick bite to eat in a nearby café.

The April day was bright, but the breeze carried with it a chill off the unseen sea.

"Not overselling themselves, are they?" he muttered as he saw the name of the café: The Last Resort. It stood opposite Second Chance, which sold old clothing, and a flourishing pawnbroker's. Notwithstanding its unpropitious name, The Last Resort was cozy and clean, full of chattering old ladies, and they returned to the car park feeling pleasantly well fed.

"His house won't be easy to watch if no one's home," said Strike, showing Robin the map when they were back in the Land Rover. "It's in a dead straight dead end. Nowhere to lurk."

"Has it occurred to you," said Robin, not entirely flippantly, as they drove away, "that Holly *is* Noel? That he's had a sex change?"

"If he has, he'll be a cinch to find," said Strike. "Six foot eight in high heels, with a cauliflower ear. Take a right here," he added as they passed a nightclub called Skint. "Christ, they tell it like it is in Barrow, don't they?"

Ahead, a gigantic cream building with the name BAE SYSTEMS on it blocked any view of the seafront. The edifice was windowless and seemed to stretch a mile across, blank, faceless, intimidating.

"I think Holly's going to turn out to be a sister, or maybe a new wife," said Strike. "Hang a left...she's the same age as him. Right, we're looking for Stanley Road...we're going to end up right by BAE Systems, by the look of it."

As Strike had said, Stanley Road ran in a straight line with houses on one side and a high brick wall topped with barbed wire on the other. Beyond this uncompromising barrier rose the strangely sinister factory building, white and windowless, intimidating in its sheer size.

"'Nuclear Site Boundary'?" Robin read from a sign on the wall, slowing the Land Rover to a crawl as they proceeded up the road.

"Building submarines," said Strike, looking up at the barbed wire. "Police warnings everywhere—look."

The cul-de-sac was deserted. It terminated in a small parking area beside a children's play park. As she parked, Robin noticed a number of objects stuck in the barbed wire on top of the wall. The ball had undoubtedly landed there by accident, but there was also a small pink doll's pushchair, tangled up and irretrievable. The sight of it gave her an uncomfortable feeling: somebody had deliberately thrown that out of reach.

"What are you getting out for?" asked Strike, coming around the back of the vehicle.

"I was—"

"I'll deal with Brockbank, if he's in there," said Strike, lighting up. "You're not going anywhere near him."

Robin got back into the Land Rover.

"Try not to punch him, won't you?" she muttered at Strike's retreating figure as he walked with a slight limp towards the house, his knee stiff from the journey.

Some of the houses had clean windows and ornaments neatly arranged behind the glass; others had net curtains in various states of cleanliness. A few were shabby and, on the evidence of grimy interior windowsills, dirty. Strike had almost reached a maroon door when he suddenly stopped in his tracks. Robin noticed that a group of men in blue overalls and hard hats had appeared at the end of the street. Was one of them Brockbank? Was that why Strike had stopped?

No. He was merely taking a phone call. Turning his back on both the door and the men, he moved slowly back towards Robin, his stride no longer purposeful but with the aimless ramble of a man intent only on the voice in his ear.

One of the men in the overalls was tall, dark and bearded. Had Strike seen him? Robin slipped out of the Land Rover again and, on pretext of texting, took several photographs of the workmen, zooming in on them as closely as she could. They turned a corner and walked out of sight.

Strike had paused ten yards away from her, smoking and listening to the person talking on his mobile. A gray-haired woman was squinting at the pair of them from an upstairs window of the nearest house. Thinking to allay her suspicions, Robin turned away from the houses and took a picture of the huge nuclear facility, playing the tourist.

"That was Wardle," said Strike, coming up behind her. He looked grim. "The body isn't Oxana Voloshina's."

"How do they know?" asked Robin, stunned.

"Oxana's been home in Donetsk for three weeks. Family wedding—they haven't spoken to her personally, but they've talked to her mother on the phone and she says Oxana's there. Meanwhile, the landlady's recovered enough to tell police that she was especially shocked when she found the body because she thought Oxana had gone back to Ukraine for a holiday. She also mentioned that the head didn't look very like her."

Strike slid his phone back into his pocket, frowning. He hoped this news would focus Wardle's mind on someone other than Malley.

"Get back in the car," said Strike, lost in thought, and he set off towards Brockbank's house again.

Robin returned to the driver's seat of the Land Rover. The woman in the upper window was still staring.

Two policewomen in high-visibility tabards came walking down the street. Strike had reached the maroon door. The rap of metal on wood echoed down the street. Nobody answered. Strike was preparing to knock again when the policewomen reached him.

Robin sat up, wondering what on earth the police wanted with him. After a brief conversation all three of them turned and headed towards the Land Rover.

Robin pushed down the window, feeling suddenly and unaccountably guilty.

"They want to know," Strike called, when within earshot, "whether I'm Mr. Michael Ellacott."

"What?" said Robin, completely confused by the mention of her father's name.

The ludicrous thought came to her that Matthew had sent the police after them—but why would he have told them that Strike was her father? And then the realization came to her, voiced as soon as understood.

"The car's registered in Dad's name," she said. "Have I done something wrong?"

"Well, you're parked on a double yellow line," said one of the policewomen drily, "but that's not why we're here. You've been taking photographs of the facility. It's all right," she added, as Robin looked panicked. "People do it every day. You were caught on the security cameras. Can I see your driving license?"

"Oh," said Robin weakly, aware of Strike's quizzical look. "I only—I thought it would make an arty picture, you know? The barbed wire and the white building and—and the clouds..."

She handed over her documentation, studiously avoiding Strike's eye, mortified.

"Mr. Ellacott's your father, is he?"

"He lent us the car, that's all," said Robin, dreading the idea of the police contacting her parents and them finding out that she was in Barrow, without Matthew, ring-less and single...

"And where do you two live?"

"We don't—not together," said Robin.

They gave their names and addresses.

"You're visiting someone, are you, Mr. Strike?" asked the second policewoman.

"Noel Brockbank," said Strike promptly. "Old friend. Passing, thought I'd look him up."

"Brockbank," repeated the policewoman, handing Robin her

license, and Robin hoped that the woman might know him, which would surely go a long way to repairing her gaffe. "Good Barrovian surname, that. All right, on you go. No more photos round here."

"I'm. So. Sorry," Robin mouthed at Strike as the policewomen walked away. He shook his head, grinning through his annoyance.

"'Arty photo'...the wire...the sky..."

"What would you have said?" she demanded. "I could hardly tell them I was taking pictures of workmen because I thought one of them might be Brockbank—look—"

But when she brought up the picture of the workmen she realized that the tallest of them, with his ruddy cheeks, short neck and large ears, was not the man they sought.

The door of the nearest house opened. The gray-haired woman who had been watching from the upper window appeared, pulling a tartan shopping trolley. Her expression was now cheery. Robin was sure that the woman had observed the police arrive and depart, and was satisfied that they were not spies.

"It's always 'appening," she called loudly, her voice ringing across the street. She pronounced "always" "orlwuz." The accent was unfamiliar to Robin, who had thought she knew Cumbrian, hailing from the next county. "They've gor cameraz orl awwer. Teeking registrations. We're orl used to it."

"Spot the Londoners," said Strike pleasantly, which made her pause, curious.

"From London? Wha' brings th'all the way to Barra?"

"Looking for an old friend. Noel Brockbank," said Strike, pointing down the street, "but there's no answer at his house. He'll be at work, I expect."

She frowned a little.

"Noel, did th'say? Not Holly?"

"We'd love to see Holly, if she's around," said Strike.

"She'll be at work noo," said the neighbor, checking her watch. "Bak'ry awwer in Vickerstown. Or," said the woman, with a trace of grim humor, "tha can try the Crow's Nest tonight. She's usually there."

"We'll try the bakery—surprise her," said Strike. "Where is it exactly?"

"Little white one, just up the road from Vengeance Street."

They thanked her and she set off along the road, pleased to have been helpful.

"Did I hear that right?" Strike muttered, shaking open his map once they were safely back in the Land Rover. " 'Vengeance Street'?"

"That's what it sounded like," said Robin.

The short journey took them across a bridge spanning the estuary, where sailing boats bobbed on dirty-looking water or sat marooned on mudflats. Utilitarian, industrial buildings along the shore gave way to more streets of terraced houses, some pebble-dashed, some of red brick.

"Ships' names," guessed Strike as they drove up Amphitrite Street.

Vengeance Street ran up a hill. A few minutes' exploration of its vicinities revealed a little white-painted bakery.

"That's her," said Strike at once, as Robin pulled in with a clear view of the glass door. "Got to be his sister, look at her."

The bakery worker looked, thought Robin, harder than most men. She had the same long face and high forehead as Brockbank; her flinty eyes were outlined in thick kohl, her jet-black hair scraped back into a tight, unflattering ponytail. The cap-sleeved black T-shirt, worn under a white apron, revealed thick bare arms that were covered in tattoos from shoulder to wrist. Multiple gold hoops hung from each ear. A vertical frown line between her eyebrows gave her a look of perpetual bad temper.

The bakery was cramped and busy. Watching Holly bag up pasties, Strike remembered his venison pies from Melrose and his mouth watered.

"I could eat again."

"You can't talk to her in there," said Robin. "We'd do better to approach her at home, or in the pub."

"You could nip in and get me a pasty."

"We had rolls less than an hour ago!"

"So? I'm not on a bloody diet."

"Nor am I, anymore," said Robin.

The brave words brought to mind the strapless wedding dress still waiting for her in Harrogate. Did she really not intend to fit into it?

The flowers, the catering, the bridesmaids, the choice of first dance—would none of it be needed anymore? Deposits lost, presents returned, the faces of stunned friends and relatives when she told them...

The Land Rover was chilly and uncomfortable, she was very tired after hours of driving and for a few seconds—the time it took for a weak, treacherous lurch of her heart—the thought of Matthew and Sarah Shadlock made her want to cry all over again.

"D'you mind if I smoke?" said Strike, pushing down the window and letting in the cold air without waiting for an answer. Robin swallowed an affirmative answer; he had forgiven her for the police, after all. Somehow the chilly breeze helped brace her for what she needed to tell him.

"You can't interview Holly."

He turned to her, frowning.

"Taking Brockbank by surprise is one thing, but if Holly recognizes you she'll warn him you're after him. I'll have to do it. I've thought of a way."

"Yeah—that's not going to happen," said Strike flatly. "Odds are he's either living with her or a couple of streets away. He's a nutcase. If he smells a rat he'll turn nasty. You're not doing it alone."

Robin drew her coat more tightly around her and said coolly:

"D'you want to hear my idea or not?"

25

There's a time for discussion and a time for a fight.

Blue Öyster Cult, "Madness to the Method"

Strike didn't like it, but he was forced to concede that Robin's plan was a good one and that the danger of Holly tipping off Noel outweighed the probable risk to Robin. Accordingly, when Holly left work with a colleague at five o'clock, she was followed on foot by Strike, although unaware of his presence. Robin, meanwhile, drove to a deserted stretch of road beside a wide stretch of marshy wasteland, retrieved her holdall from the back of the car, wriggled out of her jeans and dragged on a smarter, though creased, pair of trousers.

She was driving back across the bridge towards central Barrow when Strike called to inform her that Holly had not returned home, but headed straight to the pub at the end of her street.

"Great, I think that'll be easier anyway," shouted Robin in the direction of her mobile, which was lying on the front passenger seat, set to speakerphone. The Land Rover vibrated and rattled around her.

"What?"

"I said, I think—never mind, I'm nearly there!"

Strike was waiting outside the Crow's Nest car park. He had just opened the passenger door when Robin gasped:

"Get down, get down!"

Holly had appeared in the doorway of the pub, pint in hand. She was taller than Robin and twice as broad in her black cap-sleeved T-shirt and jeans. Lighting a cigarette, she squinted around at what must have been a view she knew by heart, and her narrowed eyes rested briefly on the unfamiliar Land Rover.

Strike had scrambled into the front seat as best he could, keeping his head low. Robin put her foot down and drove away at once.

"She didn't give me a second look when I was following her," Strike pointed out, hoisting himself into a sitting position.

"You still shouldn't let her see you if you can help it," said Robin sententiously, "in case she noticed you and it reminds her."

"Sorry, forgot you're Highly Commended," said Strike.

"Oh sod off," said Robin with a flash of temper. Strike was surprised.

"I was joking."

Robin turned into a parking space further up the street, out of sight of the Crow's Nest entrance, then checked her handbag for a small package she had bought earlier in the afternoon.

"You wait here."

"The hell I will. I'll be in the car park, keeping an eye out for Brockbank. Give me the keys."

She handed them over with ill grace and left. Strike watched her walking towards the pub, wondering about that sudden spurt of temper. Perhaps, he thought, Matthew belittled what he probably saw as meager achievements.

The Crow's Nest stood where Ferry and Stanley Roads met and formed a hairpin bend: a large, drum-shaped building of red brick. Holly was still standing in the doorway, smoking and drinking her pint. Nerves fluttered in the pit of Robin's stomach. She had volunteered for this: now hers was the sole responsibility for finding out where Brockbank was. Her stupidity at bringing the police down on them earlier had made her touchy, and Strike's ill-timed humor had reminded her of Matthew's subtly belittling comments about her countersurveillance training. After formal congratulations on her top marks Matthew had implied that what she had learned was, after all, no more than common sense.

Robin's mobile rang in her coat pocket. Aware of Holly's eyes on her as she approached, Robin pulled out the phone to check the caller's name. It was her mother. On the basis that it would look slightly more unusual to switch off the call than to take it, she raised it to her ear.

"Robin?" came Linda's voice as Robin passed Holly in the doorway without looking at her. "Are you in Barrow-in-Furness?"

"Yes," said Robin. Confronted by two inner doors, she chose the one on the left, which brought her into a large, high-ceilinged and dingy bar room. Two men in the now-familiar blue overalls were playing pool at a table just inside the door. Robin sensed, rather than saw, the turning of several heads towards the stranger. Avoiding all eye contact, she drifted towards the bar as she continued her call.

"What are you doing there?" asked Linda and, without waiting for a response, "We've had the police on the phone, checking whether Dad lent you the car!"

"It was all a misunderstanding," said Robin. "Mum, I can't really talk now."

The door opened behind her and Holly walked past, thickly tattooed arms folded, giving Robin a sideways look of appraisal and, she sensed, animosity. Apart from the short-haired barmaid, they were the only two females in the place.

"We called the flat," her mother went on, unheeding, "and Matthew said you'd gone away with Cormoran."

"Yes," said Robin.

"And when I asked whether you'd have time to drop round for lunch this weekend—"

"Why would I be in Masham this weekend?" Robin asked, confused. Out of the corner of her eye she saw Holly taking a bar stool and chatting to several more blue-overalled men from the BAE factory.

"It's Matthew's dad's birthday," said her mother.

"Oh, of course it is," said Robin. She had completely forgotten. There was to be a party. It had been on the calendar so long that she had got used to the sight of it and forgotten that the trip back to Masham was actually going to happen.

"Robin, is everything all right?"

"Like I said, Mum, I can't really talk right now," said Robin.

"Are you all right?"

"Yes!" said Robin impatiently. "I'm absolutely fine. I'll ring you later."

She hung up and turned to the bar. The barmaid, who was waiting to take her order, wore the same look of shrewd appraisal as the watching neighbor in Stanley Road. There was an extra layer to their caginess around here, but Robin understood, now, that theirs was not the chauvinistic antagonism of the local for the stranger. Rather, it was the protectiveness of a people whose business was confidential. With her heart beating slightly faster than usual, Robin said with an air of forced confidence:

"Hi, I don't know whether you can help me. I'm looking for Holly Brockbank. I was told she might be in here."

The barmaid considered Robin's request, then said, unsmiling:

"Tha's 'er, down the bar. Can A get th'somethin'?"

"Glass of white wine, please," said Robin.

The woman whom she was impersonating would drink wine, Robin knew. She would also be unfazed by the edge of mistrust she saw in the barmaid's eyes, by Holly's reflexive antagonism, by the up-and-down stares of the pool players. The woman whom she was pretending to be was cool, clearheaded and ambitious.

Robin paid for her drink then headed directly for Holly and the three men chatting to her at the bar. Curious but cagey, they fell silent when it became clear that they were Robin's destination.

"Hello," said Robin, smiling. "Are you Holly Brockbank?"

"Yeah," said Holly, her expression grim. "Whee're thoo?"

"Sorry?"

Aware of several pairs of amused eyes on her, Robin kept her smile in place by sheer force of will.

"Who—are—yew?" asked Holly, in a mock London accent.

"My name's Venetia Hall."

"Ooh, unlucky," said Holly with a broad grin at the closest workman, who sniggered.

Robin pulled a business card out of her handbag, freshly printed that afternoon on a machine in a shopping center, while Strike remained behind, keeping an eye on Holly in the bakery. It had been Strike's suggestion that she use her middle name. ("Makes you sound like a poncy southerner.")

Robin handed over the business card, looked boldly into Holly's heavily kohled eyes and repeated: "Venetia Hall. I'm a lawyer."

Holly's grin evaporated. Scowling, she read the card, one of two hundred Robin had had printed for £4.50.

"I'm looking for your brother Noel," said Robin. "We—"

"'Ow did thoo know A was 'ere?"

In her mistrust she seemed to be swelling, bristling like a cat.

"A neighbor said you might be."

Holly's blue-overalled companions smirked.

"We might have some good news for your brother," Robin plowed on bravely. "We're trying to find him."

"A dunno where 'e is and A don' care."

Two of the workmen slid away from the bar towards a table, leaving only one behind, who smiled faintly as he observed Robin's discomfiture. Holly drained her pint, slid a fiver sideways at the remaining man and told him to get her another, clambered off her bar stool and strode away towards the Ladies, her arms held stiffly like a man's.

"'Er boyo an' 'er don' speak," said the barmaid, who had drifted up the bar to eavesdrop. She seemed to feel vaguely sorry for Robin.

"I don't suppose *you* know where Noel is?" Robin asked, feeling desperate.

"'E's not been in 'ere for a year or more," said the barmaid vaguely. "You know where 'e is, Kev?"

Holly's friend answered only with a shrug and ordered Holly's pint. His accent revealed him to be Glaswegian.

"Well, it's a pity," said Robin, and her clear, cool voice did not betray the frantic pounding of her heart. She dreaded going back to Strike with nothing. "There could be a big payout for the family, if only I can find him."

She turned to go.

"For the family, or for him?" asked the Glaswegian sharply.

"It depends," said Robin coolly, turning back. She did not imagine that Venetia Hall would be particularly chummy with people unconnected to the case she was building. "If family members have had to take on a carer role—but I'd need details to judge. Some relatives," lied Robin, "have had very significant compensation."

Holly was coming back. Her expression turned thunderous when she saw Robin talking to Kevin. Robin walked off to the Ladies herself, her heart pounding in her chest, wondering whether the lie she had just told would bear fruit. By the look on Holly's face as they passed each other, Robin thought there was an outside chance that she might be cornered by the sinks and beaten up.

However, when she came out of the bathroom she saw Holly and Kevin nose to nose at the bar. Robin knew not to push any harder: either Holly bit, or she did not. She tied her coat belt more tightly and walked, unhurriedly but purposefully, back past them towards the door.

"Oi!"

"Yes?" Robin said, still a little coolly, because Holly had been rude and Venetia Hall was used to a certain level of respect.

"Orlrigh', wha's it all abou'?"

Though Kevin seemed keen to participate in their conversation, his relationship with Holly was apparently not far enough advanced to permit listening in on private financial matters. He drifted away to a fruit machine looking disgruntled.

"We can yatter over 'ere," Holly told Robin, taking her fresh pint and pointing Robin to a corner table beside a piano.

The pub's windowsill bore ships in bottles: pretty, fragile things compared to the huge, sleek monsters that were being constructed beyond the windows, behind that high perimeter wall. The heavily patterned carpet would conceal a thousand stains; the plants behind the curtains looked droopy and sad, yet the mismatched ornaments and sporting trophies gave a homey feel to the large room, the bright blue overalls of its customers an impression of brotherhood.

"Hardacre and Hall is representing a large group of servicemen who suffered serious and preventable injury outside the field of combat," said Robin, sliding into her pre-rehearsed spiel. "While we were reviewing records we came across your brother's case. We can't be sure until we talk to him, of course, but he'd be very welcome to add his name to our pool of litigants. His would be very much the type of case we're expecting to win. If he joins us, it'll add to the pressure on the army to pay. The more complainants we can get, the better. It would be at no cost to Mr. Brockbank, of course. No win," she said, mimicking the TV adverts, "no fee."

Holly said nothing. Her pale face was hard and set. There were cheap rings of yellow gold on every digit except her wedding-ring finger.

"Kevin said summa' abou' the family gettin' money."

"Oh yes," said Robin blithely. "If Noel's injuries have impacted you, as a family—"

"Ower righ' they 'ave," snarled Holly.

"How?" asked Robin, taking a notebook out of her shoulder bag and waiting, pencil poised.

She could tell that alcohol and a sense of grievance were going to be her greatest allies in extracting maximum information from Holly, who was now warming to the idea of telling the story she thought the lawyer wanted to hear.

The first thing to be done was to soften that first impression of animosity towards her injured brother. Carefully she took Robin over Noel joining the army at sixteen. He had given it everything: it had been his life. Oh yeah, people didn't realize the sacrifices soldiers made…did Robin know Noel was her twin? Yeah, born on Christmas Day…Noel and Holly…

To tell this bowdlerized story of her brother was to elevate herself. The man with whom she had shared a womb had sallied forth into the world, traveled and fought and been promoted through the ranks of the British Army. His bravery and sense of adventure reflected back on her, left behind in Barrow.

"…'n 'e married a woman called Irene. Widow. Took 'er on with two kids. Jesus. No good turn goes unpunished, don't they say?"

"What do you mean?" asked Venetia Hall politely, clasping half an inch of warm vinegary wine.

"Married 'er, 'ad a son with 'er. Lovely little boy…Ryan… Lovely. We've not seen him for…six years, is it? Seven years? Bitch. Yeah, Irene jus' fucked off when 'e was at the doctor's one day. Took the kids—and his son was everything to Noel, mind. Everything—so much for in sickness and in fuckin' health, eh? Some fuckin' wife. When 'e needed support most. Bitch."

So Noel and Brittany had long since parted company. Or had he made it his business to track down the stepdaughter whom he surely blamed as much as Strike for his life-changing injuries? Robin maintained an impassive expression, although her heart was racing. She wished she could text Strike right there and then.

After his wife had left, Noel had turned up uninvited at the old family home, the tiny two up, two down on Stanley Road in which Holly had lived all her life and which she had occupied alone since her stepfather had died.

"A took 'im in," said Holly, straightening her back. "Family's family."

There was no mention of Brittany's allegation. Holly was playing the concerned relative, the devoted sister, and if it was a ham performance Robin was experienced enough, now, to know that there were usually nuggets of truth to be sifted from even the most obvious dross.

She wondered whether Holly knew about the accusation of child abuse: it had happened in Germany, after all, and no charges had been brought. Yet if Brockbank had been truly brain damaged on his discharge, would he have been canny enough to remain silent about the reason for his ignominious exit from the army? If he had been innocent and not of sound mind, wouldn't he have talked, perhaps endlessly, of the injustice that had brought him to such a low ebb?

Robin bought Holly a third pint and turned her deftly to the subject of what Noel had been like after he had been invalided out.

"'E wasn' 'imself. Fits. Seizures. 'E was on a load o' medication. I jus' go'rover nursin' my stepfather—'e 'ad a stroke—an' then A gets Noel comin' 'ome, with 'is convulsions and..."

Holly buried the end of her sentence in her pint.

"That's tough," said Robin, who was now writing in a small notebook. "Any behavioral difficulties? Families often mention those kinds of challenges as the worst."

"Yeah," said Holly. "Well. 'Is temper wasn' improved by gettin' 'is brain knocked outta his skull for 'im. 'E smashed up the 'ouse for us twice. 'E was orlwuz ragin' at us.

"'E's famous now, tha knows," said Holly darkly.

"Sorry?" said Robin, thrown.

"The gadgee that beat 'im up!"

"The gadg—"

"Cameron fuckin' Strike!"

"Ah, yes," said Robin. "I think I've heard of him."

"Oh yeah! Fuckin' private detective now, in orl the papers! Fuckin' military policeman when 'e beat the shit outta Noel... fuckin' damaged him for fuckin' life..."

The rant went on for some time. Robin made notes, waiting for Holly to tell her why the military police had come for her brother, but she either did not know or was determined not to say. All that was certain was that Noel Brockbank had attributed his epilepsy entirely to the actions of Strike.

After what sounded like a year of purgatory, during which Noel had treated both his twin sister and her house as convenient outlets for his misery and his temper, he left for a bouncer's job in Manchester obtained for him by an old Barrovian friend.

"He was well enough to work, then?" asked Robin, because the picture Holly had painted was of a man totally out of control, barely able to contain explosions of temper.

"Yeah, well, 'e was orlrigh' by then as long as 'e didn't drink and took his meds. A were glad to see the back of 'im. Took it outta me, 'avin' 'im 'ere," said Holly, suddenly remembering that there was a payout promised to those whose lives had been badly affected by their relative's injuries. "I 'ad panic attacks. Wen' to my GP. It's in my records."

The full impact of Brockbank's bad behavior on Holly's life filled the next ten minutes, Robin nodding seriously and sympathetically and interjecting encouraging phrases such as "Yes, I've heard that from other relatives," and "Oh yes, that would be very valuable in a submission." Robin offered the now-tractable Holly a fourth pint.

"A'll ge' you one," said Holly, with a vague show of getting to her feet.

"No, no, this is all on expenses," said Robin. As she waited for the fresh pint of McEwan's to be poured, she checked her mobile. There was another text from Matthew, which she did not open, and one from Strike, which she did.

All OK?

Yes, she texted back.

"So your brother's in Manchester?" she asked Holly on her return to the table.

"No," said Holly, after taking a large swig of McEwan's. " 'E was sacked."

"Oh, really?" said Robin, pencil poised. "If it was as a result of his medical condition, you know, we can help with an unfair dismissal—"

"It weren't coz of tha'," said Holly.

A strange expression crossed the tight, sullen face: a flash of silver between storm clouds, of something powerful trying to break through.

" 'E come back 'ere," said Holly, "an' it all started again—"

More stories of violence, irrational rages, broken furniture, at the end of which Brockbank had secured another job, vaguely described as "security," and taken off for Market Harborough.

"An' then he come back again," said Holly, and Robin's pulse quickened.

"So he's here in Barrow?" she asked.

"No," said Holly. She was drunk now and finding it harder to retain a hold on the line she was supposed to be peddling. "'E jus' come back for a coupla weeks but this time A told him A'd 'ave the police on 'im if 'e come back again an' 'e lef' f'r good. Need a slash," said Holly, "an' a fag. D'you smoke?"

Robin shook her head. Holly got a little unsteadily to her feet and proceeded to the Ladies, leaving Robin to pull her mobile out of her pocket and text Strike.

Says he's not in Barrow, not with family. She's drunk. Still working on her. She's about to go outside for a cig, lie low.

She regretted the last two words as soon as she had pressed "send," in case they elicited another sarcastic reference to her countersurveillance course, but her phone buzzed almost immediately and she saw two words:

Will do.

When Holly finally returned to the table, smelling strongly of Rothmans, she was carrying a white wine, which she slid across to Robin, and her fifth pint.

"Thanks very much," said Robin.

"See," said Holly plaintively, as though there had been no break in the conversation, "it was havin' a real impact on me 'ealth, 'aving 'im 'ere."

"I'm sure," said Robin. "So does Mr. Brockbank live—?"

"'E was violent. A told you abou' the time he shoved me head into the fridge door."

"You did, yes," said Robin patiently.

"An' 'e blacked me eye when A tried to stop him smashing up me mam's plates—"

"Awful. You'd certainly be in line for some kind of payout," lied

Robin and, ignoring a tiny qualm of guilt, she plunged straight towards the central question. "We assumed Mr. Brockbank was here in Barrow because this is where his pension's being paid."

Holly's reactions were slower after four and a half pints. The promise of compensation for her suffering had given her a glow: even the deep line that life had graven between her eyebrows, and which gave her a look of permanent fury, seemed to have diminished. However, the mention of Brockbank's pension turned her muzzily defensive.

"No, it's not," said Holly.

"According to our records, it is," said Robin.

The fruit machine played a synthetic jingle and flashed in the corner; the pool balls clicked and thudded off the baize; Barrovian accents mingled with Scots. Robin's flash of intuition came to her like certain knowledge. Holly was helping herself to the military pension.

"Of course," said Robin, with a convincing lightness, "we know Mr. Brockbank might not be picking it up for himself. Relatives are sometimes authorized to collect money when the pensioner is incapacitated."

"Yeah," said Holly at once. A blush was creeping blotchily up her pale face. It made her look girlish, notwithstanding the tattoos and multiple piercings. "A collected it for 'im when 'e was first out. When 'e was 'avin' fits."

Why, thought Robin, *if he was so incapacitated, did he transfer the pension to Manchester, and then to Market Harborough, and then back to Barrow again?*

"So are you sending it on to him now?" asked Robin, her heart beating fast again. "Or can he pick it up for himself now?"

"Lissen," said Holly.

There was a Hell's Angels tattoo on her upper arm, a wing-helmeted skull that rippled as she leaned in towards Robin. Beer, cigarettes and sugar had turned her breath rancid. Robin did not flinch.

"Lissen," she said again, "you get people payouts, like, if they've been... if they've been hurt, like, or... wharrever."

"That's right," said Robin.

"Wharriff someone'd been...wharriff social services shoulda... shoulda done somethin' an' they never?"

"It would depend on the circumstances," said Robin.

"Our mam lef' when we was nine," said Holly. "Lef' us with oor stepfather."

"I'm sorry," said Robin. "That's tough."

"Nineteen-seventies," said Holly. "Nobody gave a shit. Child abuse."

A lead weight dropped inside Robin. Holly's bad breath was in her face, her mottled face close. She had no idea that the sympathetic lawyer who had approached her with the promise of sacks of free cash was only a mirage.

" 'E done it to both of us," said Holly. "Me step. Noel gorrit an' all. From when we wuz tiny. We useter hide under ower beds together. An' then Noel did it to me. Mind," she said, suddenly earnest, " 'e could be orlright, Noel. We wuz close and tha' when we wuz little. Anyway," her tone revealed a sense of double betrayal, "when 'e wor sixteen, he lef' us to join the army."

Robin, who had not meant to drink any more, picked up her wine and took a large slug. Holly's second abuser had also been her ally against her first: the lesser of two evils.

"Bastard, he wor," she said, and Robin could tell she meant the stepfather, not the twin who had abused her then disappeared abroad. "He had an accident at work when A was sixteen, though, an' after tha' A could manage 'im better. Industrial chemicals. Fucker. Couldn't get it up after that. On so many painkillers an' shit. An' then 'e 'ad his stroke."

The look of determined malice on Holly's face told Robin exactly what kind of care the stepfather might have received at her hands.

"Fucker," she said quietly.

"Have you received counseling at all?" Robin heard herself ask.

I do *sound like a poncy southerner.*

Holly snorted.

"Fuck, no. You're the firs' person A've ever told. S'pose you've heard a lot of stories like this?"

"Oh, yes," said Robin. She owed Holly that.

"A told Noel, last time 'e come back," said Holly, five pints to the bad now and slurring her words badly, "fuck off an' stay away from us. You leave or A'm going to the p'lice about what you did to us before, an' see what they think o' that, after all these little girls keep sayin' you've fiddled with 'em."

The phrase turned the warm wine rancid in Robin's mouth.

"Tha's 'ow he lost the job in Manchester. Groped a thirteen-year-ould. Prob'bly the same in Market 'Arborough. 'E wouldn' tell me why 'e was back, but A know 'e'll've done summat like that again. 'E learned from the best," said Holly. "So, could A sue?"

"I think," said Robin, fearful of giving advice that would cause further damage to the wounded woman beside her, "that the police would probably be your best bet. Where *is* your brother?" she asked, desperate, now, to extract the information she wanted and leave.

"Dunno," said Holly. "When A told 'im A'd go to the p'lice 'e wen' beserk, bu' then…"

She mumbled something indistinct, something in which the word "pension" was just audible.

He told her she could keep the pension if she didn't go to the police.

So there she sat, drinking herself into an early grave with the money her brother had given her not to reveal his abuse. Holly knew he was almost certainly still "fiddling" with other young girls…had she ever known about Brittany's accusation? Did she care? Or had the scar tissue grown so thick over her own wounds that it rendered her impervious to other little girls' agony? She was still living in the house where it had all happened, with the front windows facing out on barbed wire and bricks…why hadn't she run, Robin wondered. Why hadn't she escaped, like Noel? Why stay in the house facing the high, blank wall?

"You haven't got a number for him, or anything like that?" Robin asked.

"No," said Holly.

"There could be big money in this if you can find me any kind of contact," said Robin desperately, throwing finesse to the wind.

" 'S'old place," Holly slurred, after a few minutes' muddled thought and fruitless staring at her phone, " 'n Market 'Arborough…"

It took a long time to locate the telephone number of Noel's last place of work, but at last they found it. Robin made a note, then dug ten pounds out of her own purse and thrust it into Holly's willing hand.

"You've been very helpful. Very helpful indeed."

"It's jus' gadgees, isn't i'? All th'same."

"Yes," said Robin, without a clue what she was agreeing to. "I'll be in touch. I've got your address."

She stood up.

"Yeah. See thoo. Jus' gadgees. All th'same."

"She means men," said the barmaid, who had come over to collect some of Holly's many empty glasses, and was smiling at Robin's clear bewilderment. "A gadgee is a man. She's saying men are all the same."

"Oh yes," said Robin, barely aware of what she was saying. "So true. Thanks very much. Good-bye, Holly…take care of yourself…"

26

Desolate landscape,
Storybook bliss...

Blue Öyster Cult, "Death Valley Nights"

"Psychology's loss," said Strike, "is private detection's gain. That was bloody good going, Robin."

He raised his can of McEwan's and toasted her. They were sitting in the parked Land Rover, eating fish and chips a short distance away from the Olympic Takeaway. Its bright windows intensified the surrounding darkness. Silhouettes passed regularly across the rectangles of light, metamorphosed into three-dimensional humans as they entered the bustling chip shop, and turned back into shadows as they left.

"So his wife left him."

"Yep."

"And Holly says he hasn't seen the kids since?"

"Right."

Strike sipped his McEwan's, thinking. He wanted to believe that Brockbank really had lost contact with Brittany, but what if the evil bastard had somehow tracked her down?

"We still don't know where he is, though," Robin sighed.

"Well, we know he isn't here and that he hasn't been here for around a year," said Strike. "We know he still blames me for what's wrong with him, that he's still abusing little girls and that he's a fuck sight saner than they thought he was in the hospital."

"Why d'you say that?"

"Sounds like he's kept the accusation of child abuse quiet. He's holding down jobs when he could be sitting at home claiming disability benefit. I suppose working gives him more opportunities to meet young girls."

"Don't," murmured Robin as the memory of Holly's confession suddenly gave way to that of the frozen head, looking so young, so plump, so dimly surprised.

"That's Brockbank and Laing both at large in the UK, both hating my guts."

Chomping chips, Strike rummaged in the glove compartment, extracted the road atlas and for a while was quiet, turning pages. Robin folded the remainder of her fish and chips in its newspaper wrappings and said:

"I've got to ring my mother. Back in a bit."

Leaning against a streetlamp a short distance away she called her parents' number.

"Are you all right, Robin?"

"Yes, Mum."

"What's going on between you and Matthew?"

Robin looked up at the faintly starry sky.

"I think we've split up."

"You *think?*" said Linda. She sounded neither shocked nor sad, merely interested in the full facts.

Robin had been worried that she might cry when she had to say it aloud, yet no tears stung her eyes, nor did she need to force herself to speak calmly. Perhaps she was toughening up. The desperate life story of Holly Brockbank and the gruesome end of the unknown girl in Shepherd's Bush certainly gave a person perspective.

"It only happened on Monday night."

"Was this because of Cormoran?"

"No," said Robin. "Sarah Shadlock. It turns out Matt was sleeping with her while I was...at home. When—you know when. After I dropped out."

Two young men meandered out of the Olympic, definitely the

worse for drink, shouting and swearing at each other. One of them spotted Robin and nudged the other. They veered towards her.

"Thoo orlrigh', darlin'?"

Strike got out of the car and slammed the door, looming darkly, a head taller than both of them. The youths swayed away in sudden silence. Strike lit a cigarette leaning up against the car, his face in shadow.

"Mum, are you still there?"

"He told you this on Monday night?" asked Linda.

"Yes," said Robin.

"Why?"

"We were rowing about Cormoran again," Robin muttered, aware of Strike yards away. "I said, 'It's a platonic relationship, like you and Sarah'—and then I saw his face—and then he admitted it."

Her mother gave a long, deep sigh. Robin waited for words of comfort or wisdom.

"Dear God," said Linda. There was another long silence. "How are you really, Robin?"

"I'm all right, Mum, honestly. I'm working. It's helping."

"Why are you in Barrow, of all places?"

"We're trying to trace one of the men Strike thinks might've sent him the leg."

"Where are you staying?"

"We're going to go to the Travelodge," said Robin. "In separate rooms, obviously," she hastened to add.

"Have you spoken to Matthew since you left?"

"He keeps sending me texts telling me he loves me."

As she said it, she realized that she had not read his last. She had only just remembered it.

"I'm sorry," Robin told her mother. "The dress and the reception and everything...I'm so sorry, Mum."

"They're the last things I'm worried about," said Linda and she asked yet again: "Are you all right, Robin?"

"Yes, I promise I am." She hesitated, then said, almost defiantly, "Cormoran's been great."

"You're going to have to talk to Matthew, though," said Linda. "After all this time...you can't not talk to him."

Robin's composure broke; her voice trembled with rage and her hands shook as the words poured out of her.

"We were at the rugby with them just two weekends ago, with Sarah and Tom. She's been hanging around ever since they were at uni—they were sleeping together while I was—while I—he's never cut her out of his life, she's always hugging him, flirting with him, shit-stirring between him and me—at the rugby it was Strike, *oh, he's so attractive, just the two of you in the office, is it?*—and all this time I've thought it just went one way, I *knew* she'd tried to get him into bed at uni but I never—eighteen months, they were sleeping together—and you know what he said to me? She was *comforting* him...I had to give in and say she could come to the wedding because I'd asked Strike without telling Matt, that was my punishment, because I didn't want her there. Matt has lunch with her whenever he's near her offices—"

"I'm going to come down to London and see you," said Linda.

"No, Mum—"

"For a day. Take you out for lunch."

Robin gave a weak laugh.

"Mum, I don't take a lunch hour. It isn't that kind of job."

"I'm coming to London, Robin."

When her mother's voice became firm like that, there was no point arguing.

"I don't know when I'll be back."

"Well, you can let me know and I'll book the train."

"I...oh, OK," said Robin.

When they had bidden each other good-bye she realized that she had tears in her eyes at last. Much as she might pretend otherwise, the thought of seeing Linda brought much comfort.

She looked over at the Land Rover. Strike was still leaning up against it, and he too was on the phone. Or was he merely pretending? She had been talking loudly. He could be tactful when he chose.

She looked down at the mobile in her hands and opened Matthew's message.

Your mother called. I told her you're away with work. Let me know whether you want me to tell Dad you're not going to his birthday thing. I love you, Robin. Mxxxxxx

There he went again: he did not really believe that the relationship was at an end. **Let me know whether you want me to tell Dad...** as though it were a storm in a teacup, as though she would never take it so far as not to attend his father's party... *I don't even like your bloody father...*

Angry, she typed and sent the response.

Of course I'm not coming.

She got back into the car. Strike seemed to be genuinely talking on the phone. The road atlas lay open on the passenger seat: he had been looking at the Leicestershire town of Market Harborough.

"Yeah, you too," she heard Strike say. "Yeah. See you when I get back."

Elin, she thought.

He climbed back into the car.

"Was that Wardle?" she asked innocently.

"Elin," he said.

Does she know you've gone away with me? Just the two of us?

Robin felt herself turn red. She did not know where that thought had come from. It wasn't as though...

"You want to go to Market Harborough?" she asked, holding up the map.

"Might as well," said Strike, taking another swig of beer. "It's the last place Brockbank worked. Could get a lead; we'd be stupid not to check it out...and if we're going through there..."

He lifted the book out of her hands and flicked over a few pages.

"It's only twelve miles from Corby. We could swing by and see whether the Laing who was shacked up with a woman there in 2008 is our Laing. She's still living there: Lorraine MacNaughton's the name."

Robin was used to Strike's prodigious memory for names and details.

"OK," she said, pleased to think that the morning would bring more investigation, not simply a long drive back to London. Perhaps, if they found something interesting, there would be a second night on the road and she need not see Matthew for another twelve hours—but then she remembered that Matthew would be heading north the following night, for his father's birthday. She would have the flat to herself in any case.

"Could he have tracked her down?" Strike wondered aloud, after a silence.

"Sorry—what? Who?"

"Could Brockbank have tracked Brittany down and killed her after all this time? Or am I barking up the wrong tree because I feel so fucking guilty?"

He gave the door of the Land Rover a soft thump with his fist.

"The leg, though," said Strike, arguing against himself. "It's scarred just like hers was. That was a thing between them: 'I tried to saw off your leg when you were little and your mum walked in.' Fucking evil bastard. Who else would send me a scarred leg?"

"Well," said Robin slowly, "I can think of a reason a leg was chosen, and it might not have anything at all to do with Brittany Brockbank."

Strike turned to look at her.

"Go on."

"Whoever killed that girl could have sent you any part of her and achieved the same result," said Robin. "An arm, or—or a breast"—she did her best to keep her tone matter-of-fact—"would have meant the police and the press swarming all over us just the same. The business would still have been compromised and we'd have been just as shaken up—but he chose to send a right leg, cut exactly where your right leg was amputated."

"I suppose it ties in with that effing song. Although—" Strike reconsidered. "No, I'm talking crap, aren't I? An arm would've worked just as well for that. Or a neck."

"He's making clear reference to your injury," Robin said. "What does your missing leg mean to him?"

"Christ knows," said Strike, watching her profile as she talked.

"Heroism," said Robin.

Strike snorted.

"There's nothing heroic about being in the wrong place at the wrong time."

"You're a decorated veteran."

"I wasn't decorated for being blown up. That happened before."

"You've never told me that."

She turned to face him, but he refused to be sidetracked.

"Go on. Why the leg?"

"Your injury's a legacy of war. It represents bravery, adversity overcome. Your amputation's mentioned every single time they talk about you in the press. I think—for him—it's tied up with fame and achievement and—and honor. He's trying to denigrate your injury, to tie it to something horrible, divert the public's perception away from you as hero towards you as a man in receipt of part of a dismembered girl. He wants to cause you trouble, yes, but he wants to diminish you in the process. He's somebody who wants what you've got, who wants recognition and importance."

Strike bent down and took a second can of McEwan's out of the brown bag at his feet. The crack of the ring pull reverberated in the cold air.

"If you're right," said Strike, watching his cigarette smoke curl away into the darkness, "if what's riling this maniac is that I got famous, Whittaker goes to the top of the list. That was all he ever wanted: to be a celebrity."

Robin waited. He had told her virtually nothing about his stepfather, although the internet had supplied her with many of the details that Strike had withheld.

"He was the most parasitic fucker I've ever met," said Strike. "It'd be like him to try and siphon off a bit of fame from someone else."

She could feel him becoming angry again beside her in the small space. He reacted consistently at every mention of each of the three suspects: Brockbank made him guilty, Whittaker angry. Laing was the only one he discussed with anything like objectivity.

"Hasn't Shanker come up with anything yet?"

"Says he's in Catford. Shanker'll track him down. Whittaker'll be there, somewhere, in some filthy corner. He's definitely in London."

"Why are you so sure?"

"Just London, isn't it?" said Strike, staring across the car park at the terraced houses. "He came from Yorkshire originally, Whittaker, you know, but he's pure cockney now."

"You haven't seen him for ages, have you?"

"I don't need to. I know him. He's part of the junk that washes up in the capital looking for the big time and never leaves. He thought London was the only place that deserved him. Had to be the biggest stage for Whittaker."

Yet Whittaker had never managed to claw his way out of the dirty places of the capital where criminality, poverty and violence bred like bacteria, the underbelly where Shanker still dwelled. Nobody who had not lived there would ever understand that London was a country unto itself. They might resent it for the fact that it held more power and money than any other British city, but they could not understand that poverty carried its own flavor there, where everything cost more, where the relentless distinctions between those who had succeeded and those who had not were constantly, painfully visible. The distance between Elin's vanilla-columned flat in Clarence Terrace and the filthy Whitechapel squat where his mother had died could not be measured in mere miles. They were separated by infinite disparities, by the lotteries of birth and chance, by faults of judgment and lucky breaks. His mother and Elin, both beautiful women, both intelligent, one sucked down into a morass of drugs and human filth, the other sitting high over Regent's Park behind spotless glass.

Robin, too, was thinking about London. It had Matthew in its spell, but he had no interest in the labyrinthine worlds she probed daily during her detective work. He looked excitedly towards the surface glitter: the best restaurants, the best areas to live, as though London were a huge Monopoly board. He had always had a divided allegiance to Yorkshire, to their hometown Masham. His father was Yorkshire-born, while his late mother had come from Surrey and had carried with her an air of having gone north on sufferance. She had persistently corrected any Yorkshire turns of speech in Matthew and his sister Kimberley. His carefully neutral accent had been one of the reasons that Robin's brothers had not been impressed when they had started dating: in spite of her protestations, in spite of his Yorkshire name, they had sensed the wannabe southerner.

"It'd be a strange place to come from, this, wouldn't it?" said Strike, still looking out over the terraces. "It's like an island. I've never heard that accent before either."

A man's voice sounded somewhere nearby, singing a rousing song. Robin thought at first that the tune was a hymn. Then the man's unique voice was joined by more voices and the breeze changed direction so that they heard a few lines quite distinctly:

> "Friends to share in games and laughter
> Songs at dusk and books at noon..."

"School song," said Robin, smiling. She could see them now, a group of middle-aged men in black suits, singing loudly as they walked up Buccleuch Street.

"Funeral," guessed Strike. "Old schoolmate. Look at them."

As the black-suited men drew level with the car, one of them spotted Robin looking.

"Barrow Boys' Grammar School!" he shouted at her, fist raised as though he had just scored a goal. The men cheered, but there was melancholy to their drink-fueled swagger. They began singing the song again as they passed out of sight.

> "Harbor lights and clustered shipping
> Clouds above the wheeling gulls..."

"Hometowns," said Strike.

He was thinking about men like his Uncle Ted, a Cornishman to his bones, who lived and would die in St. Mawes, part of the fabric of the place, remembered as long as there were locals, beaming out of fading photographs of the Life Boat on pub walls. When Ted died—and Strike hoped it would be twenty, thirty years hence—they would mourn him as the unknown Barrovian Grammar boy was being mourned: with drink, with tears, but in celebration that he had been given to them. What had dark, hulking Brockbank, child rapist, and fox-haired Laing, wife-torturer, left behind in the towns of their birth? Shudders of relief that they had gone, fear that they had returned, a trail of broken people and bad memories.

"Shall we go?" Robin asked quietly and Strike nodded, dropping the burning stub of his cigarette into his last inch of McEwan's, where it emitted a small, satisfying hiss.

27

A dreadful knowledge comes...

Blue Öyster Cult, "In the Presence of Another World"

They were given rooms five doors apart in the Travelodge. Robin had dreaded the man behind the desk offering a double room, but Strike had headed that off with a peremptory "two singles" before he had time to open his mouth.

Ridiculous, really, to feel suddenly self-conscious, because they had been physically closer all day in the Land Rover than they were in the lift. It felt odd saying goodnight to Strike when she reached the door of her room; not that he lingered. He merely said " 'night" and walked on to his own room, but he waited outside his door until she managed to work the key card and let herself inside with a flustered wave.

Why had she had waved? Ridiculous.

She dropped her holdall on the bed and moved to the window, which offered only a bleak view of the same industrial warehouses they had passed on their way into town a few hours earlier. It felt as though they had been away from London for much longer than they had.

The heating was turned up too high. Robin forced open a stiff window, and the cool night air surged inside, eager to invade the stuffy square box of a room. After putting her phone on to charge, she undressed, pulled on a nightshirt, brushed her teeth and slid down between the cool sheets.

She still felt strangely unsettled, knowing that she was sleeping five rooms away from Strike. That was Matthew's fault, of course. *If you sleep with him, we're over for good.*

Her unruly imagination suddenly presented her with the sound of a knock on the door, Strike inviting himself in on some slim pretext...

Don't be ridiculous.

She rolled over, pressing her flushed face into the pillow. What was she thinking? Damn Matthew, putting things in her head, judging her by himself...

Strike, meanwhile, had not yet made it into bed. He was stiff all over from the long hours of immobility in the car. It felt good to get the prosthesis off. Even though the shower was not particularly handy for a man with one leg, he used it, carefully holding on to the bar inside the door, trying to relax his sore knee with hot water. Towel-dried, he navigated his way carefully back to the bed, put his mobile on to charge and climbed, naked, beneath the covers.

Lying with his hands behind his head he stared up at the dark ceiling and thought about Robin, lying five rooms away. He wondered whether Matthew had texted again, whether they were on the phone together, whether she was capitalizing on her privacy to cry for the first time all day.

The sounds of what was probably a stag party reached him through the floor: loud male laughter, shouting, whoops, slamming doors. Somebody put on music and the bass pounded through his room. It reminded him of the nights he had slept in his office, when the music playing in the 12 Bar Café below had vibrated through the metal legs of his camp bed. He hoped the noise was not as loud in Robin's room. She needed her rest—she had to drive another two hundred and fifty miles tomorrow. Yawning, Strike rolled over and, in spite of the thudding music and yells, fell almost immediately asleep.

They met by agreement in the dining room next morning, where Strike blocked Robin from view as she surreptitiously refilled their flask from the urn at the buffet and both loaded their plates with toast. Strike resisted the full English and rewarded himself for his restraint by sliding several Danish pastries into his backpack. At eight o'clock they were back in the Land Rover, driving through the glorious Cumbrian countryside, a rolling panorama of heather moors and peat lands under a hazy blue sky, and joining the M6 South.

"Sorry I can't share the driving," said Strike, who was sipping coffee. "That clutch would kill me. It'd kill both of us."

"I don't care," said Robin. "I love driving, you know that."

They sped on in companionable silence. Robin was the only person whom Strike could stand to be driven by, notwithstanding the fact that he had an ingrained prejudice against women drivers. This was something that he generally kept quiet, but which had its roots in many a negative passenger experience, from his Cornish aunt's nervous ineptitude, to his sister Lucy's distractibility, to Charlotte's reckless courting of danger. An ex-girlfriend from the SIB, Tracey, had been competent behind the wheel and yet had become so paralyzed with fear on a high, narrow alpine road that she had stopped, on the verge of hyperventilating, refusing to cede the wheel to him but unable to drive further.

"Matthew like the Land Rover?" Strike asked as they trundled over a flyover.

"No," said Robin. "He wants an A3 Cabriolet."

"Course he does," said Strike under his breath, inaudible in the rattling car. "Wanker."

It took them four hours to reach Market Harborough, a town which, as they established en route, neither Strike nor Robin had ever visited. The approach wound through a number of pretty little villages with thatched roofs, seventeenth-century churches, topiary gardens and residential streets with names like Honeypot Lane. Strike remembered the stark, blank wall, barbed wire and looming submarine factory that had formed the view from Noel Brockbank's childhood home. What could have brought Brockbank here, to bucolic prettiness and charm? What kind of business owned the telephone number that Holly had given Robin, and which was now residing in Strike's wallet?

The impression of genteel antiquity only increased when they reached Market Harborough itself. The ornate and aged church of

St. Dionysius rose proudly in the heart of the town, and beside it, in the middle of the central thoroughfare, stood a remarkable structure resembling a small timbered house on wooden stilts.

They found a parking space to the rear of this peculiar building. Keen to smoke and to stretch his knee, Strike got out, lit up and went to examine a plaque that informed him the stilted edifice was a grammar school that had been built in 1614. Biblical verses painted in gold ran around the structure.

Man looketh on the outward appearance, but the Lord looketh on the heart.

Robin had remained in the Land Rover, examining the map for the best route to Corby, their next stop. When Strike had finished his cigarette he hoisted himself back into the passenger seat.

"OK, I'm going to try the number. If you fancy stretching your legs, I'm nearly out of fags."

Robin rolled her eyes, but took the proffered tenner and left in search of Benson & Hedges.

The number was engaged the first time Strike tried it. On his second attempt, a heavily accented female voice answered:

"Thai Orchid Massage, how can I help you?"

"Hi," said Strike. "I've been given your number by a friend. Whereabouts are you?"

She gave him a number in St. Mary's Road, which he saw, after a brief consultation of the map, was mere minutes away.

"Any of your ladies free for me this morning?" he asked.

"What kind you like?" said the voice.

He could see Robin coming back in the wing mirror, her strawberry-blonde hair blowing freely in the breeze, a gold pack of Benson & Hedges glinting in her hand.

"Dark," said Strike, after a fractional hesitation. "Thai."

"We have two Thai ladies free for you. What service you look for?"

Robin pulled open the driver's door and got back in.

"What have you got?" asked Strike.

"One-lady sensual massage with oils, ninety pound. Two-lady sensual massage with oil, one hundred twenty. Full body-to-body naked massage with oil, one hundred fifty. You negotiate extras with lady, OK?"

"OK, I'd like the—er—one lady," said Strike. "Be with you in a bit."

He hung up.

"It's a massage parlor," he told Robin, examining the map, "but not the kind you'd take your bad knee to."

"Really?" she said, startled.

"They're everywhere," he said. "You know that."

He understood why she was disconcerted. The scene beyond the windscreen—St. Dionysius, the godly grammar school on stilts, a busy and prosperous high street, a St. George's Cross rippling in the breeze outside a nearby pub—might have appeared on a poster advertising the town.

"What are you going to—where is it?" asked Robin.

"Not far away," he said, showing her on the map. "I'm going to need a cashpoint first."

Was he actually going to pay for a massage? Robin wondered, startled, but she did not know how to frame the question, and nor was she sure that she wanted to hear the answer. After pulling in at a cashpoint to enable Strike to increase his overdraft by another two hundred pounds, she followed his directions onto St. Mary's Road, which lay at the end of the main street. St. Mary's Road proved to be a perfectly respectable-looking thoroughfare lined with estate agents, beauty spas and solicitors, most of them in large detached buildings.

"That's it," said Strike, pointing, as they drove past a discreet establishment that sat on a corner. A glossy purple and gold sign read THAI ORCHID MASSAGE. Only the dark blinds on the windows hinted at activities beyond the medically sanctioned manipulation of sore joints. Robin parked in a side street and watched Strike until he passed out of sight.

Approaching the massage parlor's entrance, Strike noticed that the orchid depicted on the glossy sign overhead looked remarkably like a vulva. He rang the bell and the door was opened instantly by a long-haired man almost as tall as himself.

"I just phoned," Strike said.

The bouncer grunted and nodded Strike through a pair of thick black inner curtains. Immediately inside was a small, carpeted lounge area with two sofas, where an older Thai woman sat along with two Thai girls, one of whom looked about fifteen. A TV in the corner was showing *Who Wants to Be a Millionaire?* The girls' expressions changed from bored to alert as he entered. The older woman stood up. She was vigorously chewing gum.

"You call, yeah?"

"That's right," said Strike.

"You want drink?"

"No thanks."

"You like Thai girl?"

"Yep," said Strike.

"Who you want?"

"Her," said Strike, pointing at the younger girl, who was dressed in a pink halterneck, suede miniskirt and cheap-looking patent stilettos. She smiled and stood up. Her skinny legs reminded him of a flamingo's.

"OK," said his interlocutor. "You pay now, go private booth after, OK?"

Strike handed over ninety pounds and his chosen girl beckoned, beaming. She had the body of an adolescent boy except for the clearly fake breasts, which reminded him of the plastic Barbies on Elin's daughter's shelf.

The private booth was accessed down a short corridor: a small room with a single black-blinded window and low lighting, it was suffused with the smell of sandalwood. A shower had been crammed into the corner. The massage table was of fake black leather.

"You want shower first?"

"No thanks," said Strike.

"OK, you take off clothes in there," she said, pointing at a tiny curtained-off corner in which Strike would have had great difficulty concealing his six foot three frame.

"I'm happier with my clothes on. I want to talk to you."

She did not seem fazed. She had seen all sorts.

"You want top off?" she offered brightly, reaching for the bow behind her neck. "Ten pound extra, top off."

"No," said Strike.

"Hand relief?" she offered, eyeing his flies. "Hand relief with oil? Twenty extra."

"No, I just want to talk to you," said Strike.

Doubt crossed her face, and then a sudden flash of fear.

"You police."

"No," said Strike, holding up his hands as though surrendering to her. "I'm not police. I'm looking for a man called Noel Brockbank. He used to work here. On the door, I expect—probably the bouncer."

He had chosen this particular girl because she looked so young. Knowing Brockbank's proclivities, he thought Brockbank might have sought contact with her rather than any of the other girls, but she shook her head.

"He gone," she said.

"I know," said Strike. "I'm trying to find out where he went."

"Mama sack him."

Was the owner her mother, or was it an honorary title? Strike preferred not to involve Mama in this. She looked shrewd and tough. He had an idea he would be forced to pay well for what might turn out to be no information at all. There was a welcome naivety about his chosen girl. She could have charged him for confirmation that Brockbank had once worked there, that he had been sacked, but it had not occurred to her.

"Did you know him?" Strike asked.

"He sacked week I come," she said.

"Why was he sacked?"

The girl glanced at the door.

"Would anyone here have a contact number for him, or know where he went?"

She hesitated. Strike took out his wallet.

"Twenty," he said, "if you can introduce me to someone who's got information on where he is now. That's yours to keep."

She stood playing with the hem of her suede skirt like a child, staring at him, then tweaked the tenners out of his hand and tucked them deep into her skirt pocket.

"Wait here."

He sat down on the fake-leather massage table and waited. The little room was as clean as any spa, which Strike liked. He found dirt deeply anaphrodisiac; it always reminded him of his mother and Whittaker in that fetid squat, of stained mattresses and the miasma of his stepfather thick in his nostrils. Here beside the oils neatly lined up on a side cabinet, erotic thoughts could hardly fail to occur. The idea of a full body-to-body naked massage with oil was far from unpleasing.

For no reason that he could think of, his thoughts jumped to Robin, sitting outside in the car. He got briskly to his feet again, as though he had been discovered doing something compromising, and then angry Thai voices sounded close at hand. The door burst open to reveal Mama and his chosen girl, who looked frightened.

"You pay for one girl massage!" said Mama angrily.

Like her protégée, her eyes found his flies. She was checking to see whether any business had already been done, whether he was trying to get more on the cheap.

"He change mind," said the girl desperately. "He want two girl, one Thai, one blonde. We do nothing. He change mind."

"You pay for one girl only," shouted Mama, pointing at Strike with a talon-tipped finger.

Strike heard heavy footsteps and guessed that the long-haired doorman was approaching.

"I'm happy," he said, inwardly cursing, "to pay for the two-girl massage as well."

"One hundred twenty more?" Mama shouted at him, unable to believe her ears.

"Yes," he said. "Fine."

She made him come back out into the lounge area to pay. An overweight redhead was sitting there in a cut-out black lycra dress. She looked hopeful.

"He want blonde," said Strike's accomplice as he handed over another hundred and twenty pounds, and the redhead's face fell.

"Ingrid with client," said Mama, shoving Strike's cash in a drawer. "You wait here 'til she finish."

So he sat between the skinny Thai girl and the redhead and watched *Who Wants to Be a Millionaire?* until a small, suited man with a white beard came scurrying out of the corridor and, avoiding eye contact with everybody, disappeared through the black curtains and escaped onto the street. Five minutes later a slim peroxide blonde who, Strike thought, must be around his own age appeared in purple lycra and thigh-high boots.

"You go with Ingrid," said Mama and Strike and the Thai girl traipsed obediently back to the private parlor.

"He no want massage," Strike's first girl told the blonde breathlessly when the door was closed. "He want know where Noel went."

The blonde eyed Strike, frowning. She might be more than twice the age of her companion, but she was good-looking, with dark brown eyes and high cheekbones.

"What d'you want *'im* for?" she asked in pure Essex and then, calmly, "Are you police?"

"No," said Strike.

Sudden comprehension was illuminating her pretty face.

" 'Ang on," she said slowly. "I know 'oo you are—you're that Strike! You're Cameron Strike! The detective 'oo solved the Lula Landry case and—Jesus—didn't someone just send you a *leg?*"

"Er—yeah, they did."

"Noel was fucking *obsessed* with you!" she said. "All I ever heard 'im talk about, practically. After you was on the news."

"Is that right?"

"Yeah, 'e kept saying you give 'im a brain injury!"

"I can't take full credit. You knew him well, did you?"

"Not *that* well!" she said, correctly interpreting Strike's meaning. "I knew 'is friend from up north, John. He was a great guy, one of my regular punters before 'e went off to Saudi. Yeah, they was at school together, I fink. 'E felt sorry for Noel 'cause 'e was ex-forces and 'e'd 'ad a few problems, so 'e recommended him for 'ere. Said 'e was down on his luck. 'E got me to rent Noel a room at my place an' all."

Her tone said plainly that she felt John's sympathy for Brockbank had been misplaced.

"How did that go?"

" 'E was all right at first, but once 'is guard come down 'e just ranted all the time. About the army, about you, about 'is son—'e's obsessed with 'is son, getting 'is son back. 'E says it's your fault he can't see 'im, but I don't see 'ow 'e works that out. Anyone could see why his ex-wife didn't want 'im near the kid."

"And why's that?"

"Mama found 'im with 'er granddaughter on 'is lap and 'is 'and up 'er skirt," said Ingrid. "She's six."

"Ah," said Strike.

" 'E left owing me two weeks' rent and that's the last I ever saw of 'im. Good bloody riddance."

"D'you know where he went after he was sacked?"

"No idea."

"So you haven't got any contact details?"

"I've prob'bly still got his mobile number," she said. "I don't know whether 'e'll still be using it."

"Could you give—?"

"Do I look like I've got a mobile on me?" she asked, raising her arms high. The lycra and boots outlined every curve. Her erect nipples were clearly visible through the thin fabric. Invited to look, Strike forced himself to maintain eye contact.

"Could you meet me later and give it to me?"

"We're not allowed to exchange contact details with punters. Terms and conditions, sweet'art: why we're not allowed to carry phones. Tell you what," she said, eyeing him up and down, "seeing as it's you and seeing as 'ow I know you punched the bastard and you're a war 'ero and everyfing, I'll meet you up the road when I clock off."

"That," said Strike, "would be great. Thanks very much."

He did not know whether he imagined a flirtatious glint in her eye. Possibly he was distracted by the smell of massage oil and his recent thoughts of warm, slippery bodies.

Twenty minutes later, having waited long enough for Mama to

assume that relief had been sought and given, Strike left the Thai Orchid and crossed the road to where Robin was waiting in the car.

"Two hundred and thirty quid for an old mobile number," he said as she pulled away from the curb and accelerated towards the town center. "I hope it's bloody worth it. We're looking for Adam and Eve Street—she says it's just up here on the right—the café's called Appleby's. She's going to meet me there in a bit."

Robin found a parking space and they waited, discussing what Ingrid had said about Brockbank while eating the Danish pastries that Strike had stolen from the breakfast buffet. Robin was starting to appreciate why Strike was carrying extra weight. She had never before undertaken an investigation that lasted more than twenty-four hours. When every meal had to be sourced in passing shops and eaten on the move, you descended quickly to fast food and chocolate.

"That's her," said Strike forty minutes later, clambering out of the Land Rover and heading for the interior of Appleby's. Robin watched the blonde approach, now in jeans and a fake-fur jacket. She had the body of a glamour model and Robin was reminded of Platinum. Ten minutes passed, then fifteen; neither Strike nor the girl reappeared.

"How long does it take to hand over a telephone number?" Robin asked the interior of the Land Rover crossly. She felt chilly in the car. "I thought you wanted to get on to Corby?"

He had told her nothing had happened, but you never knew. Perhaps it had. Perhaps the girl had covered Strike in oil and...

Robin drummed her fingers on the steering wheel. She thought about Elin, and how she would feel if she knew what Strike had done that day. Then, with a slight jolt, she remembered that she had not checked her phone to see whether Matthew had been in contact again. She took it out of her coat pocket and saw no new messages. Since telling him she was definitely not going to his father's birthday party, he had gone quiet.

The blonde and Strike emerged from the café. Ingrid did not seem to want to let Strike go. When he waved farewell she leaned forward and kissed him on the cheek, then sashayed away. Strike caught Robin watching and got back into the car with a kind of bashful grimace.

"That looked interesting," said Robin.

"Not really," said Strike, showing her the number now keyed into his phone: **NOEL BROCKBANK MOBILE**. "She was just chatty."

If Robin had been a male colleague he would have found it impossible not to add: "I was in there." Ingrid had flirted shamelessly across the table, scrolling slowly through the contacts on her phone, wondering aloud whether she still had the number so that he started to feel anxious that she had nothing, asking him whether he had ever had a proper Thai massage, probing about what he wanted Noel for, about the cases he had solved, especially that of the beautiful dead model, which had first brought him to public notice, and finally insisting, with a warm smile, that he take her number too, "just in case."

"D'you want to try Brockbank's number now?" Robin asked, recalling Strike's attention from the back view of Ingrid as she walked away.

"What? No. That wants thinking about. We might only have one shot if he picks up." He checked his watch. "Let's get going, I don't want to be too late in Cor—"

The phone in his hand rang.

"Wardle," said Strike.

He answered, putting the phone onto speaker so that Robin could listen.

"What's going on?"

"We've ID'd the body," said Wardle. A note in his voice warned them that they were about to recognize a name. The tiny pause that followed allowed the image of that little girl with her small bird-like eyes to slide in panic through Strike's mind.

"She's called Kelsey Platt and she's the girl who wrote to you for advice on how to cut off her leg. She was genuine. Sixteen years old."

Equal amounts of relief and disbelief crashed over Strike. He groped for a pen, but Robin was already writing.

"She was doing a City and Guilds in childcare at some vocational college, which is where she met Oxana Voloshina. Kelsey usually lived in Finchley with her half-sister and the sister's partner. She told them she was going away on a college placement for two weeks. They didn't report her missing—they weren't worried. She wasn't expected back until tonight.

"Oxana says Kelsey didn't get on with her sister and asked whether she could stay there for a couple of weeks, get some space. Looks like the girl had it all planned out, writing to you from that address. The sister's a total mess, understandably. I can't get much sense out of her yet, but she's confirmed the handwriting on the letter was genuine and the thing the girl had about wanting to get rid of her leg didn't seem to come as a total shock to her. We got DNA samples off the girl's hairbrush. It matches. It's her."

With a creak of the passenger seat, Strike leaned closer to Robin to read her notes. She could smell the cigarette smoke on his clothes and a tiny whiff of sandalwood.

"There's a partner living with the sister?" he asked. "A man?"

"You won't pin it on him," said Wardle, and Strike could tell that Wardle had already had a good try. "Forty-five, retired fireman, not in great nick. Knackered lungs and a watertight alibi for the weekend in question."

"The weekend—?" began Robin.

"Kelsey left her sister's on the night of April first. We know she must've died on the second or third—you got handed her leg on the fourth. Strike, I'm going to need you back in here for more questions. Routine, but we're going to have to take a formal statement about those letters."

There seemed little else to be said. After accepting Strike's thanks for letting them know, Wardle rang off, leaving a silence that seemed to Robin to quiver with aftershocks.

28

> ...oh Debbie Denise was true to me,
> She'd wait by the window, so patiently.
>
> Blue Öyster Cult, "Debbie Denise"
> Lyrics by Patti Smith

"This whole trip's been a wasted detour. It isn't Brittany. It can't be Brockbank."

Strike's relief was stupendous. The colors of Adam and Eve Street seemed suddenly washed clean, the passersby brighter, more likable than they had been before he had taken the call. Brittany must, after all, be alive somewhere. This was not his fault. The leg had not been hers.

Robin said nothing. She could hear the triumph in Strike's voice, feel his release. She, of course, had never met or seen Brittany Brockbank, and while she was glad the girl was safe, the fact remained that a girl had died in horrific circumstances. The guilt that had tumbled from Strike seemed to have fallen heavily into her own lap. She was the one who had skim-read Kelsey's letter and simply filed it in the nutter drawer without response. Would it have made a difference, Robin wondered, if she had contacted Kelsey and advised her to get help? Or if Strike had called her and told her that he had lost his leg in battle, that whatever she had been told about his injury was a lie? Robin's insides ached with regret.

"Are you sure?" she said aloud after a full minute's silence, both of them lost in their own private thoughts.

"Sure about what?" asked Strike, turning to look at her.

"That it can't be Brockbank."

"If it's not Brittany—" began Strike.

"You've just told me that girl—"

"Ingrid?"

"Ingrid," said Robin, with a trace of impatience, "yes. You've just told me she says Brockbank's obsessed with you. He holds you accountable for his brain damage and the loss of his family."

Strike watched her, frowning, thinking.

"Everything I said last night about the killer wanting to denigrate you and belittle your war record would sit comfortably with everything we know about Brockbank," Robin went on, "and don't you think that meeting this Kelsey and perhaps seeing the scarring on her leg that was like Brittany's, or hearing that she wanted to get rid of it could have—I don't know—triggered something in him? I mean," said Robin tentatively, "we don't know exactly how the brain damage—"

"He's not that fucking brain damaged," snapped Strike. "He was faking in the hospital. I know he was."

Robin said nothing, but sat behind the wheel and watched shoppers moving up and down Adam and Eve Street. She envied them. Whatever their private preoccupations, they were unlikely to include mutilation and murder.

"You make some good points," said Strike at last. Robin could tell that she had taken the edge off his private celebration. He checked his watch. "C'mon, we'd better get off to Corby if we're going to do it today."

The twelve miles between the two towns were swiftly covered. Robin guessed from his surly expression that Strike was mulling over their discussion about Brockbank. The road was nondescript, the surrounding countryside flat, hedgerows and occasional trees lining the route.

"So, Laing," said Robin, trying to move Strike out of what seemed an uncomfortable reverie. "Remind me—?"

"Laing, yeah," said Strike slowly.

She was right to think that he had been lost in thoughts of Brockbank. Now he forced himself to focus, to regroup.

"Well, Laing tied up his wife and used a knife on her; accused of rape twice that I know of, but never done for it—and he tried to bite half my face off in the boxing ring. Basically, a violent, devious bastard," said Strike, "but, like I told you, his mother-in-law reckons he was ill when he got out of jail. She says he went to Gateshead, but he can't have stayed there long if he was living in Corby with this woman in 2008," he said, checking the map again for Lorraine MacNaughton's road. "Right age, right time frame... we'll see. If Lorraine's not in, we'll go back after five o'clock."

Following Strike's directions, Robin drove through the very center of Corby town, which proved to be a sprawl of concrete and brick dominated by a shopping center. A massive block of council offices, on which aerials bristled like iron moss, dominated the skyline. There was no central square, no ancient church and certainly no stilted, half-timbered grammar school. Corby had been planned to house its explosion of migrant workers in the 1940s and 1950s; many of the buildings had a cheerless, utilitarian air.

"Half the street names are Scottish," said Robin as they passed Argyll Street and Montrose Street.

"Used to call it Little Scotland, didn't they?" said Strike, noting a sign for Edinburgh House. He had heard that in its industrial heyday, Corby had had the largest Scottish population south of the border. Saltires and lions rampant fluttered from balconies of flats. "You can see why Laing might've felt more at home here than in Gateshead. Could've had contacts in the area."

Five minutes later they found themselves in the old part of town, whose pretty stone buildings retained traces of the village that Corby had been before the steelworks arrived. Shortly afterwards they came upon Weldon Road, where Lorraine MacNaughton lived.

The houses stood in solid blocks of six, each pair a mirror image of the other, so that their front doors sat side by side and the layout of the windows was reversed. Carved into the stone lintel over each door was a name.

"That's hers," said Strike, pointing at Summerfield, which was twinned with Northfield.

Summerfield's front garden had been covered in fine gravel.

Northfield's grass needed mowing, which reminded Robin of her own flat back in London.

"I think we'd both better go in," Strike said, unbuckling his seatbelt. "She'll probably be more comfortable with you there."

The doorbell seemed to be out of order. Strike therefore rapped sharply on the door with his knuckles. An explosion of furious barking told them that the house had at least one living inhabitant. Then they heard a woman's voice, angry but somehow ineffectual.

"Shh! Be quiet! Stop it! Shh! No!"

The door opened and Robin had just caught a glimpse of a hard-faced woman of around fifty when a rough-coated Jack Russell came pelting out, growling and barking with ferocity, and sank its teeth into Strike's ankle. Fortunately for Strike, but less so for the Jack Russell, its teeth connected with steel. It yelped and Robin capitalized on its shock by stooping swiftly, grabbing it by the scruff of the neck and lifting it up. So surprised was the dog at finding itself dangling in midair that it simply hung there.

"No biting," said Robin.

Apparently deciding that a woman brave enough to pick it up was worthy of respect, the dog allowed her to take a firmer grip, twisted in midair and attempted to lick her hand.

"Sorry," said the woman. "He was my mother's. He's a bloody nightmare. He likes you, look. Miracle."

Her shoulder-length brown hair had gray roots. Deep marionette lines lay either side of a thin-lipped mouth. She was leaning on a stick, one of her ankles swollen and bandaged, the foot encased in a sandal that displayed yellowing toenails.

Strike introduced himself, then showed Lorraine his driving license and a business card.

"Are you Lorraine MacNaughton?"

"Yeah," she said hesitantly. Her eyes flickered to Robin, who smiled reassuringly over the Jack Russell's head. "You're a—what did you say?"

"A detective," said Strike, "and I was wondering whether you could tell me anything about Donald Laing. Telephone records show he was living here with you a couple of years ago."

"Yeah, he was," she said slowly.

"Is he still here?" Strike asked, although he knew the answer.

"No."

Strike indicated Robin.

"Would it be all right if my colleague and I come in and ask you a few questions? We're trying to find Mr. Laing."

There was a pause. Lorraine chewed her inner lip, frowning. Robin cradled the Jack Russell, which was now enthusiastically licking her fingers where, no doubt, it could taste traces of Danish pastry. Strike's torn trouser leg flapped in a light breeze.

"All right, come in," said Lorraine, and she backed away on her crutches to admit them.

The frowzy front room smelled strongly of stale cigarette smoke. There were countless old-ladyish touches: crocheted tissue-box covers, cheap frilled cushions and an array of fancily dressed teddy bears arranged on a polished sideboard. One wall was dominated by a painting of a saucer-eyed child dressed as a pierrot. Strike could no more imagine Donald Laing living here than he could visualize a bullock bedded down in the corner.

Once inside, the Jack Russell scrabbled to get down out of Robin's arms, then started barking at Strike again.

"Oh, shut up," groaned Lorraine. Sinking down onto the faded brown velvet sofa, she used both arms to lift her bandaged ankle back onto a leather pouffe, reached sideways to retrieve her packet of Superkings and lit up.

"I'm supposed to keep it raised," she explained, cigarette waggling in her mouth as she picked up a full cut-glass ashtray and set it on her lap. "District nurse is in every day to change the dressings. Sit down."

"What have you done?" asked Robin, squeezing past the coffee table to sit beside Lorraine on the sofa. The Jack Russell immediately jumped up beside her and, mercifully, stopped barking.

"I got a load of chip fat dropped on me," said Lorraine. "At work."

"Christ," said Strike, settling himself in the armchair. "That must've been agony."

"Yeah, it was. They say I'll be off at least a month. Least it wasn't far to go to casualty."

Lorraine, it transpired, worked in the canteen of the local hospital.

"So what's Donnie done?" Lorraine muttered, puffing smoke, once the subject of her injury had been thoroughly aired. "Robbery again, is it?"

"Why do you say that?" asked Strike carefully.

"He robbed me," she said.

Robin saw, now, that the brusqueness was a façade. Lorraine's long cigarette trembled as she said it.

"When was this?" asked Strike.

"When he walked out. Took all my jewelry. Mum's wedding ring, everything. He knew what that meant to me. She'd not been dead a year. Yeah, one day he just walks out of the house and never comes back. I called the police, I thought he'd had an accident. Then I realized my purse was empty and my jewelry was gone."

The humiliation had not left her. Her sunken cheeks flushed as she said it.

Strike felt in the inside pocket of his jacket.

"I want to make sure we're talking about the same man. Does this picture look familiar?"

He handed her one of the photographs Laing's ex-mother-in-law had given him in Melrose. Big and broad in his blue and yellow kilt, with his dark ferret-like eyes and that low-sprouting crop of fox-red hair, Laing was standing outside a registry office. Rhona clung to his arm, less than half his width in what looked like a poorly fitting, possibly secondhand wedding gown.

Lorraine examined the photograph for what seemed like a very long time. At last she said:

"I *think* it's him. It could be."

"You can't see it, but he had a big tattoo of a yellow rose on his left forearm," said Strike.

"Yeah," said Lorraine heavily. "That's right. He did."

She smoked, staring at the picture.

"He'd been married, had he?" she asked, with a slight quaver in her voice.

"Didn't he tell you?" asked Robin.

"No. Told me he'd never been."

"How did you meet him?" asked Robin.

"Pub," said Lorraine. "He didn't look much like that when I knew him."

She turned in the direction of the sideboard behind her and made a vague attempt to get up.

"Can I help?" Robin offered.

"In that middle drawer. There might be a picture."

The Jack Russell began barking again as Robin opened a drawer containing an assortment of napkin rings, crocheted doilies, souvenir teaspoons, toothpicks and loose photographs. Robin extracted as many of the latter as she could and brought them back to Lorraine.

"That's him," said Lorraine, after sorting through many pictures that mostly featured a very elderly woman whom Robin assumed to be Lorraine's mother. Lorraine passed the picture straight to Strike.

He would not have recognized Laing if he had passed him in the street. The former boxer was massively swollen, especially around the face. His neck was no longer visible; his skin seemed tight, his features distorted. One arm was around a smiling Lorraine's shoulders, the other hung loose at his side. He was not smiling. Strike peered closer. The yellow rose tattoo was visible, but partially obscured by angry red skin plaques that mottled the whole expanse of his forearm.

"Is there something wrong with his skin?"

"Psoriatic arthritis," said Lorraine. "He was bad with it. That's why he was on the sick benefit. Had to stop work."

"Yeah?" said Strike. "What had he been working as before?"

"He come down here as a manager for one of the big construction firms," she said, "but then he got ill and couldn't work. He'd had his own building company up in Melrose. He was the managing director."

"Really?" said Strike.

"Yeah, family business," said Lorraine, searching her stack of photographs. "He inherited it from his dad. There he is again, look."

They were holding hands in this picture, which looked as though it had been taken in a beer garden. Lorraine beamed and Laing looked blank, his moon face shrinking his dark eyes to slits. He had the characteristic look of a man on medically prescribed steroids. The hair like a fox's pelt was the same, but otherwise Strike was hard pressed to make out the features of the fit young boxer who had once bitten his face.

"How long were you together?"

"Ten months. I met him right after Mum died. She was ninety-two—she lived here with me. I was helping with Mrs. Williams next door and all; she was eighty-seven. Senile. Her son's in America. Donnie was good to her. He mowed her lawn and got shopping."

Bastard knew which side his bread was buttered, thought Strike. Ill, unemployed and broke as Laing had been at the time, a lonely middle-aged woman without dependents who could cook, who had her own house, who had just inherited money from her mother, must have been a godsend. It would have been worth faking a bit of compassion to get his feet under the table. Laing had had charm when he chose to use it.

"He seemed all right when we met," said Lorraine morosely. "Couldn't do enough for me then. He wasn't well himself. Joints swollen and everything. He had to have injections off the doctor... He got a bit moody later, but I thought that was just his health. You don't expect ill people to be always cheerful, do you? Not everyone's like Mum. She was a bloody marvel, her health was that bad and she was always smiling and...and..."

"Let me get you a tissue," said Robin and she leaned slowly towards the crochet-covered box, so as not to disarrange the Jack Russell, which had its head on her lap.

"Did you report the theft of your jewelry?" Strike asked, once Lorraine had received her tissue, which she plied between deep drags on her Superking.

"No," she said gruffly. "What was the point? They were never going to find it."

Robin guessed that Lorraine had not wanted to draw official attention to her humiliation, and sympathized.

"Was he ever violent?" Robin asked gently.

Lorraine looked surprised.

"No. Is that why you're here? Has he hurt someone?"

"We don't know," said Strike.

"I don't think he'd *hurt* anyone," she said. "He wasn't that kind of man. I said that to the police."

"Sorry," said Robin, stroking the now-dozing Jack Russell's head. "I thought you didn't report the robbery?"

"This was later," said Lorraine. "Month or so after he'd gone. Somebody broke into Mrs. Williams's place, knocked her out and robbed the house. The police wanted to know where Donnie was. I said, 'He's long gone, moved out.' Anyway, he wouldn't do that, I told them. He'd been good to her. He wouldn't punch an old lady."

They had once held hands in a beer garden. He had mowed the old lady's lawn. She refused to believe Laing had been all bad.

"I assume your neighbor couldn't give the police a description?" Strike asked.

Lorraine shook her head.

"She never came back, after. Died in a home. Got a family in Northfield now," said Lorraine. "Three little kids. You should hear the noise—and they've got the bloody cheek to complain about the dog!"

They had hit a complete dead end. Lorraine had no idea where Laing had gone next. She could not remember him mentioning any place to which he was connected other than Melrose and she had never met any of his friends. Once she had realized that he was never coming back, she had deleted his mobile number from her phone. She agreed to let them take the two photographs of Laing, but other than that, had no more help to offer.

The Jack Russell protested loudly at Robin withdrawing her warm lap and showed every sign of wishing to take his displeasure out on Strike as the detective rose from his chair.

"*Stop it,* Tigger," said Lorraine crossly, holding the struggling dog on the sofa with difficulty.

"We'll see ourselves out," Robin shouted over the dog's frenzied barking. "Thanks so much for all your help!"

They left her there in her cluttered, smoky sitting room, bandaged ankle raised, probably a little sadder and more uncomfortable for their visit. The sound of the hysterical dog followed them all the way up the garden path.

"I feel like we could at least have made her a cup of tea or something," said Robin guiltily as they got back into the Land Rover.

"She doesn't know what a lucky escape she's had," said Strike bracingly. "Think about the poor old dear in there," he pointed at Northfield, "beaten to shit for a couple of extra quid."

"You think that was Laing?"

"Of course it was bloody Laing," said Strike as Robin turned on the engine. "He'd cased the joint while he was supposedly helping her out, hadn't he? And you notice that, for all he was supposed to be so ill with his arthritis, he was still capable of mowing lawns and half killing old women."

Hungry and tired, her head aching from the stale cigarette smoke, Robin nodded and said that she supposed so. It had been a depressing interview and the prospect of a further two and a half hours' drive to get back home was not appealing.

"D'you mind if we get going?" said Strike, checking his watch. "I told Elin I'll be over tonight."

"No problem," said Robin.

Yet for some reason—perhaps due to her headache, perhaps because of the lonely woman sitting in Summerfield among the memories of loved ones who had left her—Robin could easily have wept all over again.

29

I Just Like to Be Bad

Sometimes he found it hard to be with the people who thought themselves his friends: the men with whom he associated when he needed money. Theft was their main occupation, tomming of a Saturday night their recreation; he was popular among them, a mate, so they thought, a fellow, an equal. An equal!

The day the police had found her, all he had wanted was to be alone to savor the coverage. The stories in the paper made good reading. He felt proud: this was the first time he'd been able to kill in private, to take his time, to organize things as he'd wanted. He intended to do the same with The Secretary; to have time to enjoy her alive before he killed her.

His one frustration was there was no mention of the letters that were supposed to point the police to Strike, to make them interrogate and badger the fucker, drag his name through the mud in the papers, make the dumb public think he'd had something to do with it.

However, there were columns and columns of coverage, photographs of the flat where he'd done her, interviews with the pretty-boy police officer. He saved the stories: they were souvenirs, just like the bits of her he had taken for his private collection.

Of course, his pride and enjoyment had to be hidden from It, because It required very careful handling at the moment. It wasn't happy, not happy at all. Life wasn't panning out the way It had expected and he had to pretend to give a flying fuck, to be concerned, be a nice guy, because It was useful to him: It brought in money and It might have to give him alibis. You never knew whether they might be needed. He'd had a close call once before.

That had been the second time he had killed, in Milton Keynes. You didn't shit on your own doorstep: that had always been one of his guiding principles. He had never been to Milton Keynes before or since and had no connection with the place. He had stolen a car, away from the boys, a solo job. He had had fake plates ready for a while. Then he had simply driven, wondering whether he would get lucky. There had been a couple of failed attempts since his first murder: trying to chat up girls in pubs, in clubs, trying to isolate them, was not working as well as it had in the past. He didn't look as good as he once had, he knew that, but he didn't want to establish a pattern of doing prostitutes. The police started to put two and two together if you went for the same type every time. Once he had managed to track a tipsy girl down an alleyway, but before he'd even drawn his knife out a pack of giggling kids had burst into view and he had taken off. After that he had given up on trying to pick up a girl in the usual way. It would have to be force.

He had driven for hours in increasing frustration; not a whiff of a victim in Milton Keynes. At ten to midnight he was on the verge of caving and sniffing out a hooker when he'd spotted her. She was arguing with her boyfriend on a roundabout in the middle of the road, a short-haired brunette in jeans. As he passed he kept an eye on the couple in his rearview mirror. He watched her storm away, as good as intoxicated by her own anger and tears. The infuriated man she had left behind shouted after her, then, with a gesture of disgust, stumbled off in the opposite direction.

He did a U-turn and drove back up the road towards her. She was sobbing as she walked, wiping her eyes on her sleeve.

He had wound down the window.

"You all right, love?"

"Piss off!"

She sealed her fate by plunging angrily into bushes beside the road to get away from his crawling car. Another hundred yards would have taken her to a well-lit stretch of road.

All he had to do was turn off the road and park. He pulled on the balaclava before getting out of the car, the knife ready in his hand, and walked calmly back to the place where she had disappeared. He could hear her trying to fight her way back out of the dense patch of trees and shrubs, placed there by town planners to soften the contours of the wide gray dual carriageway. There was no streetlamp here. He was invisible to passing drivers as he skirted the dark foliage. As she beat her way back onto the pavement, he was standing ready to force her back in at knifepoint.

He had spent an hour in the bushes before leaving the body. He ripped her earrings from her lobes and then wielded his knife with abandon, hacking off bits of her. A gap in the traffic and he scurried, panting, back to the stolen car in the darkness, balaclava still in place.

He drove away, every particle of him elated and sated, his pockets seeping. Only then did the mist lift.

Last time, he had used a car from work, which he had subsequently cleaned thoroughly in full view of his workmates. He doubted anyone would be able to get the blood out of these cloth seats and his DNA would be on everything. What was he going to do? That was the closest he had ever come to panicking.

He drove miles north before abandoning the car in a lonely field far from the main road, not overlooked by any buildings. Here, shivering in the cold, he took off the fake plates, soaked one of his socks in the petrol tank, then chucked it into the bloody front seat and lit it. It took a long time for the car to properly catch; he had to reapproach it several times to help it along until finally, at three in the morning while he watched, shivering, from the cover of trees, it exploded. Then he ran.

It was winter, which meant at least that the balaclava did not look out of place. He buried the fake plates in a wood and hurried on, head bowed, hands in his pockets on his treasured souvenirs. He had considered burying them too, but he could not bring himself to do it. He had covered the bloodstains on his trousers with mud, kept his balaclava on at the station, acting drunk in a corner of the train carriage to keep people away from him, muttering to himself, projecting that aura of menace and madness that acted like a cordon when he wished to be left alone.

By the time he reached home they had found her body. He watched it on the TV that night, eating off a tray in his lap. They found the burnt-out car, but not the plates and—this really was proof of his own inimitable luck, the strange protective blessing the cosmos gave him—the boyfriend with whom she had argued was arrested, charged and, though the evidence against him was transparently weak, convicted! The thought of that dickhead serving his time still made him laugh sometimes...

Nevertheless, those long hours of driving through the darkness when he had known an encounter with the police might be fatal, when he had feared a request to turn out his pockets or a shrewd-eyed passenger noticing dried blood on him had taught him a powerful lesson. Plan every detail. Leave nothing to chance.

That was why he needed to nip out for some Vicks VapoRub. The number-one priority right now was to make sure that Its stupid new scheme did not interfere with his own.

30

I am gripped, by what I cannot tell...

Blue Öyster Cult, "Lips in the Hills"

Strike was inured to the shifts between frenetic activity and enforced passivity demanded by investigations. Nevertheless, the weekend following their round-trip to Barrow, Market Harborough and Corby found him in a strange state of tension.

The gradual re-immersion in civilian life that had taken place over the past couple of years had brought with it pressures from which he had been protected while in the military. His half-sister Lucy, the only sibling with whom he had shared a childhood, called early on Saturday morning to ask why he had not responded to her invitation to his middle nephew's birthday party. He explained that he had been away, unable to access mail sent to the office, but she barely listened.

"Jack hero-worships you, you know," she said. "He really wants you to come."

"Sorry, Lucy," said Strike, "can't make it. I'll send him a present."

Had Strike still been in the SIB, Lucy would not have felt entitled to exert emotional blackmail. It had been easy to avoid family obligations then, while he was traveling the world. She had seen him as an inextricable part of the army's immense and implacable machine. When he steadily refused to yield to her word picture of a desolate eight-year-old nephew looking in vain for Uncle Cormoran at the garden gate, she desisted, asking instead how the hunt for the man who had sent the leg was progressing. Her tone implied that there was something disreputable about being sent a leg. Keen to get her off the phone, Strike told her untruthfully that he was leaving everything up to the police.

Fond as he was of his younger sister, he had come to accept that their relationship rested almost entirely on shared and largely traumatic memories. He never confided in Lucy unless forced to do so by external events, for the simple reason that confidences usually elicited alarm or anxiety. Lucy lived in a state of perennial disappointment that he was still, at the age of thirty-seven, holding out against all those things that she believed necessary to make him happy: a job with regular hours, more money, a wife and children.

Glad to have got rid of her, Strike made himself his third mug of tea of the morning and laid back down on the bed with a pile of newspapers. Several of them displayed a photograph of MURDER VICTIM KELSEY PLATT, wearing a navy school uniform, a smile on her plain, pimply face.

Dressed only in boxers, his hairy belly no smaller for the plentiful takeaways and chocolate bars that had filled it in the last fortnight, he munched his way through a packet of Rich Tea biscuits and skimmed several of the stories, but they told him nothing he did not already know, so he turned instead to the anticipatory comment about the next day's Arsenal–Liverpool match.

His mobile rang while he was reading. He had not realized how tightly wound he was: he reacted so fast that Wardle was taken by surprise.

"Bloody hell, that was quick. What were you doing, sitting on it?"

"What's going on?"

"We've been over to Kelsey's sister's place—name's Hazel, she's a nurse. We're looking into all Kelsey's day-to-day contacts, we've gone through her room and we've got her laptop. She'd been online, on some message board for people who want to hack bits off themselves, and she was asking about you."

Strike scratched his dense, curly hair, staring at the ceiling, listening.

"We've got personal details for a couple of the people she was interacting with regularly on the boards. I should have pictures by Monday—where will you be?"

"Here, in the office."

"Her sister's boyfriend, the ex-fireman, says Kelsey kept asking him about people trapped in buildings and car accidents and all sorts. She really wanted to get rid of that leg."

"Jesus," muttered Strike.

After Wardle had hung up, Strike found himself unable to focus on the backroom reshuffles at the Emirates. After a few minutes he abandoned the pretense that he was absorbed in the fate of Arsène Wenger's management team and resumed his staring at the cracks in the ceiling, absently turning his mobile over and over.

In the blinding relief that the leg had not been Brittany Brockbank's, he had given less thought to the victim than he would ordinarily have done. Now, for the first time, he wondered about Kelsey and the letter that she had sent him, which he had not bothered to read.

The idea of anybody seeking amputation was repugnant to Strike. Round and round in his hand he turned his mobile, marshaling everything he knew about Kelsey, trying to build a mental picture out of a name and mingled feelings of pity and distaste. She had been sixteen; she had not got on with her sister; she had been studying childcare...Strike reached for his notebook and began to write: *Boyfriend at college? Lecturer?* She had gone online, asking about him. Why? Where had she got the idea that he, Strike, had amputated his own leg? Or had she evolved a fantasy out of newspaper reports about him?

Mental illness? Fantasist? he wrote.

Wardle was already looking into her online contacts. Strike paused in his writing, remembering the photograph of Kelsey's head with its full cheeks in the freezer, staring out of its frosted eyes. Puppy fat. He had thought all along that she looked far too young for twenty-four. In truth, she had looked young for sixteen.

He let his pencil fall and continued to turn his mobile over and over in his left hand, thinking...

Was Brockbank a "true" pedophile, as a psychologist Strike had met in the context of another military rape case had put it? Was he a man who was only sexually attracted to children? Or was he a different kind of violent abuser, a man who targeted young girls merely because they were most readily available and easiest to cow into silence, but who had wider sexual tastes if an easy victim became available? In short, was a babyish-looking sixteen-year-old too old to appeal sexually to Brockbank, or would he rape any easily silenced female if he got the chance? Strike had once had to deal with a nineteen-year-old soldier who had attempted to rape a sixty-seven-year-old. Some men's violent sexual nature required only opportunity.

Strike had not yet called the number that Ingrid had given him for Brockbank. His dark eyes drifted to the tiny window that showed a feebly sunlit sky. Perhaps he should have passed Brockbank's number to Wardle. Perhaps he ought to call it now...

Yet even as Strike began to scroll down the list of contacts, he reconsidered. What had he achieved so far by confiding his suspicions to Wardle? Nothing. The policeman was busy in his operations room, doubtless sifting leads, busy with his own lines of inquiry and giving Strike's—as far as the private detective could tell—only slightly more credence than he would have given anyone who had hunches but no proof. The fact that Wardle, with all his resources, had not yet located Brockbank, Laing or Whittaker, did not suggest that he was prioritizing the men.

No, if Strike wanted to find Brockbank he ought surely to maintain the cover that Robin had created: that of the lawyer looking to win the ex-major compensation. The traceable backstory they had created with his sister in Barrow might prove valuable. In fact, thought Strike, sitting up on the bed, it might be an idea to call Robin right now and give her Brockbank's number. She was alone, he knew, in the Ealing flat, while Matthew was home in Masham. He could call and perhaps—

Oh no you don't, you silly fucker.

A vision of himself and Robin in the Tottenham had bloomed in his head, a vision of where a phone call might lead. They were both at a loose end. A drink to discuss the case...

On a Saturday night? Piss off.

Strike got up suddenly, as though the bed had become painful to lie on, dressed and headed out to the supermarket.

On his way back into Denmark Street carrying bulging plastic bags he thought he spotted Wardle's plainclothes policeman, stationed in the area to keep an eye out for large men in beanie hats. The young man in a donkey jacket was hyperaware, his eyes lingering a tad too long on the detective as he walked past, his shopping swinging.

Elin called Strike much later, after he had eaten a solitary evening meal in his flat. As usual, Saturday night was out of bounds for a meeting. He could hear her daughter playing in the background as she talked. They had already arranged to see each other for dinner on Sunday, but she had called to ask whether he fancied meeting her earlier. Her husband was determined to force the sale of the valuable flat in Clarence Terrace and she had started looking for a new property.

"Do you want to come and look at it with me?" she asked. "I've got an appointment at the show flat tomorrow at two."

He knew, or thought he knew, that the invitation sprang, not from some eager hope that he would one day be living with her there—they had only been dating for three months—but because she was a woman who would always choose company when possible. Her air of cool self-sufficiency was misleading. They might never have met had she not preferred to attend a party full of her brother's unknown colleagues and friends rather than spend a few hours alone. There was nothing wrong with that, of course, nothing wrong with being sociable, except that for a year now Strike had organized his life to suit himself and the habit was hard to break.

"Can't," he said, "sorry. I'm on a job until three."

The lie convincingly told. She took it reasonably well. They agreed to meet at the bistro on Sunday evening as previously planned, which meant that he would be able to watch Arsenal–Liverpool in peace.

After he had hung up, he thought again of Robin, alone in the flat she shared with Matthew. Reaching for a cigarette, he turned on the TV and sank back onto his pillows in the dark.

Robin was having a strange weekend. Determined not to sink into moroseness just because she was alone and Strike had gone off to Elin's (where had that thought come from? Of course he had gone; after all, it was the weekend, and it was no business of hers where he chose to spend it), she had spent hours on her laptop, doggedly pursuing one old line of inquiry, and one new.

Late on Saturday night she made an online discovery that caused her to jog three victory laps of the tiny sitting room and almost phone Strike to tell him. It took several minutes, with her heart thumping and her breath coming fast, to calm down, and to tell herself that the news would keep until Monday. It would be much more satisfying to tell him in person.

Knowing that Robin was alone, her mother called her twice over the weekend, both times pressing for a date when she could come down to London.

"I don't know, Mum, not just now," sighed Robin on Sunday morning. She was sitting in her pajamas on the sofa, laptop open in front of her again, trying to hold an online conversation with a member of the BIID community who called themselves <<Δēvōŧėė>>. She had only picked up her mother's call because she was afraid ignoring it might result in an unannounced visit.

<<Δēvōŧėė>>: where do you want to be cut?
TransHopeful: mid-thigh
<<Δēvōŧėė>>: both legs?

"What about tomorrow?" asked Linda.

"No," said Robin at once. Like Strike, she lied with fluent conviction, "I'm midway through a job. The following week's better."

TransHopeful: Yes, both. Do you know anyone who's done it?
<<Δēvōŧėė>>: Can't share that on msj board. Where you live?

"I haven't seen him," said Linda. "Robin, are you typing?"

"No," lied Robin again, her fingers suspended over the keyboard. "Who haven't you seen?"

"Matthew, of course!"

"Oh. Well, no, I didn't think he'd come calling this weekend."

She tried typing more quietly.

TransHopeful: London
<<Δēvōtėė>>: Me too. Got a pic?

"Did you go to Mr. Cunliffe's birthday party?" she asked, trying to drown out the sound of the laptop keys.

"Of course we didn't!" said Linda. "Well, let me know what day's best week after next, and I'll book my ticket. It's Easter; it'll be busy."

Robin agreed, returned Linda's affectionate good-bye and directed her full attention to <<Δēvōtėė>>. Unfortunately, after Robin refused to give him or her (she was almost positive that he was male) a picture, <<Δēvōtėė>> lost interest in their back and forth on the noticeboards and went quiet.

She had expected Matthew to return from his father's on Sunday evening, but he did not. When she checked the calendar in the kitchen at eight, she realized that he had always intended to take Monday off. Presumably she had agreed to this, back when the weekend had been planned, and told Matthew that she would ask Strike for a day's holiday, too. It was lucky that they had split up, really, she told herself bracingly: she had dodged one more row about her working hours.

However, she cried later, alone in the bedroom that was thick with relics of their shared past: the fluffy elephant he had given her on their first Valentine's Day together—he had not been so suave in those days; she could remember him turning red as he had produced it—and the jewelry box he had given her for her twenty-first. Then there were all the photographs showing them beaming during holidays in Greece and Spain, and dressed up at Matthew's sister's wedding. The biggest picture of the lot showed them arm in arm on Matthew's graduation day. He was in his academic gown and Robin stood beside him in a summer dress, beaming as she celebrated an achievement of which she had been robbed by a man in a gorilla mask.

31

Nighttime flowers, evening roses,
Bless this garden that never closes.

Blue Öyster Cult, "Tenderloin"

Robin's mood was buoyed next day by the glorious spring morning that greeted her outside her front door. She did not forget to remain aware of her surroundings as she traveled by Tube towards Tottenham Court Road, but saw no sign of any large man in a beanie hat. What leapt to the eye on her morning commute was the mounting journalistic excitement about the royal wedding. Kate Middleton seemed to be on the front of virtually every newspaper held by her fellow travelers. It made Robin hyperaware all over again of that naked, sensitive place on her third finger where an engagement ring had sat for a year. However, excited as she was about sharing the results of her solo investigative work with Strike, Robin refused to be downcast.

She had just left Tottenham Court Road station when she heard a man shout her name. For a split second she feared an ambush by Matthew, then Strike appeared, forging a path through the crowd, backpack on his shoulder. Robin deduced that he had spent the night with Elin.

"Morning. Good weekend?" he asked. Then, before she could answer: "Sorry. No. Crap weekend, obviously."

"Bits of it were all right," said Robin as they wended their way through the usual obstacle course of barriers and holes in the road.

"What have you got?" Strike asked loudly over the interminable drills.

"Sorry?" she shouted.

"What. Have. You. Found. Out?"

"How do you know I've found anything out?"

"You've got that look," he said. "The look you get when you're dying to tell me something."

She grinned.

"I need a computer to show you."

They turned the corner into Denmark Street. A man dressed all in black stood outside their office door, holding a gigantic bunch of red roses.

"Oh, for God's sake," breathed Robin.

A spasm of fear receded: her mind had momentarily edited out the armful of blooms and seen only the man in black—but it wasn't the courier, of course. This, she saw as they approached him, was a youth with long hair, an Interflora deliveryman wearing no helmet. Strike doubted the boy had ever handed over fifty red roses to a less enthusiastic recipient.

"His father's put him up to this," Robin said darkly, as Strike held open the door for her and she pushed her way inside, being none too gentle with the quivering floral display. "'All women love roses,' he'll have said. That's all it takes—a bunch of bloody flowers."

Strike followed her up the metal staircase, amused but careful not to show it. He unlocked the office door and Robin crossed to her desk and dropped the roses unceremoniously onto it, where they quivered in their beribboned polythene bag of greenish water. There was a card. She did not want to open it in front of Strike.

"Well?" he asked, hanging his backpack on the peg beside the door. "What have you found out?"

Before Robin could say a word there was a rap on the door. Wardle's shape was easily recognizable through the frosted glass: his wavy hair, his leather jacket.

"I was in the area. Not too early, is it? Bloke downstairs let me in."

Wardle's eyes traveled immediately to the roses on Robin's desk.

"Birthday?"

"No," she said shortly. "Do either of you want coffee?"

"I'll do it," said Strike, moving over to the kettle and still speaking to Robin. "Wardle's got some stuff to show us."

Robin's spirits sank: was the policeman about to preempt her? Why hadn't she called Strike on Saturday night, when she'd found it?

Wardle sat down on the mock-leather sofa that always emitted loud farting noises whenever anyone over a certain weight sat on it. Clearly startled, the policeman repositioned himself gingerly and opened a folder.

"It turns out Kelsey was posting on a website for other people who wanted to get limbs taken off," Wardle told Robin.

Robin sat down in her usual seat behind her desk. The roses impeded her view of the policeman; she picked them up impatiently and deposited them on the floor beside her.

"She mentioned Strike," Wardle went on. "Asked if anyone else knew anything about him."

"Was she using the name Nowheretoturn?" asked Robin, trying to keep her voice casual. Wardle looked up, astonished, and Strike turned, a coffee spoon suspended in midair.

"Yeah, she was," said the policeman, staring. "How the hell did you know that?"

"I found that message board last weekend," said Robin. "I thought Nowheretoturn might be the girl who wrote the letter."

"Christ," said Wardle, looking from Robin to Strike. "We should offer her a job."

"She's got a job," said Strike. "Go on. Kelsey was posting…"

"Yeah, well, she ended up exchanging email addresses with these two. Nothing particularly helpful, but we're looking to establish whether they actually met her—you know, in Real Life," said Wardle.

Strange, thought Strike, how that phrase—so prevalent in childhood to differentiate between the fantasy world of play and the dull adult world of fact—had now come to signify the life that a person had outside the internet. He handed Wardle and Robin their coffees, then went through to his inner office to fetch a chair, preferring not to share the farting sofa with Wardle.

When he returned, Wardle was showing Robin printed screen-shots of the Facebook pages of two people.

She examined each of them carefully, then passed them on to Strike. One was a thick-set young woman with a round, pale face, bobbed black hair and glasses. The other was a light-haired man in his twenties with lopsided eyes.

"*She* blogs about being 'transabled,' whatever the fuck that is, and *he's* all over message boards asking for help in hacking bits off himself. Both of them have got serious issues, if you ask me. Recognize either of them?"

Strike shook his head, as did Robin. Wardle sighed and took the pictures back.

"Long shot."

"What about other men she's been knocking around with? Any boys or lecturers at college?" asked Strike, thinking of the questions that had occurred to him on Saturday.

"Well, the sister says Kelsey claimed to have a mysterious boyfriend they were never allowed to meet. Hazel doesn't believe he existed. We've spoken to a couple of Kelsey's college friends and none of them ever saw a boyfriend, but we're following it up.

"Speaking of Hazel," Wardle went on, picking up his coffee and drinking some before continuing, "I've said I'll pass on a message. She'd like to meet you."

"Me?" said Strike, surprised. "Why?"

"I dunno," said Wardle. "I think she wants to justify herself to everyone. She's in a real state."

"Justify herself?"

"She's guilt-ridden because she treated the leg thing as weird and attention-seeking, and feels that's why Kelsey went looking for someone else to help her with it."

"She understands I never wrote back? That I never had actual contact with her?"

"Yeah, yeah, I've explained that to her. She still wants to talk to you. I dunno," said Wardle slightly impatiently, "you got sent her sister's leg—you know what people are like when they're in shock. Plus, it's you, isn't it?" said Wardle, with a faint edge in his voice.

"She probably thinks the Boy Wonder will solve it while the police are blundering."

Robin and Strike avoided looking at each other and Wardle added grudgingly:

"We could've handled Hazel better. Our guys interrogated her partner a bit more aggressively than she liked. It put her on the defensive. She might like the idea of having you on the books: the detective who's already saved one poor innocent from the nick."

Strike decided to ignore the defensive undertone.

"Obviously, we had to question the bloke who was living with her," Wardle added for Robin's benefit. "That's routine."

"Yes," said Robin. "Of course."

"No other men in her life, except the sister's partner and this alleged boyfriend?" asked Strike.

"She was seeing a male counselor, a skinny black guy in his fifties who was visiting family in Bristol on the weekend she died, and there's a church youth group leader called Darrell," said Wardle, "fat guy in dungarees. He cried his eyes out all through the interview. He was present and correct at the church on the Sunday; nothing checkable otherwise, but I can't see him wielding a cleaver. That's everyone we know about. Her course is nearly all girls."

"No boys in the church youth group?"

"They're nearly all girls as well. Oldest boy's fourteen."

"How would the police feel about me seeing Hazel?" Strike asked.

"We can't stop you," Wardle said, shrugging. "I'm for it, on the understanding that you'll pass on anything useful, but I doubt there's anything else there. We've interviewed everyone, we've been through Kelsey's room, we've got her laptop and personally I'd bet none of the people we've talked to knew anything. They all thought she was off on a college placement."

After thanks for the coffee and a particularly warm smile for Robin, which was barely returned, Wardle left.

"Not a word about Brockbank, Laing or Whittaker," Strike grumbled as Wardle's clanging footsteps faded from earshot. "And you never told me you'd been ferreting around on the net," he added to Robin.

"I had no proof she was the girl who'd written the letter," said Robin, "but I did think Kelsey might have gone online looking for help."

Strike heaved himself to his feet, took her mug from her desk and was heading for the door when Robin said indignantly:

"Aren't you interested in what I was going to tell you?"

He turned, surprised.

"That wasn't it?"

"No!"

"Well?"

"I think I've found Donald Laing."

Strike said nothing at all, but stood looking blank, a mug in each hand.

"You've—what? How?"

Robin turned on her computer, beckoned Strike over and began typing. He moved around to look over her shoulder.

"First," she said, "I had to find out how to spell psoriatic arthritis. Then...look at this."

She had brought up a JustGiving charity page. A man glared out of the small picture at the top.

"Bloody hell, that's him!" said Strike, so loudly that Robin jumped. He set the mugs down and dragged his chair around the desk to look at the monitor. In doing so, he knocked over Robin's roses.

"Shit—sorry—"

"I don't care," said Robin. "Sit here, I'll clear them up."

She moved out of the way and Strike took her place on the swivel chair.

It was a small photograph, which Strike enlarged by clicking on it. The Scot was standing on what seemed to be a cramped balcony with a balustrade of thick, greenish glass, unsmiling, with a crutch under his right arm. The short, bristly hair still grew low on his forehead, but it seemed to have darkened over the years, no longer red as a fox's pelt. Clean-shaven, his skin looked pockmarked. He was less swollen in the face than he had been in Lorraine's picture, but he had put on weight since the days when he had been muscled like a marble Atlas and had bitten Strike on the face in the boxing ring. He was wearing a yellow T-shirt and on his right forearm was the rose tattoo, which had undergone a modification: a dagger now ran through it, and drops of blood fell out of the flower towards the wrist. Behind Laing on his balcony was what looked like a blurry, jagged pattern of windows in black and silver.

He had used his real name:

Donald Laing Charity Appeal
I am a British veteran now suffering from psoriatic arthritis. I am raising money for Arthritis Research. Please give what you can.

The page had been created three months previously. He had raised 0 percent of the one thousand pounds he was hoping to meet.

"No rubbish about doing anything for the money," Strike noted. "Just 'gimme.'"

"Not give *me,*" Robin corrected him from the floor, where she was mopping up spilled flower water with bits of kitchen roll. "He's giving it to the charity."

"So he says."

Strike was squinting at the jagged pattern behind Laing on the balcony.

"Does that remind you of anything? Those windows behind him?"

"I thought of the Gherkin at first," said Robin, throwing the sodden towels in the bin and getting to her feet, "but the pattern's different."

"Nothing about where he's living," said Strike, clicking everywhere he could on the page to see what further information he might uncover. "JustGiving must have his details somewhere."

"You somehow never expect evil people to get ill," said Robin.

She checked her watch.

"I'm supposed to be on Platinum in fifteen. I'd better get going."

"Yeah," said Strike, still staring at Laing's picture. "Keep in touch and—oh yeah: I need you to do something."

He pulled his mobile out of his pocket.

"Brockbank."

"So you *do* still think it might be him?" Robin said, pausing in the act of putting on her jacket.

"Maybe. I want you to call him, keep the Venetia Hall, personal injury lawyer thing going."

"Oh. OK," she said, pulling out her own mobile and keying in the number that he had shown her, but beneath her matter-of-fact manner she was quietly elated. Venetia had been her own idea, her creation, and now Strike was turning the whole line of inquiry over to her.

She was halfway up Denmark Street in the sunshine before Robin remembered that there had been a card with the now-battered roses, and that she had left it behind, unread.

32

What's that in the corner?
It's too dark to see.

Blue Öyster Cult, "After Dark"

Surrounded all day long by the sounds of traffic and loud voices, Robin did not have a good opportunity to call Noel Brockbank until five o'clock that afternoon. Having seen Platinum to work as usual, she turned into the Japanese restaurant beside the lap-dancing club and took her green tea to a quiet corner table. There, she waited for five minutes to satisfy herself that any background noises Brockbank might hear could plausibly belong to a busy office situated on a main road, and keyed in the number, her heart hammering.

It was still in service. Robin listened to it ringing for twenty seconds and then, just when she had guessed that nobody was going to pick up, somebody did.

Very heavy breathing roared down the line. Robin sat still, the mobile tight against her ear. Then she jumped, as a shrill toddler's voice said:

"HELLO!"

"Hello?" said Robin cautiously.

In the background a woman's muffled voice said:

"What've you got, Zahara?"

A scraping noise and then, much louder:

"That's Noel's, he's been look—"

The line went dead. Robin lowered the phone slowly, her heart still racing. She could almost see the sticky little finger that had accidentally cut the call.

The phone began to vibrate in her hand: Brockbank's number, calling back. She took a steadying breath and answered.

"Hello, Venetia Hall."

"What?" said a woman's voice.

"Venetia Hall—Hardacre and Hall," said Robin.

"What?" said the woman again. "Did you just call this number?"

She had a London accent. Robin's mouth was dry.

"Yes, I did," said Robin-as-Venetia. "I'm looking for Mr. Noel Brockbank."

"Why?"

After an almost imperceptible pause Robin said:

"Could I ask who I'm speaking to, please?"

"Why?" The woman was sounding increasingly belligerent. "Who are you?"

"My name's Venetia Hall," said Robin, "and I'm a lawyer specializing in personal injury compensation."

A couple sat down in front of her and began to talk loudly in Italian.

"What?" said the woman on the end of the line again.

Inwardly cursing her neighbors, Robin raised her voice and gave the same story that she had told Holly back in Barrow.

"Money for *him?*" said the unknown woman, with a degree less animosity.

"Yes, if his case is successful," said Robin. "Can I ask—?"

"How did you find out about him?"

"We came across Mr. Brockbank's records while we were researching other—"

"How much money?"

"That depends." Robin took a deep breath. "Where is Mr. Brockbank?"

"At work."

"Can I ask where—?"

"I'll get him to call you. This number, yeah?"

"Yes, please," said Robin. "I'll be here in the office tomorrow from nine."

"Vene—Ven—what was your name?"

Robin spelled Venetia for her.

"Yeah, all right, then. I'll get him to call. Bye, then."

Robin rang Strike to tell him what had happened as she walked towards the Tube, but his number was engaged.

Her spirits ebbed as she descended into the Underground. Matthew would be at home by now. It felt as though it had been a long time since she had seen her ex-fiancé and she dreaded their reunion. Her mood sank still further as she traveled home, wishing she had a valid reason to stay away, but grudgingly obedient to her promise to Strike that she would not stay out after dark.

Forty minutes later she arrived at West Ealing station. Walking towards the flat with dread in her heart, her second attempt to call Strike went through.

"Bloody good work!" he said when she told him that she had successfully contacted Brockbank's phone. "You say this woman had a London accent?"

"I think so," said Robin, feeling that Strike was missing a more important point, "and a small daughter, by the sounds of it."

"Yeah. Expect that's why Brockbank's there."

She had expected him to show more concern for a child in close proximity with a man he knew to be a child rapist, but no; he briskly changed the subject.

"I've just been on the phone to Hazel Furley."

"Who?"

"Kelsey's sister, remember? Who wants to meet me? I'm going to see her on Saturday."

"Oh," said Robin.

"Can't do it before then—Mad Dad's back from Chicago. Just as well. Two-Times won't support us forever."

Robin did not respond. She was still thinking about the toddler who had answered the phone. Strike's reaction to that news had disappointed her.

"Are you all right?" asked Strike.

"Yes," said Robin.

She had reached the end of Hastings Road.

"Well, I'll see you tomorrow," she said.

He agreed to it and hung up. Feeling unexpectedly worse for having spoken to Strike, she headed with some trepidation towards her front door.

She need not have worried. The Matthew who had returned from Masham was no longer the man who begged Robin hourly to talk to him. He slept on the sofa. Over the next three days they moved carefully around each other, Robin with cool politeness, he with an air of ostentatious devotion that tipped, at times, into parody. He hurried to wash up cups as soon as she had finished drinking from them and on Thursday morning asked her respectfully how work was going.

"Oh, *please,*" was Robin's only response as she strode past him to the front door.

His family, she guessed, had told him to back off, to give her time. They had not yet discussed how they were going to tell everyone else that the wedding was off: Matthew clearly did not wish to have that discussion. Day to day, Robin stopped short of initiating the conversation. Sometimes she asked herself whether this cowardice revealed her own secret desire to put her ring back on. At others, she was sure that her reluctance sprang from exhaustion, disinclination for what she knew would be the worst and most painful confrontation yet, and a need to marshal her forces before the final break. Little though she had encouraged her mother's forthcoming visit, Robin was subconsciously hoping to draw enough strength and comfort from Linda to do what had to be done.

The roses on her desk shriveled slowly. Nobody had bothered to put them in fresh water, so they died quietly in the wrappings in which they had arrived, but Robin was not there to throw them out and Strike, who visited the office infrequently to fetch things, felt it would be out of place for him to dispose of them, or of the still-unopened card.

After the previous week of regular contact Robin and Strike had resumed a work pattern that meant they rarely saw each other, taking it in turns to follow Platinum and Mad Dad, who had returned from America and immediately resumed the stalking of his young sons. On Thursday afternoon they discussed by phone the question of whether Robin should try Noel Brockbank again, because he had still not called her back. After consideration, Strike told her that Venetia Hall, busy lawyer, would have other fish to fry.

"If he hasn't contacted you by tomorrow you can try again. That'll be a full working week. Course, his lady friend might have lost the number."

When Strike had hung up, Robin resumed her wanderings in Edge Street in Kensington, which was where Mad Dad's family lived. The location did nothing to lift Robin's spirits. She had begun looking online for somewhere else to live, but the places she would be able to afford on the salary Strike paid her were even worse than she had feared, single rooms in shared houses the best she could expect.

The beautiful Victorian mews houses that surrounded her, with glossy front doors, leafy climbing plants, window boxes and bright sash windows, spoke of the comfortable, prosperous existence to which Matthew had aspired back in the days that Robin seemed ready to embrace a more lucrative career. She had told him all along that she did not care about money, or at least not as much as he did, and that remained true, but it would be a strange human being, she thought, who could linger among these pretty, quiet houses and not compare them, to the others' detriment, with "small room in strictly vegan household, mobile phone tolerated if used in bedroom" that was just within her price range, or the cupboard-sized room in Hackney in "friendly and respectful household ready to TAKE YOU ON BOARD!"

Her mobile rang again. She tugged the phone out of her jacket pocket, expecting Strike, and her stomach turned over: Brockbank. Taking a deep breath, she answered.

"Venetia Hall."

"You th'lawyer?"

She did not know what she had expected him to sound like. He had taken monstrous form in her mind, this rapist of children, the long-jawed thug with his broken bottle and what Strike believed to be fake amnesia. His voice was deep and his accent, though by no means as thick as his twin's, remained distinctly Barrovian.

"Yes," said Robin. "Is that Mr. Brockbank?"

"Aye, tha's righ'."

The quality of his silence was somehow threatening. Robin hastened to tell her fictitious story of the compensation that might await him if he were happy to meet her. When she had finished, he said nothing. Robin held her nerve, because Venetia Hall had the self-confidence not to rush to fill a silence, but the crackling of the slack line between them unnerved her.

"An' where did you find ou' abou' us, eh?"

"We came across your case notes while we were investigating—"

"Investigatin' wha'?"

Why did she have such a feeling of menace? He couldn't be anywhere near her, but she scanned her surroundings all the same. The sunny, gracious street was deserted.

"Investigating similar non-combat-related injuries to other servicemen," she said, wishing that her voice had not risen to such a high pitch.

More silence. A car rolled towards her round the corner.

Damn it, Robin thought desperately as she realized that the driver was the obsessive father she was supposed to be observing covertly. He had looked her full in the face as she turned towards his car. She ducked her head and walked slowly away from the school.

"So wha' do I 'ave ter do then, eh?" asked Noel Brockbank in her ear.

"Could we meet and have a chat about your history?" Robin asked, her chest actually painful, so fast was her heart pounding.

"I though' you'd read our 'istory?" he said and the hairs on the back of Robin's neck stood up. "A cun' called Cameron Strike gave us brain damage."

"Yes, I saw that in your file," said Robin breathlessly, "but it's important to take a statement so we can—"

"Take a statemen'?"

There was a pause that felt suddenly dangerous.

"Sure you're no' a horney?"

Robin Ellacott, northerner, understood; Venetia Hall, Londoner, almost certainly would not. "Horney" was the Cumbrian word for policeman.

"Not a what—I'm sorry?" she said, doing her best to sound politely confused.

Mad Dad had parked outside his estranged wife's house. Any moment now, his sons would be leaving with their nanny for a play date. If he accosted them, Robin needed to photograph the encounter. She was falling down on the paying job: she ought to be photographing Mad Dad's movements.

"Police," said Brockbank aggressively.

"Police?" she said, still striving for that tone of mingled disbelief and amusement. "Of course not."

"You sure abou' tha', are you?"

The front door of Mad Dad's wife's house had opened. Robin saw the nanny's red hair and heard a car door open. She forced herself to sound offended and confused.

"Yes, of course I am. Mr. Brockbank, if you're not interested—"

Her hand was slightly damp on the phone. Then, taking her by surprise, he said:

"All right, I'll mee' you."

"Excellent," said Robin as the nanny led the two little boys onto the pavement. "Whereabouts are you?"

"Shoreditch," said Brockbank.

Robin felt every nerve tingle. He was in London.

"So, where would be convenient to—?"

"Wha's tha' noise?"

The nanny was screaming at Mad Dad, who was advancing on her and the boys. One of his sons began wailing.

"Oh, I'm actually—it's just my day for picking up my son from school," said Robin loudly over the background shrieks and shouts.

Silence again on the end of the line. Matter-of-fact Venetia Hall would surely break it, but Robin found herself paralyzed by what she tried to tell herself was an irrational fear.

Then he spoke in a voice more menacing than Robin had ever heard, the more so because he half crooned the words, so close to the receiver that he seemed to be breathing into her ear.

"Do A know you, little girl?"

Robin tried to speak, but no sound came out. The line went dead.

33

Then the door was open and the wind appeared...

Blue Öyster Cult, "(Don't Fear) The Reaper"

"I messed up with Brockbank," said Robin. "I'm really sorry—but I don't know *how* I messed up! Plus I didn't dare take pictures of Mad Dad, because I was too close."

It was nine o'clock on Friday morning and Strike had arrived, not from the upstairs flat but from the street, fully dressed and carrying his backpack again. Robin had heard him humming as he came up the stairs. He had stayed overnight at Elin's. Robin had called him the previous evening to tell him about the Brockbank call, but Strike had not been at liberty to talk for long and had promised that they would do so today.

"Never mind Mad Dad. We'll get him another day," said Strike, busy at the kettle. "And you did great with Brockbank. We know he's in Shoreditch, we know I'm on his mind and we know he was suspicious that you might be police. So is that because he's been fiddling with kids up and down the country, or because he's recently hacked a teenager to death?"

Ever since Brockbank had spoken his last six words into her ear, Robin had felt slightly shaken. She and Matthew had barely talked to each other the previous evening and, having no outlet for a sudden feeling of vulnerability that she did not entirely understand, she had placed all her reliance on seeing Strike face to face and getting to discuss the meaning of those six ominous words: *Do A know you, little girl?* Today, she would have welcomed the serious, cautious Strike who had taken the sending of the leg as a threat and warned her about staying out after dark. The man now cheerfully making himself coffee and talking about child abuse and murder in a matter-of-fact tone was bringing her no comfort. He could have no idea what Brockbank had sounded like, crooning inside her ear.

"We know something else about Brockbank," she said in a tight voice. "He's living with a little girl."

"He might not be living with her. We don't know where he left the phone."

"All right, then," said Robin, feeling even more tightly wound. "If you want to be pedantic: we know he's in close contact with a little girl."

She turned away on the pretext of dealing with the mail she had scooped from the doormat on her arrival. The fact that he had arrived humming had irked her. Presumably his night with Elin had been a welcome distraction, providing recreation and recuperation. Robin would have loved a respite from her hypervigilant days and evenings of frigid silence. The knowledge that she was being unreasonable did nothing to diminish her resentment. She scooped the dying roses in their dry plastic bag off the desk and pushed them headfirst into the bin.

"There's nothing we can do about that kid," said Strike.

A most enjoyable stab of anger shot through Robin.

"I won't worry about her, then," she snapped.

Trying to extract a bill from an envelope, she accidentally ripped the whole thing in two.

"You think she's the only child at risk from an abuser? There'll be hundreds of them, right now, just in London."

Robin, who had half expected him to soften now that she had revealed how angry she was, looked round. He was watching her, eyes slightly narrowed, with no air of sympathy.

"Keep worrying all you want, but it's wasted energy. There's nothing you or I can do about that kid. Brockbank's not on any registers. He hasn't got any convictions. We don't even know where she is or what she's—"

"Her name's Zahara," said Robin.

To her horror, her voice turned to a strangled squeal, her face flooded with color and tears started in her eyes. She turned away again, although not fast enough.

"Hey," said Strike kindly, but Robin made a wild flapping gesture with her hand to stop him talking. She refused to break down; all that was holding her together was her ability to keep moving forwards, to keep doing the job.

"I'm fine," she said through clenched teeth. "I am. Forget it."

She could not now confess how menacing she had found Brockbank's sign-off. "Little girl," he had called her. She was *not* a little girl. She was not broken or childlike—not anymore—but Zahara, whoever she was...

She heard Strike leave for the landing, and a moment later a large wad of toilet paper appeared in her swimming sights.

"Thank you," she said thickly, taking it from Strike's hand and blowing her nose.

Several silent minutes passed while Robin periodically dabbed at her eyes and blew her nose, avoiding looking at Strike, who was perversely remaining in her part of the office rather than heading for his own.

"*What?*" Robin said at last, anger rising again at the fact that he was simply standing there watching her.

He grinned. In spite of everything, she experienced a sudden desire to laugh.

"Are you going to stand there all morning?" she asked, trying to sound cross.

"No," said Strike, still grinning, "I just wanted to show you something."

He ferreted in his backpack and pulled out a glossy property brochure.

"Elin's," he said. "She went to see it yesterday. She's thinking of buying a flat there."

All desire to laugh fled. How exactly did Strike think that it would cheer Robin up, to know that his girlfriend was thinking of buying a ludicrously expensive flat? Or was he about to announce

(Robin's fragile mood began to collapse in on itself) that he and Elin were moving in together? Like a film flickering rapidly before her eyes she saw the upstairs flat empty, Strike living in luxury, herself in a tiny box room on the edge of London, whispering into her mobile so that her vegan landlady did not hear her.

Strike laid the brochure on the desk in front of her. The cover showed a tall modern tower topped by a strange shield-like face in which wind turbines were set like three eyes. The legend read: "Strata SE1, London's most desirable residential property."

"See?" said Strike.

His triumphant air was aggravating Robin beyond measure, not least because it seemed so unlike him to gloat about the prospect of borrowed luxury, but before she could respond there was a knock on the glass door behind him.

"Bloody hell," said Strike in frank astonishment as he opened the door to Shanker, who walked in, clicking his fingers and bringing with him the usual fug of cigarette smoke, cannabis and body odor.

"I was in the area," said Shanker, unconsciously echoing Eric Wardle. "I've found him for you, Bunsen."

Shanker dropped down onto the mock-leather sofa, legs spread out in front of him, and took out a packet of Mayfairs.

"You've found Whittaker?" asked Strike, whose dominant emotion was astonishment that Shanker was awake so early in the morning.

"'Oo else did you ask me to find?" said Shanker, inhaling deeply on his cigarette and clearly enjoying the effect he was creating. "Catford Broadway. Flat over a chip shop. The brass lives with 'im."

Strike held out his hand and shook Shanker's. Notwithstanding his gold tooth and the scar that twisted his upper lip, their visitor's grin was strangely boyish.

"Want a coffee?" Strike asked him.

"Yeah, go on then," said Shanker, who seemed disposed to bask in his triumph. "All right?" he added cheerfully to Robin.

"Yes, thanks," she said with a tight smile, returning to the unopened mail.

"Talk about on a roll," Strike said quietly to Robin while the kettle boiled loudly and an oblivious Shanker smoked and checked texts on his phone. "That's all three of them in London. Whittaker in Catford, Brockbank in Shoreditch and now we know Laing's in Elephant and Castle—or he was three months ago."

She had agreed to it before doing a double take.

"How do we know Laing was in Elephant and Castle?"

Strike tapped the glossy brochure of the Strata on her desk.

"What d'you think I'm showing you that for?"

Robin had no idea what he meant. She looked blankly at the brochure for several seconds before its significance struck her. Panels of silver punctuated the long jagged lines of darkened windows all down the rounded column: this was the background visible behind Laing as he stood on his concrete balcony.

"*Oh,*" she said weakly.

Strike wasn't moving in with Elin. She did not know why she was blushing again. Her emotions seemed totally out of control. What on earth was wrong with her? She turned on her swivel chair to concentrate on the post yet again, hiding her face from both men.

"I dunno if I've got enough dosh on me to pay you, Shanker," Strike said, looking through his wallet. "I'll walk you down to a cashpoint."

"Fair enough, Bunsen," said Shanker, leaning over to Robin's bin to dispose of the ash trickling from his cigarette. "You need 'elp wiv Whittaker, y'know where I am."

"Yeah, cheers. I can probably handle it, though."

Robin reached for the last envelope in the post pile, which felt stiff and had an additional thickness at one corner, as though it contained a card with some kind of novelty attached. On the point of opening it, Robin noticed that it had been addressed to her, not Strike. She paused, uncertain, looking at it. Her name and the address of the office had been typed. The postmark was from central London and the letter had been sent the previous day.

Strike and Shanker's voices rose and fell but she could not have said what they were saying.

It's nothing, she told herself. *You're overwrought. It couldn't happen again.*

Swallowing hard, she opened the envelope and gingerly removed the card.

The image showed a Jack Vettriano painting of a blonde sitting in profile on a chair, which was draped in a dustsheet. The blonde was holding a teacup and her elegant black stockinged, stilettoed legs were crossed and raised on a footstool. There was nothing pinned to the front of the card. The object that she had felt through the card was taped inside it.

Strike and Shanker were still talking. A whiff of decay caught her nostrils through the fug of Shanker's body odor.

"Oh God," said Robin quietly, but neither man heard her. She flipped over the Vettriano print.

A rotting toe was taped to the inner corner of the card. Carefully printed in capital letters were the words:

SHE'S AS BEAUTIFUL AS A FOOT

She dropped it onto the desk and stood up. In slow motion, it seemed, she turned to Strike. He looked from her stricken face to the obscene object lying on the desk.

"Get away from it."

She obeyed, sick and trembling and wishing that Shanker was not there.

"What?" Shanker kept saying. "What? What is it? What?"

"Somebody's sent me a severed toe," said Robin in a collected voice that was not her own.

"You're fucking kidding me," said Shanker, moving forwards with eager interest.

Strike physically restrained Shanker from picking up the card, which lay where it had fallen from Robin's hand. Strike recognized the phrase "She's as Beautiful as a Foot." It was the title of another Blue Öyster Cult song.

"I'll call Wardle," Strike said, but instead of taking out his mobile he scribbled a four-digit code on a Post-it note and extracted his credit card from his wallet. "Robin, go and get the rest of Shanker's money out for him, then come back here."

She took the note and the credit card, absurdly grateful for the prospect of fresh air.

"And Shanker," said Strike sharply, as the two of them reached the glass door, "you walk her back here, all right? Walk her back to the office."

"You got it, Bunsen," said Shanker, energized, as he always had been, by strangeness, by action, by the whiff of danger.

34

The lies don't count, the whispers do.

Blue Öyster Cult, "The Vigil"

Strike sat alone at the kitchen table in his attic flat that night. The chair was uncomfortable and the knee of his amputated leg aching after several hours tailing Mad Dad, who had taken time out of work today to stalk his younger son on a trip to the Natural History Museum. The man owned his own company or he would surely have been fired for the working hours he spent intimidating his children. Platinum, however, had gone unwatched and unphotographed. On learning that Robin's mother was due to visit that evening, Strike had insisted on Robin taking three days off, overriding all her objections, walking her to the Tube and insisting that she text him once safely back at her flat.

Strike yearned for sleep, yet felt too weary to get up and go to bed. He had been more disturbed by the second communication from the killer than he had been prepared to admit to his partner. Appalling though the arrival of the leg had been, he now acknowledged that he had nourished a vestige of hope that the addressing of the package to Robin had been a nasty embellishment, but an afterthought. The second communication with her, sly sideways wink at Strike notwithstanding ("She's as Beautiful as a Foot"), had told him for certain that this man, whoever he was, had Robin in his sights. Even the name of the painting on the front of the card he had selected—the image of the solitary, leggy blonde—was ominous: *In Thoughts of You.*

Rage burgeoned in the motionless Strike, chasing away his tiredness. He remembered Robin's white face and knew that he had witnessed the death of her faint hope that the sending of the leg had not been the random act of a madman. Even so, she had argued vociferously against taking time off, pointing out that their only two paying jobs frequently clashed: Strike would be unable to cover both properly on his own and would consequently have to choose on a daily basis whether to follow Platinum or Mad Dad. He had been adamant: she should return to work only when her mother returned to Yorkshire.

Their persecutor had now succeeded in reducing Strike's business to two clients. He had just endured a second incursion of police into his office and was worried that the press would get wind of what had happened, even though Wardle had promised not to release news of the card and the toe. Wardle agreed with Strike that one of the killer's objectives was to focus press and police attention on the detective, and that it was playing into the killer's hands to alert the media.

His mobile rang loudly in the small kitchen. Glancing at his watch, he saw that it was twenty past ten. He seized it, barely registering Wardle's name as he raised it to his ear, because his mind had been on Robin.

"Good news," Wardle told him. "Well, of a kind. He hasn't killed another woman. The toe's Kelsey's. Off the other leg. Waste not, want not, eh?"

Strike, who was not in the mood for humor, replied brusquely. After Wardle had hung up, he continued to sit at his kitchen table, lost in thought while the traffic growled past in Charing Cross Road below. Only the recollection that he had to get to Finchley the next morning to meet Kelsey's sister finally motivated him to begin the usual onerous process of dealing with his prosthesis before bed.

Strike's knowledge of London was, thanks to his mother's peripatetic habits, extensive and detailed, but there were gaps, and Finchley was one of them. All he knew about the area was that it had been Margaret Thatcher's constituency in the 1980s, while he, Leda and

Lucy had been moving between squats in places like Whitechapel and Brixton. Finchley would have been too far away from the center to suit a family entirely reliant on public transport and takeaways, too expensive for a woman who frequently ran out of coins for the electricity meter: the kind of place, as his sister Lucy might once have wistfully put it, where proper families lived. In marrying a quantity surveyor and producing three impeccably turned-out sons, Lucy had fulfilled her childhood yearning for neatness, order and security.

Strike took the Tube to West Finchley and endured a long walk to Summers Lane rather than find a taxi, because his finances were so bad. Sweating slightly in the mild weather, he moved through road after road of quiet detached houses, cursing the place for its leafy quiet and its lack of landmarks. Finally, thirty minutes after he had left the station, he found Kelsey Platt's house, smaller than many of its fellows, with a whitewashed exterior and a wrought-iron gate.

He rang the doorbell and immediately heard voices through the pane of frosted glass like the one in his own office door.

"Ah think it's the detective, pet," said a Geordie voice.

"You get it!" said a woman's high-pitched voice.

A large red mass bloomed behind the glass and the door opened onto the hall, which was mostly concealed by a burly, barefoot man in a scarlet toweling robe. He was bald, but his bushy gray beard, coupled with the scarlet robe, would have suggested Santa had he looked jolly. However, he was frantically mopping his face with the sleeve of his dressing gown. The eyes behind his glasses were swollen into bee-stung slits and his ruddy cheeks were shining with tears.

"Sorry," he said gruffly, moving aside to let Strike in. "Working nights," he added in explanation of his attire.

Strike sidled past. The man smelled strongly of Old Spice and camphor. Two middle-aged women were locked in a tight embrace at the foot of the stairs, one blonde, the other dark, both sobbing. They broke apart as Strike watched, wiping their faces.

"Sorry," gasped the dark-haired woman. "Sheryl's our neighbor. She's been in Magaluf, she's only just h-heard about Kelsey."

"Sorry," echoed red-eyed Sheryl. "I'll give you space, Hazel. Anything you need. Anything, Ray—anything."

Sheryl squeezed past Strike—"sorry"—and hugged Ray. They swayed together briefly, both big people, their bellies pressed together, arms stretched around each other's necks. Ray began sobbing again, his face in her broad shoulder.

"Come through," hiccoughed Hazel, dabbing at her eyes as she led the way into the sitting room. She had the look of a Bruegel peasant, with her rounded cheeks, prominent chin and wide nose. Eyebrows as thick and bushy as tiger moth caterpillars overhung her puffy eyes. "It's been like this all week. People hearing and coming over and…sorry," she finished on a gasp.

He had been apologized to half a dozen times in the space of two minutes. Other cultures would have been ashamed of an insufficient display of grief; here in quiet Finchley, they were ashamed to have him witness it.

"Nobody knows what to say," Hazel whispered, pressing away her tears as she gestured him to the sofa. "It's not like she was hit by a car, or was ill. They don't know what you say when someone's been—" She hesitated, but balked at the word and her sentence ended in a gargantuan sniff.

"I'm sorry," said Strike, taking his turn. "I know this is a terrible time for you."

The sitting room was immaculate and somehow unwelcoming, perhaps because of its chilly color scheme. A three-piece suite covered in striped silvery-gray cloth, white wallpaper with a thin gray stripe, cushions angled on their points, ornaments on the mantelpiece perfectly symmetrical. The dust-free television screen gleamed with reflected light from the window.

Sheryl's misty form trotted past on the other side of the net curtains, wiping her eyes. Ray shuffled past the sitting-room door on his bare feet, dabbing under his glasses with the end of his toweling-robe belt, his shoulders stooped. As though she had read Strike's mind, Hazel explained:

"Ray broke his back trying to get a family out of a boarding house that caught fire. Wall gave way and his ladder fell. Three stories."

"Christ," said Strike.

Hazel's lips and hands were trembling. Strike remembered what Wardle had said: that the police had mishandled Hazel. Suspicion or rough questioning of her Ray would have seemed unforgivable cruelty to her in this state of shock, an inexcusable exacerbation of their appalling ordeal. Strike knew a lot about the brutal intrusion of officialdom into private devastation. He had been on both sides of the fence.

"Anyone want a brew?" Ray called huskily from what Strike assumed was the kitchen.

"Go to bed!" Hazel called back, clutching a sodden ball of tissues. "I can make 'em! Go to bed!"

"You sure?"

"Get to bed, I'll wake you at three!"

Hazel wiped her whole face with a fresh tissue, as though it were a face cloth.

"He's not one for disability pay and all that, but nobody wants to give him a proper job," she told Strike quietly as Ray shuffled, sniffing, back past the door. "Not with his back and his age and his lungs not being the best. Cash in hand...shift work..."

Her voice trailed away, her mouth trembled, and for the first time she looked Strike directly in the eye.

"I don't really know why I asked you to come," she confessed. "It's all confused in my head. They said she wrote to you but you never wrote back and then you got sent her—her—"

"It must have been an appalling shock to you," said Strike, fully aware that anything he could say would understate the case.

"It's been—" she said feverishly "—terrible. Terrible. We didn't know anything, anything at all. We thought she was on a college placement. When the police came to the door—she said she was going away with college and I believed her, some residential placement at a school. It sounded right—I never thought—but she was such a liar. She lied all the time. Three years she's been living with me and I still haven't—I mean, I couldn't get her to stop."

"What did she tell lies about?" asked Strike.

"Anything," said Hazel, with a slightly wild gesture. "If it was

Tuesday she'd say it was Wednesday. Sometimes there was no point to it at all. I don't know why. I don't know."

"Why was she living with you?" Strike asked.

"She's my—she was my half-sister. Same mum. We lost Dad when I was twenty. Mum married a guy from work and had Kelsey. There were twenty-four years between us—I'd left home—I was more like an auntie to her than a sister. Then Mum and Malcolm had a car crash out in Spain three years ago. Drunk driver. Malcolm died outright, Mum was in a coma for four days and then she passed, too. There isn't any other family, so I took Kelsey in."

The extreme tidiness of their surroundings, the cushions on their points, surfaces clear and highly polished, made Strike wonder how a teenager had fitted in here.

"Me and Kelsey didn't get on," said Hazel, again seeming to read Strike's thoughts. Tears flowed once more as she pointed upstairs, where Ray had gone to bed. "He was much more patient with all her moodiness and her sulks. He's got a grown-up son who's working abroad. He's better with kids than me. Then the police come jack-booting in here," she said on a sudden rush of fury, "and tell us she's been—they start questioning Ray like he'd—like he'd *ever,* in a million *years*—I said to him, it's like a nightmare. You see people on the news, don't you, appealing for kids to come home—people put on trial for things they never did—you never think...you never think...but we never even knew she was missing. We'd have looked. We never knew. The police asking Ray questions—where he was and I don't know what—"

"They've told me he didn't have anything to do with it," Strike said.

"Yeah, they believe that *now,*" said Hazel through angry tears, "after three men told them he was with them every minute of the stag weekend and showed them the bloody photos to prove it..."

She would never think it reasonable that the man who had been living with Kelsey should be questioned about her death. Strike, who had heard the testimony of Brittany Brockbank and Rhona Laing and many others like them, knew that most women's rapists and killers were not strangers in masks who reached out of the dark spacc under the stairs. They were the father, the husband, the mother's or the sister's boyfriend...

Hazel wiped the tears away as fast as they fell onto her round cheeks, then suddenly asked:

"What did you do with her silly letter anyway?"

"My assistant put it in the drawer where we keep unusual correspondence," said Strike.

"The police said you never wrote back to her. They say they was forged, the letters they found."

"That's right," said Strike.

"So whoever done it must've known she was interested in you."

"Yes," said Strike.

Hazel blew her nose vigorously, then asked:

"D'you want a cuppa, then?"

He accepted only because he thought she wanted a chance to pull herself together. Once she had left the room he looked around openly. The only photograph stood on a small nest of tables in the corner beside him. It showed a beaming woman in her sixties wearing a straw hat. This, he assumed, was Hazel and Kelsey's mother. A slightly darker stripe on the surface of the table beside the picture suggested that another had stood beside it, preventing the sun bleaching that small strip on the cheap wood. Strike guessed that this had been the school photograph of Kelsey, the picture that all the papers had printed.

Hazel returned carrying a tray bearing mugs of tea and a plate of biscuits. After she had carefully positioned his tea on a coaster beside her mother's photograph, Strike said:

"I hear Kelsey had a boyfriend."

"Rubbish," retorted Hazel, dropping back into her armchair. "More porkies."

"What makes you—?"

"She said his name was Niall. Niall. *Honestly.*"

Her eyes leaked more tears. Strike was at a loss to understand why Kelsey's boyfriend might not have been called Niall and his incomprehension showed.

"One Direction," she said over the top of her tissue.

"Sorry," said Strike, completely at sea. "I don't—"

"The band. They're a band that came third on *The X Factor.* She's obsessed—she was obsessed—and Niall was her favorite. So when she says she's met a boy called Niall and he's eighteen and he's got a motorbike, I mean, what were we supposed to think?"

"Ah. I see."

"She said she met him at the counselor's. She's been seeing a counselor, see. Claimed she met Niall in the waiting room, that he was there because his mum and dad died, like hers. *We* never saw hide nor hair of him. I said to Ray, 'She's at it again, she's fibbing,' and Ray said to me, 'Let it go, it keeps her happy,' but I didn't like her lying," said Hazel with a fanatic glare. "She lied *all* the time, came home with a plaster on her wrist, said it was a cut and it turned out to be a One Direction tattoo. Look at her saying she was going away on a college placement, look at that...she kept lying and lying and look where it got her!"

With an enormous, visible effort she controlled a fresh eruption of tears, holding her trembling lips together and pressing the tissues hard across her eyes. Taking a deep breath, she said:

"Ray's got a theory. He wanted to tell the police, but *they* didn't care, they were more interested in where *he'd* been when she was—but Ray's got a friend called Ritchie who puts a bit of gardening his way, see, and Kelsey met Ritchie—"

The theory was rolled out with a huge amount of extraneous detail and repetition. Strike, who was well used to the rambling style of unpracticed witnesses, listened attentively and politely.

A photograph was produced out of a dresser drawer, which did double duty in proving to Strike that Ray had been with three friends on a stag weekend in Shoreham-by-Sea when Kelsey was killed, and also revealed young Ritchie's injuries. Ritchie and Ray sat on the shingle beside a patch of sea holly, grinning, holding beers and squinting in the sunlight. Sweat glistened on Ray's bald pate and illuminated young Ritchie's swollen face, his stitches and bruising. His leg was in a surgical boot.

"—and, see, Ritchie came round here right after he'd had his smash and Ray thinks it put the idea in her head. He thinks she was planning to do something to her leg and then pretend she'd had a traffic accident."

"Ritchie couldn't be the boyfriend, could he?" asked Strike.

"Ritchie! He's a bit simple. He'd have told us. Anyway, she barely knew him. It was all a fantasy. I think Ray's right. She was planning to do something to her leg again and pretend she'd come off some boy's bike."

It would have been an excellent theory, thought Strike, if Kelsey had been lying in hospital, pretending to have suffered a motorbike accident and refusing to give more details under the pretense of protecting a fictitious boyfriend. He did Ray the credit of agreeing that this was exactly the kind of plan a sixteen-year-old might have come up with, mingling grandiosity and short-sightedness in dangerous measure. However, the point was moot. Whether or not Kelsey had once planned a fake motorbike crash, the evidence showed that she had abandoned the plan in preference for asking Strike for instructions on leg removal.

On the other hand, this was the first time that anyone had drawn any connection between Kelsey and a motorcyclist, and Strike was interested in Hazel's absolute conviction that any boyfriend must be fictional.

"Well, there was hardly any boys on her childcare course," said Hazel, "and where else was she going to meet him? *Niall.* She'd never had a boyfriend at school or anything. She went to the counselor and sometimes she went to the church up the road, they've a youth group, but there's no Niall-with-a-motorbike *there,*" said Hazel. "The police checked, asked her friends if they knew anything. Darrell who runs the group, he was that upset. Ray saw him this morning on his way home. Says Darrell burst into tears when he saw him from across the road."

Strike wanted to take notes, but knew it would change the atmosphere of confidence he was trying to nurture.

"Who's Darrell?"

"He didn't have anything to do with it. Youth worker at the church. He's from Bradford," said Hazel obscurely, "and Ray's sure he's gay."

"Did she talk about her—" Strike hesitated, unsure what to call it. "Her problem with her leg at home?"

"Not to me," said Hazel flatly. "I wouldn't have it, I didn't want to hear it, I hated it. She told me when she was fourteen and I told her exactly what I thought. Attention-seeking, that's all it was."

"There was old scarring on her leg. How did that—?"

"She did it right after Mum died. Like I didn't have enough to worry about. She tied wire round it, tried to cut off the circulation."

Her expression revealed a mixture, it seemed to Strike, of revulsion and anger.

"She was in the car when Mum and Malcolm died, in the back. I had to get a counselor and all that for her. He thought it was a cry for help or something, what she did to her leg. Grief. Survivors' guilt, I can't remember. She said not, though, said she'd wanted the leg gone for a while…I don't know," said Hazel, shaking her head vigorously.

"Did she talk to anyone else about it? Ray?"

"A bit, yeah. I mean, he knew what she was like. When we first got together, when he moved in, she told him some real whoppers—her dad being a spy, that was one of them, and that was why their car had crashed, and I don't know what else. So he knew what she was like, but he didn't get angry with her. He just used to change the subject, chat to her about school and that…"

She had turned an unattractive dark red.

"I'll tell you what she wanted," she burst out. "To be in a wheelchair—pushed around like a baby and to be pampered and the center of attention. That's what it was all about. I found a diary, must have been a year or so ago. The things she'd written, what she liked to imagine, what she fantasized about. Ridiculous!"

"Such as?" asked Strike.

"Such as having her leg cut off and being in a wheelchair and being pushed to the edge of the stage and watching One Direction and having them come and make a big fuss of her afterwards because she was disabled," said Hazel on a single breath. "Imagine that. It's disgusting. There are people who are really disabled and they never wanted it. I'm a nurse. I know. I see them. Well," she said, with a glance at Strike's lower legs, "*you* don't need telling.

"You didn't, did you?" she asked suddenly, point blank. "You *didn't*—you *didn't* cut—do it—yourself?"

Was that why she had wanted to see him, Strike wondered. In some confused, subconscious manner, trying to find her moorings in the sea on which she was suddenly adrift, had she wanted to prove a point—even though her sister was gone and beyond understanding—that people didn't *do* that, not in the real world where cushions stood neatly on points and disability came only by mischance, through crumbling walls or roadside explosives?

"No," he said. "I was blown up."

"There you are, you see!" she said, tears erupting again, savagely triumphant. "I could have told her that—I could have told her if she'd only...if she'd asked me...but what she claimed," said Hazel, gulping, "was that her leg felt like it shouldn't be there. Like it was wrong to have it and it needed to come off—like a tumor or something. I wouldn't listen. It was all nonsense. Ray says he tried to talk sense into her. He told her she didn't know what she was asking for, that she wouldn't want to be in hospital like he was after he broke his back, laid up for months in plaster, skin sores and infections and all the rest of it. He didn't get angry with her, though. He'd say to her, come and help me in the garden or something, distract her.

"The police told us she was talking to people online who were like her. We had no idea. I mean, she was sixteen, you can't go looking on their laptops, can you? Not that I'd know what to look for."

"Did she ever mention me to you?" Strike asked.

"The police asked that. No. I can't remember her ever talking about you and nor can Ray. I mean, no offense, but—I remember the Lula Landry trial, but I wouldn't have remembered your name from that, or recognized you. If she'd brought you up I'd remember. It's a funny name—no offense."

"What about friends? Did she go out much?"

"She hardly had any friends. She wasn't the popular sort. She lied to all the kids at school too, and nobody likes that, do they? They bullied her for it. Thought she was strange. She hardly ever went out. When she was meeting this supposed *Niall,* I don't know."

Her anger did not surprise Strike. Kelsey had been an unplanned addition to her spotless household. Now, for the rest of her life, Hazel would carry guilt and grief, horror and regret, not least that her sister's life had been ended before she could grow out of the peculiarities that had helped estrange them.

"Would it be all right if I used your bathroom?" Strike asked.

Dabbing her eyes, she nodded.

"Straight ahead, top of the stairs."

Strike emptied his bladder while reading a framed citation for "brave and meritorious conduct," awarded to firefighter Ray Williams, which was hanging over the cistern. He strongly suspected that Hazel had hung that there, not Ray. Otherwise the bathroom displayed little of interest. The same meticulous attention to cleanliness and neatness displayed in the sitting room extended all the way to the inside of the medicine cabinet, where Strike learned that Hazel was still menstruating, that they bulk-bought toothpaste and that one or both of the couple had hemorrhoids.

He left the bathroom as quietly as he could. Faintly, from behind a closed door, came a soft rumbling indicating that Ray was asleep. Strike took two decisive steps to the right and found himself in Kelsey's box room.

Everything matched, covered in the same shade of lilac: walls, duvet, lampshade and curtains. Strike thought he might have guessed that order had been forcibly imposed on chaos in here, even had he not seen the rest of the house.

A large cork noticeboard ensured that there would be no unsightly pin marks on the walls. Kelsey had plastered the cork with pictures of five pretty young boys whom Strike assumed were One Direction. Their heads and legs protruded outside the frame of the board. There was a particular recurrence of a blond boy. Other than the pictures of One Direction, she had cut out puppies, mostly shih-tzus, random words and acronyms: OCCUPY, FOMO and AMAZEBALLS, and many recurrences of the name NIALL, often stuck onto hearts. The slapdash, random collage told of an attitude completely at odds with the precision with which the duvet had been laid on the bed and the exactly square position of the lilac rug.

Prominent on the narrow bookshelf was what looked like a new *One Direction: Forever Young—Our Official X Factor Story.* Otherwise the shelves held the *Twilight* series, a jewelry box, a mess of small trinkets that not even Hazel had managed to make look symmetrical, a plastic tray of cheap makeup and a couple of cuddly toys.

Banking on the fact that Hazel was heavy enough to make a noise coming upstairs, Strike swiftly opened drawers. The police would have taken away anything of interest, of course: the laptop, any scrap of scribbled paper, any telephone number or jotted name, any diary, if she had continued to keep one after Hazel had gone snooping. A mishmash of belongings remained: a box of writing paper like that on which she had written to him, an old Nintendo DS, a pack of false nails, a small box of Guatemalan worry dolls and, in the very bottom drawer of her bedside table, tucked inside a fluffy pencil case, several stiff foil-covered strips of pills. He pulled them out: ovoid capsules in mustard yellow labeled Accutane. He took one of the strips and pocketed it, closed the drawer and headed to her wardrobe, which was untidy and slightly fusty. She had liked black and pink. He felt swiftly among the folds of material, rifling through the pockets of the clothes, but found nothing until he tried a baggy dress in which he found what looked like a crumpled raffle or coat check ticket, numbered 18.

Hazel had not moved since Strike had left her. He guessed that he could have stayed away longer and she would not have noticed. When he reentered the room she gave a little start. She had been crying again.

"Thank you for coming," she said thickly, getting to her feet. "I'm sorry, I—"

And she began to sob in earnest. Strike put a hand on her shoulder and before he knew it, she had her face on his chest, sobbing, gripping the lapels of his coat, with no trace of coquettishness, but in pure anguish. He put his arms around her shoulders and they stood so for a full minute until, with several heaving breaths, she stepped away again and Strike's arms fell back to his sides.

She shook her head, no words left, and walked him to the door. He reiterated his condolences. She nodded, her face ghastly in the daylight now falling into the dingy hall.

"Thanks for coming," she gulped. "I just needed to see you. I don't know why. I'm ever so sorry."

35

Dominance and Submission

Since leaving home, he had cohabited with three women, but this one—It—was testing him to his limits. All three dirty bitches had claimed to love him, whatever that was supposed to mean. Their so-called love had turned the first two tractable. At heart, of course, all women were cheating cunts, determined to take more than they gave, but the first two hadn't been anything like It. He was forced to put up with more than he'd ever put up with before, because It was an essential part of his grand plan.

Nevertheless, he constantly fantasized about killing It. He could imagine Its stupid face slackening as the knife sank deep into her belly, unable to believe that Baby (It called him Baby) was killing her, even as the hot blood began pouring over his hands, the rusty smell filling the air still shivering with her screams…

Having to play nice was playing havoc with his self-control. Switching on the charm, drawing them in and keeping them sweet was easy, second nature to him, always had been. Sustaining the pose over long periods, though, was something else. The pretense was bringing him to his breaking point. Sometimes, even the sound of Its breathing was enough to make him want to grab his knife and puncture her fucking lungs…

Unless he got to do one soon, he'd fucking explode.

Early on Monday morning he made an excuse to get out, but as he approached Denmark Street, intending to pick up The Secretary's trail as she arrived for work, something quivered in him, like the twitching of a rat's whiskers.

He paused beside a telephone box on the opposite side of the road, squinting at a figure standing on the corner of Denmark Street, right outside an instrument shop painted in the garish colors of a circus poster.

He knew the police, knew their moves, their games. The young man standing with his hands in the pockets of his donkey jacket was pretending to be casual, a mere bystander...

He'd invented that fucking game. He could make himself practically invisible. Look at that dickhead, standing on the corner thinking his donkey jacket made him one of the lads... *never shit a shitter, pal.*

Slowly he turned and walked out of sight behind the telephone box, where he slid the beanie hat off his head... He'd been wearing it when Strike chased him. Donkey Jacket might have a description. He should have thought of that, should have guessed Strike would call in his police mates, cowardly fucker...

There's been no photofit issued, though, he thought, his self-esteem rising again as he walked back down the street. Strike had come within feet of him, though he didn't realize it, and still had no fucking idea who he was. God, it would feel good, after he'd done The Secretary, to watch Strike and his fucking business sinking out of sight under the mudslide of the publicity, police and press crawling all over him, tainted by association, unable to protect his staff, suspected of her death, utterly ruined...

He was already planning his next move. He would go to the LSE, where The Secretary often followed the other blonde tart around, and hook up with her there. In the meantime, he'd need a different hat and, perhaps, new sunglasses. He felt in his pockets for money. He had hardly any, as fucking usual. He'd need to force It back out to work. He'd had enough of It whining and bleating and making excuses at home.

In the end he bought two new hats, a baseball cap and a gray woolen beanie to replace the black fleece version he put in a bin at Cambridge Circus. Then he caught the Tube to Holborn.

She wasn't there. Nor were any students. After searching fruitlessly for a glimpse of red-gold hair, he remembered that today was Easter Monday. The LSE was closed for the bank holiday.

After a couple of hours he returned to Tottenham Court Road, looked for her in the Court and skulked for a while near the entrance to Spearmint Rhino, but could not find her anywhere.

After a run of days when he had been unable to get out and look for her, the disappointment caused him almost physical pain. Agitated, he began walking quiet side streets, hoping that some girl would stroll across his path, any woman at all, it didn't have to be The Secretary; the knives beneath his jacket would be happy with anything now.

Perhaps she had been so shaken up by his little greetings card that she had resigned. That wasn't what he wanted at all. He wanted her terrified and off balance, but working for Strike, because she was his means of getting the bastard.

In bitter disappointment, he returned in the early evening to It. He knew he was going to have to remain with It for the next two days and the prospect was draining him of his last vestiges of control. If he could have used It in the way he planned to use The Secretary, it would have been a different matter, a release: he would have hurried home, knives at the ready—but he dared not. He needed It alive and in thrall to him.

Before forty-eight hours had passed, he was ready to explode with rage and violence. On Wednesday evening he told It that he would have to leave early next day to do a job and advised It bluntly that it was time It got back to work too. The resultant whining and mewling wore at him until he became angry. Cowed by his sudden rage, It tried to placate him. It needed him, It wanted him, It was sorry...

He slept apart from It on the pretense of still being angry. This left him free to masturbate, but that left him unsatisfied. What he wanted, what he needed, was contact with female flesh through sharp steel, to feel his dominance as the blood spurted, to hear total submission in her screams, her pleas, her dying gasps and whimpers. Memories of the times when he had done it were no comfort; they merely inflamed his need. He burned to do it again: he wanted The Secretary.

He rose on Thursday morning at a quarter to five, got dressed, pulled on his baseball cap and left to make his way across London to the flat that she shared with Pretty Boy. The sun had risen by the time he reached Hastings Road. An ancient Land Rover parked a short way from the house gave him cover. He leaned against it, keeping watch through the windscreen at the windows of her flat.

There was movement behind the sitting-room windows at seven and shortly afterwards Pretty Boy left in his suit. He looked drawn and unhappy. *You think you're unhappy now, you silly bastard . . . wait until I've had my fun with your girlfriend . . .*

Then at last she appeared, accompanied by an older woman who greatly resembled her.

For fuck's sake.

What was she doing, going on outings with her fucking mother? It felt like mockery. Sometimes the whole world seemed like it was out to get him, to stop him doing things he wanted, to keep him down. He fucking hated this feeling that his omnipotence was seeping away, that people and circumstances were hemming him in, reducing him to just another thwarted, seething mortal. Somebody was going to pay for this.

36

I have this feeling that my luck is none too good...

Blue Öyster Cult, "Black Blade"

When his alarm went off on Thursday morning, Strike extended one heavy arm and slapped the button on top of the old clock so hard that it toppled off his bedside table onto the floor. Squinting, he had to concede that the sunlight glowing through his thin curtains seemed to confirm the alarm's raucous assertion. The temptation to roll over and sink back into sleep was almost overwhelming. He lay with his forearm over his eyes for a few more seconds, blocking out the day, then, with a mingled sigh and groan, he threw back the covers. As he groped for the handle of the bathroom door shortly afterwards, he reflected that he must have averaged three hours' sleep over the preceding five nights.

As Robin had foreseen, sending her home had meant he had to choose between tailing Platinum and Mad Dad. Having recently witnessed the latter jumping out at his small sons unexpectedly, and seen their tears of fright, Strike had decided that Mad Dad ought to be prioritized. Leaving Platinum to her blameless routine, he had spent large parts of the week covertly photographing the skulking father, racking up image after image of the man spying on his boys and accosting them whenever their mother was not present.

When not covering Mad Dad, Strike had been busy with his own investigations. The police were moving far too slowly for his liking so, still without the slightest proof that Brockbank, Laing or Whittaker had any connection with Kelsey Platt's death, Strike had packed almost every free hour of the preceding five days with the kind of relentless, round-the-clock police work that he had previously only given the army.

Balanced on his only leg, he wrenched the dial on the shower clockwise and allowed the icy water to pummel him awake, cooling his puffy eyes and raising gooseflesh through the dark hair on his chest, arms and legs. The one good thing about his tiny shower was that, if he slipped, there was no room to fall. Once clean, he hopped back to the bedroom, where he toweled himself roughly and turned on the TV.

The royal wedding would take place the following day and the preparations dominated every news channel he could find. While he strapped on his prosthesis, dressed and consumed tea and toast, presenters and commentators kept up a constant, excitable stream of commentary about the people who were already sitting out in tents along the route and outside Westminster Abbey, and the numbers of tourists pouring into London to witness the ceremony. Strike turned off the television and headed downstairs to the office, yawning widely and wondering how this multimedia barrage of wedding talk would be affecting Robin, whom he had not seen since the previous Friday, when the Jack Vettriano card containing a grisly little surprise had arrived.

In spite of the fact that he had just finished a large mug of tea upstairs, Strike automatically switched on the kettle when he arrived in the office, then put down on Robin's desk the list of strip joints, lap-dancing clubs and massage parlors he had begun compiling in his few free hours. When Robin arrived, he intended to ask her to continue researching and telephoning all the places she could find in Shoreditch, a job she could do safely from her own home. If he could have enforced her cooperation, he would have sent her back to Masham with her mother. The memory of her white face had haunted him all week.

Stifling a second enormous yawn, he slumped down at Robin's desk to check his emails. In spite of his intention to send her home, he was looking forward to seeing her. He missed her presence in the office, her enthusiasm, her can-do attitude, her easy, unforced kindness, and he wanted to tell her about the few advances he had made during his dogged pursuit of the three men currently obsessing him.

He had now notched up nearly twelve hours in Catford, trying to glimpse Whittaker entering or leaving his flat over the chip shop, which stood on a busy pedestrian street running along the rear of the Catford Theatre. Fishmongers, wig shops, cafés and bakeries curved around the perimeter of the theater, and each had a flat above it boasting three arched windows in triangular formation. The thin curtains of the flat where Shanker believed Whittaker to be living were constantly closed. Market stalls filled the street by day, providing Strike with useful cover. The mingled smells of incense from the dream-catcher stall and the slabs of raw fish lying on ice nearby filled his nostrils until he barely noticed them.

For three evenings Strike had watched from the stage door of the theater, opposite the flat, seeing nothing but shadowy forms moving behind the flat's curtains. Then, on Wednesday evening, the door beside the chip shop had opened to reveal an emaciated teenage girl.

Her dark, dirty hair was pulled back off a sunken, rabbity face, which had the violet-shadowed pallor of a consumptive. She wore a crop top, a zip-up gray hoodie and leggings that gave her thin legs the look of pipe cleaners. Arms crossed tightly across her thin torso, she entered the chip shop by leaning on the door until it gave, then half falling into it. Strike hurried across the road so fast that he caught the door as it swung closed and took a place immediately behind her in the queue.

When she reached the counter the man serving addressed her by name.

"All right, Stephanie?"

"Yeah," she said in a low voice. "Two Cokes, please."

She had multiple piercings in her ears, nose and lip. After counting out payment in coins she left, head bowed, without looking at Strike.

He returned to his darkened doorway across the road where he ate the chips he had just bought, his eyes never moving from the lit windows above the chippy. Her purchase of two Cokes suggested that Whittaker was up there, perhaps sprawled naked on a mattress, as Strike had so often seen him in his teens. Strike had thought himself detached, but the awareness as he had stood in the chip-shop queue that he might be mere feet from the bastard, separated only by a flimsy wood and plaster ceiling, had made his pulse race. Stubbornly he watched the flat until the lights in the windows went off around one in the morning, but there had been no sign of Whittaker.

He had been no luckier with Laing. Careful perusal of Google Street View suggested that the balcony on which the fox-haired Laing had posed for his JustGiving photograph belonged to a flat in Wollaston Close, a squat, shabby block of flats that stood a short distance from the Strata. Neither phone nor voter registration records for the property revealed any trace of Laing, but Strike still held out hope that he might be living there as the guest of another, or renting and living without a landline. He had spent hours on Tuesday evening keeping watch over the flats, bringing with him a pair of night-vision goggles that enabled him to peer through uncurtained windows once darkness fell, but saw no hint of the Scot entering, leaving or moving around inside any of the flats. Having no wish to tip Laing off that he was after him, Strike had decided against door-to-door inquiries, but had lurked by day near the brick arches of a railway bridge nearby, which had been filled in to create tunnel-like spaces. Small businesses lived here: an Ecuadorian café, a hairdresser's. Eating and drinking silently among cheerful South Americans, Strike had been conspicuous by his silence and moroseness.

Strike's fresh yawn turned into another groan of tiredness as he stretched in Robin's computer chair, so that he did not hear the first clanging footsteps on the stairs in the hallway. By the time he had realized that somebody was approaching and checked his watch—it was surely too early for Robin, who had told him her mother's train would leave at eleven—a shadow was climbing the wall outside the frosted glass. A knock on the door, and to Strike's astonishment, Two-Times entered the office.

A paunchy middle-aged businessman, he was considerably wealthier than his crumpled, nondescript appearance would suggest. His face, which was entirely forgettable, neither handsome nor homely, was today screwed up in consternation.

"She's dumped me," he told Strike without preamble.

He dropped onto the mock-leather sofa in an eruption of fake flatulence that took him by surprise; for the second time, Strike assumed, that day. It must have been a shock to the man to be dumped, when his usual procedure was to collect evidence of infidelity and present it to the blonde in question, thus severing the connection. The better Strike had got to know his client, the more he had understood that, for Two-Times, this constituted some kind of satisfying sexual climax. The man appeared to be a peculiar mixture of masochist, voyeur and control freak.

"Really?" said Strike, getting to his feet and heading towards the kettle; he needed caffeine. "We've been keeping a very close eye on her and there hasn't been a hint of another man."

In fact, he had done nothing about Platinum all week except to take Raven's calls, a few of which he had allowed to go to voicemail while he had been tailing Mad Dad. He now wondered whether he had listened to all of them. He hoped to Christ that Raven had not been warning him that another rich man had shown up, ready to defray some of Platinum's student expenses in return for exclusive privileges, or he would have to say good-bye to Two-Times's cash for good.

"Why's she dumped me then?" demanded Two-Times.

Because you're a fucking weirdo.

"Well, I can't swear there isn't someone else," said Strike, choosing his words carefully as he poured instant coffee into a mug. "I'm just saying she's been bloody clever about it if there is. We've been tailing her every move," he lied. "Coffee?"

"I thought you were supposed to be the best," grumbled Two-Times. "No, I don't drink instant."

Strike's mobile rang. He pulled it out of his pocket and checked the caller: Wardle.

"Sorry, I need to take this," he told his disgruntled client, and did so.

"Hi, Wardle."

"Malley's ruled out," said Wardle.

It was a mark of Strike's exhaustion that these words meant nothing to him for a second or two. Then the realization dawned that Wardle was talking about the gangster who had once cut off a man's penis, and of whose probable guilt in the matter of the leg Wardle had seemed convinced.

"Digger—right," said Strike, to show that he was paying attention. "He's out, is he?"

"It can't've been him. He was in Spain when she was killed."

"Spain," repeated Strike.

Two-Times drummed his thick fingers on the arm of the sofa.

"Yeah," said Wardle, "bloody Menorca."

Strike took a swig of coffee so strong he might as well have emptied boiling water straight into the jar. A headache was building in the side of his skull. He rarely got headaches.

"But we've made progress with those two whose pictures I showed you," said Wardle. "The bloke and the girl who were posting on that freaks' website where Kelsey was asking questions about you."

Strike dimly remembered the pictures Wardle had shown him of a young man with lopsided eyes and a woman with black hair and glasses.

"We've interviewed them and they never met her; they only had online contact. Plus, *he's* got a rock-solid alibi for the date she died: he was doing a double shift at Asda—in Leeds. We've checked.

"But," said Wardle, and Strike could tell he was leading up to something he thought promising, "there's a bloke who's been hanging round the forum, calls himself 'Devotee,' who's been freaking them all out a bit. He's got a thing for amputees. He liked to ask the women where they wanted to be amputated and apparently he tried to meet a couple of them. He's gone very quiet lately. We're trying to track him down."

"Uh huh," said Strike, very conscious of Two-Times's mounting irritation. "Sounds hopeful."

"Yeah, and I haven't forgotten that letter you got from the bloke who liked your stump," said Wardle. "We're looking into him, too."

"Great," said Strike, hardly aware of what he was saying, but holding up a hand to show Two-Times—who was on the verge of getting up from the sofa—that he was almost done. "Listen, I can't talk now, Wardle. Maybe later."

When Wardle had hung up, Strike attempted to placate Two-Times, who had worked himself up into a state of weak anger while forced to wait for the phone call to end. Precisely what he thought Strike could do about the fact that his girlfriend had chucked him was a question that the detective, who could not afford to jettison possible repeat business, did not ask. Swigging tar-black coffee while the pain built in his head, Strike's dominant emotion was a fervent wish that he was in a position to tell Two-Times to fuck off.

"So what," asked his client, "are you going to do about it?"

Strike was unsure whether he was being asked to force Platinum back into the relationship, track her all over London in the hopes of discovering another boyfriend or refund Two-Times's money. Before he could answer, however, he heard more footsteps on the metal stairs, and female voices. Two-Times barely had time for more than a startled, questioning look at Strike before the glass door opened.

Robin looked taller to Strike than the Robin he kept in his memory: taller, better-looking and more embarrassed. Behind her—and under normal circumstances he would have been interested and amused by the fact—was a woman who could only be her mother. Though a little shorter and definitely broader, she had the same strawberry-blonde hair, the same blue-gray eyes and an expression of beneficent shrewdness that was deeply familiar to Robin's boss.

"I'm so sorry," said Robin, catching sight of Two-Times and halting abruptly. "We can wait downstairs—come on, Mum—"

Their unhappy client got to his feet, definitely cross.

"No, no, not at all," he said. "I didn't have an appointment. I'll go. Just my final invoice, then, Strike."

He pushed his way out of the office.

An hour and a half later, Robin and her mother were sitting in silence as their taxi moved towards King's Cross, Linda's suitcase swaying a little on the floor.

Linda had been insistent that she wanted to meet Strike before she left for Yorkshire.

"You've been working for him for over a year. Surely he won't mind if I look in to say hello? I'd like to see *where* you work, at least, so I can picture it when you're talking about the office..."

Robin had resisted as hard as she could, embarrassed by the very idea of introducing her mother to Strike. It felt childish, incongruous and silly. She was particularly concerned that appearing with her mother in tow would reinforce Strike's evident belief that she was too shaken up to deal with the Kelsey case.

Bitterly did Robin now regret betraying her distress when the Vettriano card had arrived. She ought to have known better than to let any hint of fear show, especially after telling him about the rape. He said it had made no difference, but she knew better: she'd had plenty of experience of people telling her what was, and wasn't, good for her.

The taxi bowled along the Inner Circle and Robin had to remind herself that it was not her mother's fault that they had blundered in on Two-Times. She ought to have called Strike first. The truth was that she had hoped that Strike would be out, or upstairs; that she would be able to show Linda around the office and take her away without having to introduce them. She had been afraid that, if she phoned him, Strike would make a point of being there to meet her mother, out of a characteristic blend of mischief and curiosity.

Linda and Strike had chatted away while Robin made tea, keeping deliberately quiet. She strongly suspected that one of the reasons Linda wanted to meet Strike was to assess the precise degree of warmth that existed between him and her daughter. Helpfully, Strike looked appalling, a good ten years older than his real age, with that blue-jawed, sunken-eyed look that he got when he forfeited sleep for work. Linda would surely be hard pressed to imagine that Robin was nursing a secret infatuation now she had seen her boss.

"I liked him," said Linda as the red-brick palace of St. Pancras came into view, "and I have to say, he might not be pretty, but he's got something about him."

"Yes," said Robin coldly. "Sarah Shadlock feels the same way."

Shortly before they had left for the station, Strike had asked for five minutes with her alone in the inner office. There, he had handed her the beginnings of a list of massage parlors, strip joints and lap-dancing clubs in Shoreditch and asked her to begin the laborious process of ringing them all in search of Noel Brockbank.

"The more I think about it," Strike had said, "the more I think he'll still be working as a heavy or a bouncer. What else is there for him, big bloke with brain damage and his history?"

Out of deference to the listening Linda, Strike had omitted to add that he was sure Brockbank would still be working in the sex industry, where vulnerable women might be most easily found.

"OK," Robin had replied, leaving Strike's list where he had put it on her desk. "I'll see Mum off and come back—"

"No, I want you to do it from home. Keep a record of all the calls; I'll reimburse you."

A mental picture of the Destiny's Child *Survivor* poster had flickered in Robin's mind.

"When do I come back into the office?"

"Let's see how long that takes you," he said. Correctly reading her expression, he had added: "Look, I think we've just lost Two-Times for good. I can cover Mad Dad alone—"

"What about Kelsey?"

"You're trying to trace Brockbank," he said, pointing at the list in her hand. Then (his head was pounding, though Robin did not know it), "Look, everyone'll be off work tomorrow, it's a bank holiday, the royal wedding—"

It could not have been clearer: he wanted her out of the way. Something had changed while she had been out of the office. Perhaps Strike was remembering that, after all, she had not been trained by the military police, had never seen dismembered limbs before a leg was delivered to their door, that she was not, in short, the kind of partner who was of use to him in this extremity.

"I've just had five days off—"

"For Christ's sake," he said, losing patience, "you're only making lists and phone calls—why d'you have to be in here to do it?"

You're only making lists and phone calls.

She remembered how Elin had called her Strike's secretary.

Sitting in the taxi with her mother, a lava slide of anger and resentment swept away rationality. He had called her his partner in front of Wardle, back when he had needed her to look at the photographs of a dismembered body. There had been no new contract, though, no formal renegotiation of their working relationship. She was a faster typist than Strike, with his wide hairy fingers: she dealt with the bulk of the invoices and emails. She did most of the filing too. Perhaps, Robin thought, Strike himself had told Elin that she was his secretary. Perhaps calling her partner had been a sop to her, a mere figure of speech. Maybe (she was deliberately inflaming her own resentment now, and she knew it) Strike and Elin discussed Robin's inadequacies during their sneaky dinners away from Elin's husband. He might have confided in Elin how much he now regretted taking on a woman who, after all, had been a mere temp when she had come to him. He had probably told Elin about the rape too.

It was a difficult time for me too, you know.

You're only making lists and phone calls.

Why was she crying? Tears of rage and frustration were trickling down her face.

"Robin?" said Linda.

"It's nothing, nothing," said Robin savagely, wiping under her eyes with the heels of her hands.

She had been desperate to get back to work after five days in the house with her mother and Matthew, after the awkward three-cornered silences in the tiny space, the whispered conversations she knew that Linda had had with Matthew while she was in the bathroom, and about which she had chosen not to ask. She did not want to be trapped at home all over again. Irrational though it might have been, she felt safer in the middle of London, keeping an eye out for that large figure in the beanie hat, than she did in her flat in Hastings Road.

They pulled up at last outside King's Cross. Robin was trying hard to keep her emotions under control, conscious of Linda's sideways looks as they crossed the crowded station towards her platform. She and Matthew would be alone again tonight, with the looming prospect of that final, definitive talk. She had not wanted Linda to come and stay, yet her imminent departure forced Robin to admit that there had been a comfort in her mother's presence that she had barely acknowledged.

"Right," said Linda once her case had been safely stowed in the luggage rack and she had returned to the platform to spend the last couple of minutes with her daughter. "This is for you."

She was holding out five hundred pounds.

"Mum, I can't take—"

"Yes, you can," said Linda. "Put it towards a deposit on a new place to live—or a pair of Jimmy Choos for the wedding."

They had gone window-shopping in Bond Street on Tuesday, staring through the shop windows at flawless jewels, at handbags that cost more than secondhand cars, at designer clothing to which neither woman could even aspire. It felt a long way from the shops of Harrogate. Robin had gazed most covetously through the shoe-shop windows. Matthew did not like her to wear very high heels; defiantly, she had voiced a hankering for some five-inch spikes.

"I can't," repeated Robin as the station echoed and bustled around them. Her parents were sharing the expense of her brother Stephen's wedding later in the year. They had already paid a sizable deposit on her reception, which had been postponed once; they had bought the dress and paid for its alterations, lost one deposit on the wedding cars...

"I want you to," said Linda sternly. "Either invest it in your single life or buy wedding shoes."

Fighting more tears, Robin said nothing.

"You've got Dad's and my full support whatever you decide," said Linda, "but I want you to ask yourself why you haven't let anyone else know why the wedding's off. You can't keep living in limbo like this. It's not good for either of you. Take the money. Decide."

She wrapped Robin in a tight embrace, kissed her just beneath the ear and got back on the train. Robin managed to smile all the time she was waving good-bye, but when the train had finally pulled away, taking her mother back to Masham, to her father, to Rowntree the Labrador and everything that was friendly and familiar, Robin dropped down on a cold metal bench, buried her face in her hands and wept silently into the banknotes Linda had given her.

"Cheer up, darling. Plenty more fish in the sea."

She looked up. An unkempt man stood in front of her. His belly spilled widely over his belt and his smile was lascivious.

Robin got slowly to her feet. She was as tall as he was. Their eyes were on a level.

"Sod off," she said.

He blinked. His smile turned to a scowl. As she strode away, stuffing Linda's money into her pocket, she heard him shout something after her, but she neither knew nor cared what it had been. A vast unfocused rage rose in her, against men who considered displays of emotion a delicious open door; men who ogled your breasts under the pretense of scanning the wine shelves; men for whom your mere physical presence constituted a lubricious invitation.

Her fury billowed to encompass Strike, who had sent her home to Matthew because he now considered her a liability; who would rather endanger the business that she had helped build up, soldiering on single-handedly, than let her do what she was good at, what she sometimes outshone him at, because of the permanent handicap she had in his eyes acquired by being in the wrong stairwell at the wrong time, seven years previously.

So yes, she would ring his bloody lap-dancing clubs and his strip joints in search of the bastard who had called her "little girl," but there was something else she would do too. She had been looking forward to telling Strike about it, but there had been no time with Linda's train due, and she had felt no inclination after he told her to stay at home.

Robin tightened her belt and marched on, frowning, feeling fully justified in continuing to follow one lead, unbeknownst to Strike, alone.

37

This ain't the garden of Eden.

Blue Öyster Cult, "This Ain't the Summer of Love"

If she had to be at home, she supposed she would watch the wedding. Robin staked out a position on the sitting-room sofa early next morning, her laptop open on her knees, her mobile beside her, the TV on in the background. Matthew, too, had the day off work, but he was in the kitchen, keeping out of her way. There had been no solicitous offers of tea today, no questions about her work, no obsequious attentiveness. Robin sensed a change in him since her mother had left. He seemed anxious, wary, more serious. Somehow, during their quiet conversations, Linda appeared to have convinced Matthew that what had happened might never be reparable.

Robin knew perfectly well that she needed to deliver the *coup de grâce*. Linda's parting words had increased her sense of urgency. She had not yet found another place to live, but she must nevertheless tell Matthew that she was moving out and agree a form of words to issue to their friends and family. Yet here she sat on the sofa, working rather than dealing with the subject that seemed to fill the small flat, pressing against the walls, keeping the atmosphere perpetually stiff with tension.

Commentators wearing buttonholes and corsages were babbling on screen about the decorations in Westminster Abbey. Famous guests snaked towards the entrance and Robin half listened as she noted down the telephone numbers for lap-dancing clubs, strip joints and massage parlors in and around Shoreditch. Every now and then she scrolled down a page to look through the client reviews on the remote chance that somebody might have mentioned a bouncer called Noel, but no individual was named except the women who worked there. Punters often recommended them on the basis of their reported enthusiasm for their jobs. Mandy from one massage parlor "gives full thirty minutes" with "never any sense of being rushed"; the gorgeous Sherry of Beltway Strippers was always "willing, accommodating and up for a laugh." "I can thoroughly recommend Zoe," said one punter, "gorgeous figure and a very 'happy ending'!!!"

In a different mood—or, perhaps, in a different life—Robin might have found the way they talked about the women funny. So many of the men handing over cash for sex needed to believe that the women's enthusiasm was real, that they took their time for pleasure, that they were really laughing at punters' jokes, genuinely enjoying the body-to-body massages and the hand jobs. One reviewer had posted a poem about his favorite girl.

Even as she diligently compiled her list of numbers, Robin thought it unlikely that Brockbank, with his insalubrious record, would have been hired by any of the more upmarket places, whose websites featured artistically lit, airbrushed naked girls and invitations for couples to attend together.

Brothels, Robin knew, were illegal, but you did not have to travel too far into cyberspace to find mention of them. She had become adept at nosing information from out-of-the-way corners of the internet since going to work for Strike and was soon painstakingly cross-referencing mentions of local establishments on ramshackle sites dedicated to the exchange of such information. Here, at the cheapest end of the market, there were no poems: "£60 for anal going rate round here." "All forigen girls ,no english." "Very young probably still clean. Wouldn put your dick in some of wht you see."

Often, only an approximate location was available. She knew that Strike would not let her go looking for any of these basements and tenements where "mostly east european grils" or "all Chinese tail" were working.

Taking a break and subconsciously hoping to loosen the tight knot in her chest, she looked up at the television. Princes William and Harry were walking up the aisle together. As Robin watched, the door to the sitting room opened and Matthew walked in, carrying a mug of tea. He had not offered to make her one. He sat down in the armchair, saying nothing, and stared at the television screen.

Robin returned to her work, hyperconscious of Matthew beside her. Joining her without talking was a departure. Acceptance of her separateness—not interrupting her, even with the offer of tea—was also new. So was the fact that he did not pick up the remote control and change the channel.

The cameras returned to the outside of the Goring Hotel, where they were keeping vigil for the first glimpse of Kate Middleton in her wedding dress. Robin took covert glimpses over the top of her laptop while scrolling slowly down a series of barely literate comments about a brothel near Commercial Road.

An outburst of excitable comment and cheering made Robin look up in time to see Kate Middleton climbing into a limousine. Long lace sleeves, just like the ones she had removed from her own wedding dress...

The limousine moved slowly away. Kate Middleton was just visible beside her father in the car. So she had chosen to wear her hair down. Robin had planned to keep her hair down too. Matthew liked it that way. Not that that mattered anymore...

The crowds were cheering all the way down the Mall, Union Jacks as far as the eye could see.

As Matthew turned towards her, Robin pretended to be immersed in her laptop again.

"D'you want tea?"

"No," she said. "Thanks," she added grudgingly, aware how aggressive she had sounded.

Her mobile beeped beside her. Matthew often scowled or sulked when this happened on her days off: he expected it to be Strike, which it sometimes was. Today he merely turned back to watch the television.

Robin picked up her mobile and read the text that had just arrived:

How do I know you're not press?

It was the lead she was pursuing without Strike's knowledge and she had her answer ready. While the crowds cheered the limousine's slow progress on screen, she typed in:

If the press knew about you, they'd already be outside your house. I told you to look me up online. There's a picture of me going into court to give evidence in Owen Quine's murder case. Have you found it?

She put the mobile down again, her heart beating faster.

Kate Middleton was getting out of her limousine at the Abbey. Her waist looked tiny in the lace dress. She looked so happy... genuinely happy... Robin's heart hammered as she watched the beautiful woman in a tiara proceed towards the Abbey entrance.

Her mobile beeped again.

Yes I've seen the picture. So?

Matthew made a peculiar noise into his mug of tea. Robin ignored him. He probably thought that she was texting Strike, usually the cause of his little grimaces and noises of exasperation. Switching her mobile to camera mode, Robin held it up in front of her face and took a photo.

The flash startled Matthew, who looked around. He was crying.

Robin's fingers trembled as she sent the photograph of herself off in a text. After that, not wanting to look at Matthew, she watched the television again.

Kate Middleton and her father were now walking slowly up the scarlet-carpeted aisle that divided a sea of hatted guests. The culmination of a million fairy tales and fables was being played out in front of her: the commoner walking slowly towards her prince, beauty moving inexorably towards high rank...

Against her will, Robin remembered the night that Matthew had proposed under the statue of Eros at Piccadilly Circus. There had been tramps sitting on the steps, jeering as Matthew sank to his knees. She had been caught completely off guard by that unexpected scene on the grimy steps, Matthew risking his best suit on the damp, dirty stone, alcoholic fumes wafting towards them over the smell of exhaust fumes: the little blue velvet box and then the winking sapphire, smaller and paler than Kate Middleton's. Matthew later told her he'd chosen it because it matched her eyes. One of the tramps had got to his feet and applauded drunkenly when she said yes. She remembered the flashing neon lights of Piccadilly reflected on Matthew's beaming face.

Nine years of shared life, of growing up together, of arguing and reconciling, of loving. Nine years, holding fast to each other through trauma that ought to have broken them apart.

She remembered the day after the proposal, the day she had been sent by the temping agency to Strike. It seemed much, much longer ago than it was. She felt like a different person... at least, she *had* felt like a different person, until Strike told her to stay at home and copy down phone numbers, evading the question of when she would return to work as his partner.

"*They* split up."

"What?" said Robin.

"*They* did," said Matthew, and his voice broke. He nodded at the screen. Prince William had just turned to look at his bride. "They broke up for a bit."

"I know they did," said Robin.

She tried to speak coldly, but Matthew's expression was bereft.

Maybe on some level I think you deserve better than me.

"Is it—are we really over?" he asked.

Kate Middleton had drawn level with Prince William at the altar. They looked delighted to be reunited.

Staring at the screen, Robin knew that today her answer to Matthew's question would be taken as definitive. Her engagement ring was still lying where she had left it, on top of old accountancy textbooks on the bookcase. Neither of them had touched it since she had taken it off.

"Dearly beloved..." began the Dean of Westminster on screen.

She thought of the day that Matthew had asked her out for the very first time and remembered walking home from school, her insides on fire with excitement and pride. She remembered Sarah Shadlock giggling, leaning against him in a pub in Bath, and Matthew frowning slightly and pulling away. She thought of Strike and Elin... *what have they got to do with anything?*

She remembered Matthew, white-faced and shaking, in the hospital where they had kept her for twenty-four hours after the rape. He had missed an exam to be with her, simply taken off without leaving word. His mother had been annoyed about that. He had had to resit in the summer.

I was twenty-one and I didn't know then what I know now: that there's nobody like you and that I could never love anyone else as much as I love you...

Sarah Shadlock, arms around him when he was drunk, no doubt, while he poured out his confused feelings about Robin, agoraphobic, unable to be touched...

The mobile beeped. Automatically, Robin picked it up and looked at it.

All right, I believe it's you.

Robin could not take in what she was reading and set the mobile down on the sofa without responding. Men looked so tragic when they cried. Matthew's eyes were scarlet. His shoulders heaved.

"Matt," she said in a low voice over his silent sobs. "Matt..."

She held out her hand.

38

Dance on Stilts

The sky was marbled pink, but the streets were still heaving with people. A million Londoners and out-of-towners swarmed the pavements: red, white and blue hats, Union Jacks and plastic crowns, beer-swilling buffoons clutching the hands of children with painted faces, all of them bobbing and eddying on a tide of mawkish sentiment. They filled the Tube, they packed the streets, and as he forced his way through them, looking for what he needed, he heard more than once the refrain of the national anthem, sung tunelessly by the tipsy, and once with virtuosity by a gaggle of rollicking Welsh women who blocked his way out of the station.

He had left It sobbing. The wedding had lifted It temporarily out of Its misery, led to cloying affection and self-pitying tears, to plaintive hints about commitment and companionship. He had kept his temper only because his every nerve, every atom of his being focused on what he was going to do tonight. Focused on the release that was coming, he had been patient and loving, but his reward had been It taking the biggest liberty yet and trying to prevent him leaving.

He had already put on the jacket that accommodated his knives, and he had cracked. Although he had not laid a finger on It, he knew how to terrify and intimidate with words alone, with body language, with a sudden revelation of the beast inside. He had slammed his way out of the house, leaving It cowed and appalled behind him.

He would have to work hard to make up for that, he reflected as he pushed his way through a crowd of drinkers on a pavement. A bunch of poxy flowers, some fake regret, some bullshit about being stressed...the thought turned his expression mean. Nobody dared challenge him, not with his size and demeanor, though he knocked into several of them plowing his way through them. They were like skittles, fleshy ninepins, and they had about as much life and meaning to him. People had significance in his life only in what they could do for him. That was how The Secretary had come to assume such importance. He had never tracked a woman for so long.

Yes, the last one had taken a while too, but that had been different: that dumb little bitch had toppled so gleefully into his clutches you'd have thought getting hacked to pieces was her life's ambition. Which, of course, it had been...

The thought of it made him smile. The peach towels and the stink of her blood...He was starting to get the feeling again, that feeling of omnipotence. He was going to get one tonight, he could feel it...

Headin' for a meeting, shining up my greeting...

He was on the lookout for a girl who had become separated from the massing throngs, addled with drink and sentimentality, but they moved in herds through the streets, so he was starting to think he'd be better with a whore after all.

Times had changed. It wasn't how it had been in the old days. Hookers didn't need to walk the streets anymore, not with mobile phones and the internet. Buying yourself a woman was as easy as dialing up a takeaway nowadays, but he didn't want to leave a trail online or on some bitch's mobile records. Only the dregs were left on the streets and he knew all the areas, but it had to be somewhere that he had no association with, somewhere a long way from It...

By ten to midnight he was in Shacklewell, walking the streets with his lower face concealed by the upturned collar of his jacket, his hat low on his forehead, the knives bouncing heavily against his chest as he walked, one a straightforward carving knife, the other a compact machete. Lit windows of curry houses and more pubs, Union Jack bunting everywhere...if it took all night, he would find her...

On a dark corner stood three women in tiny skirts, smoking,

talking. He passed by on the other side of the street and one of them called out to him, but he ignored her, passing on into the darkness. Three was too many: two witnesses left.

Hunting was both easier and more difficult on foot. No worries about number plates caught on camera, but the difficulty was where he took her, not to mention the getaway being so much harder.

He prowled the streets for another hour until he found himself back on that stretch of road where the three whores had stood. Only two of them now. More manageable. A single witness. His face was almost entirely covered. He hesitated, and as he did so a car slowed and the driver had a brief conversation with the girls. One of them got in and the car drove away.

The glorious poison flooded his veins and his brain. It was exactly like the first time he'd killed: then, too, he had been left with the uglier one, to do with whatever he wanted.

No time for hesitation. Either of her mates could come back.

"Back again, babes?"

Her voice was guttural, although she looked young, with red hennaed hair in a shabby bob, piercings in both ears and her nose. Her nostrils were wet and pink, as though she had a cold. Along with her leather jacket and rubber miniskirt, she wore vertiginous heels on which she seemed to have trouble balancing.

"How much?" he asked, barely listening to her answer. What mattered was where.

"We can go to my place if you want."

He agreed, but he was tense. It had better be a self-contained room or a bedsit: nobody on the stairs, no one to hear or see, just some dirty, dark little nook where a body begged to be. If it turned out to be a communal place, some actual brothel, with other girls and a fat old bitch in charge or, worse, a pimp...

She wobbled out onto the road before the pedestrian light turned green. He seized her arm and yanked her back as a white van went hurtling past.

"My savior!" she giggled. "Ta, babes."

He could tell she was on something. He'd seen plenty like her. Her raw, weeping nose disgusted him. Their reflection in the dark shop windows they passed could have been father and daughter, she was so short and skinny and he so large, so burly.

"See the wedding?" she asked.

"What?"

"Royal wedding? She looked lovely."

Even this dirty little whore was wedding-crazy. She babbled on about it as they walked, laughing far too often, teetering on her cheap stilettos, while he remained entirely silent.

"Shame 'is mum never saw 'im marry, though, innit? 'Ere we go," said the girl, pointing to a tenement a block ahead. "That's my gaff."

He could see it in the distance: there were people standing around the lit door, a man sitting on the steps. He stopped dead.

"No."

"'Smatter? Don't worry about them, babes, they know me," she said earnestly.

"No," he said again, his hand tight around her thin arm, suddenly furious. What was she trying to pull? Did she think he was born yesterday?

"Down there," he said, pointing to a shadowy space between two buildings.

"Babes, there's a bed—"

"Down there," he repeated angrily.

She blinked at him out of heavily made-up eyes, a little fazed, but her thought processes were fogged, the silly bitch, and he convinced her silently, by sheer force of personality.

"Yeah, all right, babes."

Their footsteps crunched on a surface that seemed to be part gravel. He was afraid there might be security lights or sensors, but a thicker, deeper darkness awaited them twenty yards off the road.

He handed over the notes. She unzipped his trousers for him. He was still soft. While she was busy on her knees in the darkness, trying to persuade him into tumescence, he was pulling his knives silently from their hiding place inside his jacket. A slither of nylon lining, one in each hand, his palms sweaty on the plastic handles...

He kicked her so hard in the stomach that she flew backwards through the air. A choking, wheezing gasp then a crunch of gravel told him where she had landed. Lurching forward, his flies still open, his trousers sliding down his hips, he found her by tripping over her and was on her.

The carving knife plunged and plunged: he hit bone, probably rib, and stabbed again. A whistle from her lungs and then, shocking him, she screamed.

Though he was straddling her she was fighting and he could not find her throat to finish her. He gave a mighty left-handed swing with the machete, but incredibly she still had enough life in her to shriek again—

A stream of obscenities poured from his mouth—stab, stab and stab again with the carving knife—he punctured her palm as she tried to stop him and that gave him an idea—slamming her arm down, kneeling on it, he raised his knife—

"You fucking little cocksucking..."

"Who's down there?"

Fucking hell and shit.

A man's voice, coming out of the dark from the direction of the street, said again:

"Who's there?"

He scrambled off her, pulling up his pants and his trousers, backing away as quietly as he could, two knives in his left hand and what he thought were two of her fingers in his right, still warm, bony and bleeding...She was still moaning and whimpering...then, with a last long wheeze, she fell silent...

He hobbled away into the unknown, away from her motionless form, every sense as sharp as a cat's to the distant approach of a hound.

"Everything all right down there?" said an echoing male voice.

He had reached a solid wall. He felt his way along it until it turned into wire mesh. By the distant light of a streetlamp he saw the outlines of what looked like a ramshackle car repair shop beyond the fence, the hulking forms of vehicles eerie in the gloom. Somewhere in the space he had just left he heard footsteps: the man had come to investigate the screams.

He must not panic. He must not run. Noise would be fatal. Slowly he edged along the wire enclosure containing the old cars, towards a patch of darkness that might be either an opening onto an adjoining street or a dead end. He slid the bloody knives back inside his jacket, dropped her fingers into his pocket and crept along, trying not to breathe.

An echoing shout from the alleyway:

"Fucking hell! Andy—ANDY!"

He began to run. They would not hear him now, not with their yells echoing off the walls, and as though the universe were once again his friend, it laid soft grassy ground beneath his feet as he lumbered into the new darkness of the opening...

A dead end, a six-foot wall. He could hear traffic on the other side. Nothing else for it: panting, scrambling, wishing he were what he had once been, fit and strong and young, he tried to hoist himself up, his feet trying to find some purchase, his muscles screaming in protest...

Panic can do wonderful things. He was on top of the wall and down again. He landed heavily; his knees protested, but he staggered then regained his balance.

Walk on, walk on... normal... normal... normal...

Cars whooshed past. Surreptitiously he wiped his bloody hands on his jacket. Distant shouting, too muffled to hear... he needed to get away from here as quickly as possible. He would go to the place that It didn't know about.

A bus stop. He jogged a short distance and joined the queue. It didn't matter where he went as long as it took him out of here.

His thumb made a bloody mark on the ticket. He pushed it deep into his pocket and made contact with her severed fingers.

The bus rumbled away. He took long slow breaths, trying to calm himself.

Somebody upstairs began singing the national anthem again. The bus sped up. His heart jolted. Slowly his breathing returned to normal.

Staring at his own reflection in the filthy window, he rolled her still-warm little finger between his own. As panic receded, elation took its place. He grinned at his dark reflection, sharing his triumph with the only one who could understand.

39

The door opens both ways...

Blue Öyster Cult, "Out of the Darkness"

"Look at this," said Elin on Monday morning, standing aghast in front of the television with a bowl of granola in her hands. "Can you believe it!"

Strike had just entered the kitchen, freshly washed and dressed, after their usual Sunday night rendezvous. The spotless cream and white space was full of stainless steel surfaces and subdued lighting, like a space age operating theater. A plasma TV hung on the wall behind the table. President Obama was on screen, standing at a podium, talking.

"They've killed Osama bin Laden!" said Elin.

"Bloody hell," said Strike, stopping dead to read the tickertape running across the bottom of the screen.

Clean clothes and a shave had made little difference to his hang-dog look of exhaustion. The hours he was putting in trying to catch a glimpse of Laing or Whittaker were beginning to take their painful toll: his eyes were bloodshot and his skin was tinged with gray.

He crossed to the coffee maker, poured himself a mugful and gulped it down. He had almost fallen asleep on top of Elin last night, and counted it among the week's few small achievements that he had finished that job, at least. Now he leaned against the steel-topped island, watching the immaculate President and envying him from his soul. He, at least, had got his man.

The known details of bin Laden's death gave Elin and Strike something to talk about while she was dropping him off at the Tube.

"I wonder how sure they were it was him," she said, pulling up outside the station, "before they went in."

Strike had been wondering that, too. Bin Laden had been physically distinctive, of course: well over six feet tall...and Strike's thoughts drifted back to Brockbank, Laing and Whittaker, until Elin recalled them.

"I've got work drinks on Wednesday, if you fancy it." She sounded slightly self-conscious. "Duncan and I have nearly agreed everything. I'm sick of sneaking around."

"Sorry, no can do," he said. "Not with all these surveillance jobs on, I told you."

He had to pretend to her that the pursuit of Brockbank, Laing and Whittaker were paid jobs, because she would never have understood his so far fruitless persistence otherwise.

"OK, well, I'll wait for you to ring me, then," she said, and he caught, but chose to ignore, a cool undertone in her voice.

Is it worth it? he asked himself as he descended into the Underground, backpack over his shoulder, with reference not to the men he was pursuing but to Elin. What had begun as an agreeable diversion was starting to assume the status of onerous obligation. The predictability of their rendezvous—same restaurants, same nights—had started to pall, yet now that she offered to break the pattern he found himself unenthusiastic. He could think offhand of a dozen things he would rather do with a night off than have drinks with a bunch of Radio Three presenters. Sleep headed the list.

Soon—he could feel it coming—she would want to introduce him to her daughter. In thirty-seven years, Strike had successfully avoided the status of "Mummy's boyfriend." His memories of the men who had passed through Leda's life, some of them decent, most of them not—the latter trend reaching its apotheosis in Whittaker—had left him with a distaste that was almost revulsion. He had no desire to see in another child's eyes the fear and mistrust that he had read in his sister Lucy's every time the door opened onto yet another male stranger. What his own expression had been, he had no idea.

For as long as he had been able to manage it, he had closed his mind willfully to that part of Leda's life, focusing on her hugs and her laughter, her maternal delight in his achievements.

As he climbed out of the Tube at Notting Hill Gate on his way to the school, his mobile buzzed: Mad Dad's estranged wife had texted.

Just checking you know boys not at school today because of bank holiday. They're with grandparents. He won't follow them there.

Strike swore under his breath. He had indeed forgotten about the bank holiday. On the plus side, he was now free to return to the office, catch up with some paperwork, then head out to Catford Broadway by daylight for a change. He only wished that the text could have arrived before he made the detour to Notting Hill.

Forty-five minutes later, Strike was tramping up the metal staircase towards his office and asking himself for the umpteenth time why he had never contacted the landlord about getting the birdcage lift fixed. When he reached the glass door of his office, however, a far more pressing question presented itself: why were the lights on?

Strike pushed open the door so forcefully that Robin, who had heard his laborious approach, nevertheless jumped in her chair. They stared at each other, she defiant, he accusing.

"What are you doing here?"

"Working," said Robin.

"I told you to work from home."

"I've finished," she said, tapping a sheaf of papers that lay on the desk beside her, covered with handwritten notes and telephone numbers. "Those are all the numbers I could find in Shoreditch."

Strike's eyes followed her hand, but what caught his attention was not the small stack of neatly written papers she was showing him, but the sapphire engagement ring.

There was a pause. Robin wondered why her heart was pummeling her ribs. How ridiculous to feel defensive . . . it was up to her whether she married Matthew . . . ludicrous even to feel she had to state that to herself . . .

"Back on, is it?" Strike said, turning his back on her as he hung up his jacket and backpack.

"Yes," said Robin.

There was a short pause. Strike turned back to face her.

"I haven't got enough work for you. We're down to one job. I can cover Mad Dad on my own."

She narrowed her gray-blue eyes.

"What about Brockbank and Laing and Whittaker?"

"What about them?"

"Aren't you still trying to find them?"

"Yes, but that's not the—"

"So how are you going to cover four cases?"

"They're not cases. No one's paying—"

"So they're a kind of hobby, are they?" said Robin. "That's why I've been looking for numbers all weekend?"

"Look—I want to trace them, yes," said Strike, trying to marshal his arguments through heavy fatigue and other, less easily definable emotions (the engagement was back on . . . he had suspected all along that it might happen . . . sending her home, giving her time with Matthew would have helped, of course), "but I don't—"

"You were happy enough to let me drive you to Barrow," said Robin, who had come prepared for argument. She had known perfectly well he didn't want her back in the office. "You didn't mind me questioning Holly Brockbank and Lorraine MacNaughton, did you? So what's changed?"

"*You got sent another fucking body part, that's what's fucking changed, Robin!*"

He had not intended to shout, but his voice echoed off the filing cabinets.

Robin remained impassive. She had seen Strike angry before, heard him swear, seen him punch those very metal drawers. It didn't bother her.

"Yes," she said calmly, "and it shook me up. I think most people would have been shaken up by getting a toe stuck inside a card. You looked pretty sick about it yourself."

"Yeah, which is why—"

"—you're trying to cover four cases single-handedly and you sent me home. I didn't ask for time off."

In the euphoric aftermath of replacing her ring, Matthew had actually helped her rehearse her case for returning to work. It had been quite extraordinary, looking back on it, he pretending to be Strike and she putting her arguments, but Matthew had been ready to help her do anything at all, so long as she agreed to marry him on the second of July.

"I wanted to get straight back to—"

"Just because you wanted to get back to work," said Strike, "doesn't mean it was in your best interests to do so."

"Oh, I didn't realize you're a qualified occupational therapist," said Robin, delicately sarcastic.

"Look," said Strike, more infuriated by her aloof rationality than he would have been with rage and tears (the sapphire sparkling coolly from her finger again), "I'm your employer and it's down to me if—"

"I thought I was supposed to be your partner," said Robin.

"Makes no difference," said Strike, "partner or not, I've still got a responsibility—"

"So you'd rather see this business fail than let me work?" said Robin, an angry flush rising in her pale face, and while Strike felt he was losing on points he took an obscure pleasure in the fact that she was losing her cool. "I helped you build it up! You're playing right into his hands, whoever he is, sidelining me, neglecting paying cases and working yourself into the—"

"How do you know I've—?"

"Because you look like shit," said Robin baldly and Strike, caught off guard, almost laughed for the first time in days.

"Either," she resumed, "I'm your partner or I'm not. If you're going to treat me like some piece of special-occasion china that gets taken out when you don't think I'll get hurt, we're—we're doomed. The business is doomed. I'd do better to take Wardle up on—"

"On what?" said Strike sharply.

"On his suggestion that I apply to the police," said Robin, looking Strike squarely in the face. "This isn't a game to me, you know. I'm not a little girl. I've survived far worse than being sent a toe. So—" She screwed up her courage. She had hoped it would not come to an ultimatum. "—decide. Decide whether I'm your partner or a—a liability. If you can't rely on me—if you can't let me run the same risks you do—then I'd rather—"

Her voice nearly broke, but she forced herself onwards.

"—rather get out," she finished.

In her emotion, she swung her chair round to face her computer a little too forcefully and found herself facing the wall. Mustering what dignity she felt she had left, she adjusted her seat to face the monitor and continued opening emails, waiting for his answer.

She had not told him about her lead. She needed to know whether she was reinstated as his partner before she either shared her spoils or gave it to him as a farewell gift.

"Whoever he is, he butchers women for pleasure," said Strike quietly, "and he's made it clear he'd like to do the same to you."

"I've grasped that," said Robin in a tight voice, her eyes on the screen, "but have *you* grasped the fact that if he knows where I work, he probably also knows where I live, and if he's that determined he'll follow me anywhere I go? Can't you understand that I'd much rather help catch him than sit around waiting for him to pounce?"

She was not going to beg. She had emptied the inbox of twelve spam emails before he spoke again, his voice heavy.

"All right."

"All right what?" she asked, looking around cautiously.

"All right... you're back at work."

She beamed. He did not return the smile.

"Oh, cheer up," she said, getting to her feet and moving around the desk.

For one crazy moment Strike thought she might be about to hug him, she looked so happy (and with the protective ring back on her finger, perhaps he had become a safely huggable figure, a de-sexed noncompetitor), but she was merely heading for the kettle.

"I've got a lead," she told him.

"Yeah?" he said, still struggling to make sense of the new situation. (What was he going to ask her to do that wasn't too dangerous? Where could he send her?)

"Yes," she said. "I've made contact with one of the people on the BIID forum who was talking to Kelsey."

Yawning widely, Strike dropped down into the fake-leather sofa, which made its usual flatulent noises under his weight, and tried to remember whom she was talking about. He was so sleep-deprived that his usually capacious and accurate memory was becoming unreliable.

"The... bloke or the woman?" he asked, with the vague remembrance of the photographs Wardle had shown them.

"The man," said Robin, pouring boiling water onto tea bags.

For the first time in their relationship Strike found himself relishing an opportunity to undermine her.

"So you've been going onto websites without telling me? Playing games with a bunch of anonymous punters without knowing who you're messing with?"

"I told you I'd been on there!" said Robin indignantly. "I saw Kelsey asking questions about you on a message board, remember? She was calling herself Nowheretoturn. I *told* you all this when Wardle was here. *He* was impressed," she added.

"He's also way ahead of you," said Strike. "He's questioned both of those people she was talking to online. It's a dead end. They never met her. He's working on a guy called Devotee now, who was trying to meet women off the site."

"I already know about Devotee."

"How?"

"He asked to see my picture and when I didn't send it, he went quiet—"

"So you've been flirting with these nutters, have you?"

"Oh, for God's sake," said Robin impatiently, "I've been pretending I've got the same disorder they have, it's hardly flirting—and I don't think Devotee's anything to worry about."

She passed Strike a mug of tea, which was precisely his preferred shade of creosote. Perversely, this aggravated rather than soothed him.

"So you don't think Devotee's anything to worry about? What are you basing that on?"

"I've been doing some research into acrotomophiliacs ever since that letter came in addressed to you—the man who was fixated on your leg, remember? As paraphilias go, it's hardly ever associated with violence. I think Devotee's much more likely to be masturbating over his keyboard at the idea of all the wannabes."

Unable to think of any response to this, Strike drank some tea.

"Anyway," said Robin (his lack of thanks for his tea had rankled), "the guy Kelsey was talking to online—he wants to be an amputee too—lied to Wardle."

"What do you mean, he lied?"

"He *did* meet Kelsey in real life."

"Yeah?" said Strike, determinedly casual. "How do you know that?"

"He's told me all about it. He was terrified when the Met contacted him—none of his family or his friends knows about his obsession with getting rid of his leg—so he panicked and said he'd never met Kelsey. He was afraid that if he admitted he had, there would be publicity and he'd have to give evidence in court.

"Anyway, once I'd convinced him that I am who I am, that I'm not a journalist or a policewoman—"

"You told him the truth?"

"Yes, which was the best thing I could have done, because once he was convinced I was really me, he agreed to meet."

"And what makes you think he's genuinely going to meet you?" asked Strike.

"Because we've got leverage with him that the police haven't."

"Like what?"

"Like," she said coldly, wishing that she could have returned a different answer, "you. Jason's absolutely desperate to meet you."

"Me?" said Strike, completely thrown. "Why?"

"Because he believes you cut your leg off yourself."

"*What?*"

"Kelsey convinced him that you did it yourself. He wants to know how."

"Jesus fucking Christ," said Strike, "is he mentally ill? Of course he is," he answered himself immediately. "Of course he's mentally ill. He wants to cut his fucking leg off. Jesus fucking Christ."

"Well, you know, there's debate about whether BIID is a mental illness or some kind of brain abnormality," said Robin. "When you scan the brain of someone suffering—"

"Whatever," said Strike, waving the topic away. "What makes you think this nutter's got anything useful—?"

"*He met Kelsey,*" said Robin impatiently, "who must have told him why she was so convinced you were one of them. He's nineteen years old, he works in an Asda in Leeds, he's got an aunt in London and he's going to come down, stay with her and meet me. We're trying to find a date. He needs to find out when he can get the time off.

"Look, he's two removes from the person who convinced Kelsey you were a voluntary amputee," she went on, both disappointed and annoyed by Strike's lack of enthusiasm for the results of her solo work, but still holding out a faint hope that he would stop being so tetchy and critical, "and that person is almost certainly the killer!"

Strike drank more tea, allowing what she had told him to percolate slowly through his exhausted brain. Her reasoning was sound. Persuading Jason to meet her was a significant achievement. He ought to offer praise. Instead he sat in silence, drinking his tea.

"If you think I should call Wardle and pass this over to him—" said Robin, her resentment palpable.

"No," said Strike, and the haste with which he answered gave Robin some small satisfaction. "Until we've heard what he's... we won't waste Wardle's time. We'll let him know once we've heard what this Jason's got. When did you say he's coming to London?"

"He's trying to get time off; I don't know yet."

"One of us could go up to Leeds and meet him."

"He wants to come down. He's trying to keep all this away from anyone who knows him."

"OK," said Strike gruffly, rubbing his bloodshot eyes and trying to formulate a plan that would keep Robin simultaneously busy and out of harm's way. "You keep the pressure on him, then, and start ringing round those numbers, see whether you can get a lead on Brockbank."

"I've already started doing that," she said and he heard the latent rebelliousness, the imminent insistence that she wanted to be back on the street.

"And," said Strike, thinking fast, "I want you to stake out Wollaston Close."

"Looking for Laing?"

"Exactly. Keep a low profile, don't stay there after dark and if you see the beanie bloke you get out of there or set off your bloody rape alarm. Preferably both."

Even Strike's surliness could not douse Robin's delight that she was back on board, a fully equal partner in the business.

She could not know that Strike believed and hoped that he was sending her up a dead end. By day and by night he had watched the entrances to the small block of flats, shifting position regularly, using night-vision goggles to scan the balconies and windows. Nothing he had seen indicated that Laing was lurking within: no broad shadow moving behind a curtain, no hint of a low-growing hairline or dark ferret-like eyes, no massive figure swaying along on crutches or (because Strike took nothing for granted when it came to Donald Laing) swaggering along like the ex-boxer he was. Every man who had passed in and out of the building had been scrutinized by Strike for a hint of resemblance to Laing's JustGiving photograph or to the faceless figure in the beanie hat, and none of them had come close to a match.

"Yeah," he said, "you get onto Laing and—give me half those Brockbank numbers—we'll divide them up. I'll stick with Whittaker. Make sure you check in regularly, OK?"

He heaved himself out of the sofa.

"Of course," said Robin, elated. "Oh, and—Cormoran—"

He was already on the way to the inner office, but turned.

"—what are these?"

She was holding up the Accutane pills that he had found in Kelsey's drawer and which he had left in Robin's in-tray after looking them up online.

"Oh, them," he said. "They're nothing."

Some of her cheeriness seemed to evaporate. A faint guilt stirred.

He knew he was being a grumpy bastard. She didn't deserve it. He tried to pull himself together.

"Acne medication," he said. "They were Kelsey's."

"Of course—you went to the house—you saw her sister! What happened? What did she say?"

Strike did not feel equal to telling her all about Hazel Furley now. The interview felt a long time ago, he was exhausted and still felt unreasonably antagonistic.

"Nothing new," he said. "Nothing important."

"So why did you take these pills?"

"I thought they might be birth control...maybe she was up to something her sister didn't know about."

"Oh," said Robin. "So they really are nothing."

She tossed them into the bin.

Ego made Strike go on: ego, pure and simple. She had found a good lead and he had nothing except a vague idea about the Accutane.

"And I found a ticket," he said.

"A what?"

"Like a coat check ticket."

Robin waited expectantly.

"Number eighteen," said Strike.

Robin waited for a further explanation, but none came. Strike yawned and conceded defeat.

"I'll see you later. Keep me posted on what you're up to and where you are."

He let himself into his office, closed the door, sat down at his desk and slumped backwards in his chair. He had done all he could to stop her getting back on the street. Now, he wanted nothing more than to hear her leave.

40

...love is like a gun
And in the hands of someone like you
I think it'd kill.

Blue Öyster Cult, "Searchin' for Celine"

Robin was a decade younger than Strike. She had arrived in his office as a temporary secretary, unsought and unwelcome, at the lowest point of his professional life. He had only meant to keep her on for a week, and that because he had almost knocked her to her death down the metal stairs when she arrived, and he felt he owed her. Somehow she had persuaded him to let her stay, firstly for an extra week, then for a month and, finally, forever. She had helped him claw his way out of near insolvency, worked to make his business successful, learned on the job and now asked nothing more than to be allowed to stand beside him while that business crumbled again, and to fight for its survival.

Everyone liked Robin. *He* liked Robin. How could he fail to like her, after everything they had been through together? However, from the very first he had told himself: this far and no further. A distance must be maintained. Barriers must remain in place.

She had entered his life on the very day that he had split from Charlotte for good, after sixteen years of an on-off relationship that he still could not say had been more pleasurable than painful. Robin's helpfulness, her solicitousness, her fascination with what he did, her admiration for him personally (if he was going to be honest with himself, he should do it thoroughly) had been balm to those wounds that Charlotte had inflicted, those internal injuries that had long outlasted her parting gifts of a black eye and lacerations.

The sapphire on Robin's third finger had been a bonus, then: a safeguard and a full stop. In preventing the possibility of anything more, it set him free to...what? Rely on her? Befriend her? Allow barriers to become imperceptibly eroded, so that as he looked back it occurred to him that they had each shared personal information that hardly anybody else knew. Robin was one of only three people (he suspected) who knew about that putative baby that Charlotte claimed to have lost, but which might never have existed, or was aborted. He was one of a mere handful who knew that Matthew had been unfaithful. For all his determination to keep her at arm's length, they had literally leaned on each other. He could remember exactly what it felt like to have his arm around her waist as they had meandered towards Hazlitt's Hotel. She was tall enough to hold easily. He did not like having to stoop. He had never fancied very small women.

Matthew would not *like this,* she had said.

He would have liked it even less had he known how much Strike had liked it.

She was nowhere near as beautiful as Charlotte. Charlotte had had the kind of beauty that made men forget themselves midsentence, that stunned them into silence. Robin, as he could hardly fail to notice when she bent over to turn off her PC at the wall, was a very sexy girl, but men were not struck dumb in her presence. Indeed, remembering Wardle, she seemed to make them more loquacious.

Yet he liked her face. He liked her voice. He liked being around her.

It wasn't that he wanted to *be* with her—that would be insanity. They could not run the business together and have an affair. In any case, she wasn't the kind of girl you had an affair with. He had only ever known her engaged or else bereft at the demise of her engagement and therefore saw her as the kind of woman who was destined for marriage.

Almost angrily, he added together those things he knew and had observed that marked her as profoundly different from him, as embodying a safer, more cloistered, more conventional world. She had had the same pompous boyfriend since sixth form (although he understood that a little better now), a nice middle-class family back in Yorkshire, parents married for decades and apparently happy, a Labrador and a Land Rover and a *pony,* Strike reminded himself. A bloody pony!

Then other memories intruded and a different Robin peeled away from this picture of a safe and ordered past: and there in front of him stood a woman who would not have been out of place in the SIB. This was the Robin who had taken advanced driving courses, who had concussed herself in the pursuit of a killer, who had calmly wrapped her coat like a tourniquet around his bleeding arm after he was stabbed and taken him to hospital. The Robin who had improvised so successfully in interrogating suspects that she had winkled out information that the police had not managed to get, who had invented and successfully embodied Venetia Hall, who had persuaded a terrified young man who wanted his leg amputated to confide in her, who had given Strike a hundred other examples of initiative, resourcefulness and courage that might have turned her into a plainclothes police officer by now, had she not once walked into a dark stairwell where a bastard in a mask stood waiting.

And that woman was going to marry Matthew! Matthew, who had been banking on her working in human resources, with a nice salary to complement his own, who sulked and bitched about her long, unpredictable hours and her lousy paycheck . . . couldn't she *see* what a stupid bloody thing she was doing? Why the fuck had she put that ring back on? Hadn't she tasted freedom on that drive up to Barrow, which Strike looked back on with a fondness that discomposed him?

She's making a fucking huge mistake, that's all.

That was all. It wasn't personal. Whether she was engaged, married or single, nothing could or ever would come of the weakness he was forced to acknowledge that he had developed. He would reestablish the professional distance that had somehow ebbed away with her drunken confessions and the camaraderie of their trip up north, and temporarily shelve his half-acknowledged plan to end the relationship with Elin. It felt safer just now to have another woman within reach, and a beautiful one at that, whose enthusiasm and expertise in bed ought surely to compensate for an undeniable incompatibility outside it.

He fell to wondering how long Robin would continue working for him after she became Mrs. Cunliffe. Matthew would surely use every ounce of his husbandly influence to pry her away from a profession as dangerous as it was poorly paid. Well, that was her lookout: her bed, and she could lie in it.

Except that once you had broken up, it was much easier to do so again. He ought to know. How many times had he and Charlotte split? How many times had their relationship fallen to pieces, and how many times had they tried to reassemble the wreckage? There had been more cracks than substance by the end: they had lived in a spider's web of fault lines, held together by hope, pain and delusion.

Robin and Matthew had just two months to go before the wedding.

There was still time.

41

See there a scarecrow who waves through the mist.

Blue Öyster Cult, "Out of the Darkness"

It happened quite naturally that Strike saw Robin very little over the following week. They were staking out different locations and exchanged information almost exclusively over their mobiles.

As Strike had expected, neither Wollaston Close nor its environs had revealed any trace of the ex-King's Own Royal Borderer, but he had been no more successful in spotting his man in Catford. The emaciated Stephanie entered and left the flat over the chip shop a few more times. Although he could not be there around the clock, Strike was soon pretty sure that he had seen her entire wardrobe: a few pieces of dirty jersey and one tatty hoodie. If, as Shanker had confidently asserted, she was a prostitute, she was working infrequently. While he took care never to let her see him, Strike doubted that her hollow eyes would retain much of an impression even if he had moved into plain view. They had become shuttered, full of inner darkness, no longer taking in the outside world.

Strike had tried to ascertain whether Whittaker was almost permanently inside or almost constantly absent from the flat in Catford Broadway, but there was no landline registered for the address and the property was listed online as owned by a Mr. Dareshak, who was either renting it or unable to get rid of his squatters.

The detective was standing smoking beside the stage door one evening, watching the lit windows and wondering whether he was imagining movement behind them, when his mobile buzzed and he saw Wardle's name.

"Strike here. What's up?"

"Bit of a development, I think," said the policeman. "Looks like our friend's struck again."

Strike moved the mobile to his other ear, away from the passing pedestrians.

"Go on."

"Someone stabbed a hooker down in Shacklewell and cut off two of her fingers as a souvenir. Deliberately cut 'em off—pinned her arm down and hacked at them."

"Jesus. When was this?"

"Ten days ago—twenty-ninth of April. She's only just come out of an induced coma."

"She survived?" said Strike, now taking his eyes entirely off the windows behind which Whittaker might or might not have been lurking, his attention all Wardle's.

"By a fucking miracle," said Wardle. "He stabbed her in the abdomen, punctured her lung, then hacked off her fingers. Miracle he missed major organs. We're pretty sure he thought she was dead. She'd taken him down a gap between two buildings for a blow job, but they were disturbed: two students walking down Shacklewell Lane heard her scream and went down the alley to see what was going on. If they'd been five minutes later she'd've been a goner. It took two blood transfusions to keep her alive."

"And?" said Strike. "What's she saying?"

"Well, she's drugged up to the eyeballs and can't remember the actual attack. She thinks he was a big, beefy white guy wearing a hat. Dark jacket. Upturned collar. Couldn't see much of his face, but she thinks he was a northerner."

"She does?" said Strike, his heart pounding faster than ever.

"That's what she said. She's groggy, though. Oh, and he stopped her getting run over, that's the last thing she can remember. Pulled her back off the road when a van was coming."

"What a gent," said Strike, exhaling smoke at the starry sky.

"Yeah," said Wardle. "Well, he wanted his body parts pristine, didn't he?"

"Any chance of a photofit?"

"We're going to get the artist in to see her tomorrow, but I haven't got high hopes."

Strike stood in the darkness, thinking hard. He could tell that Wardle had been shaken by the new attack.

"Any news on any of my guys?" he asked.

"Not yet," said Wardle tersely. Frustrated, Strike chose not to push it. He needed this open line into the investigation.

"What about your Devotee lead?" Strike asked, turning back to look at the windows of Whittaker's flat, where nothing seemed to have changed. "How's that coming along?"

"I'm trying to get the cybercrime lot after him, but I'm being told they've got bigger fish to fry just now," said Wardle, not without bitterness. "Their view is he's just a common or garden pervert."

Strike remembered that this had also been Robin's opinion. There seemed little else to say. He said good-bye to Wardle, then sank back into his niche in the cold wall, smoking and watching Whittaker's curtained windows as before.

Strike and Robin met in the office by chance the following morning. Strike, who had just left his flat with a cardboard file of pictures of Mad Dad under his arm, had intended to head straight out without entering the office, but the sight of Robin's blurred form through the frosted glass changed his mind.

"Morning."

"Hi," said Robin.

She was pleased to see him and even more pleased to see that he was smiling. Their recent communication had been full of an odd constraint. Strike was wearing his best suit, which made him look thinner.

"Why are you so smart?" she asked.

"Emergency lawyer's appointment: Mad Dad's wife wants me to show them everything I've got, all the pictures of him lurking outside the school and jumping out at the kids. She called me late last night; he'd just turned up at the house pissed and threatening: she's going to throw the book at him, try and get an injunction out."

"Does this mean we're stopping surveillance on him?"

"I doubt it. Mad Dad won't go quietly," said Strike, checking his watch. "Anyway, forget that—I've got ten minutes and I've got news."

He told her about the attempted murder of the prostitute in Shacklewell. When he had finished, Robin looked sober and thoughtful.

"He took fingers?"

"Yeah."

"You said—when we were in the Feathers—you said you didn't see how Kelsey could have been his first murder. You said you were sure he'd worked up to—what he did to her."

Strike nodded.

"Do you know whether the police have looked for any other killings where a bit of the woman was cut off?"

"Bound to have," said Strike, hoping he was right and making a mental note to ask Wardle. "Anyway," he said, "after this one, they will."

"And she doesn't think she'd recognize him again?"

"Like I said, he'd obscured his face. Big white guy, black jacket."

"Did they get any DNA evidence from her?" asked Robin.

Simultaneously, both of them thought of what Robin herself had been subjected to in hospital after her attack. Strike, who had investigated rapes, knew the form. Robin had a sudden miserable memory of having to pee into a sample bottle, one eye completely closed from where he had punched her, aching all over, her throat swollen from the strangulation, then having to lie down on the examination couch, and the female doctor's gentleness as she parted Robin's knees…

"No," said Strike. "He didn't—no penetration. Anyway, I'd better get going. You can forget about tailing Mad Dad today: he'll know he's blotted his copybook, I doubt he'll show up at school. If you can keep an eye on Wollaston—"

"Wait! I mean, if you've got time," she added.

"Couple more minutes," he said, checking his watch again. "What's up? You're haven't spotted Laing?"

"No," she said, "but I think—just possibly—we might have a lead on Brockbank."

"You're kidding!"

"It's a strip club off Commercial Road; I've had a look at it on Google Street View. Looks pretty grotty. I called and asked for Noel Brockbank and a woman said 'Who?' and then, 'Nile, you mean?' And she put her hand over the mouthpiece and had a bit of discussion with another woman about what the new bouncer was called. He's obviously only just arrived. So I described him physically and she said, 'Yeah, that's Nile.' Of course," said Robin self-deprecatingly, "it might not be him at all, it *could* be a dark man who really is called Nile, but when I described the long jaw, she said immediately—"

"You've played your usual blinder," said Strike, checking his watch. "Gotta go. Text me the details of this strip club, will you?"

"I thought I might—"

"No, I want you to stick to Wollaston Close," said Strike. "Keep in touch."

As the glass door closed behind him and he clanged away down the metal stairs, she tried to feel pleased that he had said she'd played a blinder. Nevertheless, she had hoped for a chance to do something other than stare pointlessly at the flats of Wollaston Close for hours. She was starting to suspect that Laing was not there and, worse still, that Strike knew it.

The visit to the lawyers was brief but productive. The solicitor was delighted with the copious evidence that Strike had laid in front of him, which vividly documented Mad Dad's constant violations of the custody agreements.

"Oh, excellent," he beamed over an enlarged picture of the youngest son cowering tearfully behind his nanny as his father snarled and pointed, almost nose to nose with the defiant woman. "Excellent, excellent…"

And then, catching sight of his client's expression, he had hurried to conceal his glee at this vision of her child's distress and offered tea.

An hour later Strike, still in his suit but with his tie now stuffed in his pocket, was following Stephanie into Catford shopping center. This meant passing under a gigantic fiberglass sculpture of a grinning black cat, which sat on top of the girder that spanned the alley leading into the mall. Two stories high from its dangling paw to the tip of its jaunty tail, which pointed skywards, it seemed poised to pounce upon or scoop up shoppers as they passed beneath.

Strike had decided to follow Stephanie on a whim, never having tracked her before, and intended to return to keep watch over the flat once he had satisfied himself as to where she was going and whom she might be meeting. She walked, as she almost always did, with her arms wrapped tightly around her torso, as though holding herself together, wearing the familiar gray hoodie on top of a black miniskirt and leggings. The slenderness of her twig-like legs was emphasized by her clumpy trainers. She visited a pharmacy and Strike watched through the window as she sat huddled in a chair waiting for a prescription, making eye contact with nobody, staring at her feet. Once she had collected her white paper bag she left the way she had come, passing back beneath the giant cat with its dangling paw, apparently returning to the flat. However, she walked straight past the chippy in Catford Broadway and shortly afterwards took a right at the Afro Caribbean Food Centre and disappeared into a small pub called the Catford Ram, which was built into the rear of the shopping center. The pub, which appeared to have only one window, had a wood-clad exterior that would have given it the look of a large Victorian kiosk had it not been plastered with signs advertising fast food, Sky Sports and a Wi-Fi connection.

The entire area was paved for pedestrians, but a battered gray transit van had been parked a short distance from the pub entrance, giving Strike useful cover as he lurked, debating his options. No purpose would be served at this juncture by coming face to face with Whittaker and the pub looked too small to avoid being seen by his ex-stepfather, if that was whom Stephanie was meeting. All he really wanted was a chance to measure Whittaker's current appearance against that of the figure in the beanie hat and, perhaps, the man in the camouflage jacket who had been watching the Court.

Strike leaned up against the van and lit a cigarette. He had just resolved to find a vantage point that was a little further away, so that he might observe whom Stephanie left the pub with, when the rear doors of the van behind which he was lurking suddenly opened.

Strike took several hasty steps backwards as four men clambered out of the back, along with a smoky haze that gave out a powerful, acrid smell of burned plastic that the ex-SIB man recognized immediately as crack.

All four were unkempt, their jeans and T-shirts filthy, their age hard to gauge because each of them was sunken-faced and prematurely wrinkled. The mouths of two of them had collapsed inwards onto gums that had lost teeth. Momentarily taken aback to find the clean-suited stranger at such close quarters, they seemed to understand from his startled expression that he had not known what was happening inside and slammed the van doors.

Three of them swaggered off towards the pub, but the fourth man did not leave. He was staring at Strike, and Strike was staring right back at him. It was Whittaker.

He was bigger than Strike remembered. Although he had known that Whittaker was almost as tall as he was, he had forgotten the scale of him, the breadth of his shoulders, the heft of the bones beneath his heavily tattooed skin. His thin T-shirt, emblazoned with the logo of the band Slayer, which was both militaristic and occult, blew back against him as they stood facing each other, revealing the outline of ribs.

His yellow face looked freeze-dried like an old apple, the flesh wasted, the skin shrunken against the bone, with cavities beneath the high cheekbones. His matted hair was thinning at the temples: it hung in rats' tails around his stretched earlobes, each of which was adorned with a silver flesh tunnel. There they stood, Strike in his Italian suit, abnormally well groomed, and Whittaker, stinking of crack fumes, his heretic priest's golden eyes now set beneath wrinkled, sagging lids.

Strike could not have said how long they stared at each other, but a stream of perfectly coherent thoughts passed through his mind while they did...

If Whittaker were the killer, he might be panicked but not too surprised to see Strike. If he were not the killer, his shock at finding Strike right outside his van ought to be extreme. Yet Whittaker had never behaved like other people. He always liked to appear unshockable and omniscient.

Then Whittaker reacted and Strike felt at once that it would have been unreasonable to expect him to do anything other than what he did. Whittaker grinned, revealing blackened teeth, and instantly the hatred of twenty years ago rose in Strike, and he yearned to put his fist through Whittaker's face.

"Looky look," said Whittaker quietly. "It's Sergeant Sherlock facking Holmes."

He turned his head and Strike saw scalp shining through the thinning roots and took some petty pleasure in the fact that Whittaker was going bald. He was a vain fucker. He wouldn't like that.

"Banjo!" shouted Whittaker at the last of his three companions, who had only just reached the pub. "Bring 'er out 'ere!"

His smile remained insolent, although the mad eyes flickered from the van to Strike and back to the pub. His filthy fingers were flexing. For all his assumed insouciance, he was edgy. Why didn't he ask why Strike was there? Or did he already know?

The friend called Banjo reappeared, dragging Stephanie out of the pub by her thin wrist. In her free hand she was still clutching the pharmacist's white paper bag. It looked glaringly pristine against her and Banjo's cheap and dirty clothes. A gold necklace bounced around her neck.

"Why're you—? What—?" she whimpered, uncomprehending.

Banjo deposited her beside Whittaker.

"Go get us a pint," Whittaker instructed Banjo, who shuffled obediently away. Whittaker slid a hand around the back of Stephanie's thin neck and she looked up at him with the slavish adoration of a girl who, like Leda before her, saw in Whittaker wonderful things that were totally invisible to Strike. Then Whittaker's fingers gripped her neck until the skin around them went white and began to shake her, not so vigorously as to attract the attention of a passer-by, but with sufficient force to change her expression instantly to one of abject fear.

"Know anything about this?"

"'Bout w-what?" she stammered. The pills were rattling in her white paper bag.

"'Im!" said Whittaker quietly. "'Im that you're so interested in, you filthy little bitch—"

"Get off her," said Strike, speaking for the first time.

"Do I take orders?" Whittaker asked Strike quietly, his grin wide, his eyes manic.

With sudden, shocking strength, he seized Stephanie around the neck with both hands and lifted her bodily into the air, so that she dropped the white bag on the pavement to try to fight free, her feet scrabbling, her face growing purple.

No thought, no reflection. Strike punched Whittaker hard in the gut and he fell backwards, taking Stephanie with him; before Strike could do anything to prevent it, he heard the smack of her head on the concrete. Temporarily winded, Whittaker tried to get to his feet, a stream of whispered filth pouring from between his black teeth, while out of the corner of his eye Strike saw Whittaker's three friends, Banjo at the fore, pushing their way out of the pub: they had seen everything through its one dingy window. One of them was holding a short, rusty blade.

"Do it!" Strike taunted them, standing his ground and opening his arms wide. "Bring the cops round your mobile crack den!"

The winded Whittaker made a gesture from the ground that had the effect of holding his friends at bay, which was the most common sense Strike had ever known him show. Faces were peering out of the pub window.

"You fucking mother…you motherfucker…" Whittaker wheezed.

"Yeah, let's talk about mothers," Strike said, jerking Stephanie to her feet. The blood was pounding in his ears. He itched to punch Whittaker until the yellow face was pulp. "He killed mine," he told the girl, looking into her hollow eyes. Her arms were so thin that his hands almost met around them. "Did you hear that? He's already killed one woman. Maybe more."

Whittaker tried to grab Strike around his knees and bring him down; Strike kicked him off, still holding Stephanie. Whittaker's red handprints stood out on her white neck, as did the imprint of the chain, from which hung the outline of a twisted heart.

"Come with me, now," Strike told her. "He's a fucking killer. There are women's refuges. Get away from him."

Her eyes were like boreholes into a darkness he had never known. He might have been offering her a unicorn: his proposal was madness, outside the realm of the possible, and incredibly, though Whittaker had squeezed her throat until she could not speak, she wrenched away from Strike as if he were a kidnapper, stumbled over to Whittaker and crouched protectively over him, the twisted heart swinging.

Whittaker allowed Stephanie to help him to his feet and turned to face Strike, rubbing his stomach where the punch had landed and then, in his manic way, he began cackling like an old woman. Whittaker had won: they both knew it. Stephanie was clinging to him as though he had saved her. He pushed his filthy fingers deep into the hair at the back of her head and pulled her hard towards him, kissing her, his tongue down her throat, but with his free hand he gestured to his still-watching friends to get back in the van. Banjo climbed into the driver's seat.

"See ya, mummy's boy," Whittaker whispered to Strike, pushing Stephanie in front of him into the back of the van. Before the doors shut on the obscenities and jeers of his male companions, Whittaker looked directly into Strike's eyes and made the familiar throat-slashing gesture in midair, grinning. The van moved away.

Strike became suddenly aware that a number of people were standing around him, staring, all gazing at him with the vacant yet startled expressions of an audience when the lights go up unexpectedly. Faces were still pressed up against the pub window. There was nothing left for him to do except memorize the registration number of the battered old van before it turned the corner. As he departed the scene, furious, the onlookers scattered, clearing his way.

42

I'm living for giving the devil his due.

Blue Öyster Cult, "Burnin' for You"

Fuck-ups happen, Strike told himself. His military career had not been entirely devoid of mishap. You could train as hard as you liked, check every piece of equipment, plan for every contingency and still some random mischance would screw you. Once, in Bosnia, a faulty mobile phone had unexpectedly dumped all its power, triggering a train of mishaps that culminated in a friend of Strike's barely escaping with his life after driving up the wrong street in Mostar.

None of this altered the fact that if a subordinate in the SIB had been running surveillance and leaned up against the back of a carelessly parked van without first checking that it was empty, Strike would have had a lot to say about it, and loudly. He had not meant to confront Whittaker, or so he told himself, but a period of sober reflection forced him to admit that his actions told a different story. Frustrated by the long hours watching Whittaker's flat, he had taken few pains to hide himself from the pub windows, and while he could not have known that Whittaker was inside the van, there was a savage retrospective pleasure in knowing that, at last, he had punched the fucker.

God, he had wanted to hurt him. The gloating laugh, the rat's-tail hair, the Slayer T-shirt, the acrid smell, the clutching fingers around the thin white neck, the taunting talk of mothers: the feelings that had erupted in Strike at the unexpected sight of Whittaker had been those of his eighteen-year-old self, eager to fight, careless of consequences.

Setting aside the pleasure it had been to hurt Whittaker, the encounter had not produced much meaningful information. Try though he might to effect a retrospective comparison, he could neither identify nor rule out Whittaker as the large figure in the beanie hat on looks alone. While the dark silhouette that Strike had chased through Soho had not had Whittaker's matted locks, long hair can be tied back or tucked into a hat; it had looked burlier than Whittaker, but padded jackets easily add substance. Nor had Whittaker's reaction on finding Strike outside his van given the detective real clues. The more he thought about it, the less he could decide whether he had read triumph in Whittaker's gloating expression, or whether the last gesture, the dirty fingers slashing through the air, had been his usual play-acting, a toothless threat, the infantile retaliation of a man determined at all costs to be the worst, the scariest.

In brief, their encounter had revealed that Whittaker remained narcissistic and violent, and given Strike two small pieces of additional information. The first was that Stephanie had aggravated Whittaker by showing curiosity about Strike, and while Strike assumed that this was merely because he had once been Whittaker's stepson, he did not entirely rule out the possibility that it had been triggered by Whittaker mentioning a desire for retribution, or letting slip that he was seeking it. Secondly, Whittaker had managed to make himself some male friends. While he had always had a, to Strike, incomprehensible attraction for certain women, Whittaker had been almost universally disliked and despised by men in the days that Strike had known him. His own gender had tended to deplore his histrionics, the Satanic bullshit, his craving to be first in all company and, of course, to resent his strange magnetic pull over females. Now, though, Whittaker seemed to have found a crew of sorts, men who shared drugs with him and allowed him to boss them around.

Strike concluded that the one thing he could profitably do in the short term was tell Wardle what had happened and give him the registration number of the van. He did this in the hope that the police would think it worth their while to check for drugs and any other incriminating evidence within the vehicle or, even better, inside that flat over the chippy.

Wardle listened to Strike's insistence that he had smelled crack fumes without any form of enthusiasm. Strike was forced to admit, when their call had concluded, that if he were in Wardle's position he would not have considered his own evidence grounds for a search warrant. The policeman clearly thought that Strike had it in for his ex-stepfather, and no amount of pointing out the Blue Öyster Cult connection between himself and Whittaker seemed likely to change Wardle's mind.

When Robin phoned that night with her usual progress report, Strike found relief and solace in telling her what had happened. Although she had news of her own, she was instantly distracted by the announcement that he had come face to face with Whittaker, and listened to the whole story in eager silence.

"Well, I'm glad you hit him," she said when Strike had finished castigating himself for allowing the altercation to happen.

"You are?" said Strike, taken aback.

"Of course I am. He was strangling the girl!"

The moment the words left Robin's mouth she wished she had not said them. She did not want to give Strike any further reason for remembering the thing that she wished she had never told him.

"As knights errant go, I was on the crap side. She fell over with him and cracked her head on the pavement. What I don't get," he added, after a short pause for reflection, "is *her.* That was her chance. She could've left: I'd've got her to a refuge, I'd've seen her right. Why the fuck did she go back to him? Why do women do that?"

In the fractional hesitation before Robin replied, Strike realized that a certain personal interpretation could be put on these words.

"I suppose," began Robin, and simultaneously Strike said, "I didn't mean—"

Both stopped.

"Sorry, go on," said Strike.

"I was only going to say that abused people cling to their abusers, don't they? They've been brainwashed to believe there's no alternative."

I was the bloody alternative, standing there, right in front of her!

"Any sign of Laing today?" Strike asked.

"No," said Robin. "You know, I *really* don't think he's there."

"I still think it's worth—"

"Look, I know who's in every flat except for one of them," said Robin. "People go in and out of all the others. The last one's either unoccupied, or someone's lying in there dead, because the door never opens. I haven't even seen carers or nurses visit."

"We'll give it another week," said Strike. "It's the only lead we've got for Laing. Listen," he added irritably, as she tried to protest, "I'll be in the same position, staking out that strip club."

"Except we know that Brockbank's there," said Robin sharply.

"I'll believe it when I see him," retorted Strike.

They said good-bye a few minutes later in poorly concealed mutual dissatisfaction.

All investigations had their slumps and droughts, when information and inspiration ran dry, but Strike was finding it difficult to take a philosophical view. Thanks to the unknown sender of the leg, there was no longer any money coming in to the business. His last paying client, Mad Dad's wife, no longer needed him. In the hope of persuading a judge that the restraining order was not required, Mad Dad was actually complying with it.

The agency could not survive much longer if the twin stenches of failure and perversity continued to emanate from his office. As Strike had foreseen, his name was now multiplying across the internet in connection with the killing and dismemberment of Kelsey Platt, and the gory details were not only obliterating all mention of his previous successes, they were also eclipsing the simple advertisement of his detective services. Nobody wanted to hire a man so notorious; nobody liked the idea of a detective so intimately connected with unsolved murder.

It was therefore in a mood of determination and slight desperation that Strike set out for the strip club where he hoped to find Noel Brockbank. It turned out to be another converted old pub, which lay on a side street off Commercial Road in Shoreditch. The brick façade was crumbling in parts; its windows had been blacked out and crude white silhouettes of naked women painted upon them. The original name ("The Saracen") was still picked out in wide golden letters across the peeling black paint over the double doors.

The area had a large proportion of Muslim residents. Strike passed them in their hijabs and taqiyahs, browsing the many cheap clothes shops, all bearing names like International Fashion and Made in Milan and displaying sad mannequins in synthetic wigs wearing nylon and polyester. Commercial Road was crammed with Bangladeshi banks, tatty estate agents, English schools and ramshackle grocers that sold past-its-prime fruit behind grimy windows, but it had no benches to sit on, not even a low, cold wall. Even though he frequently changed his vantage point, Strike's knee soon began to complain about long stretches spent standing, waiting for nothing, because Brockbank was nowhere to be seen.

The man on the door was squat and neckless, and Strike saw nobody enter or leave the place except punters and strippers. The girls came and went, and like their place of employment, they were shabbier and less polished than those who worked at Spearmint Rhino. Some were tattooed or pierced; several were overweight, and one, who looked drunk as she entered the building at eleven in the morning, appeared distinctly grubby viewed through the window of the kebab shop that lay directly opposite the club. After watching the Saracen for three days, Strike, whose hopes had been high, whatever he had said to Robin, reluctantly concluded that either Brockbank had never worked there, or that he had already been sacked.

Friday morning arrived before the depressing pattern of no leads changed. As he was lurking in the doorway of an especially dismal clothing store named World Flair, Strike's mobile rang and Robin spoke in his ear:

"Jason's coming to London tomorrow. The leg guy. From the wannabe amputee website."

"Great!" said Strike, relieved at the mere prospect of interviewing someone. "Where are we meeting him?"

"It's 'them,'" said Robin, with a definite note of reservation in her voice. "We're meeting Jason *and* Tempest. She's—"

"Excuse me?" interrupted Strike. "*Tempest?*"

"I doubt it's her birth name," said Robin drily. "She's the woman Kelsey was interacting with online. Black hair and glasses."

"Oh, yeah, I remember," repeated Strike, supporting the mobile between jaw and shoulder while he lit a cigarette.

"I've just got off the phone with her. She's a big activist in the transabled community and she's pretty overwhelming, but Jason thinks she's wonderful and he seems to feel safer with her there."

"Fair enough," said Strike. "So where are we meeting Jason and Tempest?"

"They want to go to Gallery Mess. It's the café at the Saatchi Gallery."

"Really?" Strike seemed to remember that Jason worked in an Asda, and was surprised that his first craving on arriving in London was contemporary art.

"Tempest's in a wheelchair," said Robin, "and apparently it's got really good disabled access."

"OK," said Strike. "What time?"

"One," said Robin. "She—er—asked whether we'd be paying."

"I suppose we'll have to."

"And listen—Cormoran—would it be all right if I took the morning off?"

"Yeah, of course. Everything OK?"

"Everything's fine, I've just got some—some wedding stuff to sort out."

"No problem. Hey," he added, before she could hang up, "shall we meet up somewhere first, before we question them? Agree our interviewing strategy?"

"That'd be great!" said Robin, and Strike, touched by her enthusiasm, suggested they meet in a sandwich shop on the King's Road.

43

Freud, have mercy on my soul.

Blue Öyster Cult, "Still Burnin' "

The next day, Strike had been in Pret A Manger on the King's Road for five minutes when Robin arrived, carrying a white bag over her shoulder. He was as uninformed about female fashion as most male ex-soldiers, but even he recognized the name Jimmy Choo.

"Shoes," he said, pointing, after he had ordered her a coffee.

"Well done," said Robin, grinning. "Shoes. Yes. For the wedding," she added, because after all, they ought to be able to acknowledge that it was happening. A strange taboo had seemed to exist around the subject since she had resumed her engagement.

"You're still coming, right?" she added as they took a table beside the window.

Had he ever agreed that he was attending her wedding, Strike wondered. He had been given the reissued invitation, which like the first had been of stiff cream card engraved in black, but he could not remember telling her that he would be there. She watched him expectantly for an answer, and he was reminded of Lucy and her attempts to coerce him into attending his nephew's birthday party.

"Yeah," he said unwillingly.

"Shall I RSVP for you?" Robin asked.

"No," he said. "I'll do it."

He supposed that it would entail calling her mother. This, he thought, was how women roped you in. They added you to lists and forced you to confirm and commit. They impressed upon you that if you didn't show up a plate of hot food would go begging, a gold-backed chair would remain unoccupied, a cardboard place name would sit shamefully upon a table, announcing your rudeness to the world. Offhand, he could think of literally nothing he wanted to do less than watch Robin marry Matthew.

"D'you want—would you like me to invite Elin?" Robin asked valiantly, hoping to see his expression become a degree or two less surly.

"No," said Strike without hesitation, but he read in her offer a kind of plea, and his real fondness for her caused his better nature to reassert itself. "Let's see the shoes then."

"You don't want to see the—!"

"I asked, didn't I?"

Robin lifted the box out of its bag with a reverence that amused Strike, took off the lid and unfolded the tissue paper inside. They were high, glittery champagne-colored heels.

"Bit rock 'n' roll for a wedding," said Strike. "I thought they'd be . . . I dunno . . . flowery."

"You'll hardly see them," she said, stroking one of the stilettos with a forefinger. "They had some platforms, but—"

She did not finish the sentence. The truth was that Matthew did not like her too tall.

"So how are we going to handle Jason and Tempest?" she said, pushing the lid back down on the shoes and replacing them in the bag.

"You're going to take the lead," said Strike. "You're the one who's had contact with them. I'll jump in if necessary."

"You realize," said Robin awkwardly, "that Jason's going to ask you about your leg? That he thinks you—you lied about how you lost it?"

"Yeah, I know."

"OK. I just don't want you to get offended or anything."

"I think I can handle it," said Strike, amused by her look of concern. "I'm not going to hit him, if that's what's worrying you."

"Well, good," said Robin, "because from his pictures you'd probably break him in two."

They walked side by side up the King's Road, Strike smoking, to the place where the entrance to the gallery sat a little retired from the road, behind the statue of a bewigged and stockinged Sir Hans Sloane. Passing through an arch in the pale brick wall, they entered a grassy square that might, but for the noise of the busy street behind them, have belonged to a country estate. Nineteenth-century buildings on three sides surrounded the square. Ahead, contained in what might once have been barracks, was Gallery Mess.

Strike, who had vaguely imagined a canteen tacked on to the gallery, now realized that he was entering a far more upmarket space and remembered with some misgivings both his overdraft and his agreement to pay for what was almost certainly going to be lunch for four.

The room they entered was long and narrow, with a second, wider area visible through arched openings to their left. White tablecloths, suited waiters, high-vaulted ceilings and contemporary art all over the walls increased Strike's dread of how much this was going to cost him as they followed the maître d' into the inner portion of the room.

The pair they sought was easy to spot among the tastefully dressed, mostly female clientele. Jason was a stringy youth with a long nose who wore a maroon hoodie and jeans and looked as though he might take flight at the slightest provocation. Staring down at his napkin, he resembled a scruffy heron. Tempest, whose black bob had certainly been dyed and who wore thick, square black-rimmed spectacles, was his physical opposite: pale, dumpy and doughy, her small, deep-set eyes like raisins in a bun. Wearing a black T-shirt with a multicolored cartoon pony stretched across an ample chest, she was sitting in a wheelchair adjacent to the table. Both had menus open in front of them. Tempest had already ordered herself a glass of wine.

When she spotted Strike and Robin approaching, Tempest beamed, stretched out a stubby forefinger and poked Jason on the shoulder. The boy looked around apprehensively; Strike registered the pronounced asymmetry of his pale blue eyes, one of which was a good centimeter higher than the other. It gave him an oddly vulnerable look, as though he had been finished in a hurry.

"Hi," said Robin, smiling and reaching out a hand to Jason first. "It's nice to meet you at last."

"Hi," he muttered, proffering limp fingers. After one quick glance at Strike he looked away, turning red.

"Well, hello!" said Tempest, sticking her own hand out to Strike, still beaming. Deftly she reversed her wheelchair a few inches and suggested that he pull up a chair from a neighboring table. "This place is great. It's so easy to get around in, and the staff are really helpful. Excuse me!" she said loudly to a passing waiter, "Could we have two more menus, please?"

Strike sat down beside her, while Jason shunted up to make room for Robin beside him.

"Lovely space, isn't it?" said Tempest, sipping her wine. "And the staff are wonderful about the wheelchair. Can't help you enough. I'm going to be recommending it on my site; I do a list of disability-friendly venues."

Jason drooped over his menu, apparently afraid to make eye contact with anyone.

"I've told him not to mind what he orders." Tempest told Strike comfortably. "He didn't realize how much you'll have made from solving those cases. I've told him: the press will have paid you loads just for your story. I suppose that's what you do now, try and solve the really high-profile ones?"

Strike thought of his plummeting bank balance, his glorified bedsit over the office and the shattering effect the severed leg had had on his business.

"We try," he said, avoiding looking at Robin.

Robin chose the cheapest salad and a water. Tempest ordered a starter as well as a main course, urged Jason to imitate her, then collected in the menus to return them to the waiter with the air of a gracious hostess.

"So, Jason," Robin began.

Tempest at once talked over Robin, addressing Strike.

"Jason's nervous. He hadn't really thought through what the repercussions of meeting you might be. I had to point them out to him; we've been on the phone day and night, you should see the bills—I should charge you, ha, ha! But seriously—"

Her expression became suddenly grave.

"—we'd really like your assurance up front that we're not going to be in trouble for not telling the police everything. Because it wasn't as though we had any useful information. She was just a poor kid with problems. We don't know anything. We only met up with her once, and we haven't got a clue who killed her. I'm sure you know much more about it than we do. I was pretty worried when I heard Jason had been talking to your partner, to be honest, because I don't think anyone really appreciates how much we're persecuted as a community. I've had death threats myself—I should hire you to investigate them, ha ha."

"Who's made death threats against you?" asked Robin in polite surprise.

"It's *my* website, you see," said Tempest, ignoring Robin and addressing Strike. "I run it. It's like I'm den mother—or Mother Superior, ha ha . . . anyway, I'm the one everyone confides in and comes to for advice, so obviously, *I'm* the one who gets attacked when ignorant people target us. I suppose I don't help myself. I fight other people's battles a lot, don't I, Jason? Anyway," she said, pausing only to take a greedy sip of wine, "I can't advise Jason to talk to you without a guarantee he's not going to get in any trouble."

Strike wondered what possible authority she thought he had in the matter. The reality was that both Jason and Tempest had concealed information from the police and, whatever their reasons for doing so, and whether or not the information turned out to be valuable, their behavior had been foolish and potentially harmful.

"I don't think either of you will be in trouble," he lied easily.

"Well, OK, that's good to hear," said Tempest with some complacency, "because we *do* want to help, obviously. I mean, I said to Jason, if this man's preying on the BIID community, which is possible—I mean, bloody hell, it's our *duty* to help. It wouldn't surprise me, either, the abuse we get on the website, the hatred. It's unbelievable. I mean, obviously it stems from ignorance, but we get abuse from people you'd expect to be on our side, who know exactly what it's like to be discriminated against."

Drinks arrived. To Strike's horror, the Eastern European waiter upended his bottle of Spitfire beer into a glass containing ice.

"Hey!" said Strike sharply.

"The beer isn't cold," said the waiter, surprised by what he clearly felt was Strike's overreaction.

"For fuck's sake," muttered Strike, fishing the ice out of his glass. It was bad enough that he was facing a hefty lunch bill, without ice in his beer. The waiter gave Tempest her second glass of wine with a slightly huffy air. Robin seized her chance:

"Jason, when you first made contact with Kelsey—"

But Tempest set down her glass and drowned Robin out.

"Yeah, I checked all my records, and Kelsey first visited the site back in December. Yeah, I told the police that, I let them see everything. She asked about *you*," Tempest told Strike in a tone that suggested he ought to be flattered to have secured a mention on her website, "and then she got talking to Jason and they exchanged email addresses, and from then on they were in direct contact, weren't you, Jason?"

"Yeah," he said weakly.

"Then she suggested meeting up and Jason got in touch with me—didn't you, Jason?—and basically he thought he'd feel more comfortable if I came along, because after all, it's the internet, isn't it? You never know. She could've been anyone. She could've been a man."

"What made you want to meet Kel—?" Robin began to ask Jason, but again, Tempest talked over her.

"They were both interested in *you,* obviously," said Tempest to Strike. "Kelsey got Jason interested, didn't she, Jason? She knew *all* about you," said Tempest, smiling slyly as though they shared disreputable secrets.

"So what did Kelsey tell you about me, Jason?" Strike asked the boy.

Jason turned scarlet at being addressed by Strike and Robin

wondered suddenly whether he could be gay. From her extensive perusal of the message boards she had detected an erotic undertone to some, though not all, of the posters' fantasies, <<Δēvōŧėė>> being the most blatant of them.

"She said," mumbled Jason, "her brother knew you. That he'd worked with you."

"Really?" said Strike. "Are you sure she said her brother?"

"Yeah."

"Because she didn't have one. Only a sister."

Jason's lopsided eyes traveled nervously over the objects on the table before returning to Strike.

"I'm pretty sure she said brother."

"Worked with me in the army, did he?"

"No, not in the army, I don't think. Later."

She lied all the time... If it was Tuesday she'd say it was Wednesday.

"Now, *I* thought she said her boyfriend told her," said Tempest. "She told us she had a boyfriend called Neil, Jason—remember?"

"Niall," mumbled Jason.

"Oh, was it? All right, Niall. He picked her up after we had coffee, remember?"

"Hang on," said Strike, raising a hand, and Tempest paused obediently. "You *saw* Niall?"

"Yes," said Tempest. "He picked her up. On his motorbike."

There was a brief silence.

"A man on a motorbike picked her up from—where did you meet her?" asked Strike, his calm tone belying his suddenly pounding pulse.

"Café Rouge on Tottenham Court Road," said Tempest.

"That's not far from our office," said Robin.

Jason turned an even darker red.

"Oh, Kelsey and Jason knew that, ha ha! You were hoping to see Cormoran pop in, weren't you, Jason? Ha ha ha," laughed Tempest merrily as the waiter returned with her starter.

"A man on a motorbike picked her up, Jason?"

Tempest's mouth was full and, at last, Jason was able to speak.

"Yeah," he said with a furtive look at Strike. "He was waiting for her along the road."

"Could you see what he looked like?" asked Strike, correctly anticipating the answer.

"No, he was sort of—sort of tucked around the corner."

"He kept his helmet on," said Tempest, washing down a mouthful with wine, the quicker to rejoin the conversation.

"What color was the motorbike, can you remember?" Strike asked.

Tempest rather thought it had been black and Jason was sure it had been red, but they agreed that it had been parked far too far away to recognize the make.

"Can you remember anything else Kelsey said about her boyfriend?" asked Robin.

Both shook their heads.

Their main courses arrived midway through a lengthy explanation by Tempest of the advocacy and support services offered by the website she had developed. Only with her mouth full of chips did Jason finally find the courage to address Strike directly.

"Is it true?" he said suddenly. His face again grew bright red as he said it.

"Is what true?" asked Strike.

"That you—that—"

Chewing vigorously, Tempest leaned towards Strike in her wheelchair, placed her hand on his forearm and swallowed.

"That you did it yourself," she whispered, with the ghost of a wink.

Her thick thighs had subtly readjusted themselves as she lifted them off the chair, bearing their own weight, instead of hanging behind the mobile torso. Strike had been in Selly Oak Hospital with men left paraplegic and quadriplegic by the injuries they had sustained in war, seen their wasted legs, the compensations they had learned to make in the movement of their upper bodies to accommodate the dead weight below. For the first time, the reality of what Tempest was doing hit him forcibly. She did not need the wheelchair. She was entirely able-bodied.

Strangely, it was Robin's expression that kept Strike calm and polite, because he found vicarious release in the look of distaste and fury she threw Tempest. He addressed Jason.

"You'll need to tell me what you've been told before I can tell you whether it's true or not."

"Well," said Jason, who had barely touched his Black Angus burger, "Kelsey said you went to the pub with her brother and you got—got drunk and told him the truth. She reckoned you walked off your base in Afghanistan with a gun and you went as far as you could in the dark, then you—shot yourself in the leg, and then you got a doctor to amputate it for you."

Strike took a large swig of beer.

"And I did this why?"

"What?" said Jason, blinking confusedly.

"Was I trying to get invalided out of the army, or—?"

"Oh, no!" said Jason, looking strangely hurt. "No, you were"—he blushed so hard it seemed unlikely that there was enough blood left in the rest of his body—"like us. You needed it," he whispered. "You needed to be an amputee."

Robin suddenly found that she could not look at Strike and pretended to be contemplating a curious painting of a hand holding a single shoe. At least, she thought it showed a hand holding a shoe. It might equally have been a brown plant pot with a pink cactus growing out of it.

"The—brother—who told Kelsey all about me—did he know she wanted to take off her own leg?"

"I don't think so, no. She said I was the only one she'd ever told."

"So you think it was just coincidence he mentioned—?"

"People keep it quiet," said Tempest, shoehorning herself back into the conversation at the first opportunity. "There's a lot of shame, a *lot* of shame. I'm not out at work," she said blithely, waving towards her legs. "I have to say it's a back injury. If they knew I'm transabled they'd never understand. And don't get me started on the prejudice from the medical profession, which is absolutely unbelievable. I've changed GPs twice; I wasn't going to put up with being offered bloody psychiatric help *again*. No, Kelsey told us she'd never been able to tell anyone, poor little love. She had nobody to turn to. Nobody understood. That's why she reached out to us—and to you, of course," she told Strike, smiling with a little condescension because, unlike her, he had ignored Kelsey's appeal. "You're not alone, mind. Once people have successfully achieved what they're after they tend to leave the community. We get it—we understand—but it would mean a lot if people hung around just to describe what it feels like to finally be in the body you're meant to be in."

Robin was worried that Strike might explode, here in this polite white space where art lovers conversed in soft voices. However, she had reckoned without the self-control that the ex–Special Investigation Branch officer had learned through long years of interrogations. His polite smile to Tempest might have been a little grim, but he merely turned again to Jason and asked:

"So you don't think it was Kelsey's brother's idea for her to contact me?"

"No," said Jason, "I think that was all her own idea."

"So what exactly did she want from me?"

"Well, *obviously,*" interposed Tempest, half-laughing, "she wanted advice on how to do what you'd done!"

"Is that what you think, Jason?" asked Strike and the boy nodded.

"Yeah...she wanted to know how badly she'd have to injure her leg to get it taken off, and I think she had a sort of idea you'd introduce her to the doctor who did yours."

"That's the perennial problem," said Tempest, clearly oblivious to the effect she was having on Strike, "finding reliable surgeons. They're usually completely unsympathetic. People have died trying to do it themselves. There was a wonderful surgeon in Scotland who performed a couple of amputations on BIID sufferers, but then they stopped him. That was a good ten years ago. People go abroad, but if you can't pay, if you can't afford travel...you can see why Kelsey wanted to get her mitts on your contact list!"

Robin let her knife and fork fall with a clatter, feeling on Strike's behalf all the offense that she assumed him to be experiencing. *His contact list!* As though his amputation was a rare artefact that Strike had bought on the black market...

Strike questioned both Jason and Tempest for another fifteen minutes before concluding that they knew nothing more of any use. The picture they painted of their one meeting with Kelsey was of an immature and desperate girl whose urge to be amputated was so powerful that she would, by the consent of both of her cyberfriends, have done anything to achieve it.

"Yeah," sighed Tempest, "she was one of those. She'd already had a go when she was younger, with some wire. We've had people so desperate they've put their legs on train tracks. One guy tried to freeze his leg off in liquid nitrogen. There was a girl in America who deliberately botched a ski jump, but the danger with that is you might not get exactly the degree of disability you're after—"

"So what degree are *you* after?" Strike asked her. He had just put up a hand for the bill.

"I want my spinal cord severed," said Tempest with total composure. "Paraplegic, yeah. Ideally I'll have it done by a surgeon. In the meantime, I just get on with it," she said, gesturing again to her wheelchair.

"Using the disabled bathrooms and stairlifts, the works, eh?" asked Strike.

"Cormoran," said Robin in a warning voice.

She had thought this might happen. He was stressed and sleep-deprived. She supposed she ought to be glad that they had got all the information they needed first.

"It's a need," said Tempest composedly. "I've known ever since I was a child. I'm in the wrong body. I need to be paralyzed."

The waiter had arrived; Robin held out her hand for the bill, because Strike hadn't noticed him.

"Quickly, please," she said to the waiter, who looked sullen. He was the man Strike had barked at for putting ice in his beer glass.

"Know many disabled people, do you?" Strike was asking Tempest.

"I know a couple," she said. "Obviously we've got a lot in—"

"You've got fuck all in common. Fuck all."

"I knew it," muttered Robin under her breath, snatching the chip and pin machine out of the waiter's grip and shoving in her Visa card. Strike stood up, towering over Tempest, who looked suddenly unnerved, while Jason shrank back in his seat, looking as though he wanted to disappear inside his hoodie.

"C'mon, Corm—" said Robin, ripping her card out of the machine.

"Just so you know," said Strike, addressing both Tempest and Jason as Robin grabbed her coat and tried to pull him away from the table, "I was in a car that blew up around me." Jason had put his hands over his scarlet face, his eyes full of tears. Tempest merely gaped. "The driver was ripped in two—*that'd* get you some attention, eh?" he said savagely to Tempest. "Only he was dead, so not so fucking much. The other guy lost half his face—I lost a leg. There was nothing voluntary about—"

"OK," said Robin, taking Strike's arm. "We're off. Thanks very much for meeting us, Jason—"

"Get some help," said Strike loudly, pointing at Jason as he allowed Robin to pull him away, diners and waiters staring. "Get some fucking help. With your *head*."

They were out in the leafy road, nearly a block away from the gallery, before Strike's breathing began to return to normal.

"OK," he said, though Robin had not spoken. "You warned me. I'm sorry."

"That's all right," she said mildly. "We got everything we wanted."

They walked on in silence for a few yards.

"Did you pay? I didn't notice."

"Yes. I'll take it out of petty cash."

They walked on. Well-dressed men and women passed them, busy, bustling. A bohemian-looking girl with dreadlocks floated past in a long paisley dress, but a five-hundred-pound handbag revealed that her hippy credentials were as fake as Tempest's disability.

"At least you didn't punch her," said Robin. "In her wheelchair. In front of all the art lovers."

Strike began to laugh. Robin shook her head.

"I knew you'd lose it," she sighed, but she was smiling.

44

Then Came the Last Days of May

He had thought she was dead. It had not troubled him that he hadn't seen a news report, because she'd been a hooker. He'd never seen anything in the papers about the first one he'd done either. Prostitutes didn't fucking count, they were nothing, no one cared. The Secretary was the one who was going to make the big splash, because she was working for that bastard—a clean-living girl with her pretty fiancé, the kind the press went wild for...

He didn't understand how the whore could still be alive, though. He remembered the feeling of her torso beneath the knife, the popping, puncturing sound of the metal slitting her skin, the grating of steel on bone, the blood gushing. Students had found her, according to the newspaper. Fucking students.

He still had her fingers, though.

She'd produced a photofit. What a fucking joke! The police were shaven monkeys in uniforms, the lot of them. Did they think this picture would help? It looked nothing like him, nothing at all; it could have been anyone, white or black. He would have laughed out loud if It hadn't been there, but It wouldn't like him laughing over a dead hooker and a photofit...

It was pretty bolshy at the moment. He had had to work hard to make up for the fact that he had treated It roughly, had to apologize, play the nice guy. "I was upset," he had said. "Really upset." He'd had to cuddle It and buy It fucking flowers and stay home, to make up for being angry, and now It was taking advantage, the way women always did, trying to take more, as much as It could get.

"I don't like it when you go away."

I'll make YOU *fucking go away if you keep this up.*

He had told her a cock-and-bull story about the chance of a job, but for the first time ever she actually fucking dared question him: Who told you about it? How long will you be gone?

He watched It talking and he imagined drawing back a fist and punching It so hard in Its ugly fucking face that the bones splintered…

Yet he needed It a little while longer, at least until he did The Secretary.

It still loved him, that was the trump card: he knew he could bring It back into line with the threat of leaving for good. He didn't want to overplay that one, though. So he pressed on with the flowers, the kisses, the kindness that made the memory of his rage soften and dissolve in Its stupid, addled memory. He liked to add a little emollient to her drinks, a little extra something to keep her off balance, weeping into his neck, clinging to him.

Patient, kind, but determined.

At last she agreed: a week away, completely away, free to do as he liked.

45

Harvester of eyes, that's me.

Blue Öyster Cult, "Harvester of Eyes"

Detective Inspector Eric Wardle was far from delighted that Jason and Tempest had lied to his men, but Strike found him less angry than he might have expected when they met for a pint, at Wardle's invitation, on Monday evening in the Feathers. The explanation for his surprising forbearance was simple: the revelation that Kelsey had been picked up from her rendezvous in Café Rouge by a man on a motorbike fitted perfectly with Wardle's new pet theory.

"You remember the guy called Devotee who was on their website? Got a fetish for amputees, went quiet after Kelsey was killed?"

"Yeah," said Strike, who recalled Robin saying that she had had an interaction with him.

"We've tracked him down. Guess what's in his garage?"

Strike assumed, from the fact that no arrest had been made, that they had not found body parts, so he obligingly suggested: "Motorbike?"

"Kawasaki Ninja," said Wardle. "I know we're looking for a Honda," he added, forestalling Strike, "but he crapped himself when we came calling."

"So do most people when CID turn up on their doorstep. Go on."

"He's a sweaty little guy, name of Baxter, a sales rep with no alibi for the weekend of the second and third, or for the twenty-ninth. Divorced, no kids, claims he stayed in for the royal wedding, watching it. Would you have watched the royal wedding without a woman in the house?"

"No," said Strike, who had only caught footage on the news.

"He claims the bike's his brother's and he's just looking after it, but after a bit of questioning he admitted he's taken it out a few times. So we know he can ride one, and he could have hired or borrowed the Honda."

"What did he say about the website?"

"He downplayed that completely, says he's only pissing around, doesn't mean anything by it, he's not turned on by stumps, but when we asked whether we could have a look at his computer he didn't like it at all. Asked to talk to his lawyer before he gave an answer. That's where we've left it, but we're going back to see him again tomorrow. Friendly chat."

"Did he admit to talking to Kelsey online?"

"Hard for him to deny it when we've got her laptop and all Tempest's records. He asked Kelsey about her plans for her leg and offered to meet her and she brushed him off—online, anyway. Bloody hell, we've got to look into him," said Wardle in response to Strike's skeptical look, "he's got no alibi, a motorbike, a thing for amputation and he tried to meet her!"

"Yeah, of course," said Strike. "Any other leads?"

"That's why I wanted to meet you. We've found your Donald Laing. He's in Wollaston Close, in Elephant and Castle."

"He is?" said Strike, genuinely taken aback.

Savoring the fact that he had surprised Strike for once, Wardle smirked.

"Yeah, and he's a sick man. We found him through a JustGiving page. We got on to them and got his address."

That was the difference between Strike and Wardle, of course: the latter still had badges, authority and the kind of power Strike had relinquished when he left the army.

"Have you seen him?" asked Strike.

"Sent a couple of guys round and he wasn't in, but the neighbors confirmed it's his flat. He rents, lives alone and he's pretty ill, apparently. They said he's gone home to Scotland for a bit. Friend's funeral. Supposed to be back soon."

"Likely bloody story," muttered Strike into his pint. "If Laing's got a friend left in Scotland I'll eat this glass."

"Have it your own way," said Wardle, half amused, half impatient. "I thought you'd be pleased we're chasing up your guys."

"I am," said Strike. "Definitely ill, is he?"

"The neighbor reckons he needs sticks. He's been in and out of hospital a lot, apparently."

The leather-padded screen overhead was showing last month's Arsenal–Liverpool match with the sound turned down. Strike watched as van Persie sank the penalty that he had thought, watching back on his tiny portable at the flat, might help Arsenal to a desperately needed win. It hadn't happened, of course. The Gunners' fortunes were currently sinking with his own.

"You seeing anyone?" asked Wardle abruptly.

"What?" said Strike, startled.

"Coco liked the look of you," said Wardle, making sure that Strike saw him smirking as he said it, the better to impress upon Strike that he thought this ludicrous. "The wife's friend, Coco. Red hair, remember?"

Strike remembered that Coco was a burlesque dancer.

"I said I'd ask," said Wardle. "I've told her you're a miserable bastard. She says she doesn't mind."

"Tell her I'm flattered," said Strike, which was the truth, "but yeah, I'm seeing someone."

"Not your work partner, is it?" asked Wardle.

"No," said Strike. "She's getting married."

"You missed a trick there, mate," said Wardle, yawning. "*I* would."

"So, let me get this straight," said Robin in the office next morning. "As soon as we find out that Laing actually *does* live in Wollaston Close, you want me to stop watching it."

"Hear me out," said Strike, who was making tea. "He's away, according to the neighbors."

"You've just told me you don't think he's really gone to Scotland!"

"The fact that the door of his flat's been closed ever since you've been watching it suggests he's gone *somewhere*."

Strike dropped tea bags into two mugs.

"I don't buy the friend's funeral bit, but it wouldn't surprise me if he'd popped back to Melrose to try and beat some cash out of his demented mother. That could easily be our Donnie's idea of holiday fun."

"One of us should be there for when he comes back—"

"One of us *will* be there," said Strike soothingly, "but in the meantime, I want you to switch to—"

"Brockbank?"

"No, I'm doing Brockbank," said Strike. "I want you to have a bash at Stephanie."

"Who?"

"Stephanie. Whittaker's girl."

"Why?" asked Robin loudly, as the kettle boiled in its usual crescendo of rattling lid and rambunctious bubbles, condensation steaming up the window behind it.

"I want to see whether she can tell us what Whittaker was doing the day Kelsey was killed, and on the night that girl got her fingers hacked off in Shacklewell. The third and the twenty-ninth of April, to be precise."

Strike poured water on the tea bags and stirred in milk, the teaspoon pinging off the sides of the mug. Robin was not sure whether she was pleased or aggrieved by the suggested change to her routine. On balance, she thought she was glad, but her recent suspicions that Strike was trying to sideline her were not easily dispelled.

"You definitely still think Whittaker could be the killer?"

"Yep," said Strike.

"But you haven't got any—"

"I haven't got any evidence for any of them, have I?" said Strike. "I'm just going to keep going until I either get some or clear all of them."

He handed her a mug of tea and sank down on the mock-leather sofa, which for once did not fart beneath him. A minor triumph, but in the absence of others, better than nothing.

"I hoped I'd be able to rule out Whittaker on how he's looking these days," said Strike, "but, you know, it *could've* been him in that beanie hat. I know one thing: he's exactly the same bastard he was when I knew him. I've blown it completely with Stephanie, she's not going to talk to me now, but you might be able to do something with her. If she can give him an alibi for those dates, or point us towards someone else who can, we'll have to rethink. If not, he stays on the list."

"And what are you going to be doing while I'm on Stephanie?"

"Sticking with Brockbank. I've decided," said Strike, stretching out his legs and taking a fortifying drink of tea, "I'm going into the strip club today, find out what's happened to him. I'm tired of eating kebabs and hanging round clothes shops waiting for him to show up."

Robin did not say anything.

"What?" said Strike, watching her expression.

"Nothing."

"Come off it."

"OK... what if he *is* there?"

"I'll cross that bridge—I'm not going to hit him," said Strike, correctly reading her thoughts.

"OK," said Robin, but then, "you hit Whittaker, though."

"That was different," said Strike, and when she did not respond, "Whittaker's special. He's family."

She laughed, but reluctantly.

When Strike withdrew fifty pounds from a cashpoint prior to entering the Saracen off Commercial Road, the machine churlishly showed him a negative balance in his current account. His expression grim, Strike handed over a tenner to the short-necked bouncer on the door and pushed his way through the strips of black plastic masking the interior, which was dimly lit, but insufficiently to mask the overall impression of shabbiness.

The interior of the old pub had been ripped out in its entirety. The refashioned decor gave the impression of a community center gone bad, dimly lit and soulless. The floor was of polished pine, which reflected the wide neon strip running the length of the bar that took up one side of the room.

It was shortly after midday, but there was already a girl gyrating on a small stage at the far end of the pub. Bathed in red light and standing in front of angled mirrors so that every inch of dimpled flesh could be appreciated, she was removing her bra to the Rolling Stones' "Start Me Up." A grand total of four men were sitting on high stools, one to each elevated table, dividing their attention between the girl now swinging clumsily around a pole and a big-screen TV showing Sky Sports.

Strike headed straight for the bar, where he found himself facing a sign that read "Any customer caught masturbating will be ejected."

"What can I get you, love?" asked a girl with long hair, purple eye-shadow and a nose ring.

Strike ordered a pint of John Smith's and took a seat at the bar. Other than the bouncer, the only other male employee on view was the man sitting behind a turntable beside the stripper. He was stocky, blond, middle-aged and did not remotely resemble Brockbank.

"I was hoping to meet a friend here," Strike told the barmaid, who, having no further customers, was leaning on the bar, staring dreamily at the television and picking her long nails.

"Yeah?" she said, sounding bored.

"Yeah," said Strike. "He said he was working here."

A man in a fluorescent jacket approached the bar and she moved away to serve him without another word.

"Start Me Up" ended and so did the stripper's act. Naked, she hopped off the stage, grabbed a wrap and disappeared through a curtain at the back of the pub. Nobody clapped.

A woman in a very short nylon kimono and stockings slid out from behind the curtain and began walking around the pub, holding out an empty beer glass to punters, who one by one put their hands in their pockets and gave her some change. She reached Strike last. He dropped in a couple of quid. She headed straight for the stage, where she put her pint glass of coins carefully beside the DJ's turntable, wriggled out of her kimono and stepped on to the stage in bra, pants, stockings and heels.

"Gentlemen, I think you're going to enjoy this...Big welcome, please, for the lovely Mia!"

She began to jiggle to Gary Numan's "Are 'Friends' Electric?" There was not the remotest synchronicity between her movements and the track.

The barmaid resumed her lounging position near Strike. The view of the TV was clearest from where he sat.

"Yeah, like I was saying," Strike began again, "a friend of mine told me he's working here."

"Mm-hm," she said.

"Name of Noel Brockbank."

"Yeah? I don't know him."

"No," said Strike, making a show of scanning the place, although he had already established that Brockbank was nowhere to be seen. "Maybe I've got the wrong place."

The first stripper pushed her way out from behind the curtain, having changed into a bubblegum-pink spaghetti-strapped minidress that barely skimmed her crotch, and was somehow more indecent than her previous nakedness. She approached the man in the fluorescent jacket and asked him something, but he shook his head. Looking around, she caught Strike's eye, smiled and approached him.

"Hiya," she said. Her accent was Irish. Her hair, which he had thought blonde in the red light of the stage, turned out to be vivid copper. Beneath the thick orange lipstick and the thick false eyelashes hid a girl who looked as though she should still have been at school. "I'm Orla. Who're you?"

"Cameron," said Strike, which was what people usually called him after failing to grasp his first name.

"D'ya fancy a private dance then, Cameron?"

"Where does that happen?"

"Troo there," she said, pointing towards the curtain where she had changed. "I've never seen you in here before."

"No. I'm looking for a friend."

"What's her name?"

"It's a him."

"Yeh've come to the wrong place fer hims, darlin'," she said.

She was so young he felt mildly dirty just hearing her call him darling.

"Can I buy you a drink?" Strike asked.

She hesitated. There was more money in a private dance, but perhaps he was the kind of guy who needed warming up first.

"Go on, then."

Strike paid an exorbitant amount for a vodka and lime, which she sipped primly on a seat beside him, most of her breasts hanging out of the dress. The texture of her skin reminded him of the murdered Kelsey: smooth and firm, with plenty of youthful fat. There were three small blue stars inked on her shoulder.

"Maybe you know my friend?" Strike said. "Noel Brockbank."

She was no fool, little Orla. Suspicion and calculation mingled in the sharp sideways look she gave him. She was wondering, like the masseuse back in Market Harborough, whether he was police.

"He owes me money," said Strike.

She continued to scrutinize him for a moment, her smooth forehead furrowed, then apparently swallowed the lie.

"Noel," she repeated. "I tink he's gone. Hang on—Edie?"

The bored barmaid did not take her eyes from the TV.

"Hmm?"

"What was the name of yer man that Des sacked the other week? Guy who only lasted a few days?"

"Dunno what he was called."

"Yeah, I tink it was Noel who was sacked," Orla told Strike. Then, with a sudden and endearing bluntness, she said: "Gimme a tenner an' I'll make sure for ya."

With a mental sigh, Strike handed over a note.

"Wait there, now," said Orla cheerfully. She slipped off her bar stool, tucked the tenner into the elastic of her pants, tugged her dress down inelegantly and sauntered over to the DJ, who scowled over at Strike while Orla spoke to him. He nodded curtly, his jowly face glowing in the red light, and Orla came trotting back looking pleased with herself.

"I tort so!" she told Strike. "I wasn't here when it happened, but he had a fit or sometin'."

"A fit?" repeated Strike.

"Yeah, it was only his first week on the job. Big guy, wasn't he? Wit a big chin?"

"That's right," said Strike.

"Yeah, an' he was late, and Des wasn't happy. Dat's Des, over dare," she added unnecessarily, pointing out the DJ who was watching Strike suspiciously while changing the track from "Are 'Friends' Electric?" to Cyndi Lauper's "Girls Just Wanna Have Fun." "Des was givin' out to him about being late and your man just dropped to the floor an' started writhin' around. They say," added Orla, with relish, "he pissed himself."

Strike doubted that Brockbank would have urinated over himself to escape a dressing down from Des. It sounded as though he had genuinely had an epileptic fit.

"Then what happened?"

"Your mate's gorlfriend come runnin' out the back—"

"What girlfriend's this?"

"Hang on—Edie?"

"Hm?"

"Who's dat black gorl, now, with the extensions? The one with the great knockers? The one Des doesn't like?"

"Alyssa," said Edie.

"Alyssa," Orla told Strike. "She come runnin' out the back and was screamin' at Des to phone an ambulance."

"Did he?"

"Yeah. Dey took yer man away, and Alyssa went with him."

"And has Brock—has Noel been back since?"

"He's no bloody use as a bouncer if he's gonna fall down and piss himself just 'cause someone's shoutin' at him, is he?" said Orla. "I heard Alyssa wanted Des to give him a second chance, but Des doesn't give second chances."

"So Alyssa called Des a tight cunt," said Edie, emerging suddenly from her listlessness, "and he sacked her too. Silly bitch. She needs the money. She's got kids."

"When did all this happen?" Strike asked Orla and Edie.

"Couple of weeks ago," said Edie. "But he was a creep, that guy. Good riddance."

"In what way was he a creep?" asked Strike.

"You can always tell," said Edie with a kind of hard-bitten weariness. "Always. Alyssa's got fucking terrible taste in men."

The second stripper was now down to her thong and twerking enthusiastically towards her scanty audience. Two older men had just entered the club and hesitated before approaching the bar, their eyes on the thong, which was clearly about to come off.

"You don't know where I'd find Noel, do you?" Strike asked Edie, who seemed too bored to demand money for the information.

"He's living with Alyssa, somewhere in Bow," said the barmaid. "She got herself a council house but she was always bitching about the place. I don't know exactly where it is," she said, forestalling Strike's question. "I never went round or nothing."

"I tort she liked it," said Orla vaguely. "She said there was a good nursery."

The stripper had wriggled out of her thong and was waving it over her head, lasso-style. Having seen all there was to see, the two new punters drifted to the bar. One of them, a man old enough to be Orla's grandfather, fixed his rheumy eyes on her cleavage. She sized him up, businesslike, then turned to Strike.

"So, you wanna private dance or not?"

"I don't think I will," said Strike.

Before the words were even fully out of his mouth she had put down her glass, wriggled off the chair and slid towards the sixty-year-old, who grinned, revealing more gaps than teeth.

A hulking figure appeared at Strike's side: the neckless bouncer.

"Des wants a word," he said in what would have been a menacing tone had his voice not been surprisingly high-pitched for a man so broad.

Strike looked around. The DJ, who was glaring across the room at him, beckoned.

"Is there a problem?" Strike asked the bouncer.

"Des'll tell you, if there is," was the faintly ominous answer.

So Strike crossed the room to speak to the DJ, and stood like a massive schoolboy summoned to the headmaster at his lectern. Fully alive to the absurdity of the situation, he had to wait while a third stripper deposited her glass of coins safely beside the turntable, wriggled out of her purple robe and ascended the stage in black lace and Perspex heels. She was heavily tattooed and, beneath thick makeup, spotty.

"Gentlemen, tits, ass and class from—Jackaline!"

"Africa" by Toto began. Jackaline began to spin around the pole, at which she was far more accomplished than either of her colleagues, and Des covered the microphone with his hand and leaned forwards.

"Right, pal."

He appeared both older and harder than he had in the red light of the stage, his eyes shrewd, a scar as deep as Shanker's running along his jaw.

"What are you asking about that bouncer for?"

"He's a friend of mine."

"He never had a contract."

"I never said he had."

"Unfair dismissal my fucking arse. He never told me he had fucking fits. Have you been sent here by that Alyssa bitch?"

"No," said Strike. "I was told Noel worked here."

"She's a mad fucking cow."

"I wouldn't know. It's him I'm looking for."

Scratching an armpit, Des glowered at Strike while, four feet away, Jackaline slipped her bra straps from her shoulders and glared over her shoulder at the half-dozen punters watching.

"*Bollocks* was that bastard ever in the Special Forces," said Des aggressively, as though Strike had insisted he had been.

"Is that what he told you?"

"It's what *she* said. Alyssa. They wouldn't take a fucking wreck like that. Anyway," said Des, eyes narrowed, "there was other stuff I didn't like."

"Yeah? Like what?"

"That's my business. You tell her that from me. It wasn't just his fucking fit. You tell her to ask Mia why I didn't want him back, and you tell Alyssa if she does one more stupid fucking thing to my car, or sends one more of her friends round trying to get something on me, I'll fucking have her in court. You tell her that!"

"Fair enough," said Strike. "Got an address?"

"Fuck off, all right?" snarled Des. "Fuck off out of here."

He leaned into the microphone.

"Nice," he said, with a kind of professional leer, as Jackaline jiggled her breasts rhythmically in the scarlet light. Des made a "hop it" gesture to Strike and returned to his stack of old vinyl records.

Accepting the inevitable, Strike allowed himself to be escorted to the door. Nobody paid any attention; the audience's attention remained divided between Jackaline and Lionel Messi on the widescreen TV. At the door, Strike stood aside for a group of young men in suits to enter, all of whom seemed already a little worse for drink.

"Tits!" yelled the first of them, pointing at the stripper. "*Tits!*"

The bouncer took exception to this mode of entry. A mild altercation ensued, with the shouter cowed by his friends and the bouncer's strictures, which were delivered with several jabs of a forefinger to his chest.

Strike waited patiently for the matter to be adjusted. When the young men had finally been allowed to enter, he took his departure to the opening strains of "The Only Way Is Up" by Yazz.

46

Subhuman

Alone with his trophies, he felt himself entirely whole. They were proof of his superiority, his astonishing ability to glide through the ape-like police and the sheep-like masses, taking whatever he wanted, like a demigod.

Of course, they gave him something else too.

He never seemed to get hard when he was actually killing. Thinking about it beforehand, yes: sometimes he could drive himself into an onanistic frenzy with ideas of what he was going to do, refining and restaging the possibilities in his mind. Afterwards—now, for instance, holding in his hand the chilly, rubbery, shrunken breast he had hacked from Kelsey's torso, already turning slightly leathery with its repeated exposure to the air outside the fridge—then he had no problem at all. He was like a flagpole *now.*

He had the new one's fingers in the icebox. He took one out, pressed it against his lips then bit down on it, hard. He imagined her still connected to it, screaming in agony. He chewed deeper, relishing the feeling of the cold flesh splitting, his teeth pressing hard into the bone. One hand fumbled with the string of his tracksuit bottoms...

Afterwards he put it all back in the fridge, closed the door and gave it a little pat, grinning to himself. There'd be a lot more than that in there, soon. The Secretary wasn't small: five foot seven or eight by his reckoning.

One minor problem...he didn't know where she was. He'd lost the trail. She hadn't been to the office this morning. He'd gone to the LSE, where he'd spotted the platinum bitch, but seen no sign of The Secretary. He'd looked in the Court; he'd even checked the Tottenham. This was a temporary setback, though. He'd sniff her out. He'd pick her up again tomorrow morning at West Ealing station, if he had to.

He made himself a coffee and poured a slug of whisky into it from a bottle he'd had here for months. There was hardly anything else in the dirty hidey-hole where he hid his treasures, in his secret sanctuary: a kettle, a few chipped mugs, the fridge—the altar of his profession—an old mattress to sleep on and a docking port for him to place his iPod on. That was important. It had become part of his ritual.

He had thought they were shit when he'd first heard them, but as his obsession with bringing down Strike had grown, so had his liking for their music. He liked to listen to it through earphones while he was stalking The Secretary, while he was cleaning his knives. It was sacred music to him now. Some of their lyrics stayed with him like fragments of a religious service. The more he listened, the more he felt they understood.

Women were reduced to the elemental when they were facing the knife. They became cleansed by their terror. There was a kind of purity to them as they begged and pleaded for their lives. The Cult (as he privately called them) seemed to understand. They got it.

He put his iPod into the dock and selected one of his favorite tracks, "Dr. Music." Then he headed to the sink and the cracked shaving mirror he kept there, razor and scissors at the ready: all the tools a man needed to totally transform himself.

From the single speaker of the dock, Eric Bloom sang:

Girl don't stop that screamin'
You're sounding so sincere...

47

I sense the darkness clearer...

Blue Öyster Cult, "Harvest Moon"

Today—June the first—Robin was able to say for the first time: "I'm getting married next month." July the second suddenly seemed very close. The dressmaker back in Harrogate wanted a final fitting, but she had no idea when she would be able to fit in a trip home. At least she had her shoes. Her mother was taking the RSVPs and updating her regularly on the guest list. Robin felt strangely disconnected from it all. Her tedious hours of surveillance in Catford Broadway, staking out the flat over the chip shop, were a world away from queries on the flowers, who should sit beside whom at the reception, and (this last from Matthew) whether or not she had yet asked Strike for the fortnight off for the honeymoon, which Matthew had booked and which was to be a surprise.

She did not know how the wedding could have come so close without her realizing. Next month, the very next month, she would become Robin Cunliffe—at least, she supposed she would. Matthew certainly expected her to take his name. He was incredibly cheerful these days, hugging her wordlessly when he passed her in the hall, raising not a single objection to the long hours she was working, hours that bled into their weekends.

He had driven her to Catford on the last few mornings because it was on the way to the company he was auditing in Bromley. He was being nice about the despised Land Rover now, even while he crashed the gears and stalled it at junctions, saying what a wonderful gift it had been, how kind Linda was to have given it to them, how useful a car was when he was sent somewhere out of town. During yesterday's commute he had offered to remove Sarah Shadlock from the wedding guest list. Robin could tell that he had had to screw up his courage even to ask the question, afraid that mentioning Sarah's name might provoke a row. She had thought about it for a while, wondering how she really felt, and finally said no.

"I don't mind," she said. "I'd rather she came. It's fine."

Removing Sarah from the list would tell Sarah that Robin had found out what had happened years before. She would rather pretend that she had always known, that Matthew had confessed long ago, that it was nothing to her; she had her pride. However, when her mother, who had also queried Sarah's attendance, asked whom Robin wanted to put on Sarah's free side, now that Sarah and Matthew's mutual university friend Shaun couldn't make it, Robin answered with a question.

"Has Cormoran RSVP'd?"

"No," said her mother.

"Oh," said Robin. "Well, he says he's going to."

"You want to put him next to Sarah, do you?"

"No, of course not!" snapped Robin.

There was a short pause.

"Sorry," said Robin. "Sorry, Mum…stressed…no, could you sit Cormoran next to…I don't know…"

"Is his girlfriend coming?"

"He says not. Put him anywhere, just not near bloody—I mean, not by Sarah."

So, Robin settled in to wait for a glimpse of Stephanie on the warmest morning so far. The shoppers on Catford Broadway were wearing T-shirts and sandals; black women passed in brightly colored head wraps. Robin, who had put on a sundress under an old denim jacket, leaned back into one of her accustomed nooks in the theater building, pretending that she was talking on the mobile and killing time before she pretended to peruse the scented candles and incense sticks on the nearest stall.

It was difficult to maintain concentration when you were convinced that you had been sent on a wild goose chase. Strike might insist that he still thought Whittaker a suspect in Kelsey's killing, but Robin was quietly unconvinced. She increasingly inclined to Wardle's view that Strike had it in for his ex-stepfather and that his usually sound judgment was clouded by old grievances. Glancing up periodically at the unmoving curtains of Whittaker's flat, she remembered that Stephanie had last been seen being bundled into the back of a transit van by Whittaker, and wondered whether she was even inside the flat.

From faint resentment that this was going to be another wasted day, she fell easily to dwelling on the main grudge she currently felt against Strike: his appropriation of the search for Noel Brockbank. Somehow Robin had come to feel that Brockbank was particularly her own suspect. Had she not successfully impersonated Venetia Hall, they would never have known that Brockbank was living in London, and if she had not had the wit to recognize that Nile was Noel, they would never have traced him to the Saracen. Even the low voice in her ear—*Do A know you, little girl?*—creepy as it had been, constituted a strange kind of connection.

The mingled smells of raw fish and incense that had come to represent Whittaker and Stephanie filled her nostrils as she leaned back against chilly stone and watched the unmoving door of his flat. Like foxes to a dustbin, her unruly thoughts slunk back to Zahara, the little girl who had answered Brockbank's mobile. Robin had thought of her every day since they had spoken and had asked Strike for every detail about the little girl's mother on his return from the strip club.

He had told Robin that Brockbank's girlfriend was called Alyssa and that she was black, so Zahara must be too. Perhaps she looked like the little girl with stiff pigtails now waddling along the street, holding tight to her mother's forefinger and staring at Robin with solemn dark eyes. Robin smiled, but the little girl did not: she merely continued to scrutinize Robin as she and her mother passed. Robin kept smiling until the little girl, twisting almost 180 degrees so as not to break eye contact with Robin, tripped over her tiny sandaled feet. She hit the ground and began to wail; her impassive mother scooped her up and carried her. Feeling guilty, Robin resumed her observation of Whittaker's windows as the fallen toddler's wails reverberated down the street.

Zahara almost certainly lived in the flat in Bow that Strike had told her about. Zahara's mother complained about the flat, apparently, although Strike said that one of the girls...

One of the girls had said...

"Of course!" Robin muttered excitedly. "*Of course!*"

Strike wouldn't have thought of that—of course he wouldn't, he was a man! She began to press the keys on her phone.

There were seven nurseries in Bow. Absently replacing her mobile in her pocket and energized by her train of thought, Robin began her usual drift through the market stalls, casting the occasional glance up at the windows of Whittaker's flat and at the perennially closed door, her mind entirely given over to the pursuit of Brockbank. She could think of two possible courses of action: stake out each of these seven nurseries, watching for a black woman picking up a girl called Zahara (and how would she know which was the right mother and daughter?) or...or...She paused beside a stall selling ethnic jewelry, barely seeing it, preoccupied by thoughts of Zahara.

Entirely by chance, she looked up from a pair of feather and bead earrings as Stephanie, whom Strike had accurately described, came out of the door beside the chip shop. Pale, red-eyed and blinking in the bright light like an albino rabbit, Stephanie leaned on the chip-shop door, toppled inside and proceeded to the counter. Before Robin could collect her wits, Stephanie had brushed past her holding a can of Coke and gone back into the building through the white door.

Shit.

"Nothing," she told Strike on the phone an hour later. "She's still in there. I didn't have a chance to do anything. She was in and out in about three minutes."

"Stick with it," said Strike. "She might come out again. At least we know she's awake."

"Any luck with Laing?"

"Not while I was there, but I've had to come back to the office.

Big news: Two-Times has forgiven me. He's just left. We need the money—I could hardly refuse."

"Oh, for God's sake—how can he have another girlfriend *already?*" asked Robin.

"He hasn't. He wants me to check out some new lap-dancer he's flirting with, see whether she's already in a relationship."

"Why doesn't he just *ask* her?"

"He has. She says she isn't seeing anyone, but women are devious, cheating scum, Robin, you know that."

"Oh yes, of course," sighed Robin. "I forgot. Listen, I've had an idea about Br—Wait, something's happening."

"Everything all right?" he asked sharply.

"Fine...hang on..."

A transit van had rolled up in front of her. Keeping the mobile to her ear, Robin ambled around it, trying to see what was going on. As far as she could make out, the driver had a crew cut, but the sun on the windscreen dazzled her eyes, obscuring his features. Stephanie had appeared on the pavement. Arms wrapped tightly around herself, she trooped across the street and climbed into the back of the van. Robin stepped back to allow it to pass, pretending to talk into her mobile. Her eyes met those of the driver; they were dark and hooded.

"She's gone, got in the back of an old van," she told Strike. "The driver didn't look like Whittaker. Could've been mixed race or Mediterranean. Hard to see."

"Well, we know Stephanie's on the game. She's probably off to earn Whittaker some money."

Robin tried not to resent his matter-of-fact tone. He had, she reminded herself, freed Stephanie from Whittaker's stranglehold with a punch to the gut. She paused, looking into a newsagent's window. Royal wedding ephemera was still very much in evidence. A Union Jack was hanging on the wall behind the Asian man at the till.

"What do you want me to do? I could go and cover Wollaston Close for you, if you're off after Two-Times' new girl. It makes—oof," she gasped.

She had turned to walk away and collided with a tall man sporting a goatee, who swore at her.

"Sorry," she gasped automatically as the man shoved his way past her into the newsagent's.

"What just happened?" asked Strike.

"Nothing—I bumped into someone—listen, I'm going to go to Wollaston Close," she said.

"All right," said Strike after a perceptible pause, "but if Laing turns up, just try and get a picture. Don't go anywhere near him."

"I wasn't intending to," said Robin.

"Call me if there's any news. Or even if there isn't."

The brief spurt of enthusiasm she had felt at the prospect of going back to Wollaston Close had faded by the time she had reached Catford station. She was not sure why she felt suddenly downcast and anxious. Perhaps she was hungry. Determined to break herself of the chocolate habit that was jeopardizing her ability to fit into the altered wedding dress, she bought herself an unappetizing-looking energy bar before boarding the train.

Chewing the sawdusty slab as the train carried her towards Elephant and Castle, she found herself absentmindedly rubbing her ribs where she had collided with the large man in the goatee. Being sworn at by random people was the price you paid for living in London, of course; she could not ever remember a stranger swearing at her in Masham, not even once.

Something made her suddenly look all around her, but there did not seem to be any large man in her vicinity, neither in the sparsely occupied carriage nor peering at her from the neighboring ones. Now she came to think of it, she had jettisoned some of her habitual vigilance that morning, lulled by the familiarity of Catford Broadway, distracted by her thoughts of Brockbank and Zahara. She wondered whether she would have noticed somebody else there, watching her...but that, surely, was paranoia. Matthew had dropped her off in the Land Rover that morning; how could the killer have followed her to Catford unless he had been waiting in some kind of vehicle at Hastings Road?

Nevertheless, she thought, she must guard against complacency. When she got off the train she noticed a tall dark man walking a little behind her, and deliberately stopped to let him pass. He did not give her a second look. *I'm definitely being paranoid*, she thought, dropping the unfinished energy bar into a bin.

It was half past one before she reached the forecourt of Wollaston Close, the Strata building looming over the shabby old flats like an emissary from the future. The long sundress and the old denim jacket that had fitted in so well in the market in Catford felt a little studentish here. Yet again pretending to be on her mobile, Robin looked casually upwards and her heart gave a little skip.

Something had changed. The curtains had been pulled back.

Hyperaware now, she maintained her course in case he was looking out of the window, intending to find a place in shadow where she could keep an eye on his balcony. So intent was she on finding the perfect place to lurk, and on maintaining the appearance of a natural conversation, that she had no attention to spare for where she was treading.

"*No!*" Robin squealed as her right foot skidded out from under her, her left became caught in the hem of her long skirt and she slid into an undignified half-splits before toppling sideways and dropping her mobile.

"Oh bugger," she moaned. Whatever she had slipped in looked like vomit or even diarrhea: some was clinging to her dress, to her sandal, and she had grazed her hand on landing, but it was the precise identity of the thick, yellow-brown, glutinous lumpy stuff that worried her most.

Somewhere in her vicinity a man burst out laughing. Cross and humiliated, she tried to get up without spreading the muck further over her clothes and shoes and did not look immediately for the source of the jeering noise.

"Sorry, hen," said a soft Scottish voice right behind her. She looked around sharply and several volts of electricity seemed to pass through her.

In spite of the warmth of the day, he was wearing a windstopper hat with long earflaps, a red and black check jacket and jeans. A pair of metal crutches supported most of his substantial weight as he looked down at her, still grinning. Deep pockmarks disfigured his pale cheeks, his chin and the pouches beneath his small, dark eyes. The flesh on his thick neck spilled over his collar.

A plastic bag containing what looked like a few groceries hung from one hand. She could just see the tattooed dagger tip that she knew ran through a yellow rose higher on his forearm. The drops of tattooed blood running down his wrist looked like injuries.

"Ye'll need a tap," he said, grinning broadly as he pointed at her foot and the hem of her dress, "and a scrubbing brush."

"Yes," said Robin shakily. She bent to pick up her mobile. The screen was cracked.

"I live up there," he said, nodding towards the flat she had been watching on and off for a month. "Ye can come up if y'want. Clean yerself up."

"Oh no—that's all right. Thanks very much, though," said Robin breathlessly.

"Nae problem," said Donald Laing.

His gaze slithered down her body. Her skin prickled, as though he had run a finger down her. Turning on his crutches, he began to move away, the plastic bag swinging awkwardly. Robin stood where he had left her, conscious of the blood pounding in her face.

He did not look back. The earflaps of his hat swayed like spaniel's ears as he moved painfully slowly around the side of the flats and out of sight.

"Oh my God," whispered Robin. Hand and knee smarting where she had fallen, she absentmindedly pushed her hair out of her face. Only then did she realize, with relief, from the smell on her fingers, that the slippery substance had been curry. Hurrying to a corner out of sight of Donald Laing's windows, she pressed the keys of the cracked mobile and called Strike.

48

Here Comes That Feeling

The heatwave that had descended on London was his enemy. There was nowhere to hide his knives in a T-shirt, and the hats and high collars on which he relied for disguise looked out of place. He could do nothing but wait, fuming and impotent, in the place that It did not know about.

At last, on Sunday, the weather broke. Rain swept the parched parks, windscreen wipers danced, tourists donned their plastic ponchos and trudged on through the puddles regardless.

Full of excitement and determination, he pulled on a hat worn low over his eyes and donned his special jacket. As he walked, the knives bounced against his chest in the long makeshift pockets he'd ripped in the lining. The capital's streets were hardly less crowded now than when he'd knifed the tart whose fingers sat in his icebox. Tourists and Londoners were still swarming everywhere like ants. Some of them had bought Union Jack umbrellas and hats. He barged into some of them for the simple pleasure of knocking them aside.

His need to kill was becoming urgent. The last few wasted days had slid past, his leave of absence from It slowly expiring, but The Secretary remained alive and free. He had searched for hours, trying to trace her and then, shockingly, she had been right there in front of him, the brazen bitch, in broad daylight—but there had been witnesses everywhere...

Poor impulse control, that fucking psychiatrist would have said, knowing what he'd done at the sight of her. Poor impulse control! He could control his impulses fine when he wanted—he was a man of superhuman cleverness, who had killed three women and maimed another without the police being any the wiser, so fuck the psychiatrist and his dumb diagnoses—but when he'd seen her right in front of him after all those empty days, he'd wanted to scare her, wanted to get up close, *really* close, close enough to smell her, speak to her, look into her frightened eyes.

Then she'd strutted away and he had not dared follow her, not then, but it had almost killed him to let her go. She ought to be lying in parcels of meat in his fridge by now. He ought to have witnessed her face in that ecstasy of terror and death, when he owned them completely and they were his to play with.

So here he was, walking through the chilly rain, burning inside because it was Sunday and she had gone again, back to the place where he could never get near her, because Pretty Boy was always there.

He needed more freedom, a lot more freedom. The real obstacle was having It at home all the time, spying on him, clinging to him. All that would have to change. He'd already pushed It unwillingly back into work. Now he had decided that he would have to pretend to It that he had a new job. If necessary, he'd steal to get cash, pretend he'd earned it—he'd done that plenty of times before. Then, freed up, he'd be able to put in the time he really needed to make sure he was close at hand when The Secretary dropped her guard, when nobody was looking, when she turned the wrong corner…

The passersby had as little life as automata to him. Stupid, stupid, stupid…Everywhere he walked he looked for her, the one he'd do next. Not The Secretary, no, because the bitch was back behind her white front door with Pretty Boy, but any woman stupid enough, drunk enough, to walk a short way with a man and his knives. He had to do one before he went back to It, he had to. It would be all that could keep him going, once he was back pretending to be the man It loved. His eyes flickered from under his hat, sorting them, discarding them: the women with men, the women with kids clutching them, but no women alone, none the way he needed them…

He walked for miles until darkness fell, past lit pubs where men and women laughed and flirted, past restaurants and cinemas, looking, waiting, with a hunter's patience. Sunday night and the workers were returning home early, but it did not matter: there were still tourists everywhere, out-of-towners, drawn by the history and mystery of London...

It was nearly midnight when they leapt to his practiced eye like a cluster of plump mushrooms in long grass: a bunch of squawking, tiddly girls cackling and weaving along the pavement. They were on one of those miserable, rundown streets that were his especial delight, where a drunken tussle and a shrieking girl would be nothing out of the ordinary. He followed, ten yards behind them, watching them pass under streetlamps, elbowing each other and cackling, all except for one of them. She was the drunkest and youngest-looking of them all: ready to throw up, if he knew anything about it. She stumbled on her heels, falling slightly behind her friends, the silly little tart. None of her friends had realized what a state she was in. They were just the right side of legless, snorting and guffawing as they staggered along.

He drifted after them, casual as you please.

If she threw up in the street the noise would attract her friends, who would stop and rally around her. While she fought the urge to vomit, she could not speak. Slowly, the distance between her and her friends increased. She swayed and wobbled, reminding him of the last one, with her stupid high heels. This one must not survive to help make photofits.

A taxi was approaching. He saw the scenario play out before it did. They hailed it loudly, screeching and waving their arms, and in they piled, one by one, fat arse after fat arse. He sped up, head down, face hidden. The streetlamps reflected in the puddles, the "for hire" light extinguished, the growl of the engine...

They had forgotten her. She swayed right into the wall, holding up an arm to support herself.

He might only have seconds. One of her friends would realize any time now that she wasn't with them.

"You all right, darling? You feeling bad? Come here. This way. You'll be all right. Just down here."

She began to retch as he tugged her down a side street. Feebly she tried to pull her arm away, heaving; the vomit splattered down her, gagging her.

"Filthy bitch," he snarled, one hand already on the handle of his knife under the jacket. He was dragging her forcibly towards a darkened recess between an adult video store and a junk shop.

"No," she gasped, but she choked on her vomit, heaving.

A door opened across the street, light rippling down a flight of steps. People burst out onto the pavement, laughing.

He slammed her up against the wall and kissed her, pinning her flat while she tried to struggle. She tasted foul, of sick. The door opposite closed, the gaggle of people passed by, their voices echoing in the quiet night, the light extinguished.

"Fucking hell," he said in disgust, releasing her mouth but keeping her pinned to the wall with his body.

She drew breath to scream, but he had the knife ready and it sank deep between her ribs with ease, nothing like the last one, who'd fought so hard and so stubbornly. The noise died on her stained lips as the hot blood poured over his gloved hand, soaking the material. She jerked convulsively, tried to speak, her eyes rolled upwards into whiteness and her entire body sagged, still pinned by the knife.

"Good girl," he whispered, pulling the carving knife free as she fell, dying, into his arms.

He dragged her deeper into the recess, where a pile of rubbish sat waiting for collection. Kicking the black bags aside, he dumped her in a corner then pulled out his machete. Souvenirs were imperative, but he only had seconds. Another door might open, or her dozy bitches of friends might come back in their taxi…

He slashed and sawed, put his warm, oozing trophies in his pocket, then piled up the rubbish over and on her.

It had taken less than five minutes. He felt like a king, like a god. Away he walked, knives safely stowed, panting in the cool, clean night air, jogging a little once he was on the main road again. He was already a block away when he heard raucous female voices shouting in the distance.

"Heather! *Heather, where are you, you silly cow?*"

"Heather can't hear you," he whispered into the darkness.

He tried to stop himself laughing, burying his face in his collar, but he could not restrain his jubilation. Deep in his pockets, his sopping fingers were playing with the rubbery cartilage and skin to which her earrings—little plastic ice-cream cones—were still attached.

49

It's the time in the season for a maniac at night.

Blue Öyster Cult, "Madness to the Method"

The weather remained cool, rain-flecked and faintly blustery as June entered its second week. The blaze of sunlit pageantry that had surrounded the royal wedding had receded into memory: the giddy high tide of romantic fervor had ebbed, the wedding merchandise and congratulatory banners had been removed from shop windows and the capital's newspapers returned to more mundane matters, including an imminent Tube strike.

Then horror exploded across Wednesday's front pages. The mutilated body of a young woman had been uncovered beneath bin bags, and within a few hours of the first police appeal for information the world had been informed that a twenty-first-century Jack the Ripper was stalking the streets of London.

Three women had been attacked and mutilated, but the Met appeared to have no leads. In their stampede to cover every possible aspect of the story—maps of London showing the location of each attack, pictures of the three victims—the journalists revealed themselves determined to make up for lost time, aware that they might have arrived a little late at the party. They had previously treated the killing of Kelsey Platt as a lone act of madness and sadism, and the subsequent attack on Lila Monkton, the eighteen-year-old prostitute, had gained virtually no media coverage. A girl who had been selling herself for sex on the day of the royal wedding could hardly expect to oust a new-minted duchess from the front pages.

The murder of Heather Smart, a twenty-two-year-old building society employee from Nottingham, was an entirely different matter. The headlines virtually wrote themselves, for Heather was a wonderfully relatable heroine with her steady job, her innocent desire to see the capital's landmarks and a boyfriend who was a primary school teacher. Heather had been to see *The Lion King* the night before her death, had eaten dim sum in Chinatown and posed for photographs in Hyde Park with the Life Guards riding past in the background. Endless column inches could be spun out of the long weekend to celebrate her sister-in-law's thirtieth birthday, which had culminated in a brutal, sordid death in the back lot of an adult entertainment store.

The story, like all the best stories, split like an amoeba, forming an endless series of new stories and opinion pieces and speculative articles, each spawning its own counter chorus. There were discussions of the deplorable drunken tendencies of the young British woman, with reciprocal accusations of victim-blaming. There were horror-struck articles about sexual violence, tempered with reminders that these attacks were far less common than in other countries. There were interviews with the distraught, guilt-stricken friends who had accidentally abandoned Heather, which in turn spawned attacks and vilifications on social media, leading back to a defense of the grieving young women.

Overlaying every story was the shadow of the unknown killer, the madman who was hacking women's bodies apart. The press again descended upon Denmark Street in search of the man who had received Kelsey's leg. Strike decided that the time had come for Robin to take that much-discussed but daily postponed trip to Masham for a final fitting of her wedding dress, then decamped yet again to Nick and Ilsa's with a backpack and a crushing sense of his own impotence. A plainclothes officer remained stationed in Denmark Street in case anything suspicious turned up in the post. Wardle was concerned lest another body part addressed to Robin arrived.

Weighed down by the demands of an investigation that was being conducted under the full glare of the national media, Wardle was unable to meet Strike face to face for six days after the discovery of Heather's body. Strike journeyed again to the Feathers in the early evening, where he found Wardle looking haggard, but looking forward to talking things over with a man who was both inside and outside the case.

"Been a fucker of a week," sighed Wardle, accepting the pint Strike had bought him. "I've started bloody smoking again. April's really pissed off."

He took a long draft of lager, then shared with Strike the truth about the discovery of Heather's body. The press stories, as Strike had already noted, conflicted in many possibly important essentials, though all blamed the police for not finding her for twenty-four hours.

"She and her friends were all shitfaced," said the policeman, setting the scene with bluntness. "Four of them got into a cab, so ratted they forgot about Heather. They were a street away when they realized she wasn't with them.

"The cabbie's hacked off because they're loud and obnoxious. One of them starts swearing at him when he says he can't do a U-turn in the middle of the road. There's a big argument, so it's a good five minutes before he agrees to go back for Heather.

"When they finally reach the street where they think they left her—they're from Nottingham, remember, they don't know London at all—Heather's nowhere to be seen. They crawl up the road in the cab, shouting for her out of the open window. Then one of them thinks she sees Heather in the distance, getting onto a bus. So two of them get out—there's no bloody logic to it, they were out of their skulls—and go running down the road screaming after the bus to stop while the other two lean out of the cab screaming at them to get back in, they should follow the bus in the cab. Then the one who got into an argument with the cabbie earlier calls him a stupid Paki, he tells them to get the fuck out of his cab and drives away.

"So basically," said Wardle wearily, "all this shit we're taking for not finding her within twenty-four hours is down to alcohol and racism. The silly bitches were convinced Heather had got on that bus so we wasted a day and a half trying to track a woman wearing a similar coat. Then the owner of the Adult Entertainment Centre goes to put his bins out and finds her lying there under a load of bags, nose and ears cut off."

"So that bit was true," said Strike.

Her mutilated face had been the one detail all of the papers had agreed on.

"Yeah, that bit was true," said Wardle heavily. " 'The Shacklewell Ripper.' It's got a great ring to it."

"Witnesses?"

"Nobody saw a bloody thing."

"What about Devotee and his motorbike?"

"Ruled out," Wardle admitted, his expression grim. "He's got a firm alibi for Heather's killing—family wedding—and we couldn't make anything stick for either of the other two attacks."

Strike had the impression that Wardle wanted to tell him something else, and waited receptively.

"I don't want the press to get wind of this," Wardle said, dropping his voice, "but we think he might've done two more."

"Jesus," said Strike, genuinely alarmed. "When?"

"Historic," said Wardle. "Unsolved murder in Leeds, 2009. Prostitute, originally from Cardiff. Stabbed. He didn't cut anything off her, but he took a necklace she always wore and dumped her in a ditch out of town. The body wasn't found for a fortnight.

"Then, last year, a girl was killed and mutilated in Milton Keynes. Sadie Roach, her name was. Her boyfriend went down for it. I've looked it all up. The family campaigned hard for his release and he got out on appeal. There was nothing to tie him to it, except that they'd rowed and he once threatened a bloke with a penknife.

"We've got the psychologist and forensics on to all five attacks and the conclusion is they've got enough features in common to suggest the same perpetrator. It looks like he uses two knives, a carving knife and a machete. The victims were all vulnerable—prostitutes, drunk, emotionally off balance—and all picked up off the street except for

Kelsey. He took trophies from all of them. It's too soon to say whether we've got any similar DNA off the women. Odds are, not. It doesn't look like he had sex with any of them. He gets his kicks a different way."

Strike was hungry, but something told him not to interrupt Wardle's moody silence. The policeman drank more beer then said, without quite meeting Strike's eyes, "I'm looking into all your guys. Brockbank, Laing and Whittaker."

About fucking time.

"Brockbank's interesting," said Wardle.

"You've found him?" asked Strike, freezing with his pint at his lips.

"Not yet, but we know he was a regular attendee at a church in Brixton until five weeks ago."

"Church? Are you sure it's the same bloke?"

"Tall ex-soldier, ex-rugby player, long jaw, one of his eyes sunken, cauliflower ear, dark crew cut," reeled off Wardle. "Name Noel Brockbank. Six foot three or four. Strong northern accent."

"That's him," said Strike. "A bloody *church?*"

"Hang on," said Wardle, getting up. "Need a slash."

And yet, why not a church? Strike thought as he went to the bar for a couple of fresh pints. The pub was filling up around him. He took a menu back to the table as well as the beers, but could not concentrate on it. *Young girls in the choir . . . he wouldn't be the first . . .*

"Needed that," said Wardle, rejoining Strike. "I might go out for a fag, join you back—"

"Finish about Brockbank first," said Strike, pushing the fresh pint across the table.

"To tell you the truth, we found him by accident," said Wardle, sitting back down and accepting the pint. "One of our guys has been tailing the mother of a local drug lord. We don't think Mum's as innocent as she's claiming to be, so our guy follows her to church and there's Brockbank standing on the door handing out hymnbooks. He got talking to the copper without knowing who he was, and our guy didn't have a clue Brockbank was wanted in connection with anything.

"Four weeks later our guy hears me talking about looking for a Noel Brockbank on the Kelsey Platt case and tells me he met a bloke with the same name a month ago in Brixton. See?" said Wardle, with a ghost of his usual smirk. "I *do* pay attention to your tip-offs, Strike. Be silly not to, after the Landry case."

You pay attention when you've got nothing out of Digger Malley and Devotee, thought Strike, but he made impressed and grateful noises before returning to the main point.

"Did you say Brockbank's stopped attending church?"

"Yeah," sighed Wardle. "I went down there yesterday, had a word with the vicar. Young guy, enthusiastic, inner-city church—you know the sort," said Wardle—inaccurately, because Strike's contact with the clergy had been mostly limited to military chaplains. "He had a lot of time for Brockbank. Said he'd had a rough deal in life."

"Brain damage, invalided out of the army, lost his family, all that crap?" asked Strike.

"That was the gist," said Wardle. "Said he misses his son."

"Uh huh," said Strike darkly. "Did he know where Brockbank was living?"

"No, but apparently his girlfriend—"

"Alyssa?"

Frowning slightly, Wardle reached into the inside pocket of his jacket, pulled out a notebook and consulted it.

"Yeah, it is, as it goes," he said. "Alyssa Vincent. How did you know that?"

"They've both just been sacked from a strip club. I'll explain in a bit," said Strike hurriedly, as Wardle showed signs of becoming sidetracked. "Go on about Alyssa."

"Well, she's managed to get a council house in east London near her mother. Brockbank told the vicar he was going to move in with her and the kids."

"Kids?" said Strike, his thoughts flying to Robin.

"Two little girls, apparently."

"Do we know where this house is?" asked Strike.

"Not yet. The vicar was sorry to see him go," said Wardle, glancing restlessly towards the pavement, where a couple of men were smoking. "I did get out of him that Brockbank was in church on Sunday the third of April, which was the weekend Kelsey died."

In view of Wardle's increasing restlessness, Strike passed no comment except to suggest that they both adjourn to the pavement for a cigarette.

They lit up and smoked side by side for a couple of minutes. Workers walked past in both directions, weary from late hours at the office. Evening was drawing in. Directly above them, between the indigo of approaching night and the neon coral of the setting sun, was a narrow stretch of no-colored sky, of vapid and empty air.

"*Christ,* I've missed this," said Wardle, dragging on the cigarette as though it was mother's milk before picking up the thread of their conversation once more. "Yeah, so Brockbank was in church that weekend, making himself useful. Very good with the kids, apparently."

"I'll bet he is," muttered Strike.

"Take some nerve, though, wouldn't it?" said Wardle, blowing smoke towards the opposite side of the road, his eyes on Epstein's sculpture *Day,* which adorned the old London Transport offices. A boy stood before a throned man, his body contorted so that he both managed to embrace the king behind him and display his own penis to onlookers. "To kill and dismember a girl, then turn up in church as though nothing had happened?"

"Are you Catholic?" Strike asked.

Wardle looked startled.

"I am, as it goes," he said suspiciously. "Why?"

Strike shook his head, smiling slightly.

"I know a psycho wouldn't care," said Wardle with a trace of defensiveness. "I'm just saying... anyway, we've got people trying to find out where he's living now. If it's a council house, and assuming Alyssa Vincent's her real name, it shouldn't be too difficult."

"Great," said Strike. The police had resources that he and Robin could not match; perhaps now, at last, some definitive information would be forthcoming. "What about Laing?"

"Ah," said Wardle, grinding out his first cigarette and immediately lighting another, "we've got more on him. He's been living alone in Wollaston Close for eighteen months now. Survives on disability benefits. He had a chest infection over the weekend of the second and third and his friend Dickie came in to help him out. He couldn't get to the shops."

"That's bloody convenient," said Strike.

"Or genuine," said Wardle. "We checked with Dickie and he confirmed everything Laing told us."

"Was Laing surprised the police were asking about his movements?"

"Seemed pretty taken aback at first."

"Did he let you in the flat?"

"Didn't arise. We met him crossing the car park on his sticks and we ended up talking to him in a local café."

"That Ecuadorian place in a tunnel?"

Wardle subjected Strike to a hard stare that the detective returned with equanimity.

"You've been staking him out as well, have you? Don't mess this up for us, Strike. We're on it."

Strike might have responded that it had taken press scrutiny and the failure to make anything of his preferred leads to make Wardle commit serious resources to the tracking of Strike's three suspects. He chose to hold his silence.

"Laing's not stupid," Wardle continued. "We hadn't been questioning him long when he twigged what it was about. He knew you must've given us his name. He'd seen in the papers you got sent a leg."

"What was his view on the matter?"

"There might've been an undertone of 'couldn't've happened to a nicer bloke,'" said Wardle with a slight grin, "but on balance, about what you'd expect. Bit of curiosity, bit of defensiveness."

"Did he look ill?"

"Yeah," said Wardle. "He didn't know we were coming, and we met him shambling along on his sticks. He doesn't look good close up. Bloodshot eyes. His skin's kind of cracked. Bit of a mess."

Strike said nothing. His mistrust of Laing's illness lingered. In spite of the clear photographic evidence of steroid use, skin plaques and lesions that Strike had seen with his own eyes, he found himself stubbornly resistant to the idea that Laing was genuinely ill.

"What was he doing when the other women were killed?"

"Says he was home alone," said Wardle. "Nothing to prove or disprove it."

"Hmn," said Strike.

They turned back into the pub. A couple had taken their table so they found another beside the floor-to-ceiling window onto the street.

"What about Whittaker?"

"Yeah, we caught up with him last night. He's roadying for a band."

"Are you sure about that?" said Strike suspiciously, remembering Shanker's assertion that Whittaker claimed to be doing so, but was in fact living off Stephanie.

"Yeah, I'm sure. We called in on the druggie girlfriend—"

"Get inside the flat?"

"She talked to us at the door, unsurprisingly," said Wardle. "The place stinks. Anyway, she told us he was off with the boys, gave us the address of the concert and there he was. Old transit van parked outside and an even older band. Ever heard of Death Cult?"

"No," said Strike.

"Don't bother, they're shit," said Wardle. "I had to sit through half an hour of the stuff before I could get near Whittaker. Basement of a pub in Wandsworth. I had tinnitus all the next day.

"Whittaker seemed to be half expecting us," said Wardle. "Apparently he found you outside his van a few weeks ago."

"I told you about that," said Strike. "Crack fumes—"

"Yeah, yeah," said Wardle. "Look, I wouldn't trust him as far as I could throw him, but he reckons Stephanie can give him an alibi for the whole day of the royal wedding, so that would rule out the attack on the hooker in Shacklewell, and he claims he was off with Death Cult when both Kelsey and Heather were killed."

"All three killings covered, eh?" said Strike. "That's neat. Do Death Cult agree he was with them?"

"They were pretty vague about it, to be honest," said Wardle.

"The lead singer's got a hearing aid. I don't know whether he caught everything I asked him. Don't worry, I've got guys checking all their witness statements," he added in the face of Strike's frown. "We'll find out whether he was really there or not."

Wardle yawned and stretched.

"I've got to get back to the office," he said. "This could be an all-nighter. We've got a load of information coming in now the papers are on to it."

Strike was extremely hungry now, but the pub was noisy and he felt he would rather eat somewhere he could think. He and Wardle headed up the road together, both lighting fresh cigarettes as they walked.

"The psychologist raised something," said Wardle as the curtain of darkness unrolled across the sky above them. "If we're right, and we're dealing with a serial killer, he's usually an opportunist. He's got a bloody good m.o.—he must be a planner to a degree, or he couldn't have got away with it so often—but there was a change in the pattern with Kelsey. He knew exactly where she was staying. The letters and the fact that he knew there wouldn't be anyone there: it was totally premeditated.

"Trouble is, we've had a bloody good look, but we can't find any evidence that any of your guys have ever been in proximity with her. We virtually took her laptop apart, and there was nothing there. The only people she ever talked to about her leg were those oddballs Jason and Tempest. She had hardly any friends, and the ones she did have were all girls. There was nothing suspicious on her phone. As far as we know, none of your guys has ever lived or worked in Finchley or Shepherd's Bush, let alone gone anywhere near her school or college. They've got no known connection with any of her associates. How the hell could any of them get close enough to manipulate her without her family noticing?"

"We know she was duplicitous," said Strike. "Don't forget the pretend boyfriend who turned out to be pretty real when he picked her up from Café Rouge."

"Yeah," sighed Wardle. "We've still got no leads on that bloody bike. We've put out a description in the press, but nothing.

"How's your partner?" he added, pausing outside the glass doors of his place of work, but apparently determined to smoke the cigarette down to the last millimeter. "Not too shaken up?"

"She's fine," said Strike. "She's back in Yorkshire for a wedding dress fitting. I made her take the time off: she's been working through the weekend a lot lately."

Robin had left without complaint. What was there to stay for, with the press staking out Denmark Street, one lousy paying job and the police now covering Brockbank, Laing and Whittaker more efficiently than the agency ever could?

"Good luck," said Strike as he and Wardle parted. The policeman raised a hand in acknowledgment and farewell, and disappeared into the large building behind the slowly revolving prism glittering with the words New Scotland Yard.

Strike strolled back towards the Tube, craving a kebab and inwardly deliberating the problem that Wardle had just put to him. How could any of his suspects have got close enough to Kelsey Platt to know her movements or gain her trust?

He thought about Laing, living alone in his grim Wollaston Close flat, claiming his disability benefit, overweight and infirm, looking far older than his real age of thirty-four. He had been a funny man, once. Did he still have it in him to charm a young girl to the point that she would have ridden on motorbikes with him or taken him trustingly to a flat in Shepherd's Bush, about which her family knew nothing?

What about Whittaker, stinking of crack, with his blackened teeth and his thinning, matted hair? True, Whittaker had once had mesmeric charm, and emaciated, drug-addicted Stephanie seemed to find him appealing, but Kelsey's only known passion had been for a clean-cut blond boy just a few years older than herself.

Then there was Brockbank. To Strike, the massive, swarthy ex-flanker was downright repulsive, as unlike pretty Niall as it was possible to be. Brockbank had been living and working miles from Kelsey's home and work, and while both had attended churches, their places of worship were on opposite banks of the Thames. The police would surely have unearthed any contact between the two congregations by now.

Did the absence of any known connection between Kelsey and Strike's three suspects rule each of them out as the killer? While logic seemed to urge the answer yes, something stubborn inside Strike continued to whisper no.

50

I'm out of my place, I'm out of my mind...

Blue Öyster Cult, "Celestial the Queen"

Robin's trip home was tinged throughout with the strangest sense of unreality. She felt out of step with everybody, even her mother, who was preoccupied with the wedding arrangements and, while sympathetic to Robin's constant checking of her phone for any development on the Shacklewell Ripper, a little harassed.

Back in the familiar kitchen where Rowntree snoozed at her feet, the seating plan for the reception spread out on the scrubbed wooden table between them, Robin began to appreciate how fully she had abnegated responsibility for her wedding. Linda was constantly firing questions at her about favors, speeches, the bridesmaids' shoes, her headdress, when it would be convenient to speak to the vicar, where she and Matt wanted the presents sent, whether Matthew's Auntie Sue ought to be on the top table or not. Robin had imagined that being at home would be restful. Instead she was required to deal, on the one hand, with a tidal wave of trivial queries from her mother; on the other, a series of questions from her brother Martin, who pored over accounts of the discovery of Heather Smart's body until Robin lost her temper with what she saw as his ghoulishness, whereupon an overwrought Linda banned all mention of the killer from their house.

Matthew, meanwhile, was angry, though trying not to show it, that Robin had not yet asked Strike for two weeks off for the honeymoon.

"I'm sure it'll be fine," said Robin at dinner. "We've got hardly any work on and Cormoran says the police have taken over all our leads."

"He still hasn't confirmed," said Linda, who had been beadily watching how little Robin was eating.

"Who hasn't?" asked Robin.

"Strike. No RSVP."

"I'll remind him," said Robin, taking a large slug of wine.

She had not told any of them, not even Matthew, that she kept having nightmares that woke her gasping in the darkness, back in the bed where she had slept in the months following her rape. A massive man kept coming for her in these dreams. Sometimes he burst into the office where she worked with Strike. More frequently he loomed out of the darkness in the backstreets of London, knives shining. That morning he had been on the point of gouging out her eyes when she woke, gasping, to the sound of Matthew drowsily asking her what she had said.

"Nothing," she had said, pushing sweaty hair off her forehead. "Nothing."

Matthew had to return to work on Monday. He seemed pleased to leave her behind in Masham, helping Linda with preparations for the wedding. Mother and daughter met the vicar at St. Mary the Virgin for a final discussion about the form of the service on Monday afternoon.

Robin tried hard to concentrate on the minister's cheerful suggestions, his ecclesiastical pep talk, but all the time he was talking her eyes kept drifting to the large stone crab that appeared to be clinging to the church wall on the right of the aisle.

This crab had fascinated her in her childhood. She had not been able to understand why there was a big carved crab crawling up the stones of their church, and her curiosity on the point had ended up infecting Linda, who had gone to the local library, looked up the records and triumphantly informed her daughter that the crab had been the emblem of the ancient Scrope family, whose memorial sat above it.

Nine-year-old Robin had been disappointed by the answer. In a way, an explanation had never been the point. She had simply liked being the only one who wanted to find out the truth.

She was standing in the dressmaker's box-like changing room, with its gilt-framed mirror and its new-carpet smell, when Strike called next day. Robin knew that it was Strike because of the unique ringtone that she had attached to his calls. She lunged for her handbag, causing the dressmaker to emit a little cry of annoyance and surprise as the folds of chiffon that she was dexterously repinning were torn from her hands.

"Hello?" said Robin.

"Hi," said Strike.

The single syllable told her that something bad had happened.

"Oh God, has someone else been killed?" Robin blurted out, forgetting the dressmaker crouching at the hem of her wedding dress. The woman stared at her in the mirror, her mouth full of pins.

"Sorry, could you give me a moment? Not you!" she added to Strike, in case he hung up.

"Sorry," she repeated as the curtain closed behind the dressmaker and she sank down onto the stool in the corner in her wedding dress, "I was with someone. *Has* someone else died?"

"Yes," said Strike, "but it's not what you think. It's Wardle's brother."

Robin's tired and overwrought brain tried to join dots that refused to connect.

"It's nothing to do with the case," said Strike. "He was knocked down on a zebra crossing by a speeding van."

"God," said Robin, utterly fazed. She had temporarily forgotten that death came in any manner other than at the hands of a maniac with knives.

"It's a fucker, all right. He had three kids, and a fourth on the way. I've just spoken to Wardle. Bloody terrible thing to happen."

Robin's brain seemed to grind back into gear again.

"So is Wardle—?"

"Compassionate leave," said Strike. "Guess who's taken over from him?"

"Not Anstis?" Robin asked, suddenly worried.

"Worse than that," said Strike.

"Not—not Carver?" said Robin, with a sudden presentiment of doom.

Of the policemen whom Strike had managed to offend and upstage during his two most famous detective triumphs, Detective Inspector Roy Carver had been the most comprehensively outclassed and was consequently the most deeply embittered. His failings during the investigation into a famous model's fall from her penthouse flat had been extensively documented and, indeed, exaggerated in the press. A sweaty man with dandruff and a mottled, purple face like corned beef, he had had an antipathy towards Strike even before the detective had publicly proven that the policeman had failed to spot murder.

"Right in one," said Strike. "I've just had him here for three hours."

"Oh, God—why?"

"Come off it," said Strike, "you know why. This is a wet dream for Carver, having an excuse to interrogate me about a series of murders. He stopped just short of asking me for alibis, and he spent a hell of a lot of time on those fake letters to Kelsey."

Robin groaned.

"Why on earth would they let Carver—? I mean, with his record—"

"Hard though it might be for us to believe, he hasn't been a dickhead his entire career. His bosses must think he was unlucky with Landry. It's supposed to be only temporary, while Wardle's off, but he's already warned me to stay well away from the investigation. When I asked how inquiries into Brockbank, Laing and Whittaker were going, he as good as told me to fuck off with my ego and my hunches. We'll be getting no more inside information on the progress of the case, I can promise you that."

"He'll have to follow up Wardle's lines of investigation, though," said Robin, "won't he?"

"Given that he'd clearly rather chop off his own knob than let me solve another of his cases, you'd think he'd be careful to follow up all my leads. Trouble is, I can tell he's rationalized the Landry case as me getting lucky, and I reckon he thinks me coming up with three suspects in this case is pure showboating. I wish to hell," said Strike, "we'd got an address for Brockbank before Wardle had to leave."

As Robin had been silent for a whole minute while she listened to Strike, the dressmaker clearly thought it reasonable to check whether she was ready to resume the fitting, and poked her head in through the curtain. Robin, whose expression was suddenly beatific, waved her away impatiently.

"We *have* got an address for Brockbank," Robin told Strike in a triumphant voice as the curtains swung closed again.

"What?"

"I didn't tell you, because I thought Wardle would already have got it, but I thought, just in case—I've been ringing round the local nurseries, pretending I was Alyssa, Zahara's mum. I said I wanted to check they had our new address right. One of them read it out to me off the parent contact sheet. They're living on Blondin Street in Bow."

"Jesus Christ, Robin, that's fucking brilliant!"

When the dressmaker returned to her job at last, she found a considerably more radiant bride than she had left. Robin's lack of enthusiasm for the process of altering her dress had been diminishing the seamstress's pleasure in her job. Robin was easily the best-looking client on her books and she had hoped to get a photograph for advertising purposes once the dress was finished.

"That's wonderful," said Robin, beaming at the seamstress as she tugged the last seam straight and together they contemplated the vision in the mirror. "That's absolutely wonderful."

For the first time, she thought that the dress really didn't look bad at all.

51

Don't turn your back, don't show your profile,
You'll never know when it's your turn to go.

Blue Öyster Cult, "Don't Turn Your Back"

"The public response has been overwhelming. We're currently following up over twelve hundred leads, some of which look promising," said Detective Inspector Roy Carver. "We continue to appeal for information on the whereabouts of the red Honda CB750 used to transport part of Kelsey Platt's body and we remain interested in speaking to anybody who was in Old Street on the night of 5th June, when Heather Smart was killed."

The headline POLICE FOLLOW NEW LEADS IN HUNT FOR SHACKLEWELL RIPPER was not really justified, in Robin's view, by anything in the brief report beneath, although she supposed that Carver would not share details of genuine new developments with the press.

Five photographs of the women now believed to have been victims of the Ripper filled most of the page, their identities and their brutal fates stamped across their chests in black typeface.

Martina Rossi, 28, prostitute, stabbed to death, necklace stolen.

Martina was a plump, dark woman wearing a white tank top. Her blurry photograph looked as though it had been a selfie. A small heart-shaped harp charm hung from a chain around her neck.

Sadie Roach, 25, admin assistant, stabbed to death, mutilated, earrings taken.

She had been a pretty girl with a gamine haircut and hoops in her ears. Judging by cropped figures at the edges of her picture, it had been taken at a family gathering.

Kelsey Platt, 16, student, stabbed to death and dismembered.

Here was the familiar chubby, plain face of the girl who had written to Strike, smiling in her school uniform.

Lila Monkton, 18, prostitute, stabbed, fingers cut off, survived.

A blurred picture of a gaunt girl whose bright red hennaed hair was cut into a shaggy bob, her multiple piercings glinting in the camera flash.

Heather Smart, 22, financial services worker, stabbed to death, nose and ears removed.

She was round-faced and innocent-looking, with wavy mouse-brown hair, freckles and a timid smile.

Robin looked up from the *Daily Express* with a deep sigh. Matthew had been sent to audit a client in High Wycombe, so he had been unable to give Robin a lift today. It had taken her a full hour and twenty minutes to get to Catford from Ealing on trains crammed with tourists and commuters sweating in the London heat. Now she left her seat and headed for the door, swaying with the rest of the commuters as the train slowed and stopped, yet again, at Catford Bridge station.

Her week back at work with Strike had been strange. Strike, who clearly had no intention to comply with the instruction to keep out of Carver's investigation, was nevertheless taking the investigating officer seriously enough to be cautious.

"If he can make a case that we've buggered up the police investigation, we're finished as a business," he said. "And we know he'll try and say I've screwed things up, whether I have or not."

"So why are we carrying on?"

Robin had been playing devil's advocate, because she would have been deeply unhappy and frustrated had Strike announced that they were abandoning their leads.

"Because Carver thinks my suspects are bullshit, and I think he's an incompetent tit."

Robin's laugh had ended prematurely when Strike had told her he wanted her to return to Catford and stake out Whittaker's girlfriend.

"Still?" she asked. "Why?"

"You know why. I want to see whether Stephanie can give him alibis for any of the key dates."

"You know what?" said Robin, plucking up her courage. "I've been in Catford a lot. If it's all the same to you, I'd rather do Brockbank. Why don't I try and get something out of Alyssa?"

"There's Laing as well, if you want a change," said Strike.

"He saw me up close when I fell over," Robin countered at once. "Don't you think it would be better if you did Laing?"

"I've been watching his flat while you've been away," Strike said.

"And?"

"And he mostly stays in, but sometimes he goes to the shops and back."

"You don't think it's him anymore, do you?"

"I haven't ruled him out," said Strike. "Why are you so keen to do Brockbank?"

"Well," said Robin bravely, "I feel like I've done a lot of the running on him. I got the Market Harborough address out of Holly and I got Blondin Street out of the nursery—"

"And you're worried about the kids who're living with him," said Strike.

Robin remembered the little black girl with the stiff pigtails who had tripped over, staring at her, in Catford Broadway.

"So what if I am?"

"I'd rather you stuck to Stephanie," said Strike.

She had been annoyed; so annoyed that she had promptly asked for two weeks off rather more bluntly than she might otherwise have done.

"Two weeks off?" he said, looking up in surprise. He was far more used to her begging to stay at work than asking to leave it.

"It's for my honeymoon."

"Oh," he said. "Right. Yeah. I suppose that'll be soon, will it?"

"Obviously. The wedding's on the second."

"Christ, that's only—what—three weeks or something?"

She had been annoyed that he had not realized that it was so close.

"Yes," she had said, getting to her feet and reaching for her jacket. "And would you mind RSVP'ing if you're coming?"

So she returned to Catford and the busy market stalls, to the smell of incense and raw fish, to pointless hours of standing beneath the crouching stone bears over the stage door of the Broadway Theatre.

Robin had hidden her hair under a straw hat today and was wearing sunglasses, but she still wondered whether she did not see a hint of recognition in the eyes of stallholders as she settled once more to lurk opposite the triple windows of Whittaker and Stephanie's flat. She had only had a couple of glimpses of the girl since she had resumed her surveillance on her, and on neither occasion had there been the slightest chance of speaking to her. Of Whittaker, there had been no hint at all. Robin settled back against the cool gray stone of the theater wall, prepared for another long day of tedium, and yawned.

By late afternoon she was hot, tired and trying not to resent her mother, who had texted repeatedly throughout the day with questions about the wedding. The last, telling her to ring the florist, who had yet another finicky question for her, arrived just as Robin had decided she needed something to drink. Wondering how Linda would react if she texted back and said she'd decided to have plastic flowers everywhere—on her head, in her bouquet, all over the church—anything to stop having to make decisions—she crossed to the chip shop, which sold chilled fizzy drinks.

She had barely touched the door handle when somebody collided with her, also aiming for the chip-shop door.

"Sorry," said Robin automatically, and then, "oh my God."

Stephanie's face was swollen and purple, one eye almost entirely closed.

The impact had not been hard, but the smaller girl had been bounced off her. Robin reached out to stop her stumbling.

"Jesus—what happened?"

She spoke as though she knew Stephanie. In a sense, she felt she did. Observing the girl's little routines, becoming familiar with her body language, her clothing and her liking for Coke had fostered a one-sided sense of kinship. Now she found it natural and easy to ask a question hardly any British stranger would ask of another: "Are you all right?"

How she managed it, Robin hardly knew, but two minutes later she was settling Stephanie into a chair in the welcome shade of the Stage Door Café, a few doors along from the chip shop. Stephanie was obviously in pain and ashamed of her appearance, but at the same time she had become too hungry and thirsty to remain upstairs in the flat. Now she had simply bowed to a stronger will, thrown off balance by the older woman's solicitude, by the offer of a free meal. Robin gabbled nonsensically as she ushered Stephanie down the street, maintaining the fiction that her quixotic offer of sandwiches was due to her guilt at having almost knocked Stephanie over.

Stephanie accepted a cold Fanta and a tuna sandwich with mumbled thanks, but after a few mouthfuls she put her hand to her cheek as though in pain and set the sandwich down.

"Tooth?" asked Robin solicitously.

The girl nodded. A tear trickled out of her unclosed eye.

"Who did this?" Robin said urgently, reaching across the table for Stephanie's hand.

She was playing a character, growing into the role as she improvised. The straw hat and the long sundress she was wearing had unconsciously suggested a hippyish girl full of altruism who thought that she could save Stephanie. Robin felt a tiny reciprocal squeeze of her fingers even as Stephanie shook her head to indicate that she was not going to give away her attacker.

"Somebody you know?" Robin whispered.

More tears rolled down Stephanie's face. She withdrew her hand from Robin's and sipped her Fanta, wincing again as the cold liquid made contact with what Robin thought was probably a cracked tooth.

"Is he your father?" Robin whispered.

It would have been an easy assumption to make. Stephanie could not possibly be older than seventeen. She was so thin that she barely had breasts. Tears had washed away any trace of the kohl that usually outlined her eyes. Her grubby face was infantile, with the suggestion of an overbite, but all was dominated by the purple and gray bruising. Whittaker had pummeled her until the blood vessels in her right eye had burst: the sliver that was visible was scarlet.

"No," whispered Stephanie. "Boyfriend."

"Where is he?" Robin asked, reaching again for Stephanie's hand, now chilly from contact with the cold Fanta.

"Away," said Stephanie.

"Does he live with you?"

Stephanie nodded and tried to drink more Fanta, keeping the icy liquid away from the damaged side of her face.

"I didn't wan' 'im to go," whispered Stephanie.

As Robin leaned in, the girl's restraint suddenly dissolved in the face of kindness and sugar.

"I aksed to go wiv 'im and 'e wouldn't take me. I know 'e's out tomming, I know 'e is. 'E's got someone else, I 'eard Banjo saying sumfing. 'E's got anuvver girl somewhere."

To Robin's disbelief, Stephanie's primary source of pain, far worse than that of her cracked tooth and her bruised and broken face, was the thought that filthy, crack-dealing Whittaker might be somewhere else, sleeping with another woman.

"I on'y wan'ed to go wiv 'im," Stephanie repeated, and tears slid more thickly down her face, stinging that slit of an eye into a more furious redness.

Robin knew that the kind, slightly dippy girl she had been impersonating would now earnestly beseech Stephanie to leave a man who had beaten her so badly. The trouble was, she was sure that would be the surest way to make Stephanie walk out on her.

"He got angry because you wanted to go with him?" she repeated. "Where has he gone?"

"Says 'e's wiv the Cult like last—they're a band," mumbled Stephanie, wiping her nose on the back of her hand. " 'E roadies for 'em—bur it's just an excuse," she said, crying harder, "to go places an' find girls to fuck. I said I'd go an'—'cause last time 'e wanted me to—an' I done the 'ole band for 'im."

Robin did her very best not to look as though she understood what she had just been told. However, some flicker of anger and revulsion must have contaminated the look of pure kindliness she was trying to project, because Stephanie seemed suddenly to withdraw. She did not want judgment. She met that every day of her life.

"Have you been to a doctor?" Robin asked quietly.

"Wha'? No," said Stephanie, folding her thin arms around her torso.

"When's he due back, your boyfriend?"

Stephanie merely shook her head and shrugged. The temporary sympathy Robin had kindled between them seemed to have cooled.

"The Cult," said Robin, improvising rapidly, her mouth dry, "that isn't Death Cult, is it?"

"Yeah," said Stephanie, dimly surprised.

"Which gig? I saw them the other day!"

Don't ask me where, for God's sake...

"This was in a pub called the—Green Fiddle, or sumfing. Enfield."

"Oh, no, it wasn't the same gig," said Robin. "When was yours?"

"Need a pee," mumbled Stephanie, looking around the café.

She shuffled off towards the bathroom. When the door had closed behind her, Robin frantically keyed search terms into her mobile. It took her several attempts to find what she was looking for: Death Cult had played a pub called the Fiddler's Green in Enfield on Saturday the fourth of June, the day before Heather Smart had been murdered.

The shadows were lengthening outside the café now, which had emptied apart from themselves. Evening was drawing in. The place would surely close soon.

"Cheers for the sandwich an' ev'rything," said Stephanie, who had reappeared beside her. "I'm gonna—"

"Have something else. Some chocolate or something," Robin urged her, even though the waitress mopping table tops looked ready to throw them out.

"Why?" asked Stephanie, showing the first sign of suspicion.

"Because I really want to talk to you about your boyfriend," said Robin.

"Why?" repeated the teenager, a little nervous now.

"Please sit down. It isn't anything bad," Robin coaxed her. "I'm just worried about you."

Stephanie hesitated, then sank slowly back into the seat she had vacated. For the first time, Robin noticed the deep red mark around her neck.

"He didn't—he didn't try and strangle you, did he?" she asked.

"Wha'?"

Stephanie felt her thin neck and tears welled again in her eyes.

"Oh, tha's—tha' was my necklace. 'E give it me an' then 'e...'cause I ain't makin' enough money," she said, and began to cry in earnest. " 'E's sold it."

Unable to think what else to do, Robin stretched her other hand across the table and held on to Stephanie's with both of her own, holding tightly, as though Stephanie were on some moving plateau that was drifting away.

"Did you say he made you...with the whole band?" Robin asked quietly.

"That were f'free," said Stephanie tearfully, and Robin understood that Stephanie was still thinking of her money-making abilities. "I only blew 'em."

"After the gig?" asked Robin, releasing one hand to press paper napkins into Stephanie's.

"No," said Stephanie, wiping her nose, "next night. We stayed over in the van at the lead singer's 'ouse. 'E lives in Enfield."

Robin would not have believed that it was possible to feel simultaneously disgusted and delighted. If Stephanie had been with Whittaker on the night of the fifth of June, Whittaker could not have killed Heather Smart.

"Was he—your boyfriend—was he there?" she asked in a quiet voice. "All the time, while you were—you know—?"

"The fuck's going on 'ere?"

Robin looked up. Stephanie snatched her hand away, looking frightened.

Whittaker was standing over them. Robin recognized him immediately from the pictures she had seen online. He was tall and broad-shouldered, yet scrawny. His old black T-shirt was washed out almost to gray. The heretic priest's golden eyes were fascinating in their intensity. In spite of the matted hair, the sunken, yellowing face, in spite of the fact that he repulsed her, she could yet feel the strange, manic aura of him, a magnetic pull like the reek of carrion. He woke the urge to investigate provoked by all dirty, rotten things, no less powerful because it was shameful.

"'Oo are *you?*" he asked, not aggressively, but with something close to a purr in his voice. He was looking unabashedly right down the front of her sundress.

"I bumped into your girlfriend outside the chippy," said Robin. "I bought her a drink."

"Didjoo now?"

"We're closing," said the waitress loudly.

The appearance of Whittaker had been a little too much for her, Robin could tell. His flesh tunnels, his tattoos, his maniac's eyes, his smell would be desirable in very few establishments selling food.

Stephanie looked terrified, even though Whittaker was ignoring her completely. His attention was entirely focused on Robin, who felt absurdly self-conscious as she paid the bill, then stood and walked, Whittaker just behind her, out onto the street.

"Well—good-bye then," she said weakly to Stephanie.

She wished that she had Strike's courage. He had urged Stephanie to come away with him right underneath Whittaker's nose, but Robin's mouth was suddenly dry. Whittaker was staring at her as though he had spotted something fascinating and rare on a dung heap. Behind them, the waitress was bolting the doors. The sinking sun was throwing cold shadows across the street that Robin only knew as hot and smelly.

"Jus' bein' kind, were you, darlin'?" Whittaker asked softly, and Robin could not tell whether there was more malice or sweetness in his voice.

"I suppose I was worried," said Robin, forcing herself to look into those wide-apart eyes, "because Stephanie's injuries look quite serious."

"That?" said Whittaker, putting out a hand to Stephanie's purple and gray face. "Come off a pushbike, din'choo, Steph? Clumsy little cow."

Robin suddenly understood Strike's visceral hatred for this man. She would have liked to hit him too.

"I hope I'll see you again, Stephanie," she said.

She did not dare give the girl a number in front of Whittaker. Robin turned and began to walk away, feeling like the worst kind of coward. Stephanie was about to walk back upstairs with the man. She ought to have done more, but what? What could she say that would make a difference? Could she report the assault to the police? Would that constitute an interference with Carver's case?

Only when she was definitely out of sight of Whittaker did she lose the sensation that invisible ants were crawling up her spine. Robin pulled out her mobile and called Strike.

"I know," she said, before Strike could start telling her off, "it's getting late but I'm on my way to the station right now and when you've heard what I've got, you'll understand."

She walked fast, chilly in the increasing cool of the evening, telling him everything that Stephanie had said.

"So he's got an alibi?" said Strike slowly.

"For Heather's death, yes, if Stephanie's telling the truth, and I honestly think she is. She was with him—and the whole of Death Cult, as I say."

"She definitely said Whittaker was there while she was servicing the band?"

"I think so. She was just answering that when Whittaker turned up and—hang on."

Robin stopped and looked around. Busy talking, she had taken a wrong turning somewhere on the way back to the station. The sun was setting now. Out of the corner of her eye, she thought she saw a shadow move behind a wall.

"Cormoran?"

"Still here."

Perhaps she had imagined the shadow. She was on a stretch of unfamiliar residential road, but there were lit windows and a couple walking along in the distance. She was safe, she told herself. It was all right. She just needed to retrace her steps.

"Everything OK?" asked Strike sharply.

"Fine," she said. "I've taken a wrong turn, that's all."

"Where are you exactly?"

"Near Catford Bridge station," she said. "I don't know how I've ended up here."

She did not want to mention the shadow. Carefully she crossed the darkening road, so that she would not have to walk past the wall where she thought she had seen it, and after transferring her mobile into her left hand she took a tighter hold of the rape alarm in her right pocket.

"I'm going back the way I came," she told Strike, wanting him to know where she was.

"Have you seen something?" he demanded.

"I don't kn—maybe," she admitted.

Yet when she drew level with the gap between houses where she had thought she had seen the figure, there was nobody there.

"I'm jumpy," she said, speeding up. "Meeting Whittaker wasn't fun. There's definitely something—nasty—about him."

"Where are you now?"

"About twenty feet away from where I was the last time you asked me. Hang on, I can see a street name. I'm crossing back over, I can see where I've gone wrong, I should've turned—"

She heard the footsteps only when they were right behind her. Two massive black-clad arms closed around her, pinning hers to her sides, squeezing the air from her lungs. Her mobile slipped out of her hand and fell with a crack onto the pavement.

52

Do not envy the man with the x-ray eyes.

Blue Öyster Cult, "X-Ray Eyes"

Strike, who had been standing in the shadow of a warehouse in Bow, keeping watch on Blondin Street, heard Robin's sudden gasp, the thud of the mobile on the pavement and then the scuffling and skidding of feet on asphalt.

He began to run. The phone connection to Robin was still open, but he could hear nothing. Panic sharpened his mental processes and obliterated all perception of pain as he sprinted down a darkening street in the direction of the nearest station. He needed a second phone.

"Need to borrow that, mate!" he bellowed at a pair of skinny black youths walking towards him, one of whom was chuckling into a mobile. "Crime's being committed, need to borrow that phone!"

Strike's size and his aura of authority as he pelted towards them made the teenager surrender the phone with a look of fear and bewilderment.

"Come with me!" Strike bellowed at the two boys, running on past them towards busier streets where he might be able to find a cab, his own mobile still pressed to his other ear. "Police!" Strike yelled into the boy's phone as the stunned teenagers ran alongside him like bodyguards. "There's a woman being attacked near Catford Bridge station, I was on the line to her when it happened! It's happening right—no, I don't know the street but it's one or two away from the station—right now, I was on the line to her when he grabbed her, I heard it happen—yeah—and fucking hurry!

"Cheers, mate," Strike panted, throwing the mobile back into the hands of its owner, who continued to run alongside him for several yards without realizing that he no longer needed to.

Strike hurtled around a corner; Bow was a totally unfamiliar area of London to him. On he ran past the Bow Bells pub, ignoring the red-hot jabs of the ligaments in his knee, moving awkwardly with only one free arm to balance himself, his silent phone still clamped to his ear. Then he heard a rape alarm going off at the other end of the line.

"TAXI!" he bellowed at a distant glowing light. "ROBIN!" he yelled into the phone, sure she could not hear him over the screeching alarm. "ROBIN, I'VE CALLED THE POLICE! THE POLICE ARE ON THEIR WAY. ARE YOU LISTENING, YOU FUCKER?"

The taxi had driven off without him. Drinkers outside the Bow Bells stared at the lunatic hobbling past at high speed, yelling and swearing into his phone. A second taxi appeared.

"TAXI! TAXI!" Strike bellowed and it turned, heading towards him, just as Robin's voice spoke in his ear, gasping.

"Are... you there?"

"JESUS CHRIST! WHAT'S HAPPENED?"

"Stop... shouting..."

With enormous difficulty he modulated his volume.

"*What's happened?*"

"I can't see," she said. "I can't... see anything..."

Strike wrenched open the back door of the cab and threw himself inside.

"Catford Bridge station, hurry! What d'you mean, you can't—? What's he done to you? NOT YOU!" he bellowed at the confused cabbie. "Go! Go!"

"No... it's your bloody... rape alarm... stuff... in my face... oh... shit..."

The taxi was speeding along, but Strike had to physically restrain himself from urging the driver to floor it.

"What happened? Are you hurt?"

"A—a bit... there are people here..."

He could hear them now, people surrounding her, murmuring, talking excitedly amongst themselves.

"... hospital..." he heard Robin say, away from the phone.

"Robin? ROBIN?"

"Stop shouting!" she said. "Listen, they've called an ambulance, I'm going to—"

"WHAT'S HE DONE TO YOU?"

"Cut me... up my arm... I think it'll need stitching... God, it stings..."

"Which hospital? Let me speak to someone! I'll meet you there!"

Strike arrived at the Accident and Emergency Department at University Hospital Lewisham twenty-five minutes later, limping heavily and wearing such an anguished expression that a kindly nurse reassured him that a doctor would be with him shortly.

"No," he said, waving her away as he clumped towards the reception desk, "I'm here with someone—Robin Ellacott, she's been knifed—"

His eyes traveled frantically over the packed waiting room where a young boy was whimpering on his mother's lap and a groaning drunk cradled his bloodied head in his hands. A male nurse was showing a breathless old lady how to use an inhaler.

"Strike... yes... Miss Ellacott said you'd be coming," said the receptionist, who had checked her computer records with what Strike felt was unnecessary and provocative deliberation. "Down the corridor and to the right... first cubicle."

He slipped a little on the shining floor in his haste, swore and hurried on. Several people's eyes followed his large, ungainly figure, wondering whether he was quite right in the head.

"Robin? Fucking hell!"

Scarlet spatters disfigured her face; both eyes were swollen. A young male doctor, who was examining an eight-inch wound in her forearm, barked:

"Out until I've finished!"

"It isn't blood!" Robin called as Strike retreated behind the curtain. "It's the damn spray stuff in your rape alarm!"

"Stay still, please," Strike heard the doctor say.

He paced a little outside the cubicle. Five other curtained beds hid their secrets along the side ward. The nurses' rubber soles squeaked on the highly polished gray floor. God, how he hated hospitals: the smell of them, the institutional cleanliness underlaid with that faint whiff of human decomposition, immediately transported him back to those long months in Selly Oak after his leg had been blown off.

What had he done? *What had he done?* He had let her work, knowing the bastard had her in his sights. She could have died. She *should* have died. Nurses rustled past in their blue scrubs. Behind the curtain, Robin gave a small gasp of pain and Strike ground his teeth.

"Well, she's been extremely lucky," said the doctor, ripping the curtains open ten minutes later. "He could have severed the brachial artery. There's tendon damage, though, and we won't know how much until we get her into theater."

He clearly thought they were a couple. Strike did not put him right.

"She needs surgery?"

"To repair the tendon damage," said the doctor, as though Strike were a bit slow. "Plus, that wound needs a proper clean. I want to X-ray her ribs as well."

He left. Bracing himself, Strike entered the cubicle.

"I know I screwed up," said Robin.

"Holy shit, did you think I was going to tell you off?"

"Maybe," she said, pulling herself up a little higher on the bed. Her arm was bound up in a temporary crêpe bandage. "After dark. I wasn't paying attention, was I?"

He sat down heavily beside the bed on the chair that the doctor had vacated, accidentally knocking a metal kidney dish to the floor. It clanged and rattled; Strike put his prosthetic foot on it to silence it.

"Robin, how the fuck did you get away?"

"Self-defense," she said. Then, correctly reading his expression, she said crossly, "I *knew* you didn't believe I'd done any."

"I did believe you," he said, "but Jesus fucking Christ—"

"I had lessons from this brilliant woman in Harrogate who was ex-army," said Robin, wincing a little as she readjusted herself on her pillows again. "After—you know what."

"Was this before or after the advanced driving tests?"

"After," she said, "because I was agoraphobic for a while. It was the driving that really got me back out of my room and then, after that, I did self-defense classes. The first one I signed to was run by a man and he was an idiot," said Robin. "All judo moves and—just useless. But Louise was brilliant."

"Yeah?" said Strike.

Her composure was unnerving him.

"Yeah," said Robin. "She taught us it's not about clever throws when you're an ordinary woman. It's about reacting smartly and fast. Never let yourself get taken to a second location. Go for the weak spots and then run like hell.

"He grabbed me from behind but I heard him just before he got to me. I practiced it loads with Louise. If they grab you from behind, you bend over."

"Bend over," repeated Strike numbly.

"I had the rape alarm in my hand. I bent right over and slammed it into his balls. He was wearing tracksuit pants. He let go for a couple of seconds and I tripped on this damn dress again—he pulled out the knife—I can't remember exactly what happened then—I know he cut me as I was trying to get up—but I managed to press the button on the alarm and it went off and that scared him—the ink went all over my face and must've gone in his as well, because he was close to me—he was wearing a balaclava—I could hardly see—but I got in a good jab at his carotid artery as he bent over me—that's the other thing Louise taught us, side of the neck, you can make them collapse if you do it right—and he staggered, and then I think he realized people were coming and he ran."

Strike was speechless.

"I'm really hungry," said Robin.

Strike felt in his pockets and pulled out a Twix.

"Thanks."

But before she could take a bite, a nurse escorting an old man past the foot of her bed said sharply:

"Nil by mouth, you're going to theater!"

Robin rolled her eyes and handed the Twix back to Strike. Her mobile rang. Strike watched, dazed, as she picked it up.

"Mum... hi," said Robin.

Their eyes met. Strike read Robin's unexpressed desire to save her mother, at least temporarily, from what had just happened, but no diversionary tactics were necessary because Linda was gabbling without allowing Robin to speak. Robin laid the mobile on her knees and switched it to speakerphone, her expression resigned.

"...let her know as soon as possible, because lily of the valley is out of season, so if you want it, it'll be a special order."

"OK," said Robin. "I'll skip lily of the valley."

"Well, it would be great if you could call her directly and tell her what you *do* want, Robin, because it isn't easy being the intermediary. She says she's left you loads of voicemails."

"Sorry, Mum," said Robin. "I'll call her."

"You're not supposed to be using that in here!" said a second cross nurse.

"Sorry," said Robin again. "Mum, I'll have to go. I'll speak to you later."

"Where are you?" Linda asked.

"I'm... I'll ring you later," said Robin, and cut the call.

She looked at Strike and asked:

"Aren't you going to ask me which of them I think it was?"

"I'm assuming you don't know," said Strike. "If he was wearing a balaclava and your eyes were full of ink."

"I'm sure about one thing," said Robin. "It wasn't Whittaker. Not unless he changed into sweatpants the moment I left him. Whittaker was wearing jeans and he was—his physique wasn't right. This guy was strong, but soft, you know? Big, though. As big as you."

"Have you told Matthew what's happened?"

"He's on his w—"

He thought, when her expression changed to one of near horror, that he was about to turn and see a livid Matthew bearing down upon them. Instead, the disheveled figure of Detective Inspector

Roy Carver appeared at the foot of Robin's bed, accompanied by the tall, elegant figure of Detective Sergeant Vanessa Ekwensi.

Carver was in shirtsleeves. Large wet patches of sweat radiated out from his armpits. The constantly pink whites of his bright blue eyes always made him look as though he had been swimming in heavily chlorinated water. His thick, graying hair was full of large flakes of dandruff.

"How are—?" began Detective Sergeant Ekwensi, her almond-shaped eyes on Robin's forearm, but Carver interrupted with an accusatory bark.

"What've *you* been up to, then, eh?"

Strike stood up. Here at last was the perfect target for his so far suppressed desire to punish somebody, anybody, for what had just happened to Robin, to divert his feelings of guilt and anxiety onto a worthy target.

"I want to talk to you," Carver told Strike. "Ekwensi, you take her statement."

Before anyone could speak or move, a sweet-faced young nurse stepped obliviously between the two men, smiling at Robin.

"Ready to take you to X-ray, Miss Ellacott," she said.

Robin got stiffly off the bed and walked away, looking back over her shoulder at Strike, trying to convey warning and restraint with her expression.

"Out here," Carver growled at Strike.

The detective followed the policeman back through A&E. Carver had commandeered a small visitors' room where, Strike assumed, news of imminent or actual death was conveyed to relatives. It contained several padded chairs, a box of tissues on a small table and an abstract print in shades of orange.

"I told you to stay out of it," Carver said, taking up a position in the middle of the room, arms folded, feet wide apart.

With the door closed, Carver's body odor filled the room. He did not stink in the same way as Whittaker: not of ingrained filth and drugs, but of sweat that he could not contain through the working day. His blotchy complexion was not improved by the overhead strip lighting. The dandruff, the wet shirt, the mottled skin: he seemed to be visibly falling to pieces. Strike had undoubtedly helped him on his way, humiliating him in the press over the murder of Lula Landry.

"Sent her to stake out Whittaker, didn't you?" asked Carver, his face growing slowly redder, as though he were being boiled. "You did this to her."

"Fuck you," said Strike.

Only now, with his nose full of Carver's sweat, did he admit to himself that he had known it for a while: Whittaker was not the killer. Strike had sent Robin after Stephanie because, in his soul, he had thought it the safest place to put her, but he had kept her on the streets, and he had known for weeks that the killer was tailing her.

Carver knew that he had hit a nerve. He was grinning.

"You've been using murdered women to pay off your fucking grudge against your stepdaddy," he said, taking pleasure in Strike's rising color, grinning to see the large hands ball into fists. Carver would enjoy nothing more than running Strike in for assault; they both knew it. "We've checked out Whittaker. We checked all three of your fucking hunches. There's nothing in any of them. Now you listen to me."

He took a step closer to Strike. Though a head shorter, he projected the power of a furious, embittered but powerful man, a man with much to prove, and with the full might of the force behind him. Pointing at Strike's chest, he said:

"Stay out of it. You're fucking lucky you haven't got your partner's blood on your hands. If I find you anywhere near our investigation again, I'll fucking run you in. Understand me?"

He poked his stubby fingertip into Strike's sternum. Strike resisted the urge to knock it away, but a muscle in his jaw twitched. For a few seconds they eyeballed each other. Carver grinned more widely, breathing as though he had just triumphed in a wrestling match, then strutted to the door and left, leaving Strike to stew in rage and self-loathing.

He was walking slowly back through A&E when tall, handsome Matthew came running through the double doors in his suit, wild-eyed, his hair all over the place. For the first time in their acquaint-anceship, Strike felt something other than dislike for him.

"Matthew," he said.

Matthew looked at Strike as though he did not recognize him.

"She went for an X-ray," said Strike. "She might be back by now. That way," he pointed.

"Why's she need—?"

"Ribs," said Strike.

Matthew elbowed him aside. Strike did not protest. He felt he deserved it. He watched as Robin's fiancé tore off in her direction, then, after hesitating, turned to the double doors and walked out into the night.

The clear sky was now dusted with stars. Once he reached the street he paused to light a cigarette, dragging on it as Wardle had done, as though the nicotine were the stuff of life. He began to walk, feeling the pain in his knee now. With every step, he liked himself less.

"RICKY!" bawled a woman down the street, imploring an escaping toddler to return to her as she struggled with the weight of a large bag. "RICKY, COME BACK!"

The little boy was giggling manically. Without really thinking what he was doing, Strike bent down automatically and caught him as he sped towards the road.

"Thank you!" said the mother, almost sobbing her relief as she jogged towards Strike. Flowers toppled off the bag in her arms. "We're visiting his dad—oh God—"

The boy in Strike's arms struggled frantically. Strike put him down beside his mother, who was picking up a bunch of daffodils off the pavement.

"Hold them," she told the boy sternly, who obeyed. "You can give them to Daddy. Don't drop them! Thanks," she said again to Strike and marched away, keeping a tight grip on the toddler's free hand. The little boy walked meekly beside his mother now, proud to have a job to do, the stiff yellow flowers upright in his hand like a scepter.

Strike walked on a few paces and then, quite suddenly, stopped dead in the middle of the pavement, staring as though transfixed by something invisible hanging in the cold air in front of him. A chilly breeze tickled his face as he stood there, completely indifferent to his surroundings, his focus entirely inward.

Daffodils...lily of the valley...flowers out of season.

Then the sound of the mother's voice echoed through the night again—"Ricky, no!"—and caused a sudden explosive chain reaction in Strike's brain, lighting a landing strip for a theory that he knew, with the certainty of a prophet, would lead to the killer. As the steel joists of a building are revealed as it burns, so Strike saw in this flash of inspiration the skeleton of the killer's plan, recognizing those crucial flaws that he had missed—that everyone had missed—but which might, at last, be the means by which the murderer and his macabre schemes could be brought down.

53

> You see me now a veteran of a thousand psychic wars…
>
> Blue Öyster Cult, "Veteran of the Psychic Wars"

It had been easy to feign insouciance in the brightly lit hospital. Robin had drawn strength, not merely from Strike's amazement and admiration at her escape, but from listening to her own account of fighting off the killer. She had been the calmest of them all in the immediate aftermath of the attack, consoling and reassuring Matthew when he began to cry at the sight of her ink-stained face and the long wound in her arm. She had drawn strength from everyone else's weakness, hoping that her adrenaline-fueled bravery would carry her safely back to normality, where she would find a sure footing and move on unscathed, without having to pass through the dark mire where she had lived so long after the rape…

However, during the week that followed she found it almost impossible to sleep, and not only because of the throbbing of her injured forearm, which was now in a protective half-cast. In the short dozes she managed at night or by day, she felt her attacker's thick arms around her again and heard him breathing in her ear. Sometimes the eyes she had not seen became the eyes of the rapist when she was nineteen: pale, one pupil fixed. Behind their black balaclava and gorilla mask, the nightmare figures merged, mutated and grew, filling her mind day and night.

In the worst dreams, she watched him doing it to somebody else and was waiting her turn, powerless to help or escape. Once, the victim was Stephanie with her pulverized face. On another unbearable occasion, a little black girl screamed for her mother. Robin woke from that one shouting in the dark, and Matthew became so worried about her that he called in sick to work the following day so that he could stay with her. Robin did not know whether she was grateful or resentful.

Her mother came, of course, and tried to make her come home to Masham.

"You've got ten days until the wedding, Robin, why don't you just come home with me now and relax before—"

"I want to stay here," said Robin.

She was not a teenager anymore: she was a grown woman. It was up to her where she went, where she stayed, what she did. Robin felt as though she were fighting all over again for the identities she had been forced to relinquish the last time a man had lunged at her out of the darkness. He had transformed her from a straight-A student into an emaciated agoraphobic, from an aspiring forensic psychologist into a defeated girl who agreed with her overbearing family that police work would only exacerbate her mental problems.

That was not going to happen again. She would not let it. She could barely sleep, she did not want to eat, but furiously she dug in, denying her own needs and fears. Matthew was frightened of contradicting her. Weakly he agreed with her that there was no need for her to go home, yet Robin heard him whispering with her mother in the kitchen when they thought she could not hear them.

Strike was no help at all. He had not bothered to say good-bye to her at the hospital, nor he had come to see how she was doing, merely speaking to her on the phone. He, too, wanted her to go back to Yorkshire, safely out of the way.

"You must have a load of stuff to do for the wedding."

"Don't patronize me," said Robin furiously.

"Who's patronizing—?"

"Sorry," she said, dissolving into silent tears that he could not see and doing everything in her power to keep her voice normal.

"Sorry... uptight. I'm going home on the Thursday before; there's no need to go earlier."

She was no longer the person who had lain on her bed staring at Destiny's Child. She refused to be that girl.

Nobody could understand why she was so determined to remain in London, nor was she ready to explain. She threw away the sundress in which he had attacked her. Linda entered the kitchen just as Robin was shoving it into the bin.

"Stupid bloody thing," said Robin, catching her mother's eye. "I've learned *that* lesson. Don't run surveillance in long dresses."

She spoke defiantly. *I'm going back to work. This is temporary.*

"You're not supposed to be using that hand," said her mother, ignoring the unspoken challenge. "The doctor said to rest and elevate it."

Neither Matthew nor her mother liked her reading about the progress of the case in the press, which she did obsessively. Carver had refused to release her name. He said he did not want the media descending on her, but she and Strike both suspected that he was afraid that Strike's continued presence in the story would give the press a delicious new twist: Carver versus Strike all over again.

"In fairness," Strike said to Robin over the phone (she tried to limit herself to one call to him a day), "that's the last bloody thing anyone needs. It won't help catch the bastard."

Robin said nothing. She was lying on her and Matthew's bed with a number of newspapers that she had bought against Linda and Matthew's wishes spread around her. Her eyes were fixed on a double-page spread in the *Mirror,* where the five supposed victims of the Shacklewell Ripper were again pictured in a row. A sixth black silhouette of a woman's head and shoulders represented Robin. The legend beneath the silhouette read "26-year-old office worker, escaped." Much was made of the fact that the 26-year-old office worker had managed to spray the killer with red ink during the attack. She was praised by a retired policewoman in a side column for her foresight in carrying such a device, and there was a separate feature on rape alarms over the page.

"You've really given up on it?" she asked.

"It's not a question of giving up," said Strike. She could hear him moving around the office, and she wished she were there, even if only making tea or answering emails. "I'm leaving it to the police. A serial killer's out of our league, Robin. It always was."

Robin was looking down at the gaunt face of the only other woman who had survived the killing spree. "Lila Monkton, prostitute." Lila, too, knew what the killer's pig-like breathing sounded like. He had cut off Lila's fingers. Robin would only have a long scar on her arm. Her brain buzzed angrily in her skull. She felt guilty that she had got off so lightly.

"I wish there was something—"

"Drop it," said Strike. He sounded angry, just like Matthew. "We're done, Robin. I should never have sent you to Stephanie. I've let my grudge against Whittaker color my judgment ever since that leg arrived and it nearly got you—"

"Oh for God's sake," said Robin impatiently. "*You* didn't try and kill me, *he* did. Let's keep the blame where it belongs. You had good reason for thinking it was Whittaker—the lyrics. Anyway, that still leaves—"

"Carver's looked into Laing and Brockbank and he doesn't think there's anything there. We're staying out of it, Robin."

Ten miles away in his office, Strike hoped that he was convincing her. He had not told Robin about the epiphany that had occurred to him after his encounter with the toddler outside the hospital. He had tried to contact Carver the following morning, but a subordinate had told him that Carver was too busy to take his call and advised him not to try again. Strike had insisted on telling the irritable and faintly aggressive subordinate what he had hoped to tell Carver. He would have bet his remaining leg that not a word of his message had been passed on.

The windows in Strike's office were open. Hot June sunshine warmed the two rooms now devoid of clients and soon, perhaps, to be vacated due to an inability to afford the rent. Two-Times's interest in the new lap-dancer had petered out. Strike had nothing to do.

Like Robin, he yearned for action, but he did not tell her that. All he wanted was for her to heal and be safe.

"Police still in your street?"

"Yes," she sighed.

Carver had placed a plainclothes officer in Hastings Road around the clock. Matthew and Linda took immense comfort in the fact that he was out there.

"Cormoran, listen. I know we can't—"

"Robin, there's no 'we' just now. There's me, sitting on my arse with no work, and there's you, staying at bloody home until that killer's caught."

"I wasn't talking about the case," she said. Her heart was banging hard and fast against her ribs again. She had to say it aloud, or she would burst. "There's one thing we—*you* can do, then. Brockbank might not be the killer, but we know he's a rapist. You could go to Alyssa and warn her she's living with—"

"Forget it," said Strike's voice harshly in her ear. "For the last fucking time, Robin, you can't save everyone! He's never been convicted! If we go blundering in there, Carver will string us up."

There was a long silence.

"Are you crying?" Strike asked anxiously, because he thought her breathing had become ragged.

"No, I'm not crying," said Robin truthfully.

An awful coldness had spread through her at Strike's refusal to help the young girls living in Brockbank's vicinity.

"I'd better go, it's lunch," she said, though nobody had called her.

"Look," he said, "I get why you want—"

"Speak later," she said and hung up.

There's no "we" just now.

It had happened all over again. A man had come at her out of the darkness and had ripped from her not only her sense of safety, but her status. She had been a partner in a detective agency...

Or had she? There had never been a new contract. There had never been a pay rise. They had been so busy, so broke, that it had never occurred to her to ask for either. She had simply been delighted to think that that was how Strike saw her. Now even that was gone, perhaps temporarily, perhaps forever. *There's no "we" anymore.*

Robin sat in thought for a few minutes, then got off the bed, the newspapers rustling. She approached the dressing table where the white shoebox sat, engraved with the silver words Jimmy Choo, reached out a hand and stroked the pristine surface of the cardboard.

The plan did not come to her like Strike's epiphany outside the hospital, with the exhilarating force of flame. Instead it rose slowly, dark and dangerous, born of the hateful enforced passivity of the past week and out of ice-cold anger at Strike's stubborn refusal to act. Strike, who was her friend, had joined the enemy's ranks. He was a six-foot-three ex-boxer. He would never know what it was like to feel yourself small, weak and powerless. He would never understand what rape did to your feelings about your own body: to find yourself reduced to a thing, an object, a piece of fuckable meat.

Zahara had sounded three at most on the telephone.

Robin remained quite still in front of her dressing table, staring down at the box containing her wedding shoes, thinking. She saw the risks plainly spread beneath her, like the rocks and raging waters beneath a tightrope walker's feet.

No, she could not save everyone. It was too late for Martina, for Sadie, for Kelsey and for Heather. Lila would spend the rest of her days with two fingers on her left hand and a grisly scar across her psyche that Robin understood only too well. However, there were also two young girls who faced God knows how much more suffering if nobody acted.

Robin turned away from the new shoes, reached for her mobile and dialed a number she had been given voluntarily, but which she had never imagined she would use.

54

And if it's true it can't be you,
It might as well be me.

Blue Öyster Cult, "Spy in the House of the Night"

She had three days in which to plan, because she had to wait for her accomplice to get hold of a car and find a gap in his busy schedule. Meanwhile she told Linda that her Jimmy Choos were too tight for her, the style too flashy, and allowed her mother to accompany her as she exchanged them for cash. Then she had to decide what lie she was going to tell Linda and Matthew, to buy sufficient time away from them to put her plan into action.

She ended up telling them that she was to have another police interview. Insisting that Shanker remain in the car when he picked her up was key to maintaining that illusion, as was getting Shanker to pull up alongside the plainclothes policeman still patrolling their street and telling him that she was off to get her stitches out, which in reality would not happen for another two days.

It was now seven o'clock on a cloudless evening and apart from Robin, who was leaning up against the warm brick wall of the Eastway Business Centre, the scene was deserted. The sun was making its slow progress towards the west and on the distant, misty horizon, at the far end of Blondin Street, the Orbit sculpture was rising into existence. Robin had seen plans in the papers: it would soon look like a gigantic candlestick telephone wrapped in its own twisted cord. Beyond it, Robin could just make out the growing outline of the Olympic stadium. The distant view of the gigantic structures was impressive and somehow inhuman, worlds and worlds away from the secrets she suspected were hidden behind the newly painted front door she knew to be Alyssa's.

Perhaps because of what she had come to do, the silent stretch of houses she was watching unnerved her. They were new, modern and somehow soulless. Barring the grandiose edifices being constructed in the distance, the place lacked character and was devoid of any sense of community. There were no trees to soften the outlines of the low, square houses, many of them sporting "To Let" signs, no corner shop, neither pub nor church. The warehouse against which she was leaning, with its upper windows hung with shroud-like white curtains and its metal garage doors heavily graffitied, offered no cover. Robin's heart was thudding as though she had been running. Nothing would turn her back now, yet she was afraid.

Footsteps echoed nearby and Robin whipped around, her sweaty fingers tight on her spare rape alarm. Tall, loose-limbed and scarred, Shanker was loping towards her carrying a Mars bar in one hand and a cigarette in the other.

"She's comin'," he said thickly.

"Are you sure?" said Robin, her heart pounding faster than ever. She was starting to feel light-headed.

"Black girl, two kids, comin' up the road now. Seen 'er when I was buyin' this," he said, waving the Mars bar. "Wan' some?"

"No thanks," said Robin. "Er—d'you mind getting out of the way?"

"Sure you don't wan' me to come in wiv ya?"

"No," said Robin. "Only come if you see—him."

"You sure the cunt's not already in there?"

"I rang twice. I'm sure he's not."

"I'll be round the corner, then," said Shanker laconically and he ambled off, alternately taking drags on his cigarette and bites of his Mars bar, to a position out of sight of Alyssa's door. Robin, meanwhile, hurried off down Blondin Street so that Alyssa would not pass her as she entered the house. Drawing in beneath the overhanging balcony of a block of dark red flats, Robin watched as a tall black woman turned into the street, one hand gripping that of a toddler and trailed by an older girl whom Robin thought must be around eleven. Alyssa unlocked the front door and let herself and her daughters inside.

Robin headed back up the street towards the house. She had dressed in jeans and trainers today: there must be no tripping, no falling over. The newly reconnected tendons throbbed beneath the cast.

Her heart was thumping so hard that it hurt as she knocked on Alyssa's front door. The older daughter peeped out of the bow window to her right as she stood waiting. Robin smiled nervously. The girl ducked out of sight.

The woman who appeared less than a minute later was, by any standards, gorgeous. Tall, black and with a bikini model's figure, she wore her hair in waist-length twists. The first thought that shot through Robin's mind was that if a strip joint had been prepared to fire Alyssa, she must indeed be a tricky character.

"Yeah?" she said, frowning at Robin.

"Hi," said Robin, her mouth dry. "Are you Alyssa Vincent?"

"Yeah. Who're you?"

"My name's Robin Ellacott," said Robin, her mouth dry. "I wonder—could I have a quick word with you about Noel?"

"What about him?" demanded Alyssa.

"I'd rather tell you inside," said Robin.

Alyssa had the wary, defiant look of one perpetually braced to take the next punch life was going to throw her.

"Please. It's important," said Robin, her tongue sticking to the roof of her mouth because it was so dry. "I wouldn't ask otherwise."

Their eyes locked: Alyssa's a warm caramel brown, Robin's a clear gray-blue. Robin was sure that Alyssa was going to refuse. Then the thick-lashed eyes widened suddenly and a strange flicker of excitement passed over Alyssa's face, as though she had just experienced a pleasurable revelation. Without another word, Alyssa stepped backwards into the dimly lit hall and made a strangely extravagant flourish, pointing Robin inside.

Robin did not know why she felt a lurch of misgiving. Only the thought that the two little girls were in there pushed her over the threshold.

A minuscule hall opened onto the sitting room. A TV and a single sofa constituted the only furnishings. A table lamp sat on the floor. There were two photographs in cheap gilt frames hanging on the wall, one showing chubby Zahara, the toddler, who was wearing a turquoise dress with matching butterfly clips in her hair, the other of her big sister in a maroon school uniform. The sister was the image of her beautiful mother. The photographer had not managed to induce a smile.

Robin heard a lock being turned on the front door. She turned, her trainers screeching on the polished wood floor. Somewhere nearby a loud ping announced that a microwave had just finished its work.

"Mama!" said a shrill voice.

"Angel!" shouted Alyssa, walking into the room. "Get it out for her! All right," she said, arms folded, "what d'you wanna tell me about Noel, then?"

Robin's impression that Alyssa was gloating over some private piece of intelligence was reinforced by the nasty smirk that disfigured the lovely face. The ex-stripper stood with her arms crossed, so that her breasts were thrust up like the figurehead of a ship, the long ropes of hair hanging to her waist. She was taller than Robin by two inches.

"Alyssa, I work with Cormoran Strike. He's a—"

"I know who he is," said Alyssa slowly. The secret satisfaction she seemed to have gleaned from Robin's appearance had suddenly gone. "He's the bastard that give Noel epilepsy! Fucking hell! You've gone to *him,* have you? In it together, are you? Why didn't you go to the pigs, you lying bitch, if he—*really*—"

She smacked Robin hard in the shoulder and before Robin could defend herself, began punching her with every subsequent word.

"—done—*anything*—*TO*—*YOU!*"

Alyssa was suddenly pummeling her wherever she could land a punch: Robin threw up her left arm to defend herself, trying to protect her right, and kicked out at Alyssa's knee. Alyssa shrieked in pain and hopped backwards; from somewhere behind Robin the toddler screamed and her older sister came sliding into the room.

"Fucking bitch!" screamed Alyssa, "attacking me in front of my kids—"

And she launched herself at Robin, grabbing her hair and slamming her head into the curtainless window. Robin felt Angel, who was thin and wiry, trying to force the two women apart. Abandoning restraint, Robin managed to land a smack to Alyssa's ear, causing her to gasp in pain and retreat. Robin seized Angel under the armpits, swung her out of the way, put her own head down and charged at Alyssa, knocking her backwards onto the sofa.

"Leave my mum—*leave my mum alone!*" shouted Angel, grabbing Robin's injured forearm and yanking it so that Robin, too, yelled in pain. Zahara was screaming from the doorway, a sippy cup of hot milk held upside down in her hand.

"YOU'RE LIVING WITH A PEDOPHILE!" Robin roared over the racket as Alyssa tried to push herself back off the sofa to renew the fight.

Robin had imagined herself imparting the devastating news in a whisper and watching Alyssa crumble in shock. Not once had she visualized Alyssa looking up at her and snarling:

"Yeah, whatever. D'you think I don't know who you are, you fucking bitch? Are you not happy ruining his fucking life—"

She launched herself at Robin again: the space was so small that Robin hit the wall again. Locked together they slid sideways into the TV, which toppled off its stand with an ominous crash. Robin felt the wound on her forearm twist and let out another shriek of pain.

"Mama! Mama!" wailed Zahara, while Angel seized the back of Robin's jeans, hampering her ability to fend Alyssa off.

"Ask your daughters!" shouted Robin as fists and elbows flew and she tried to twist free of Angel's stubborn grip. "Ask your daughters whether he's—"

"Don't you—dare—fucking—bring—my kids—"

"Ask them!"

"Lying fucking bitch—you and your fucking mother—"

"My *mother?*" said Robin, and with an almighty effort she elbowed Alyssa so hard in the midriff that the taller woman doubled over and collapsed onto the sofa again. "Angel, get off me!" Robin roared, wrenching the girl's fingers off her jeans, sure that she had seconds before Alyssa returned to the attack. Zahara continued to wail from the doorway. "*Who,*" Robin panted, standing over Alyssa, "d'you think I am?"

"Very fucking funny!" gasped Alyssa, whom Robin had winded. "You're fucking Brittany! Phoning him and persecuting him—"

"*Brittany?*" said Robin in astonishment. "I'm not Brittany!"

She yanked her purse out of her jacket pocket. "Look at my credit card—look at it! I'm Robin Ellacott and I work with Cormoran Strike—"

"The fucker who gave him brain dam—"

"D'you know why Cormoran went to arrest him?"

"'Cause his fucking wife framed—"

"Nobody framed him! He raped Brittany and he's been sacked from jobs all over the country because he interferes with little girls! He did it to his own sister—I've met her!"

"Fucking liar!" shouted Alyssa, making to get up from the sofa again.

"I—am—not—LYING!" roared Robin, shoving Alyssa back against the cushions.

"You mad bitch," gasped Alyssa, "get out of my fucking house!"

"Ask your daughter whether he's hurt her! Ask her! Angel?"

"*Don't you* dare *talk to my kids, you bitch!*"

"Angel, tell your mother whether he's—"

"Th'fook's going on?"

Zahara had been screaming so loudly that they had not heard the key in the lock.

He was massive, dark-haired and bearded, wearing an all-black tracksuit. One eye socket was sunken, caved in towards his nose, making his stare intense and unnerving. His dark, shadowed eyes on Robin, he bent down slowly and picked up the toddler, who beamed and cuddled close to him. Angel, on the other hand, shrank backwards into the wall. Very slowly, his eyes on Robin, Brockbank lowered Zahara into her mother's lap.

"Nice t'see thoo," he said with a smile that was no smile, but a promise of pain.

Cold all over, Robin tried to slide her hand discreetly into her pocket for her rape alarm, but Brockbank was on her in seconds, seizing her wrist and compressing her stitches.

"You're fookin' phonin' no one, sneakly larl bitch—thought A didn' know it was thoo, din't thoo—"

She tried to twist away from him, her stitches pulling under his grasp, and screamed:

"SHANKER!"

"A shoulda fuckin' killed thoo when A 'ad th'chance, larl bitch!"

And then came a splintering crash of wood that was the front door caving in. Brockbank released Robin and whirled around to see Shanker hurtling into the room, knife to the fore.

"*Don't stab him!*" gasped Robin, clutching her forearm.

The six people crammed into the small bare box of a room froze for a fraction of a second, even the toddler clinging to her mother. Then a thin voice piped up, desperate, trembling, but liberated at last by the presence of a scarred, gold-toothed man whose tattooed knuckles were tight around a knife.

"He done it to me! He done it to me, Mum, he did! He done it to me!"

"What?" said Alyssa, looking towards Angel. Her face was suddenly slack with shock.

"He done it to me! What that lady said. He done it to me!"

Brockbank made a small, convulsive movement, swiftly curbed as Shanker raised his knife, pointing it at the bigger man's chest.

"You're all right, babes," Shanker said to Angel, his free hand shielding her, his gold tooth glinting in the sun falling slowly behind the houses opposite. " 'E ain't gonna do that no more. You fuckin' nonce," he breathed into Brockbank's face. "I'd like to skin ya."

"Whatchoo talkin' abou', Angel?" said Alyssa, still clutching Zahara, her face now a study in dread. "He never—?"

Brockbank suddenly put his head down and charged Shanker like the flanker he had once been. Shanker, who was less than half his width, was knocked aside like a dummy; they heard Brockbank pushing his way past the caved-in door as Shanker, swearing furiously, gave chase.

"Leave him—*leave him!*" Robin screamed, watching through the window as the two men streaked off down the street. "Oh God—SHANKER!—the police will—where's Angel—?"

Alyssa had already left the room in pursuit of her daughter, leaving behind her the much-tried toddler to wail and scream on the sofa. Robin, who knew she could not hope to catch the two men, felt suddenly so shivery that she dropped into a crouch, holding her head as waves of sickness passed over her.

She had done what she had meant to do and she had been aware all along that there would almost certainly be collateral damage. Brockbank escaping or being stabbed by Shanker had been possibilities she had foreseen. Her only present certainty was that she could do nothing to prevent either. After taking a couple of deep breaths she stood up again and moved to the sofa to try to comfort the terrified toddler, but unsurprisingly, given that Robin was associated in the little girl's mind with scenes of violence and hysteria, Zahara screamed harder than ever, and lashed out at Robin with a tiny foot.

"I never knew," said Alyssa. "Oh God. Oh God. Why didn't you tell me, Angel? Why didn't you tell me?"

Evening was drawing in. Robin had turned on the lamp, which threw pale gray shadows up onto the magnolia walls. Three flat hunchbacked ghosts seemed to crouch on the back of the sofa, mimicking Alyssa's every movement. Angel was curled, sobbing, on her mother's lap as the pair of them rocked backwards and forwards.

Robin, who had already made two rounds of tea and had cooked spaghetti hoops for Zahara, was sitting on the hard floor beneath the window. She had felt obliged to stay until they could get an emergency joiner to fix the door that Shanker had shouldered in. Nobody had yet called the police. Mother and daughter were still confiding in each other and Robin felt like an interloper, yet could not leave the family until she knew that they had a secure door and a new lock. Zahara was asleep on the sofa beside her mother and sister, curled up with her thumb in her mouth, one chubby hand still clutching the sippy cup.

"He said he'd kill Zahara if I told you," said Angel into her mother's neck.

"Oh, sweet Jesus," moaned Alyssa, tears splattering down her daughter's back. "Oh, sweet Lord."

The ominous feeling inside Robin was like having a bellyful of crawling, prickle-footed crabs. She had texted her mother and Matthew to say that the police needed to show her more photofits, but both were getting worried about her long absence and she was running out of plausible reasons to stop them coming to meet her. Again and again she checked the mute button on her phone in case somehow she had stopped it ringing. Where was Shanker?

The joiner arrived at last. Once Robin had given him her credit card details to pay for the damage, she told Alyssa that she had better get going.

Alyssa left Angel and Zahara curled up together on the sofa and accompanied Robin out into the dusky street.

"Listen," said Alyssa.

There were still tear tracks down her face. Robin could tell that Alyssa was unused to thanking people.

"Thanks, all right?" she said, almost aggressively.

"No problem," said Robin.

"I never—I mean—I met him at fucking *church.* I thought I'd found a good bloke at last, y'know... he was really good with the—with the kids—"

She began to sob. Robin considered reaching out to her, but decided against it. She was bruised all over her shoulders where Alyssa had pummeled her and her knife wound was throbbing more than ever.

"Has Brittany really been phoning him?" Robin asked.

" 'S'what he told me," said Alyssa, wiping her eyes on the back of her hand. "He reckoned his ex-wife framed him, got Brittany to lie... said if ever a young blonde bird turned up she was talking shit and I wasn't to believe anything she said."

Robin remembered the low voice in her ear:

Do A know you, little girl?

He had thought that she was Brittany. *That* was why he had hung up and never called back.

"I'd better be off," said Robin, worried about how long it would take her to get back to West Ealing. Her body ached all over. Alyssa had landed some powerful blows. "You'll call the police, right?"

"I s'pose," said Alyssa. Robin suspected that the idea was a novel one to Alyssa. "Yeah."

As Robin walked away in the darkness, her fist clenched tightly around her second rape alarm, she wondered what Brittany Brockbank had found to say to her stepfather, and thought she knew: "I haven't forgotten. Do it again and I'll report you." Perhaps it had been a salve to her conscience. She had been frightened that he was still doing to others what he had done to her, but could not face the consequences of a historical accusation.

I put it to you, Miss Brockbank, that your stepfather never touched you, that this story was concocted by yourself and your mother...

Robin knew how it worked. The defense barrister she had faced had been cold and sardonic, his expression vulpine.

You were coming back from the student bar, Miss Ellacott, where you had been drinking, yes?

You had made a public joke about missing the—ah—attentions of your boyfriend, yes?

When you met Mr. Trewin—

I didn't—

When you met Mr. Trewin outside the halls of residence—

I didn't meet—

You told Mr. Trewin you were missing—

We never talked—

I put it to you, Miss Ellacott, that you are ashamed of inviting Mr. Trewin—

I didn't invite—

You had made a joke, Miss Ellacott, hadn't you, in the bar, about missing the, ah, sexual attentions of—

I said I missed—

How many drinks had you had, Miss Ellacott?

Robin understood only too well why people were scared of telling, of owning up to what had been done to them, of being told that the dirty, shameful, excruciating truth was a figment of their own sick imagination. Neither Holly nor Brittany had been able to face the prospect of open court, and perhaps Alyssa and Angel would be scared away too. Yet nothing, Robin was sure, short of death or incarceration would ever stop Noel Brockbank raping little girls. Even so, she would be glad to know that Shanker had not killed him, because if he had...

"Shanker!" she shouted as a tall, tattooed figure in a shell suit passed under a streetlamp ahead.

"Couldn't fucking find the bastard, Rob!" came Shanker's echoing voice. He did not seem to realize that Robin had been sitting on a hard floor in terror for two whole hours, praying for his return. "He can move for a big fucker, can't 'e?"

"The police'll find him," said Robin, whose knees were suddenly weak. "Alyssa's going to call them, I think. Shanker, will you... please will you drive me home?"

55

Came the last night of sadness
And it was clear she couldn't go on.

Blue Öyster Cult, "(Don't Fear) The Reaper"

For twenty-four hours Strike remained in ignorance of what Robin had done. She did not answer when he phoned at lunchtime the next day, but as he was wrestling with his own dilemmas and believed her to be safe at home with her mother he neither found this strange nor troubled to call back. His injured partner was one of the few problems that he believed temporarily solved and he did not intend to encourage her in thoughts of returning to his side by confiding in her the revelation he had experienced outside the hospital.

This, however, was now his overriding preoccupation. After all, there was no longer any competition for his time or attention in the solitary, silent room where no clients called or visited. The only sound was the buzzing of a fly zooming between the open windows in the hazy sunlight, as Strike sat chain-smoking Benson & Hedges.

As he looked back over the almost three months since the severed leg had been delivered, the detective saw his mistakes only too clearly. He ought to have known the identity of the killer after visiting Kelsey Platt's home. If he had only realized, then—if he had not allowed himself to be taken in by the killer's misdirection, not been distracted by the competing scents of other deranged men—Lila Monkton would still have all ten fingers and Heather Smart might be safe at work in her Nottingham building society, vowing, perhaps, never again to be as drunk as she had been on her sister-in-law's birthday jaunt to London.

Strike had not come up through the Special Investigation Branch of the Royal Military Police without learning to manage the emotional consequences of an investigation. The previous evening had been full of self-directed anger, but even as he castigated himself for not seeing what was right in front of him he had acknowledged the killer's brazen brilliance. There had been artistry in the way that he had used Strike's background against him, forcing Strike to second guess and question himself, undermining his trust in his own judgment.

The fact that the killer was indeed one of the men whom he had suspected from the first was cold comfort. Strike could not remember ever being in such agony of mind over an investigation as he was now. Alone in his deserted office, convinced that the conclusion he had reached had neither been given credence by the officer in whom he had confided it, nor passed on to Carver, Strike felt, however unreasonably, that if another killing occurred it would indeed be his fault.

Yet if he went near the investigation again—if he started staking out or tailing his man—Carver would almost certainly see him in court for interfering with the course of a police investigation or obstructing the police in their inquiries. He would have felt the same way himself, had he been in Carver's shoes—except, thought Strike with a rush of pleasurable anger, that he would have listened to anyone, however infuriating, if he thought they had a shred of credible evidence. You did not solve a case as complex as this by discriminating against witnesses on the grounds that they have previously outwitted you.

Only when his stomach rumbled did Strike remember that he was supposed to be going out for dinner with Elin that night. The divorce settlement and custody arrangements had now been finalized, and Elin had announced over the phone that it was about time they enjoyed a decent dinner for a change and that she had booked Le Gavroche—"My treat."

Alone, smoking in his office, Strike contemplated the forthcoming evening with a dispassion he was no longer able to bring to the thought of the Shacklewell Ripper. On the plus side, there would be excellent food, which was an enticing prospect given the fact that he was skint and had last night dined on baked beans on toast. He supposed that there would be sex too, in the pristine whiteness of Elin's flat, the soon-to-be-vacated home of her disintegrating family. On the minus side—he found himself staring the bald fact in the face as he had never done before—he would have to talk to her, and talking to Elin, he had finally admitted to himself, was far from one of his favorite pastimes. He always found the conversation especially effortful when it came to his own work. Elin was interested, yet strangely unimaginative. She had none of the innate interest in and easy empathy for other people that Robin displayed. His would-be humorous word portraits of the likes of Two-Times left her perplexed rather than amused.

Then there were those two ominous words "my treat." The increasing imbalance in their respective incomes was about to become painfully obvious. When Strike had met Elin, he had at least been in credit. If she thought that he was going to be able to return the treat with dinner at Le Gavroche on another night, she was destined to be sorely disappointed.

Strike had spent sixteen years with another woman who had been far richer than he was. Charlotte had alternately brandished money as a weapon and deplored Strike's refusal to live beyond his means. Memories of Charlotte's occasional fits of pique that he could not or would not fund treats on which she had set her capricious heart made his hackles rise when Elin spoke of having a decent dinner "for a change." It had mostly been he who had footed the bills for French and Indian meals in out-of-the-way bistros and curry houses where Elin's ex-husband had been unlikely to see them. He did not appreciate the fruits of his hard-earned cash being disparaged.

His state of mind was not entirely propitious, therefore, when he headed off to Mayfair at eight o'clock that evening, wearing his best Italian suit, thoughts of a serial killer still chasing each other around his overtired brain.

Upper Brook Street comprised grand eighteenth-century houses and the frontage of Le Gavroche, with its wrought iron canopy and ivy-covered railings, the expensive solidity and security implied by its heavy mirrored front door, was dissonant to Strike's uneasy frame of mind. Elin arrived shortly after he had been seated in the green and red dining room, which was artfully lit so that puddles of light fell only where needed onto snow-white tablecloths, over gilt-framed oil paintings. She looked stunning in a pale blue form-fitting dress. As he rose to kiss her, Strike momentarily forgot his latent unease, his disgruntlement.

"This makes a nice change," she said, smiling, as she sank down onto the curved, upholstered bench at their round table.

They ordered. Strike, who craved a pint of Doom Bar, drank burgundy of Elin's choosing and wished, despite having smoked more than a pack that day, that he could have a cigarette. Meanwhile, his dinner companion launched into a barrage of property talk: she had decided against the Strata penthouse and had now looked at a property in Camberwell, which seemed promising. She showed him a picture on her phone: another columned and porticoed vision of Georgian whiteness met his tired eyes.

As Elin discussed the various pros and cons of a move to Camberwell, Strike drank in silence. He even begrudged the wine's deliciousness, throwing it back like the cheapest plonk, trying to blunt the edges of his resentment with alcohol. It did not work: far from dissolving, his sense of alienation deepened. The comfortable Mayfair restaurant with its low lighting and its deep carpet felt like a stage set: illusory, ephemeral. What was he doing here, with this gorgeous but dull woman? Why was he pretending to be interested in her expensive lifestyle, when his business was in its death throes and he alone in London knew the identity of the Shacklewell Ripper?

Their food arrived and the deliciousness of his fillet of beef did something to assuage his resentment.

"So what have you been up to?" asked Elin, punctiliously polite as usual.

Strike now found himself presented with a stark choice. Telling her the truth about what he had been up to would necessitate an admission that he had not kept her abreast of any of the recent events that would have been deemed enough news for a decade in most people's lives. He would be forced to reveal that the girl in the newspapers who had survived the Ripper's latest attack was his own business partner. He would have to tell her that he had been warned off the case by a man whom he had previously humiliated over another high-profile murder. If he were making a clean breast of all that he had been up to, he ought also to add that he now knew exactly who the killer was. The prospect of relating all this bored and oppressed him. He had not once thought to call her while any of these events had unfolded, which was revealing enough in itself.

Playing for time while he took another sip of wine, Strike came to the decision that the affair had to end. He would make an excuse not to go back to Clarence Terrace with her tonight, which ought to give her early warning of his intentions; the sex had been the best part of the relationship all along. Then, next time they met, he'd tell her it was over. Not only did he feel it would be churlish to end things over a meal for which she was paying, there was a remote chance that she would walk out, leaving him with a bill that his credit card company would undoubtedly refuse to process.

"I haven't been up to much, to be honest," he lied.

"What about the Shackle—"

Strike's mobile rang. He pulled it out of his jacket pocket and saw that the number had been withheld. Some sixth sense told him to answer it.

"Sorry," he said to Elin, "I think I need to—"

"Strike," said Carver's unmistakable South London voice. "Did you send her to do it?"

"What?" said Strike.

"Your fucking partner. Did you send her to Brockbank?"

Strike stood up so suddenly that he hit the edge of the table. A spray of bloodied brown liquid spattered across the heavy white tablecloth, his fillet of beef slid over the edge of the plate and his wineglass toppled, splashing Elin's pale blue dress. The waiter gaped, as did the refined couple at the next table.

"Where is she? What's happened?" asked Strike loudly, oblivious to everything except the voice on the end of the line.

"I warned you, Strike," said Carver, his voice crackling with rage. "I fucking warned you to stay away. You have fucked up royally this time—"

Strike lowered the mobile. A disembodied Carver bellowed into the restaurant, the "cunts" and "fucks" clearly audible to anybody standing nearby. He turned to Elin in her purple-stained dress, with her beautiful face screwed up in mingled perplexity and anger.

"I've got to go. I'm sorry. I'll call you later."

He did not stay to see how she took it; he did not care.

Limping slightly, because he had twisted his knee in his haste to get up, Strike hurried out of the restaurant, phone to his ear again. Carver was now virtually incoherent, shouting Strike down whenever he attempted to speak.

"Carver, listen," Strike shouted as he regained Upper Brook Street, "there's something I want to—fucking listen, will you!"

But the policeman's obscenity-strewn soliloquy merely became louder and filthier.

"You fucking stupid fucking cunt, he's gone to ground—I know what you were fucking up to—we've found it, you bastard, we found the church connection! If you ever—shut your fucking mouth, I'm talking!—if you *ever* come near one of my fucking investigations again..."

Strike slogged on through the warm night, his knee protesting, frustration and fury mounting with every step he took.

It took him nearly an hour to reach Robin's flat in Hastings Road, by which time he was in full possession of the facts. Thanks to Carver, he knew that the police had been with Robin this evening and were perhaps still there, interrogating her about the intrusion into Brockbank's house that had led to a report of child rape and the flight of their suspect. Brockbank's photograph had been widely disseminated across the force, but he had not, as yet, been apprehended.

Strike had not warned Robin that he was coming. Turning into Hastings Road as fast as his limp would allow, he saw through the fading light that all the windows of her flat were lit. As he approached, two police officers, unmistakable even in plain clothes, emerged from the front entrance. The sound of the front door closing echoed down the quiet street. Strike moved into the shadows as the police crossed the road to their car, talking quietly to each other. Once they had pulled safely away, he proceeded to the white front door and rang the bell.

"...thought we were done," said Matthew's exasperated voice behind the door. Strike doubted that he knew that he could be heard, because when he opened it Robin's fiancé was wearing an ingratiating smile that vanished the moment he realized who it was.

"What d'you want?"

"I need to talk to Robin," said Strike.

As Matthew hesitated, with every appearance of wishing to block Strike's entrance, Linda came out into the hall behind him.

"Oh," she said at the sight of Strike.

He thought she looked both thinner and older than the previous time he had met her, no doubt because her daughter had nearly got herself killed, then turned up voluntarily at a violent sexual predator's house and got attacked all over again. Strike could feel the fury building beneath his diaphragm. If necessary, he would shout for Robin to come and meet him on the doorstep, but he had no sooner formed this resolution than she appeared behind Matthew. She too looked paler and thinner than usual. As always, he found her better-looking in the flesh than in the memory he had of her when not present. This did not make him feel any more kindly towards her.

"Oh," she said in exactly the same colorless tone as her mother.

"I'd like a word," said Strike.

"All right," said Robin with a slightly defiant upwards jerk of her head that made her red-gold hair dance around her shoulders. She glanced at her mother and Matthew, then back at Strike. "D'you want to come into the kitchen, then?"

He followed her down the hall into the small kitchen where a table for two stood crammed into the corner. Robin closed the door carefully behind them. Neither sat down. Dirty dishes were piled by the sink; they had apparently been eating pasta before the police arrived to interrogate Robin. For some reason, this evidence that Robin had been behaving so prosaically in the wake of the chaos she had unleashed increased the rage now battling with Strike's desire not to lose control.

"I told you," he said, "not to go anywhere near Brockbank."

"Yes," said Robin in a flat voice that aggravated him still further. "I remember."

Strike wondered whether Linda and Matthew were listening at the door. The small kitchen smelled strongly of garlic and tomatoes. An England Rugby calendar hung on the wall behind Robin. The thirtieth of June was circled thickly, the words HOME FOR WEDDING written beneath the date.

"But you decided to go anyway," said Strike.

Visions of violent, cathartic action—picking up the pedal bin and throwing it through the steamy window, for instance—were rising chaotically in his mind's eye. He stood quite still, large feet planted on the scuffed lino, staring at her white and stubborn face.

"I don't regret it," she said. "He was raping—"

"Carver's convinced I sent you. Brockbank's vanished. You've driven him underground. How're you going to feel if he decides he'd better cut the next one into pieces before she can blab?"

"Don't you dare put that on me!" said Robin, her voice rising. "Don't you dare! You're the one who punched him when you went to arrest him! If you hadn't hit him he might've gone down for Brittany!"

"That makes what you did right, does it?"

He refrained from shouting only because he could hear Matthew lurking in the hall, however quiet the accountant thought he was being.

"I've stopped Angel being abused and if that's a bad thing to do—"

"You've driven my business off the edge of a fucking cliff," said Strike in a quiet voice that stopped her in her tracks. "We were warned away from those suspects, from the whole investigation, but you went storming in and now Brockbank's gone to ground. The press'll be all over me for this. Carver'll tell them I've fucked it all up. They'll bury me. And even if you don't give a shit about any of that," said Strike, his face rigid with fury, "how about the fact the police have just found a connection between Kelsey's church and the one in Brixton where Brockbank was attending?"

She looked stricken.

"I—I didn't know—"

"Why wait for the facts?" asked Strike, his eyes dark shadows in the harsh overhead lighting. "Why not just blunder in and tip him off before the police can take him in?"

Appalled, Robin said nothing. Strike was looking at her now as though he never liked her, as though they had never shared any of the experiences that, to her, had constituted a bond like no other. She had been prepared for him to punch walls and cupboards again, even, in the heat of his anger, to—

"We're finished," said Strike.

He took some satisfaction from the shrinking movement she could not hide, from the sudden blanching of her face.

"You don't—"

"I don't mean it? You think I need a partner who won't take instruction, who does what I've explicitly told her not to do, who makes me look like a trouble-making egotistical prick in front of the police and causes a murder suspect to disappear under the force's nose?"

He said it in a single breath and Robin, who had taken a step backwards, knocked the England Rugby calendar off the wall with a rustle and thud she failed to hear, so loudly was the blood pounding in her ears. She thought she might faint. She had imagined him shouting "I ought to fire you!" but not once had she considered that he might actually do it, that everything she had done for him—the risks, the injuries, the insights and the inspirations, the long hours of discomfort and inconvenience—would be washed away, rendered negligible by this one act of well-intentioned disobedience. She could not even get enough breath into her lungs to argue, because his expression was such that she knew all she could expect was further icy condemnation of her actions and an exposition of how badly she had screwed up. The memory of Angel and Alyssa holding each other on the sofa, the reflection that Angel's suffering was finished and that her mother believed and supported her, had comforted Robin through the hours of suspense during which she waited for this blow to fall. She had not dared tell Strike what she had done. Now she thought it might have been better if she had.

"What?" she said stupidly, because he had asked her something. The noises had been meaningless.

"*Who was the man you took with you?*"

"That's none of your business," she whispered after a short hesitation.

"They said he threatened Brockbank with a kni—Shanker!" said Strike, light dawning only now, and in that instant she saw a trace of the Strike she knew in the reanimated, infuriated face. "*How the fuck did you get Shanker's number?*"

But she could not speak. Nothing mattered beside the fact that she was fired. She knew that Strike did not relent when he decided that a relationship had run its course. His girlfriend of sixteen years had never heard from him again after he had ended it, although Charlotte had tried to initiate contact since.

He was already leaving. She followed him into the hall on numb legs, feeling herself to be acting like a beaten dog who still slinks after the punisher, hoping desperately for forgiveness.

"Goodnight," Strike called to Linda and Matthew, who had retreated into the sitting room.

"Cormoran," Robin whispered.

"I'll send your last month's salary on," he said without looking at her. "Quick and clean. Gross misconduct."

The door closed behind him. She could hear his size fourteens moving away up the path. With a gasp, she began to cry. Linda and Matthew both came hurrying into the hall, but too late: Robin had fled to the bedroom, unable to face their relief and delight that, at last, she would have to give up her dream of being a detective.

56

When life's scorned and damage done
To avenge, this is the pact.

Blue Öyster Cult, "Vengeance (The Pact)"

Half past four the following morning found Strike awake after virtually no sleep. His tongue ached from the amount of smoking he had done overnight at the Formica table in his kitchen, while contemplating the decimation of his business and his prospects. He could barely bring himself to think about Robin. Fine cracks, like those in thick ice during a thaw, were starting to appear in what had been implacable fury, but what lay beneath was scarcely less cold. He could understand the impulse to save the child—who couldn't? Hadn't he, as she had so injudiciously pointed out, knocked Brockbank out cold after viewing Brittany's taped evidence?—but the thought of her heading off with Shanker, without telling him, and after Carver had warned them not to go anywhere near the suspects, made rage thunder through his veins all over again as he upended his cigarette pack and found it empty.

He pulled himself to his feet, picked up his keys and left the flat, still wearing the Italian suit in which he had dozed. The sun was coming up as he trudged down Charing Cross Road in a dawn that made everything look dusty and fragile, a gray light full of pale shadows. He bought cigarettes in a corner shop in Covent Garden and continued to walk, smoking and thinking.

After two hours spent walking the streets, Strike reached a decision about his next move. Heading back towards the office, he saw a waitress in a black dress unlocking the doors to the Caffè Vergnano 1882 on Charing Cross Road, realized how hungry he was and turned inside.

The small coffee shop smelled of warm wood and espresso. As Strike sank gratefully onto a hard oak chair he became uncomfortably aware that for the past thirteen hours he had smoked ceaselessly, slept in his clothes and eaten steak and drunk red wine without cleaning his teeth. The man in the reflection beside him looked crumpled and grimy. He tried not to give the young waitress any opportunity to smell his breath as he ordered a ham and cheese panini, a bottle of water and a double espresso.

As the copper-domed coffee maker on the counter hissed into life, Strike sank into a reverie, searching his conscience for a truthful answer to an uncomfortable question.

Was he any better than Carver? Was he contemplating a high-risk and dangerous course of action because he really thought it the only way to stop the killer? Or was he inclining to the higher-stakes option because he knew that if he brought it off—if he were the one to catch and incriminate the murderer—it would reverse all the damage done to his reputation and his business, restoring to him the luster of a man who succeeded where the Met failed? Was it, in short, necessity or ego that was driving him towards what many would say was a reckless and foolish measure?

The waitress set his sandwich and coffee in front of him and Strike began to eat with the glazed stare of a man too preoccupied even to taste what he was chewing.

This was as well-publicized a series of crimes as Strike had ever come into contact with: the police would currently be flooded with information and leads, all of which needed following up and none of which (Strike was prepared to bet) would lead anywhere near the real devious and successful killer.

He still had the option of trying to make contact with one of Carver's superiors, although he was now in such poor odor with the police that he doubted he would be allowed direct speech with a superintendent, whose first loyalty would of course be to his own men. Trying to circumnavigate Carver would do nothing to diminish the impression that he was trying to undermine the head of the investigation.

What was more, Strike did not have evidence, merely a theory about where the evidence was. While there was a remote chance that somebody at the Met might take Strike seriously enough to go looking for what he promised they would find, Strike feared that further delay might cost another life.

He was surprised to find that he had finished his panini. Still extremely hungry, he ordered a second.

No, he thought, with sudden resolve, *this is the way it's got to be.*

This animal needed to be stopped as soon as possible. It was time to get out ahead of him for the first time. However, as a sop to his conscience, as a proof to himself that he was motivated primarily by catching a killer rather than by glory, Strike took out his mobile again and called Detective Inspector Richard Anstis, his oldest acquaintance on the force. He was not on the best terms with Anstis these days, but Strike wanted to be certain in his own mind that he had done all he could to allow the Met the chance to do the job for him.

After a long pause, a foreign dialing tone sounded in his ear. Nobody picked up. Anstis was on holiday. Strike debated leaving a voicemail and decided against. Leaving such a message on Anstis's phone when there was nothing the man could do would definitely ruin his holiday, and from what Strike knew of Anstis's wife and three children, the man needed one.

Hanging up, he scrolled absentmindedly through his recent calls. Carver had not left his number. Robin's name sat a few rows beneath. The sight of it stabbed the tired and desperate Strike to the heart because he was simultaneously furious with her and longing to talk to her. Setting the mobile resolutely back onto the table, he shoved his hand into his inside jacket pocket and pulled out a pen and notebook.

Eating his second sandwich as fast as his first, Strike began to write a list.

1) Write to Carver.

This was partly a further sop to his own conscience and partly what he generally termed "arse-covering." He doubted the ability of an email to find its way to Carver, whose direct address he did not have, through the tsunami of tip-offs now sure to be pouring into Scotland Yard. People were culturally disposed to take ink and paper seriously, especially when it had to be signed for: an old-fashioned letter, sent recorded delivery, would be sure to find its way to Carver's desk. Strike would then have laid a trail just as the killer had done, demonstrating very clearly that he had tried every possible route to tell Carver how the killer might be stopped. This was likely to be useful when they all found themselves in court, which Strike did not doubt would happen whether or not the plan he had formulated, walking through the dawn in sleepy Covent Garden, was successful.

2) Gas canister (propane?)
3) Fluorescent jacket
4) Woman—who?

He paused, arguing with himself, scowling over the paper. After much thought, he reluctantly wrote:

5) Shanker

This meant that the next item had to be:

6) £500 (from where?)

And finally, after a further minute's thought:

7) Advertise for Robin replacement.

57

Sole survivor, cursed with second sight,
Haunted savior, cried into the night.

Blue Öyster Cult, "Sole Survivor"

Four days passed. Numb with shock and misery, Robin at first hoped and even believed that Strike would call her, that he would regret what he had said to her, that he would realize what a mistake he had made. Linda had left, kind and supportive to the last, but, Robin suspected, secretly happy to think that Robin's association with the detective had ended.

Matthew had expressed enormous sympathy in the face of Robin's devastation. He said that Strike did not know how lucky he had been. He had enumerated for her all the things she had done for the detective, foremost of which was accepting a laughably small salary for unreasonably long hours. He reminded Robin that her status as partner in the agency had been entirely illusory, and totted up all the proofs of Strike's lack of respect for her: the absence of a partnership agreement, the lack of overtime pay, the fact that she always seemed to be the one who made tea and went out to buy sandwiches.

A week previously, Robin would have defended Strike against all such accusations. She would have said that the nature of the work necessitated long hours, that the moment to demand a pay rise was not when the business was fighting for its very survival, that Strike made her mugs of tea quite as often as she made them for him. She might have added that Strike had spent money he could ill afford training her in surveillance and countersurveillance, and that it was unreasonable to expect him, as senior partner, sole investor and founding member of the agency, to place her on absolutely equal legal footing with himself.

Yet she said none of those things, because the last two words that Strike had spoken to her were with her every day like the sound of her own heartbeat: *gross misconduct.* The memory of Strike's expression in that last moment helped her pretend that she saw things exactly as Matthew did, that her dominant emotion was anger, that the job which had meant everything to her could be easily replaced, that Strike had no integrity or moral sense if he could not appreciate that Angel's safety trumped all other considerations. Robin had neither the will nor the energy to point out that Matthew had performed an abrupt volte-face on the last point, because he had been furious, initially, when he had found out that she had gone to Brockbank's.

As the days went by without any contact from Strike, she felt unspoken pressure from her fiancé to pretend that the prospect of their wedding on Saturday not only made up for her recent sacking, but consumed all her thoughts. Having to fake excitement while he was present made Robin relieved to be alone during the day while Matthew worked. Every evening, before he returned, she deleted the search history on her laptop, so that he would not see that she was constantly looking for news about the Shacklewell Ripper online and—just as often—Googling Strike.

On the day before she and Matthew were due to leave for Masham, he arrived home holding a copy of the *Sun,* which was not his usual read.

"Why have you got that?"

Matthew hesitated before answering and Robin's insides twisted.

"There hasn't been another—?"

But she knew there had not been another killing: she had been following the news all day.

He opened the paper, folded it to a page about ten in, and handed it to her, his expression hard to read. Robin found herself staring at her own photograph. She was walking with her head down in the picture, dressed in her trench coat, leaving court after giving evidence at the well-publicized trial of the murderer of Owen Quine. Two smaller pictures were set into her own: one of Strike, looking hung-over, the other of the spectacularly beautiful model whose killer they had worked together to catch. Beneath the photo spread were the words:

LANDRY DETECTIVE SEEKS NEW GIRL FRIDAY

Cormoran Strike, the detective who solved the murder cases of both supermodel Lula Landry and author Owen Quine, has parted company with glamorous assistant Robin Ellacott, 26.

The detective has placed an advertisement for the position online: "If you have a background in police or military investigative work and would like to pursue—

There were several more paragraphs, but Robin could not bear to read them. Instead, she looked at the byline, which was that of Dominic Culpepper, a journalist whom Strike knew personally. Possibly he had called Culpepper, who often badgered Strike for stories, and let him have this one, to make sure his need for a new assistant was disseminated as widely as possible.

Robin had not thought that she could feel any worse, but now she discovered that she had been mistaken. She really was sacked, after everything that she had done for him. She had been a disposable "Girl Friday," an "assistant"—never a partner, never an equal—and now he was already looking for somebody with a background in the police or the military: somebody disciplined, someone who would take orders.

Rage gripped her; everything blurred, the hall, the newspaper, Matthew standing there trying to look sympathetic, and Robin had to physically resist the impulse to dive into the sitting room, where her mobile sat charging on a side table, and call Strike. She had thought of doing so many times in the last four days, but then it had been to ask—to beg—him to reconsider.

Not anymore. Now she wanted to shout at him, belittle him, accuse him of base ingratitude, hypocrisy, lack of honor—

Her burning eyes met Matthew's and she saw, before he rearranged his expression, how delighted he was that Strike had put himself so dramatically in the wrong. Matthew, she could tell, had looked forward to showing her the newspaper. Her anguish was nothing compared to his ecstasy at her separation from Strike.

She turned away, heading for the kitchen, resolving that she would not shout at Matthew. If they rowed it would feel like a triumph for Strike. She refused to allow her ex-boss to sully her relationship with the man whom she had to—the man whom she *wanted* to marry in three days' time. Clumsily dumping a saucepan of spaghetti into a colander, Robin spattered herself with boiling water and swore.

"Pasta again?" said Matthew.

"Yes," said Robin coldly. "Is that a problem?"

"God, no," said Matthew, approaching her from behind and putting his arms around her. "I love you," he said into her hair.

"I love you too," said Robin mechanically.

The Land Rover was packed with everything they would need for their stay up north, for the wedding night at Swinton Park Hotel and for their honeymoon "somewhere hot," which was all that Robin knew about the destination. They set off at ten o'clock the following morning, both wearing T-shirts in the bright sunshine, and as Robin got into the car she remembered that misty morning in April when she had driven away, Matthew in hot pursuit, when she had been desperate to get away, to get to Strike.

She was a much better driver than Matthew, but when the two of them made a journey together, he always took the wheel. Matthew sang Daniel Bedingfield's "Never Gonna Leave Your Side" as he turned onto the M1. An old song, it dated from the year that they had both started university.

"Could you not sing that?" said Robin suddenly, unable to bear it any longer.

"Sorry," he said, startled. "It seemed appropriate."

"Maybe it's got happy memories for you," said Robin, turning to look out of the window, "but it hasn't for me."

Out of the corner of her eye she saw Matthew look at her, then turn back to the road. After another mile or so she wished she had not said anything.

"That doesn't mean you can't sing something else."

"That's all right," he said.

The temperature had fallen slightly by the time they reached Donington Park Services, where they stopped for a coffee. Robin left her jacket hanging over the back of her chair when she went to the bathroom. Alone, Matthew stretched, his T-shirt riding up out of his jeans to reveal a few inches of flat stomach and drawing the attention of the girl serving behind the Costa Coffee bar. Feeling good about himself and life, Matthew grinned and winked at her. She turned red, giggled and turned to her smirking fellow barista, who had seen.

The phone in Robin's jacket rang. Assuming that it was Linda trying to find out how close they were to home, Matthew reached lazily across—conscious of the girls' eyes upon him—and tugged the phone out of Robin's pocket.

It was Strike.

Matthew looked at the vibrating device as though he had inadvertently picked up a tarantula. The phone continued to ring and vibrate in his hand. He looked around: Robin was nowhere to be seen. He answered the call, then immediately cut it. Now *Corm Missed Call* was written across the screen.

The big ugly bastard wanted Robin back, Matthew was sure of it. Strike had had five long days to realize he'd never get anyone better. Maybe he'd started interviewing people for the position and nobody had come close, or maybe all of them had laughed in his face at the pitiful salary he was offering.

The phone rang again: Strike was calling back, trying to make sure that the hanging up had been deliberate rather than accidental. Matthew looked at the mobile, paralyzed with indecision. He dared not answer on Robin's behalf or tell Strike to fuck off. He knew Strike: he'd keep calling back until he spoke to Robin.

The call went to voicemail. Now Matthew realized that a recorded apology was the worst thing that could happen: Robin could listen to it again and again and finally be worn down and softened by it...

He looked up: Robin was returning from the Ladies. With her phone in his hand he stood up and pretended to be talking into it.

"It's Dad," he lied to Robin, placing a hand over the mouthpiece and praying that Strike would not call back again while he was standing in front of her. "Mine's out of battery...listen, what's your passcode? I need to look something up for the honeymoon flights—it's to tell Dad—"

She gave it to him.

"Give me a sec, I don't want you to hear anything about the honeymoon," he said and walked away from her, torn between guilt and pride in his own quick thinking.

Once safe inside the men's bathroom, he opened up her phone. Getting rid of any record of Strike's calls meant deleting her entire call history—this he did. Then he called voicemail, listened to Strike's recorded message and deleted that too. Finally, he went into the settings on Robin's phone and blocked Strike.

Breathing deeply he turned to his handsome reflection in the mirror. Strike had said on the voicemail message that if he did not hear back from her he would not call again. The wedding was in forty-eight hours' time, and the anxious, defiant Matthew was counting on Strike keeping his word.

58

Deadline

He was pumped up, on edge, pretty sure he had just done something stupid. As the Tube train rattled south, his knuckles whitened because he was clutching the hanging strap so tightly. Behind his shades, his puffy, reddened eyes squinted at the station signs.

Its shrill voice still seemed to be piercing his eardrum.

"I don't believe you. Where's the money, then, if you've got night work? No—I want to talk to you—no—you're not going out again—"

He had hit her. He shouldn't have done it, he knew that: the vision of her appalled face was taunting him now, her eyes wide with shock, her hand clamped over the cheek where his fingermarks were turning red against the white.

It was her own fucking fault. He hadn't been able to stop himself, not after the last couple of weeks, during which It had become more and more strident. After he'd come home with his eyes full of red ink he'd pretended to have had an allergic reaction, but there'd been no sympathy from the cold bitch. All It had done was carp about where he'd been and—for the first time—ask where the money was that he claimed to be earning. There hadn't been much time for theft with the boys lately, not with all his time devoted to hunting.

She'd brought home a newspaper with a news story in it about the fact that the Shacklewell Ripper might now have red ink stains around his eyes. He had burned the paper in the garden, but he couldn't stop her reading the story elsewhere. The day before yesterday, he thought he'd surprised It watching him with an odd expression on her face. It wasn't stupid, not really; was It starting to wonder? This anxiety was the last thing he needed when his attempt on The Secretary had left him almost humiliated.

There was no point going after The Secretary anymore, because she had left Strike forever. He had seen the story online, in the internet café where he sometimes whiled away an hour, just to get away from It. He took some consolation from the idea that his machete had frightened her off, that she would bear forever the long scar down her forearm that he had carved there, but that wasn't good enough.

His months and months of careful planning had all been with the intention of entangling Strike in murder, tarring him with suspicion. Firstly, embroil him in the death of the stupid little bitch who'd wanted her leg cut off, so that the police swarmed all over him and the dumb public thought he'd had something to do with it. Then, murder his Secretary. Let him try and limp away from that untainted. Let him try and be the famous detective after that.

But the bastard kept wriggling free. There had been no mention of the letters in the press, the letter he had carefully written out "from" Kelsey, and which had been supposed to turn Strike into suspect number one. Then the press had colluded with the fucker, not giving out The Secretary's name, not drawing the connection between her and Strike.

Perhaps it might be wise to stop now... except that he could not stop. He had come too far. He had never in his life put so much planning into anything as he had into the ruination of Strike. The fat, crippled bastard had already advertised for somebody to replace The Secretary, and that didn't look like a man who was about to go out of business.

One good thing, though: there was no sign of a police presence around Denmark Street anymore. Someone had called them off. They probably thought nobody was needed now that The Secretary had gone.

Perhaps he ought not to have returned to Strike's place of work, but he had hoped to see the frightened Secretary leaving with a box in her hands, or get a glimpse of a downcast, beaten Strike, but no—shortly after he'd taken up a well-concealed position to watch the street, the bastard had come striding along Charing Cross Road with a stunning-looking woman, apparently completely unperturbed.

The girl had to be a temp, because Strike had not had time to interview and hire a permanent replacement. No doubt the Big Man needed somebody to open his mail. She wore heels that would not have disgraced that little hooker, teetering along, waggling a fine arse. He liked them dark, he always had. In fact, given the choice, he'd have taken someone like her any time over The Secretary.

She hadn't had surveillance training; that much was clear. He had watched Strike's office all morning after his first glimpse of her, watched her nipping out to the post and back, nearly always on the phone, oblivious to her surroundings, so busy tossing her long hair over her shoulders that she was unable to keep eye contact with anyone for long, dropping her keys, gabbling at the top of her voice on her phone or to anyone else with whom she came into casual contact. At one o'clock he had slipped into the sandwich shop behind her and heard her making noisy plans to go to Corsica Studios the following evening.

He knew what Corsica Studios was. He knew *where* it was. Excitement ripped through him: he had to turn his back on her, pretending to look out of the window, because he thought the expression on his face would give it away to all of them...If he did her while she was still working for Strike, he'd have fulfilled his plan: Strike would be connected to two hacked-up women and nobody, police or public, would ever trust him again.

This would be so much easier too. The Secretary had been a fucking nightmare to pick off, always alert and streetwise, going home by crowded, well-lit paths every evening to her pretty boyfriend, but The Temp was offering herself up on a plate. After telling the whole sandwich shop where she would be meeting her mates, she had strutted back to work on her Perspex heels, dropping Strike's sandwiches once on the way. He noticed that there was no wedding or engagement ring on her finger as she bent to pick them up. He had been hard pressed to suppress his jubilation as he peeled away, formulating his plan.

If only he hadn't slapped It, he'd be feeling good now, excited, elated. The slap hadn't been an auspicious start to the evening. No wonder he felt jumpy. There had been no time to stay and calm her down, turn her sweet: he had simply walked out, determined to get to The Temp, but he still felt jumpy... What if It called the police?

She wouldn't. It had only been a slap. She loved him, she told him so all the time. When they loved you, they let you get away with fucking murder...

He experienced a tickling sensation at the back of his neck and looked around with the wild idea that he would see Strike looking at him from the corner of the carriage, but nobody remotely resembling that fat bastard was there, only several ill-kempt men grouped together. One of them, who had a scarred face and a gold tooth, was indeed watching him, but as he squinted back through his shades the man ceased his scrutiny and returned to fiddling with his mobile...

Perhaps he should call It when he got off the Tube, before heading for Corsica Studios, and tell It he loved her.

59

With threats of gas and rose motif.

Blue Öyster Cult, "Before the Kiss"

Strike was standing in shadow, his mobile in his hand, waiting. The deep pocket of his secondhand jacket, which was far too heavy in the warmth of this June evening, bulged and sagged with the weight of an object he was keen to conceal. What he planned would be best accomplished under cover of darkness, but the sun was taking its time to sink behind the ill-assorted rooftops visible from his hiding place.

He knew he ought to be concentrating only upon the dangerous business of the night, but his thoughts kept slinking back to Robin. She had not returned his call. He had set a mental deadline for himself: if she doesn't ring by the end of this evening, she's never calling. At twelve o'clock the following day she would be getting married to Matthew in Yorkshire, and Strike was sure that constituted a fatal cut-off point. If they did not speak before that ring landed on her finger, he thought that they were unlikely ever to speak again. If anything in the world had been calculated to make him recognize what he had lost, it had been the truculent, noisy presence of the woman with whom he had shared his office for the last few days, staggeringly good-looking though she was.

To the west, the sky over the rooftops blazed with colors as bright as a parakeet's wing: scarlet, orange, even a faint trace of green.

Behind this flamboyant show came a pale wash of violet faintly strewn with stars. Almost time to move.

As though Shanker had heard his thought, Strike's mobile vibrated and he looked to see a message:

Pint tomorrow?

They had agreed on a code. If all of this came to court, which Strike thought overwhelmingly likely, his intention was to keep Shanker well away from the witness box. There must be no incriminating messages between them tonight. "Pint tomorrow?" meant "he's in the club."

Strike slid the mobile back into his pocket and emerged from his hiding place, crossing the dark car park that lay beneath the deserted flat of Donald Laing. The Strata building looked down upon him as he walked, vast and black, its jagged windows reflecting the last traces of bloody light.

Fine netting had been stretched over the front of the balconies of Wollaston Close to prevent birds landing on them and flying in through open doors and windows. Strike moved around to the side entrance, which he had earlier wedged open after a group of teenage girls had left it. Nobody had tampered with the arrangement. People assumed that somebody needed their hands free and feared triggering their wrath. An angry neighbor could be quite as dangerous as an intruder round here, and you had to live with them afterwards.

Halfway up the stairs, Strike stripped off his jacket to reveal a fluorescent one. Carrying the first so that it concealed the canister of propane inside, he proceeded on his way, emerging onto the balcony of Laing's flat.

Lights shone from the homes sharing the balcony. Laing's neighbors had opened their windows on this warm summer evening, so that their voices and the sounds of their TVs floated out into the night. Strike walked quietly past towards the dark, empty flat at the end. Outside the door he had so often watched from the car park, he shifted the gas canister wrapped in his jacket into the crook of his left arm and withdrew from his pocket firstly a pair of latex gloves, which he put on, then a mismatched assortment of tools, some of which belonged to Strike himself, but many of which had been lent for the occasion by Shanker. These included a mortice skeleton key, two sets of jigglers and assorted comb picks.

As Strike set to work on the two locks on Laing's front door a female, American voice floated out into the night through the neighboring window.

"There's the law and there's what's right. I'm gonna do what's right."

"What wouldn't I give to fuck Jessica Alba?" asked a stoned male voice, to laughter and agreement from what sounded like two other men.

"Come on, you bastard," breathed Strike, fighting with the lower of the two locks and keeping a tight grip on the concealed propane canister. "Move... *move*..."

The lock turned with a loud click. He pushed the door open.

As he had expected, the place smelled bad. Strike could make out very little in what looked like a dilapidated and unfurnished room. He needed to close the curtains before turning on the lights. Turning left, he immediately knocked into what felt like a box. Something heavy fell off the top and landed with a crash on the floor.

Fuck.

"Oi!" shouted a voice audible through the flimsy dividing wall. "That you, Donnie?"

Strike hastened back to the door, felt frantically up and down the wall beside the doorjamb and found the light switch. Flooded suddenly with light, the room proved to contain nothing except an old, stained double mattress and an orange box on which an iPod dock had clearly been standing, because it now lay on the ground where it had fallen.

"Donnie?" said the voice, now coming from the balcony outside.

Strike pulled out the propane canister, discharged it and shoved it underneath the orange box. Footsteps from the balcony outside were followed by a knock on the door. Strike opened it.

A spotty, greasy-haired man looked hazily at him. He appeared extremely stoned and was holding a can of John Smith's.

"Jesus," he said blearily, sniffing. "'S'that fucking smell?"

"Gas," said Strike in his fluorescent jacket, stern representative of the National Grid. "We've had a report from upstairs. Looks like this is where it's coming from."

"Bloody hell," said the neighbor, looking sick. "Not going to blow up, are we?"

"That's what I'm here to find out," Strike said sententiously. "You haven't got any naked flames next door? Not smoking, are you?"

"I'll go make sure," said the neighbor, looking suddenly terrified.

"All right. I might be in to check your place when I've finished here," said Strike. "I'm waiting for back-up."

He regretted that phrase as soon as it had escaped him, but his new acquaintance did not seem to find such language odd from a gas man. As he turned away, Strike asked:

"Owner's name's Donnie, is it?"

"Donnie Laing," said the jittery neighbor, clearly desperate to go and hide his stash and extinguish all naked flames. "He owes me forty quid."

"Ah," said Strike. "Can't help with that."

The man scuttled off and Strike closed the door thanking his lucky stars that he'd had the forethought to provide himself with a cover. All he needed was for the police to be tipped off now, before he could prove anything…

He lifted up the orange box, shut off the hissing propane and then replaced the iPod in its dock on top of the box. About to move deeper into the flat, he had a sudden thought and turned back to the iPod. One delicate poke of his latex-covered forefinger and the tiny screen lit up. "Hot Rails to Hell" by—as Strike knew only too well—Blue Öyster Cult.

60

Vengeance (The Pact)

The club was heaving with people. It had been constructed in two railway arches, just like those opposite his flat, and had a subterranean feel enhanced by the curved corrugated iron roof. A projector was throwing psychedelic lights across the ridges of metal. The music was deafening.

They had not been overly keen on letting him in. He'd had a bit of attitude from the bouncers: he had experienced a fleeting fear that they would pat him down, in his jacket with the knives concealed inside it.

He looked older than anybody else he could see and he resented it. That was what the psoriatic arthritis had done to him, leaving him pockmarked and blown up with steroids. His muscle had run to fat since his boxing days; he had pulled with ease back in Cyprus, but not anymore. He knew he'd have no chance with any of these hundreds of giddy little bitches crammed together beneath the glitter ball. Hardly any of them were dressed the way he expected of a club. Many of them were in jeans and T-shirts, like a bunch of lesbians.

Where was Strike's temp, with her gorgeous arse and her delicious distractibility? There weren't that many tall black women here; she ought to be easy to spot, yet he had combed bar and dance floor and seen no sign of her. It had seemed like providence, her mentioning this club so very close to his flat; he had thought it meant a return of his godlike status, the universe arranging itself once more for his benefit, but that feeling of invincibility had been fleeting and almost entirely dispelled by the argument with It.

The music thumped inside his head. He would rather have been back at home, listening to Blue Öyster Cult, masturbating over his relics, but he had *heard* her planning to be here...fuck, it was so crowded that he might be able to press up against her and stab her without anyone noticing or hearing her scream...Where was the bitch?

The tosser in the Wild Flag T-shirt had jostled him so many times he yearned to give him a good kicking. Instead he elbowed his way out of the bar to look at the dance floor again.

The shifting lights panned across a swaying carpet of arms and sweaty faces. A glint of gold—a scarred and sneering mouth—

He cleaved his way through onlookers, not caring how many little tarts he knocked aside.

That scarred guy had been on the Tube. He looked back. The man appeared to have lost someone; he was standing on tiptoe looking all around.

There was something wrong. He could feel it. Something fishy. Bending his knees slightly, the better to mingle with the crowd, he forced his way towards a fire exit.

"Sorry, mate, I need you to use the—"

"Fuck off."

He was out of it before anyone could stop him, forcing the bar across the fire door, plunging out into the night. He jogged along the exterior wall and around a corner where, alone, he breathed deeply, considering his options.

You're safe, he told himself. *You're safe. No one's got anything on you.*

But was it true?

Of all the clubs she could have mentioned, she had chosen the one two minutes from his house. What if that had not been a gift from the gods but something entirely different? What if someone was trying to set him up?

No. It couldn't be. Strike had sent the pigs to him and they hadn't been interested. He was safe for sure. There was nothing to connect him to any of them...

Except that that guy with the scarred face had been on the Tube from Finchley. The implications of that temporarily jammed his thought processes. If somebody was following not Donald Laing but a completely different man, he was totally fucked…

He began to walk, every now and then breaking into a short run. The crutches that were so useful a prop were no longer necessary except for gaining the sympathy of gullible women, fooling the disability office and, of course, maintaining his cover as a man too sick and ill to go looking for little Kelsey Platt. His arthritis had burned itself out years back, though it had proved a pleasant little earner and kept the flat in Wollaston Close ticking over…

Hurrying across the car park, he looked up at his flat. The curtains were closed. He could have sworn he had left them open.

61

And now the time has come at last
To crush the motif of the rose.

Blue Öyster Cult, "Before the Kiss"

The bulb was out in the only bedroom. Strike turned on the small torch he had brought with him and advanced slowly towards the only piece of furniture, a cheap pine wardrobe. The door creaked as he opened it.

The interior was plastered with articles from the newspapers about the Shacklewell Ripper. Taped above all of them was a picture that had been printed on a piece of A4 paper, possibly from the internet. Strike's young mother, naked, arms over her head, her long cloud of dark hair not quite covering her breasts proudly displayed, an arch of curly script clearly visible over the dark triangle of pubic hair: *Mistress of the Salmon Salt.*

He looked down at the floor of the wardrobe where a pile of hardcore pornography sat beside a black bin bag. Putting the torch under his arm, Strike opened the latter with his latex-gloved hands. Inside was a small selection of women's underclothing, some of it stiff with old brown blood. At the very bottom of the bag his fingers closed on a fine chain and a hoop earring. A heart-shaped harp charm glinted in the light of his torch. There was a trace of dry blood on the hoop.

Strike replaced everything in the black bin bag, closed the wardrobe door and continued to the kitchenette, which was clearly the source of the rotting smell that pervaded the entire place.

Somebody had turned up the TV next door. An echoing tirade of gunshots sounded through the thin wall. Strike heard faint, stoned laughter.

Beside the kettle sat a jar of instant coffee, a bottle of Bell's, a magnifying mirror and a razor. The oven was thick with grease and dust, and looked as though it had not been used for a long time. The fridge door had been wiped down with a dirty cloth that had left behind it sweeping arcs of a pinkish residue. Strike had just reached for the handle when his mobile vibrated in his pocket.

Shanker was calling him. They had agreed not to phone each other, but only to text.

"Fucking hell, Shanker," said Strike, raising the mobile to his ear. "I thought I said—"

He heard the breathing behind him a bare second before a machete came swinging through the air at his neck. Strike dived sideways, the mobile flying out of his hand, and slipped on the dirty floor. As he fell, the slashing blade sliced into his ear. The hulking shadow raised the machete again to attack Strike as he landed on the floor; Strike kicked out at its crotch and the killer grunted in pain, backed off a couple of paces, then raised the machete once more.

Scrambling to his knees, Strike punched his assailant hard in the balls. The machete slid out of Laing's fingers and fell onto Strike's back, causing him to shout out in pain even as he put his arms around Laing's knees and toppled him. Laing's head collided with the cooker door but his thick fingers were scrabbling for Strike's throat. Strike tried to land a punch but was pinned down by Laing's considerable weight. The man's large, powerful hands were closing on his windpipe. With a gigantic effort Strike mustered enough force to headbutt Laing, whose skull again clanged off the oven door—

They rolled over, Strike now on top. He tried to punch Laing in the face but the other's reactions were as quick as they had been in the ring: one hand deflected the blow and his other was under Strike's chin, forcing his face upwards—Strike swung again, unable to see where he was aiming, hit bone and heard it crack—

Then Laing's large fist came out of nowhere, bang into the middle of Strike's face, and he felt his nose shatter; blood spurted everywhere as he rocked backwards with the force of the punch, his eyes watering so that everything blurred: groaning and panting, Laing threw him off—from nowhere, like a conjuror, he produced a carving knife—

Half blinded, blood pouring into his mouth, Strike saw it glimmer in the moonlight and kicked out with his prosthetic leg—there was a muffled chink of metal on metal as the knife hit the steel rod of his ankle and was raised again—

"*No, you don't, you fucker!*"

Shanker had Laing in a headlock from behind. Ill-advisedly, Strike grabbed for the carving knife and got his palm sliced open. Shanker and Laing were wrestling, the Scot by far the larger of the two and rapidly getting the better of it. Strike took another powerful kick at the carving knife with his prosthetic foot and this time knocked it clean out of Laing's hand. Now he could help Shanker wrestle him to the ground.

"Give it up or I'll fuckin' knife ya!" bellowed Shanker, arms around Laing's neck as the Scot writhed and swore, his heavy fists still clenched, his broken jaw sagging. "You ain't the only one with a fucking blade, you fat piece of shit!"

Strike tugged out the handcuffs that were the most expensive piece of equipment he had taken away with him from the SIB. It took the combined force of both Strike and Shanker to force Laing into a position where he could be cuffed, securing the thick wrists behind his back while Laing struggled and swore nonstop.

Freed of the necessity to hold Laing down, Shanker kicked him so hard in the diaphragm that the killer emitted a long faint wheeze and was rendered temporarily speechless.

"You all right, Bunsen? Bunsen, where'd he get you?"

Strike had slumped back against the oven. The cut to his ear was bleeding copiously, as was his slashed right palm, but his rapidly swelling nose troubled him most, because the blood pouring out of it into his mouth was making it difficult to breathe.

"There y'go, Bunsen," said Shanker, returning from a brief search of the small flat with a roll of toilet paper.

"Cheers," said Strike thickly. He stuffed his nostrils with as much paper as they would hold, then looked down at Laing. "Nice to see you again, Ray."

The still-winded Laing said nothing. His bald pate was shining faintly in the moonlight that had illuminated his knife.

"Fort you said 'is name was Donald?" asked Shanker curiously as Laing shifted on the ground. Shanker kicked him in the stomach again.

"It is," said Strike, "and stop bloody kicking him; if you rupture anything I'll have to answer for it in court."

"So why you callin' 'im—?"

"Because," said Strike, "—and don't touch anything, either, Shanker, I don't want your fingerprints in here—because Donnie's been using a borrowed identity. When he's not here," Strike said, approaching the fridge and putting his left hand, with its still-intact latex glove, on the handle, "he's heroic retired firefighter Ray Williams, who lives in Finchley with Hazel Furley."

Strike pulled open the fridge door and, still using his left hand, opened the freezer compartment.

Kelsey Platt's breasts lay inside, dried up now like figs, yellow and leathery. Beside them lay Lila Monkton's fingers, the nails varnished purple, Laing's teeth marks imprinted deeply upon them. At the back lay a pair of severed ears from which little plastic ice-cream cones still hung, and a mangled piece of flesh in which nostrils were still distinguishable.

"Holy shit," said Shanker, who had also bent over to look, from behind him. "Holy shit, Bunsen, they're bits—"

Strike closed both icebox and fridge door and turned to look at his captive.

Laing lay quiet now. Strike was sure that he was already using that devious fox-like brain to see how he could work this desperate situation to his advantage, how he would be able to argue that Strike had framed him, planted or contaminated evidence.

"Should've recognized you, shouldn't I, Donnie?" said Strike, wrapping his right hand in toilet paper to stem the bleeding. Now, by the dim moonlight falling through the grubby window, Strike could just make out the features of Laing beneath the stones of extra weight that steroids and a lack of regular exercise had packed onto his once thickly muscled frame. His fatness, his dry, lined skin, the beard he had doubtless grown to hide his pockmarks, the carefully shaven head and the shuffling walk he had affected added up to a man at least ten years older than his real age. "Should've recognized you the moment you opened the front door to me at Hazel's," Strike said. "But you kept your face covered, dabbing away at your fucking tears, didn't you? What had you done, rubbed something in them to make them swell up?"

Strike offered his pack to Shanker before lighting up.

"The Geordie accent was a bit overdone, now I think about it. You'll have picked that up in Gateshead, did you? He's always been a good mimic, our Donnie," he told Shanker. "You should have heard his Corporal Oakley. Life and soul, Donnie was, apparently."

Shanker was staring from Strike to Laing, apparently fascinated. Strike continued to smoke, looking down at Laing. His nose was stinging and throbbing so badly it was making his own eyes water. He wanted to hear the killer speak, once, before he rang the police.

"Beat up and robbed a demented old lady in Corby, didn't you, Donnie? Poor old Mrs. Williams. You took her son's award for bravery and I bet you got a good bit of old documentation of his as well. You knew he'd gone abroad. It's not too hard to steal someone's identity if you've got a bit of ID to start with. Easy to parlay that into enough current identification to hoodwink a lonely woman and a careless policeman or two."

Laing lay silent on the dirty floor, but Strike could almost feel the frantic workings of his filthy, desperate mind.

"I found Accutane in the house," Strike told Shanker. "It's a drug for acne, but it's for psoriatic arthritis too. I should've known then. He kept it hidden in Kelsey's room. Ray Williams didn't have arthritis.

"I bet you had lots of little secrets together, didn't you, Donnie, you and Kelsey? Winding her up about me, getting her exactly where you wanted her? Taking her for motorbike rides to lurk near my office...pretending to post letters for her...bringing her my fake notes..."

"You sick bastard," said the disgusted Shanker. He leaned over Laing with his cigarette tip close to Laing's face, clearly yearning to hurt him.

"You're not burning him either, Shanker," said Strike, pulling out his mobile. "You'd better get out of here, I'm going to call the cops."

He rang 999 and gave the address. His story would be that he had followed Laing to the club and back to his flat, that there had been an argument and that Laing had attacked him. Nobody needed to know that Shanker had been involved, nor that Strike had picked Laing's locks. Of course, the stoned neighbor might talk, but Strike thought it likely that the young man might prefer to stay well out of it rather than have his sobriety and drug history assessed in a court of law.

"Take all this and get rid of it," Strike told Shanker, peeling off the fluorescent jacket and handing it to him. "And the gas canister through there."

"Right y'are, Bunsen. Sure you're gonna be all right with him?" Shanker added, eyes on Strike's broken nose, his bleeding ear and hand.

"Yeah, course I will," said Strike, vaguely touched.

He heard Shanker picking up the metal canister in the next room and, shortly afterwards, saw him passing the kitchen window on the balcony outside.

"SHANKER!"

His old friend was back in the kitchen so fast that Strike knew he must have sprinted; the heavy gas canister was raised, but Laing still lay handcuffed and quiescent on the floor, and Strike stood smoking beside the cooker.

"Fuckin' 'ell, Bunsen, I fort 'e'd jumped you!"

"Shanker, could you get hold of a car and drive me somewhere tomorrow morning? I'll give you—"

Strike looked down at his bare wrist. He had sold his watch yesterday for the cash that had paid for Shanker's help tonight. What else did he have to flog?

"Listen, Shanker, you know I'm going to make money out of this one. Give me a few months and I'll have clients queuing up."

"'S'all right, Bunsen," said Shanker, after brief consideration. "You can owe me."

"Seriously?"

"Yeah," said Shanker, turning to go. "Gimme a bell when you're ready to leave. I'll go get us a car."

"Don't nick one!" Strike called after him.

Mere seconds after Shanker had passed the window for the second time, Strike heard the distant sound of a police siren.

"Here they come, Donnie," he said.

It was then that Donald Laing spoke in his true voice to Strike, for the first and last time.

"Your mother," he said, in a deep Borders accent, "was a fucking whore."

Strike laughed.

"Maybe so," he said, bleeding and smoking in the darkness as the sirens grew louder, "but she loved me, Donnie. I heard yours didn't give a shit about you, little policeman's bastard that you were."

Laing began to thrash around, trying fruitlessly to free himself, but he merely spun on his side, arms still pinned behind his back.

62

A redcap, a redcap, before the kiss...

Blue Öyster Cult, "Before the Kiss"

Strike did not meet Carver that night. He suspected the man would have shot off his own kneecaps rather than face Strike now. A pair of CID officers he had never met interrogated him in a side room in Accident and Emergency, between the various medical procedures his injuries warranted. His ear had been stitched back together, his slashed palm bandaged, a dressing had been applied to his back, which the falling machete had nicked, and for the third time in his life his nose had been painfully manipulated back into approximate symmetry. At convenient intervals, Strike had given the police a lucid exposition of the line of reasoning that had led him to Laing. He was careful to tell them that he had phoned that information through to a subordinate of Carver's two weeks previously and had also tried to tell Carver directly the last time they had spoken.

"Why aren't you writing that down?" he asked the officers who sat in silence, staring at him. The younger man made a cursory note.

"I also," Strike continued, "wrote a letter and sent it to DI Carver, recorded delivery. He should have got it yesterday."

"You sent it recorded delivery?" repeated the older of the two officers, a sad-eyed man with a mustache.

"That's right," said Strike. "Thought I'd make sure it was good and hard to lose."

The policeman made a far more detailed note.

Strike's story was that, suspecting the police weren't convinced by his suspicions about Laing, he had never stopped watching him. He had followed Laing to the nightclub, worried about whether he was going to try to pick up a woman, then tailed him to his flat where he had decided to confront him. About Alyssa, who had played the part of his temp with such aplomb, and Shanker, whose enthusiastic intervention had certainly spared Strike several more stab wounds, he said nothing.

"The clincher," Strike told the officers, "is going to be finding this guy Ritchie, sometimes known as Dickie, whose motorbike Laing's been borrowing. Hazel will be able to tell you all about him. He's been giving Laing alibis all over the shop. I reckon he's a petty criminal himself and probably thought he was just helping Laing cheat on Hazel or do a bit of benefit fraud. He doesn't sound like a smart guy. I think he'll crack pretty quickly once he realizes it was murder."

The doctors and police finally decided that they needed nothing more from Strike at five o'clock in the morning. He refused the policemen's offer of a lift, which he suspected was made partly to keep tabs on him as long as they could.

"We wouldn't want this to get out before we've had a chance to speak to the families," said the younger officer, whose white-blond hair stood out in the drab dawn on the forecourt where the three men were taking leave of one another.

"I'm not going to the press," said Strike, yawning widely as he felt in his pockets for his remaining cigarettes. "I've got other stuff to do today."

He had begun to walk away when a thought occurred to him.

"What was the church connection? Brockbank—what made Carver think it was him?"

"Oh," said the mustached officer. He did not seem particularly eager to share the information. "There was a youth worker who'd transferred from Finchley to Brixton . . . didn't lead anywhere, but," he added, with an air of faint defiance, "we've got him. Brockbank. Got a tip-off from a homeless hostel yesterday."

"Nice one," said Strike. "Press love a pedophile. I'd lead with that when you talk to them."

Neither officer smiled. Strike bade them good morning and left, wondering whether he had any money on him for a taxi, smoking left-handed because the local anesthetic was wearing off in his right hand, his broken nose stinging in the cool morning air.

"Fuckin' Yorkshire?" Shanker said over the phone when he called to tell Strike he had a car and the detective had told him where he wanted to go. "*Yorkshire?*"

"Masham," Strike had replied. "Look, I've already told you: I'll pay you anything you like when I get the money. It's a wedding and I don't want to miss it. Time's going to be tight as it is—anything you like, Shanker, you've got my word on it, and I'll pay you when I can."

" 'Oo's gettin' married?"

"Robin," said Strike.

"Ah," said Shanker. He had sounded pleased. "Yeah, well, in that case, Bunsen, I'll drive ya. I toldja you shouldn't've—"

"—yeah—"

"—Alyssa toldja—"

"Yeah, she did, bloody loudly too."

Strike had a strong suspicion that Shanker was now sleeping with Alyssa. He could think of few other explanations for the speed with which he had suggested her when Strike had explained the need for a woman to play a safe but essential part in the entrapment of Donald Laing. She had demanded a hundred pounds for doing the job and had assured Strike that it would have been considerably more had she not considered herself deep in his partner's debt.

"Shanker, we can talk about all this on the way. I need food and a shower. We're going to be bloody lucky to make it."

So here they were, speeding north in the Mercedes Shanker had borrowed; from where, Strike did not inquire. The detective, who had had barely any sleep in the previous couple of nights, dozed for the first sixty miles, waking with a snort only when his mobile buzzed in his suit pocket.

"Strike," he said sleepily.

"Bloody good job, mate," said Wardle.

His tone did not match his words. After all, Wardle had been in charge of the investigation when Ray Williams had been cleared of all suspicion in relation to Kelsey's death.

"Cheers," said Strike. "You realize you're now the only copper in London still prepared to talk to me."

"Ah well," said Wardle, rallying slightly. "Quality over quantity. I thought you'd like to know: they've already found Richard and he's sung like a canary."

"Richard..." mumbled Strike.

He felt as though his exhausted brain had been purged of the details that had obsessed him for months. Trees poured soothingly past the passenger window in a rush of summer greenery. He felt as though he could sleep for days.

"Ritchie—Dickie—motorbike," said Wardle.

"Oh yeah," said Strike, absentmindedly scratching his stitched ear, then swearing. "Shit, that hurt—sorry—he's talked already, has he?"

"He's not what you'd call a bright boy," said Wardle. "We found a bunch of stolen gear at his place as well."

"I thought that might be how Donnie was funding himself. He's always been a handy thief."

"There was a little gang of them. Nothing major, just a lot of petty pilfering. Ritchie was the only one who knew Laing had a double identity; he thought he was working a benefits scam. Laing asked three of them to back him up and pretend their camping trip to Shoreham-by-Sea had been the weekend he killed Kelsey. Apparently he told them he had another bird somewhere and Hazel wasn't to know."

"He could always get people on side, Laing," said Strike, remembering the investigating officer in Cyprus who had been so ready to clear him of rape.

"How did you realize they weren't there that weekend?" asked Wardle curiously. "They had photos and everything...how did you know they weren't on the stag the weekend she died?"

"Oh," said Strike. "Sea holly."

"What?"

"Sea holly," repeated Strike. "Sea holly isn't in bloom in April. Summer and autumn—I spent half my childhood in Cornwall. The picture of Laing and Ritchie on the beach...there was sea holly. I should've realized then...but I kept getting sidetracked."

After Wardle had hung up, Strike stared through the windscreen at the passing fields and trees, thinking back over the past three months. He doubted that Laing had ever known about Brittany Brockbank, but he had probably dug around enough to know the story of Whittaker's trial, the quoting of "Mistress of the Salmon Salt" from the dock. Strike felt as though Laing had laid drag trails for him, without any idea how successful they would be.

Shanker turned on the radio. Strike, who would have preferred to go back to sleep, did not complain, but wound down the window and smoked out of it. In the steadily brightening sunshine he realized that the Italian suit he had pulled on automatically was flecked with small amounts of gravy and red wine. He rubbed off the worst of the dried-on stains, until reminded suddenly of something else.

"Oh, fuck."

"Whassamatter?"

"I forgot to ditch someone."

Shanker began to laugh. Strike smiled ruefully, which was painful. His whole face ached.

"Are we tryina stop this wedding, Bunsen?"

"Course not," said Strike, pulling out another cigarette. "I was invited. I'm a friend. A guest."

"You sacked 'er," said Shanker. "Which ain't a mark of friendship where I come from."

Strike refrained from pointing out that Shanker knew hardly anyone who had ever had a job.

"She's like your mum," said Shanker, after a long silence.

"Who is?"

"Your Robin. Kind. Wanted to save that kid."

Strike found it difficult to defend a refusal to save a child to a man who had been rescued, bleeding, from the gutter at the age of sixteen.

"Well, I'm going to try and get her back, aren't I? But the next time she calls you—if she calls you—"

"Yeah, yeah, I'll tell ya, Bunsen."

The wing mirror showed Strike a face that might have belonged to the victim of a car crash. His nose was enormous and purple and his left ear looked black. By daylight he saw that his hasty attempt to shave using his left hand had not been entirely successful. As he imagined himself sliding into the back of the church he realized how conspicuous he was going to be, what a scene it would make if Robin decided she did not want him there. He didn't want to spoil her day. At the first request to leave, he vowed inwardly, he would do so.

"BUNSEN!" shouted Shanker excitedly, making Strike jump. Shanker turned up the radio.

"*... arrest has been made in the case of the Shacklewell Ripper. After a thorough search of a flat in Wollaston Close, London, police have charged thirty-four-year-old Donald Laing with the murders of Kelsey Platt, Heather Smart, Martina Rossi and Sadie Roach, the attempted murder of Lila Monkton and a serious assault on a sixth, unnamed woman...*"

"They didn't mention you!" said Shanker when the report ended. He sounded disappointed.

"They wouldn't," said Strike, fighting an uncharacteristic nervousness. He had just seen the first sign to Masham. "But they will. Good thing too: I need the publicity if I'm gonna get my business back off the ground."

He automatically checked his wrist, forgetting that there was no watch there, and instead consulted the dashboard clock.

"Put your foot down, Shanker. We're going to miss the start as it is."

Strike became increasingly anxious as they approached their destination. The service had been scheduled to start twenty minutes before they finally tore up the hill to Masham, Strike checking his phone for the location of the church.

"It's over there," he said, pointing frantically to the opposite side of the broadest market square he had ever seen, which was packed with people at food stalls. As Shanker drove none too slowly around the periphery of the market several bystanders scowled and one man in a flat cloth cap shook his fist at the scarred man driving so dangerously in the sedate heart of Masham.

"Park here, anywhere here!" said Strike, spotting two dark blue Bentleys adorned with white ribbons parked at the far end of the square, the chauffeurs talking with their hats off in the sunshine. They looked around as Shanker braked. Strike threw off his seatbelt; he could see the church spire over the treetops now. He felt almost sick, due, no doubt, to the forty cigarettes he must have smoked overnight, the lack of sleep and Shanker's driving.

Strike had hurried several steps away from the car before dashing back to his friend.

"Wait for me. I might not be staying."

He hurried away again past the staring chauffeurs, nervously straightened his tie, then remembered the state of his face and suit and wondered why he bothered.

Through the gates and into the deserted churchyard Strike limped. The impressive church reminded him of St. Dionysius in Market Harborough, back when he and Robin had been friends. The hush over the sleepy, sunlit graveyard felt ominous. He passed a strange, almost pagan-looking column covered in carvings to his right as he approached the heavy oak doors.

Grasping the handle with his left hand he paused for a second.

"Fuck it," he breathed to himself, and opened it as quietly as he could.

The smell of roses met him: white roses of Yorkshire blooming in tall stands and hanging in bunches at the ends of the packed queues. A thicket of brightly colored hats stretched away towards the altar. Hardly anybody looked around at Strike as he shuffled inside, although those that did stared. He edged along the rear wall, staring at the far end of the aisle.

Robin was wearing a coronet of white roses in her long, wavy hair. He could not see her face. She was not wearing her cast. Even at this distance, he could see the long, purple scar running down the back of her forearm.

"Do you," came a ringing voice from an unseen vicar, "Robin Venetia Ellacott, take this man, Matthew John Cunliffe, to be your lawful wedded husband, to have and to hold, from this day forward—"

Exhausted, tense, his gaze fixed on Robin, Strike had not realized how near he was to the flower arrangement that stood on a fine, tulip-like bronze stand.

"—for better, for worse, for richer, for poorer, in sickness and in health, until death—"

"Oh shit," said Strike.

The arrangement he had hit toppled as though in slow motion and fell with a deafening clang to the floor. Congregation and couple turned and looked back.

"I'm—Christ, I'm sorry," said Strike hopelessly.

Somewhere in the middle of the congregation a man laughed. Most returned their gazes to the altar at once, but a few guests continued to glare at Strike before remembering themselves.

"—do you part," said the vicar with saintly tolerance.

The beautiful bride, who had not once smiled in the entire service, was suddenly beaming.

"I do," said Robin in a ringing voice, looking straight into the eyes, not of her stony-faced new husband, but of the battered and bloodied man who had just sent her flowers crashing to the floor.

ACKNOWLEDGMENTS

I can't remember ever enjoying writing a novel more than *Career of Evil.* This is odd, not only on account of the grisly subject matter, but also because I've rarely been busier than over the last twelve months and have had to keep switching between projects, which is not my favorite way to work. Nevertheless, Robert Galbraith has always felt like my own private playground, and he didn't let me down on this occasion.

I have to thank my usual team for ensuring that my once-secret identity remains such fun: my peerless editor, David Shelley, who has now been godfather to four of my novels and who makes the editing process so rewarding; my wonderful agent and friend, Neil Blair, who has been Robert's stalwart supporter from the first; Deeby and SOBE, who have allowed me to pick their military brains clean; the Back Door Man, for reasons best left undisclosed; Amanda Donaldson, Fiona Shapcott, Angela Milne, Christine Collingwood, Simon Brown, Kaisa Tiensu and Danni Cameron, without whose hard work I would not have any time left over to do my own; and the dream team of Mark Hutchinson, Nicky Stonehill and Rebecca Salt, without whom I would, frankly, be a wreck.

Particular thanks are due to MP, who enabled me to make a fascinating visit to 35 Section SIB (UK) RMP in Edinburgh Castle. Thanks are also due to the two policewomen who didn't arrest me for taking photographs of the perimeter of a nuclear facility in Barrow-in-Furness.

To all the lyricists who have worked with and for Blue Öyster

Cult, thank you for writing such great songs and for letting me use some of your words in this novel.

To my children, Decca, Davy and Kenz: I love you beyond words and I want to thank you for being so understanding about the times when the writing bug is particularly active.

Lastly and mostly: thank you, Neil. Nobody helped more when it came to this book.

CREDITS

"Career of Evil" (page ix) Words by Patti Smith. Music by Patti Smith and Albert Bouchard © 1974, Reproduced by permission of Sony/ATV Tunes LLC, London W1F 9LD. **"This Ain't the Summer of Love"** (pages 1, 64, and 305) Words and Music by Albert Bouchard, Murray Krugman and Donald Waller © 1975, Reproduced by permission of Sony/ATV Music Publishing (UK) Ltd, Sony/ATV Tunes LLC, London W1F 9LD and Peermusic (UK) Ltd. **"Madness to the Method"** (pages 5, 192, and 389) Words and Music by D. Trismen and Donald Roeser © 1985, Reproduced by permission of Sony/ATV Music Publishing (UK) Ltd, Sony/ATV Tunes LLC, London W1F 9LD. **"The Marshall Plan"** (page 9) Words and Music by Albert Bouchard, Joseph Bouchard, Eric Bloom, Allen Lainer and Donald Roeser © 1980, Reproduced by permission of Sony/ATV Music Publishing (UK) Ltd, Sony/ATV Tunes LLC, London W1F 9LD. **"Mistress of the Salmon Salt (Quicklime Girl)"** (pages 14–15 and 70) Words and Music by Albert Bouchard and Samuel Pearlman © 1973, Reproduced by permission of Sony/ATV Tunes LLC, London W1F 9LD. **"Astronomy"** (page 18) Words and Music by Albert Bouchard, Joseph Bouchard and Samuel Pearlman © 1974, Reproduced by permission of Sony/ATV Music Publishing (UK) Ltd, Sony/ATV Tunes LLC, London W1F 9LD. **"The Revenge of Vera Gemini"** (page 27) Words by Patti Smith. Music by Albert Bouchard and Patti Smith © 1976, Reproduced by permission of Sony/ATV Music Publishing (UK) Ltd, Sony/ATV Tunes LLC,

London W1F 9LD. **"Flaming Telepaths"** (page 31) Words and Music by Albert Bouchard, Eric Bloom, Samuel Pearlman and Donald Roeser © 1974, Reproduced by permission of Sony/ATV Music Publishing (UK) Ltd, Sony/ATV Tunes LLC, London W1F 9LD. **"Good to Feel Hungry"** (page 39) (Eric Bloom, Danny Miranda, Donald B. Roeser, Bobby Rondinelli, John P. Shirley). Reproduced by permission of Six Pound Dog Music and Triceratops Music. **"Lonely Teardrops"** (page 42) Words and Music by Allen Lanier © 1980, Reproduced by permission of Sony/ATV Music Publishing (UK) Ltd, Sony/ATV Tunes LLC, London W1F 9LD. **"One Step Ahead of the Devil"** (page 48) (Eric Bloom, Danny Miranda, Donald B. Roeser, Bobby Rondinelli, John P. Shirley). Reproduced by permission of Six Pound Dog Music and Triceratops Music. **"Shadow of California"** (page 50) Words and Music by Samuel Pearlman and Donald Roeser © 1983, Reproduced by permission of Sony/ATV Music Publishing (UK) Ltd/ Sony/ATV Tunes LLC, London W1F 9LD. **"O.D.'d On Life Itself"** (page 72) Words and Music by Albert Bouchard, Eric Bloom, Samuel Pearlman and Donald Roeser © 1973, Reproduced by permission of Sony/ATV Music Publishing (UK) Ltd, Sony/ATV Tunes LLC, London W1F 9LD. **"In the Presence of Another World"** (pages 80 and 217) Words and Music by Joseph Bouchard and Samuel Pearlman © 1988, Reproduced by permission of Sony/ATV Music Publishing (UK) Ltd, Sony/ATV Tunes LLC, London W1F 9LD. **"Showtime"** (page 93) (Eric Bloom, John P. Trivers). Reproduced by permission of Six Pound Dog Music. **"Power Underneath Despair"** (page 102) (Eric Bloom, Donald B. Roeser, John P. Shirley). Reproduced by permission of Six Pound Dog Music and Triceratops Music. **"Before the Kiss, A Redcap"** (pages 108, 468, 475, and 482) Words and Music by Donald Roeser and Samuel Pearlman © 1972, Reproduced by permission of Sony/ATV Music Publishing (UK) Ltd, Sony/ATV Tunes LLC, London W1F 9LD. Words taken from **"Here's Tae Melrose"** (page 108) by Jack Drummond (Zoo Music Ltd). **"The Girl That Love Made Blind"** (page 122) Lyrics by Albert Bouchard. **"Lips in the Hills"** (pages 124 and 244) Words and Music by Eric Bloom, Donald Roeser and Richard Meltzer © 1980,

Reproduced by permission of Sony/ATV Music Publishing (UK) Ltd, Sony/ATV Tunes LLC, London W1F 9LD. **"Workshop of the Telescopes"** (page 132) (Albert Bouchard, Allen Lanier, Donald Roeser, Eric Bloom, Sandy Pearlman). **"Debbie Denise"** (pages 136 and 230) Words by Patti Smith. Music by Albert Bouchard and Patti Smith © 1976, Reproduced by permission of Sony/ATV Music Publishing (UK) Ltd, Sony/ATV Tunes LLC, London W1F 9LD. **"Live For Me"** (page 151) (Donald B. Roeser, John P. Shirley). Reproduced by permission of Triceratops Music. **"I Just Like to Be Bad"** (pages 163 and 240) (Eric Bloom, Brian Neumeister, John P. Shirley). Reproduced by permission of Six Pound Dog Music. **"Make Rock Not War"** (page 171) Words and Music by Robert Sidney Halligan Jr. © 1983, Reproduced by permission of Screen Gems-EMI Music Inc/ EMI Music Publishing Ltd, London W1F 9LD. **"Hammer Back"** (page 184) (Eric Bloom, Donald B. Roeser, John P. Shirley). Reproduced by permission of Six Pound Dog Music and Triceratops Music. **"Death Valley Nights"** (page 207) Words and Music by Albert Bouchard and Richard Meltzer © 1977, Reproduced by permission of Sony/ATV Music Publishing (UK) Ltd, Sony/ATV Tunes LLC, London W1F 9LD. **"Outward Bound (A Song for the Grammar School, Barrow-in-Furness)"** (page 215) Words by Dr. Thomas Wood. **"Tenderloin"** (page 252) Words and Music by Allen Lainer © 1976, Reproduced by permission of Sony/ATV Music Publishing (UK) Ltd/ Sony/ ATV Tunes LLC, London W1F 9LD. **"After Dark"** (page 260) Words and Music by Eric Bloom, L. Myers and John Trivers © 1981, Reproduced by permission of Sony/ATV Music Publishing (UK) Ltd, Sony/ATV Tunes LLC, London W1F 9LD. **"(Don't Fear) The Reaper"** (pages 268 and 444) Words and Music by Donald Roeser © 1976, Reproduced by permission of Sony/ATV Music Publishing (UK) Ltd, Sony/ATV Tunes LLC, London W1F 9LD. **"She's as Beautiful as a Foot"** (page 273) (Albert Bouchard, Richard Meltzer, Allen Lanier). **"The Vigil"** (page 275) Words and Music by Donald Roeser and S. Roeser © 1979, Reproduced by permission of Sony/ATV Music Publishing (UK) Ltd, Sony/ATV Tunes LLC, London W1F 9LD. **"Dominance and Submission"** (page 289)

(Albert Bouchard, Eric Bloom, Sandy Pearlman). **"Black Blade"** (page 293) Words and Music by Eric Bloom, John Trivers and Michael Moorcock © 1980, Reproduced by permission of Sony/ATV Music Publishing (UK) Ltd, Sony/ATV Tunes LLC and Action Green Music Ltd/ EMI Music Publishing Ltd, London W1F 9LD. **"Dance on Stilts"** (pages 311–312) (Donald B. Roeser, John P. Shirley). Reproduced by permission of Triceratops Music. **"Out of the Darkness"** (pages 317 and 332) (Eric Bloom, Danny Miranda, Donald Roeser, John D. Shirley). Reproduced by permission of Six Pound Dog Music and Triceratops Music. **"Searchin' for Celine"** (page 328) Words and Music by Allen Lainer © 1977, Reproduced by permission of Sony/ATV Music Publishing (UK) Ltd, Sony/ATV Tunes LLC, London W1F 9LD. **"Burnin' for You"** (page 342) Words and Music by Donald Roeser and Richard Meltzer © 1981, Reproduced by permission of Sony/ATV Music Publishing (UK) Ltd, Sony/ATV Tunes LLC, London W1F 9LD. **"Still Burnin'"** (page 348) (Donald B. Roeser, John S. Rogers). Reproduced by permission of Triceratops Music. **"Then Came the Last Days of May"** (page 360) Words and Music by Donald Roeser © 1972, Reproduced by permission of Sony/ATV Music Publishing (UK) Ltd, Sony/ATV Tunes LLC, London W1F 9LD. **"Harvester of Eyes"** (page 362) Words and Music by Eric Bloom, Donald Roeser and Richard Meltzer © 1974, Reproduced by permission of Sony/ATV Music Publishing (UK) Ltd, Sony/ATV Tunes LLC, London W1F 9LD. **"Subhuman"** (page 374) (Eric Bloom, Sandy Pearlman). **"Dr. Music"** (page 375) Words and Music by Joseph Bouchard, R. Meltzer, Donald Roeser © 1979, Reproduced by permission of Sony/ATV Music Publishing (UK) Ltd, Sony/ATV Tunes LLC, London W1F 9LD. **"Harvest Moon"** (page 376) (Donald Roeser). Reproduced by permission of Triceratops Music. **"Here Comes That Feeling"** (page 384) (Donald B. Roeser, Dick Trismen). Reproduced by permission of Triceratops Music. **"Celestial the Queen"** (page 401) Words and Music by Joseph Bouchard and H. Robbins © 1977, Reproduced by permission of Sony/ATV Music Publishing (UK) Ltd, Sony/ATV Tunes LLC, London W1F 9LD. **"Don't Turn Your Back"** (page 406)

Words and Music by Allen Lainer and Donald Roeser © 1981, Reproduced by permission of Sony/ATV Music Publishing (UK) Ltd, Sony/ATV Tunes LLC, London W1F 9LD. **"X-Ray Eyes"** (page 417) (Donald B. Roeser, John P. Shirley). Reproduced by permission of Triceratops Music. **"Veteran of the Psychic Wars"** (page 427) Words and Music by Eric Bloom and Michael Moorcock © 1981, Reproduced by permission of Sony/ATV Music Publishing (UK) Ltd, Sony/ATV Tunes LLC and Action Green Music Ltd/ EMI Music Publishing Ltd, London W1F 9LD. **"Spy in the House of the Night"** (page 433) Words and Music by Richard Meltzer and Donald Roeser © 1985, Reproduced by permission of Sony/ATV Music Publishing (UK) Ltd, Sony/ATV Tunes LLC, London W1F 9LD. **"Vengeance (The Pact)"** (pages 454 and 472) Words and Music by Albert Bouchard and Joseph Bouchard © 1981, Reproduced by permission of Sony/ATV Music Publishing (UK) Ltd, Sony/ATV Tunes LLC, London W1F 9LD. **"Sole Survivor"** (page 458) Words and Music by Eric Bloom, L. Myers and John Trivers © 1981, Reproduced by permission of Sony/ATV Music Publishing (UK) Ltd, Sony/ATV Tunes LLC, London W1F 9LD. **"Deadline"** (page 464) (Donald Roeser).

ABOUT THE AUTHOR

ROBERT GALBRAITH is a pseudonym for J.K. Rowling, best-selling author of the Harry Potter series and *The Casual Vacancy. Career of Evil* is the third book in the highly acclaimed Cormoran Strike crime fiction series. *The Cuckoo's Calling* was published in 2013 and *The Silkworm* in 2014.